THE URBANA FREE LIBRARY
W9-BBQ-433

ALSO BY KATIE CROUCH

*Men and Dogs*
*Girls in Trucks*

# *ABROAD*

# ABROAD

*KATIE CROUCH*

*SARAH CRICHTON BOOKS*
*FARRAR, STRAUS AND GIROUX*
*NEW YORK*

Sarah Crichton Books
Farrar, Straus and Giroux
18 West 18th Street, New York 10011


Printed in the United States of America
First edition, 2014

Library of Congress Cataloging-in-Publication Data
Crouch, Katie.
Abroad / Katie Crouch. — First edition.
pages cm
ISBN 978-0-374-10036-0 (hardback) — ISBN 978-0-374-71135-1 (ebook)
1. Women college students—Crimes against—Fiction. 2. English—Italy—Fiction. I. Title.

PS3603.R683 A63 2014
813'.6—dc23

2013035411

Designed by Jonathan D. Lippincott

Farrar, Straus and Giroux books may be purchased for educational, business, or promotional use. For information on bulk purchases, please contact the Macmillan Corporate and Premium Sales Department at 1-800-221-7945, extension 5442, or write to specialmarkets@macmillan.com.

www.fsgbooks.com
www.twitter.com/fsgbooks • www.facebook.com/fsgbooks

10 9 8 7 6 5 4 3 2 1

*For Peter*

I am unbalanced—but I am not mad with snow.
I am mad the way young girls are mad,
With an offering, an offering . . .

—Anne Sexton

# *ABROAD*

# 1

In my suitcase: three pairs of jeans, six shirts, one practical travel dress, black cotton. One bra, white, trimmed with lace. Three photographs of my cousins and sister; one picture of my parents; two of Babs and me hugging, the first on the field and the other one at a pub. One photograph of Sean, taken out again. Also taken out: one worn, stuffed dog called Tobo. In, reluctantly—marmalade, because my mother wanted me to. Antibacterial soap, also at her insistence. My passport, of course. Three lipsticks. Seven pairs of underwear, all black. (I'd switched to black at thirteen under the instruction of my sister in order to hide stains.) Ibuprofen. Condoms, just in case, knicked from the uni health center. One copy of *Ripley Under Ground*, by Patricia Highsmith. One copy of *Italy, Go!*, highlighted and marked. The suitcase itself, a large Samsonite with wheels, inherited from my father when he moved to Dublin.

This case was eventually returned to my father by the authorities. It came back empty, save the marmalade, which never made it out of an inner pocket and was still carefully wrapped in a pair of clean running socks, blue.

•

I was a girl from Ireland, gone to Italy to study abroad. The country I chose for the language, the city I chose by chance. A boy I knew a little told me Grifonia was a good place for students. Much smaller than Rome, but not boring. Safer for girls than Florence. Good chocolate, a big uni.

"And there are those parties," he said, as if I should know what he meant.

My first afternoon, I wandered up to the main square and sat on the steps of the cathedral. I brought a guidebook, but I was too tired from the train ride to look anything up. The square was crowded with students and foreigners. I had never seen so many kids my age in one place, just doing nothing. They leaned against the warm stone, drinking and smoking, comparing photos from home. I tried to eavesdrop on the Italians, though unsuccessfully, then pretended to read, so as not to look too lonely.

A few steps down, a girl with hair dyed lavender, half of it slipping out of a braid. She was kissing a boy. He seemed Italian, his skin dark, his hair short. He was heavy, carefully dressed in a cheap shirt, ironed, perhaps, by his mother, his brown wrists thick and covered in fur. He whispered in the girl's ear, and she leaned over and laughed.

"I wish I knew what the hell you were saying," she said in English, and then giggled and kissed him again, more insistently this time.

I felt strange watching from so close, but in fairness, I had been there first, and besides, the two seemed not to care. I tried to pay attention to my book, but I couldn't help it—I couldn't stop looking.

The boy's hands traveled over the girl's shirt, then under. Still kissing, the girl turned slightly and seemed to smile at me slyly, as if we were sharing a secret. I blinked, looked away, then back again. Yes, she was, in fact, grinning at me. A sign, somehow? Or was she just laughing?

I stood, disoriented, my book and open purse falling to the ground.

"Hey, let me help you with your stuff," the girl said, leaping up. She was next to me now. The boy peered over, irritated. Apart, their incongruity grew. Her: shabby and a bit tough, yet possessing a silvery, enviable loveliness. Him: the sort of lump no one will go near at a dance.

"No, no. Thank you." I crouched and gathered my things. She shrugged and went back to the boy. Without turning again, I hurried away.

•

When I first arrived in this small town in Umbria, I was childishly disappointed. I'd imagined charming villas—wide, gardened boulevards lined with flowers, the permeating smell of pastries and fresh bread. Instead: walls of stone emblazoned with graffiti, a scarcity of trees. Men with dark eyes slipped through Grifonia's medieval alleys, muttering words I couldn't catch. As a newcomer, I felt clumsy and mute. Having studied Italian for three years now, I was, at least according to my university instructors, almost fluent. Yet in the beginning I was too afraid to use any of it. Mostly, I moved about silent, flattening against walls in shops and restaurants, trying to make myself as invisible as possible.

Soon enough, though, I fell into a pleasant, lazy rhythm. I had a glass of wine at ten a.m. in an overpriced café, watching the tourist families squabble by. I ate gelato twice a day and tried on handmade shirts I could never afford. One afternoon, I even sat in the cathedral for three-quarters of an hour, trying to drum up some inkling of faith, which, for the daughter of a Jew and an on-again off-again member of the Catholic Church, failed to make itself known.

Yet I was a terminally responsible person, and this sort of loafing could not go on for long. I had classes to sign up for and, more immediately, living arrangements to make. The program had provided an initial stay in a clean if charmless rooming house near the train station, but my patience with the twenty-minute hike to the city center was waning. And so my third morning in Grifonia, I went to the bulletin board at the college and, using my new cell phone, called a few numbers pinned there on scraps of paper, hanging as precariously as the frayed threads of a tattered dress.

During the course of the next day, I saw four flats. Having enjoyed a fairly large on-campus apartment back in Nottingham, I wasn't prepared for what passes for sizable in Italy. I had refrained from signing up for the Enteria housing out of allegiance to this idea I had of my new independence. The *other girls* might live in that sterile residence for foreigners, I'd boasted to Babs, my best friend back home, but I was going to live with *real* Italians. Now I was wishing I'd just filled out the damned form and split a flat with some nice girl from Glasgow. Two of the places required room sharing, which, after a couple of years of privacy, I just couldn't do. Another "four-bedroom" (there was a sagging cot in the kitchen) housed five somewhat angry-looking cats. One place looked promising and clean enough from the hallway, but when the door opened I was greeted by a stout, middle-aged woman who kept me prisoner for an hour and a half, instructing me, among other things, on where to buy the best sponges for scrubbing "our" floor.

The next morning I woke dejected with only two numbers left in my notebook. I called the first and hacked through an awkward conversation with a woman who called herself Gia, then agreed with little hope to meet in front of the university. If these two were dead ends, I told myself, I'd just go to the Enteria office. Surely someone had canceled their semester, and perhaps, with a little arranging, I could just move in with some other English-speakers after all.

Within an hour, I found myself following a ropey woman with friendly eyes and platinum hair across a dirty brown square near the entrance of the school. Grifonia's center is comprised of a maze of alleyways and tiny passages that flit back and forth between ancient buildings; places that once were mere cow trails have centuries later become crowded streets. Even though the cottage couldn't have been more than five hundred feet away, the path she took was so confusing I felt unsure I'd ever be able to find my way back.

I hurried to keep up. It was incredibly hot—Grifonian heat being different, somehow, from that of other places. Weightier. The sports park was filthy and smelled of sour milk, marijuana, and spilled wine. The yellow air shimmered around us, and sweat trickled down the sides of my face in persistent lines. Even the thin cotton dress I had on felt too heavy for the day. How did the Italians manage to look so fresh in weather like this? My bag sagged on my shoulder and I found myself thinking longingly of the deep, clean tub in my mother's bathroom, lined on the rim with glass jars of lavender salt.

Gia led me through an alley, then down some stairs and across a busy street that was all curves and no stop signs. As I trailed after her, I was already preparing myself for another disappointment, horrified in particular by the way the Italians drove. Why on earth would I want to live on a traffic artery? Besides, there seemed to be nothing across the street but decrepit buildings.

But then this potential landlady—lithe, pierced, with her cropped white hair, ripped jeans, and loose red tank top—opened a black gate, and all at once we were off the street and in a garden with a soaring view of Umbria. Vines climbed enchantingly up the side of the house; ripe lemons weighed heavily on a tree next to the door. Whether despite or because of the unpleasant walk, I was instantly, blindly smitten. It was sweet as a dollhouse, filled with miniature tables and chairs.

I suppose there's a time in life when a garden of roses and lavender fails to blind a girl to the true shabbiness of a place. I myself had not reached that moment of clarity. The color of a stale biscuit with a red tile roof and peeling shutters, the building squatted at the end of the gravel yard, looking as if, at any moment, it might slide into the ravine below. The gate behind us stood open, I saw, inviting any passerby to come in and enjoy the view. Gia jiggled the door of the cottage for a moment and then, with an apologetic smile, pushed it open without a key. Even at twenty-five, I believe I would have said no. But I was twenty-one, and to my naive eyes the whitewashed hut was a paradise.

Later, after everything, I wondered if it was the place itself that was cursed. It would make sense, after all. The cottage stood directly across from what had been a school for wayward girls. Gia later told us that in the seventies, when they tore the building down to erect a petrol station below our house, the builders found an old bureau filled with the tiny skeletons of discarded infants. Mightn't that have been enough in itself to render a spell into the ground?

There was a large, wild garden below, perhaps as much as an

acre. The cottage had once been a farmhouse, with terraced farmland that provided produce to the inhabitants within the city walls, Gia explained. The building was over three hundred years old. I could make out row upon row of fig and olive trees on the hill below us, then farther, a tangled, fragrant ravine. I'll plant vegetables and herbs, I thought. We'll have picnics. When I mentioned my idea of planting basil and rosemary, someone new behind me laughed.

"Oh, the boys downstairs already have enough plants to make their own farm."

I turned to see a woman with a warm face that was no less pleasant for the scars she'd clearly incurred in a long-running war with acne. She was not as striking as Gia, but her countenance was kinder; she looked at you as if she were about to set you down in a large chair and feed you a plate of pastina, whether you were hungry or not.

"I'm Alessandra," she said, smiling.

"I'm Tabitha, but everyone calls me Taz." I put out my hand, but she brushed it off and kissed me on both cheeks instead. It was a custom I never grew used to, even at the end. Recovering, I smiled politely and stepped back.

"I'm afraid I don't understand you, though. The neighbors are farmers?"

"I mean they grow plants, for *spinello.* Or they try."

I shook my head.

"They like drugs," Gia said, patting my arm. "You?"

"Not particularly."

"Smoke?"

"Now and then."

"Well, *bella.*" Alessandra gave me another squeeze. "I'm glad. You are very sweet. Very cool. And you want to farm? You farm! Basil, pineapples. Anything you want."

The house was tiny for four people, true. I was still comparing every space with my flat back in Nottingham, but I was heavily charmed. There was a small wood table with a bright ceramic bowl sitting on it, full of shiny apples. The walls were freshly painted white. The floor was cheap wood, but scattered with bright, clean rugs. Above the Lilliputian sitting area that consisted of a small sofa covered in a knitted blanket, van Gogh's *Starry Night* was tacked up, along with two posters of Johnny Depp. The kitchen was modest, but the countertops were scrubbed to a shine and the pots, pans, and knives hung in an orderly fashion. It was a poor house, but these were good Italian girls, clearly, and they had burrowed in and made themselves a home.

There were two free rooms right next to each other, flanking the tiniest bathroom I'd ever seen. The spaces were simple but clean, with one twin bed each, a dresser, and a desk. The two rooms were exactly the same in every respect, save that the one in the back had a window that opened up to a wide green-and-gold view of the Umbrian hills.

Gia stood behind me, looking out. She stood closer than an English or Irish girl would. I tried not to visibly stiffen—I had never been good with strangers.

"You have boyfriends?" I tried.

"Sure. You?"

"Not right now."

"Not yet," Gia said. Alessandra looked me up and down in a way that was frank, but somehow not rude. These girls were older than I was. Twenty-five, twenty-six.

"It is very easy in Grifonia," Gia said.

"But don't pick the first one you see," Alessandra said. "You are too nice for that."

"Yeah, for you it will be a barrel of fish shooting," Gia said, suddenly switching into English. I laughed, and they led me to the kitchen, where Gia poured us all a glass of wine, even though it wasn't even noon. It was terrible, worse than the cheap stuff we drank in Nottingham.

"From the *enoteca* around the corner. You take a water bottle, they fill it for you. Three euros."

"Mmmmmm." I took another sip for show. Alessandra took off her little cardigan now, revealing an emblazoned T-shirt straining against her motherly curves:

YOUR NEVER FULLY DRESED WITH OUT A SMILE!!!

"We are gone a lot," Gia said, getting back to business.

"I understand. I'll be busy as well. My Enteria exchange—"

"Ah, Enteria. Good," Alessandra said, pulling her long, dark hair up and fanning her neck. "Not that we won't be around for you. You will be welcome to be with us at any time, *bella*."

"Any time," Gia repeated.

"Still, you will have many friends."

"And there is an American girl, too, who just rented," Gia said. "She's away now, but you will be friends, I think. She is very sweet."

"Lovely." I put down my wine. "So, then, it's three hundred a month?"

"*Sì*." They gave each other a look. Obviously, they themselves were paying significantly less. But it was their lease, and though three hundred was high, between the scholarship and the money my father had given me, I could afford it. "What do you think?"

I looked around at the terrace, the little table, the warm faces of my potential flatmates. I didn't want to look too excited, but this seemed exactly the place I'd been dreaming of.

"Okay," I said. "I'll take it."

"Fantastic!" Alessandra cried. And the girls embraced me again, showering me with more cheek kisses.

"I hate to ask," Gia said, stepping away first, "but do you have . . . a deposit?"

"Certainly."

"It's okay to give it later," Alessandra said.

"No, no—it's fine," I said. I reached in my purse, pulled out the envelope, and gave them two months' worth of rent.

"Well, *bella*, here is your kingdom," Alessandra said, kicking the bedroom door open lightly with her foot. "You see? The bed, the closet, the desk. All yours. It is not big, but it has everything. Sheets and towels you can get at the co-op."

As I stood in the threshold, I heard a sudden roar, far away but insistent. The room seemed all at once airless. I leaned against the doorjamb, in order to catch my breath. I knew something was going to happen here. Something colossal. The sensation never happened again in this particular place, but that was it. My first ghost.

You see, it all started very simply. A girl packed a suitcase full of soap and clean underwear and went to Italy. She was young—open as an empty highway. She met some people there. Love happened. And then, her ending began.

"Tabitha?" Alessandra asked, touching my arm. "You okay?"

I looked at her, blinking.

"I'm fine, thank you."

"You sure?"

"Positive," I said, managing a smile. "I'll just go now and get my things."

# *Ido, 10th century BC*

Ido. She wasn't the strongest sister, nor was she the weakest. She had blue eyes, and it made those in her Umbri tribe uneasy. Though she was already thirteen, no one had claimed her for a wife.

She was good at being quiet. Living with the Umbri wasn't easy. Her survival depended on positioning herself with the hunters, with the aunts who could coax the most from the arid ground.

The Umbri tracked time by growing seasons. Ido's tribe had built a stone Sun Temple, a structure that took eighty years to construct; the three-ton boulders were heaved, one by one, up from the valley a mile below.

When Ido was fourteen, there was a blizzard. No one could remember a winter so harsh. The families huddled by their fires day and night, but the snow wouldn't stop. All their food stores were frozen. The mothers were unable to produce milk. Seven nights. Ten. By the eleventh darkness, three babies and two elders were dead.

The priests prayed day and night at the Sun Temple. Reluctantly, they sacrificed a sheep. Then a goat, already frozen to death. Twelve nights passed. Thirteen.

On the sixteenth night Ido woke to see her father bending over her. He pulled her up off her pallet. From the frightened moans of her sisters, she knew where she was going. She hoped she was wrong.

Her father didn't bother to wrap her in blankets. Her skin was coated in a thin sheet of ice.

At the temple, the priests grabbed Ido from her father and dragged her across the ground. She felt a sharp pain as her left cheek scraped against stone. She struggled, smacking at the priests. After a moment, another rock smashed her skull.

Blood ran down the frosted altar. Sharp clouds of steam rose from the snow.

*Ido, fourteen years old, 10th century BC*

# 2

The past runs deep in Grifonia, even in a topographical sense. Below the streets, a great network of black tunnels. Often I would wander into a stone opening that would evolve into a dark passageway leading to some other unfamiliar part of town. Though I knew it was silly, I had a notion of the Grifonian hill as a thin shell, bored into by former generations until it was fragile as a used beehive. In the beginning, I often woke covered in sweat from a recurring nightmare in which the whole place crumbled, throwing all of us down into one great, lethal heap.

My early days were laced with terrible loneliness and longings for home. Still, the fact that I belonged to the prestigious Enteria exchange—an elite program for Europeans only—cheered me. I said the strange word as often as I could. *Enteria.* Just uttering the term brought nods of recognition from Italians and looks of respect from the other foreigners. I wasn't a brilliant student, but the letters of recommendation from my father's heavy-hitter medical friends bolstered my application. I didn't care how it had happened. I was here, my place exchanged with some Italian who was now going to Nottingham University. Often I wondered whom it was now wandering through that cold British web, shadowing the life I'd left.

Our initial orientation was held on a Monday, in the last week of August. More than five hundred students from all over Europe gathered in the auditorium on the campus, talking to one another in eight or nine different languages, voices swelling in a sickening wave. Having gone through two years at a big uni, I was used to the bedlam of large, crowded rooms, knew to coolly look at no one, to sit near the front in order to hear, but not so close that I would be actually noticed. Still, I almost fainted with relief when I saw Jenny Cole, a girl I knew a bit. We'd been on the same hall during our first year at Nottingham. She'd even called me over the summer to "connect" before the trip, though we had never actually gotten together; I spent my summer working to save money, and whenever I could get away, she always had social engagements.

Jenny smiled and flittered her fingers at me. Is there anything better in a strange place than someone saving you a seat? To be lost, and then found, even if the girl beside you barely even knows you at all? She stood and made a show of kissing my cheeks, then removed the huge red bag she had placed on the chair beside her and patted it, indicating that I should sit. She was a large-shouldered girl with thick, covetable wheat-colored hair and skin the color of freshly poured milk. Legs a bit muscular, maybe, wide-ish hips, large breasts, often slyly exposed from within expensive blouses and dresses that wrapped. She wasn't heavy, exactly, but was the sort of healthy-looking person you could imagine gracefully surviving any sort of hardship or plague. It was the Jennies who'd rule come the apocalypse, whereas girls like me—the thin, meek reeds with quietly lovely manners—we'd all be swept away without so much as a parting word.

At university, Jenny had spoken to me only twice. I remembered each instance, because when Jennifer Cole spoke to you, it was an occasion. She leaned in slightly, as if she had the most fascinating bit of confidence in the world. Her voice was low and throaty, and if she really wanted to engage you, she spoke softly enough so that you, too, had to lean forward, in order to get that much closer to the secrets she held. Back at Nottingham, she had asked if I knew a certain boy she was interested in meeting (I didn't) and if my roommate and I would consider switching rooms with her, as she was forever getting in trouble with the hall proctor for late-night noise. (I'd been willing; my roommate hadn't.) In fact, I was surprised that someone like Jenny Cole had called me at all.

"Tabitha, thank God you're here," she said. "My other mates didn't make it this morning."

"You look well," I said as we sat.

She allowed a small, disappointed smile and looked around the room. I tried again.

"Oh, this is nice," I said, giving her purse a respectful pat.

"Yes."

I looked at the label, then moved my hand away. My sister had once pointed out the same sort in a magazine. It had cost upwards of five thousand pounds.

"Is this real?"

"Of course." Jenny gave me a frosty look.

I tried to hide my embarrassment by fumbling in my own cheap, fake-leather satchel. She looked at me for a moment more, then relented.

"It was a gift from Martin. My boyfriend back home. He's practically divorced, or so he says. I met him at a house party, you know, one of those weekend things."

I did my best to maintain a neutral expression. There was a reason I didn't know Jenny well: she ran with a posh group I'd observed only from afar. Though Nottingham was supposed to be the new utopia of student equality, the class system was alive and well on our campus, with girls like Jenny circulating imperiously at the top, waving to the underlings as they buzzed about in the passenger seats of properly worn Aston Martins and posted photos of themselves at hunts and polo matches and dinners at large country manors. Though she had lived on my hall our first year, she was away so much I had rarely seen her. The posh group rarely stayed on campus during the weekend. For them, a better, smarter world was always waiting just a jaunt away.

I pretended to write in my notebook while trying to think of something clever to say. All around us students shouted and gossiped feverishly, as if they'd known one another for years. There was a buzz in the room of being in a place where others wanted to be. The people sitting to my right—a boy and a girl with multiple nose rings—were jabbering in some mystifying Scandinavian language. I continued to scribble nonsensical notes, as if absorbed in important business.

Just then the head of the program, an impeccably dressed woman in her fifties, stepped up to give a welcome speech in blessedly slow Italian. If we didn't understand everything at first, she said, not to worry. Our Italian would improve in the course of time, and we could always take extra language classes. Thousands of students had gone successfully through this program, she assured us.

At first we listened politely, but as she went on the students began to get restless. There was no air-conditioning, and it was even hotter inside the room than out in the merciless August sun. After covering class schedules, the *directora* paused, as if not exactly sure how to approach the next topic on her agenda.

"You are here to experience our great country of Italy," she began almost regretfully. "The art, the music, the food, the people."

"*Could* this be more boring?" Jenny said—not even bothering to whisper—and took out her phone. "I mean, I can't understand a word, can you?"

"I'm actually pretty good at Italian," I said a little eagerly. "Want me to translate?"

Jenny shrugged.

The *directora* took off her glasses now and laid them on the podium. "So I must advise prudence. Grifonia, you see, is a lively city. A city of music. Of festivals and—"

"Fucking!" someone shouted, at which the entire auditorium rippled with an appreciative laugh.

"Some say so," the *directora* answered, and then paused for another moment. Some Italians, I was beginning to note, were extremely adept at the dramatic pause. "Yes. There are temptations in Grifonia. Likely, you will be offered certain opportunities. Some nice, some not so nice."

Another buzz rose in the crowd.

"Please, always keep in mind who you are. Enteria is a competitive program. You are guests of this university, and guests of Grifonia. And while we are here to help you, we are not here to save you. Be careful. You are responsible for yourselves."

As she went on, I studiously took notes: *Reputation. Emergency number, 327 368 4122. Travel in pairs. No phone out on street.*

Suddenly I felt a pressure on my shoulder. Jenny was leaning over and peering at my notebook. She laughed out loud.

"My God! Taz Deacon, I had no idea that you were such a fucking *nerd*!"

"What? I—"

"Travel in pairs? This is your year in *Italy*. Good Lord. I'm just glad we ran into each other. You need me."

The talking around us was rising now, but the *directora* wiped her forehead and pressed helplessly on. Jenny reached out and grabbed my pen.

*Italian lesson #1:* she scrawled.

"Stop!"

*FUCK THE RULES*

"Right?" she said.

"Exactly," I replied.

Jenny smiled and gave back my notebook. Then, done with me for the moment, she turned away to chat with the other, momentarily more interesting girls.

# 3

At twenty-one, I had been in love with only one person. I'd attended a Catholic girls' school on the outskirts of Dublin, which was exactly the sort of place those words can't fail to conjure: uniforms, giggling, pranks involving bras and sanitary napkins, and an early fear of talking to specimens of the opposite sex. I was extremely shy, as was my best friend, Babs. We were an awkward pair, really, and clung to each other all during primary. Even in secondary, when the grip loosened enough to allow us to make other friends, neither of us was swept up into any particular group. Early on, I believed this was because of Babs's brightly colored clothing and penchant for marine biology. Later I blamed it on the fact that my complexion was slightly darker than the other students'. Likely, it was both, yet neither. Our situation never bothered Babs, who seemed completely satisfied with the feeding habits of bivalve mollusks, but the isolation ate away at me. I dreamed of joining the cool girls at the lunch table, at the shops, at the weekend parties we knew must be taking place but we were never invited to. I would stare at myself in the mirror at home for hours, wondering what it was that made me different.

The fast girls, the ones with all the dates, steered well clear of us. Babs and I heard of the others' boyfriends and what the girls were doing with them—blow jobs in the bathroom and all that—but we assumed that we would be ignored by the male species until college, if not beyond. Then, while I was serving cinnamon cake at the Christmas fair, a boy named Sean with large brown eyes and freckles came over and asked my name.

His ears, I noticed, were inordinately delicate—fine and white as bleached seashells.

"Tabitha Deacon," I said.

"You make this cake?"

"What?"

"The cake?"

"Oh. No. Got it from the store."

"Isn't that cheating?" he asked, seemingly serious. "Aren't you afraid of hell?"

"I'm a Jew. We don't have hell."

"Lucky for you."

I looked at the cake, wanting to die. "It's just for charity. The money. And it's—it's good cake."

"You've had it?"

"Sure."

He grabbed a piece and crammed it in his mouth, then screwed up his face and pretended to choke.

"It's awful. Fucking God. I'll take four pieces."

"Four?"

"Sure. There's loads of girls I hate here. I'll give it to them."

The next few afternoons, Sean was waiting for me at the school at the end of the day. Babs politely hung back while the other girls fanned out beyond us, smirking and jealous. What exactly Sean and I talked about is now a mystery. Movies? Algebra? I can't imagine. After a while I would tell him it was time for Babs and me to go home.

The fourth day, Friday, Babs looked at me brightly.

"Taz, I can't walk you home today."

"Why not?"

"I've got a project at the lab."

"On a Friday?"

She didn't bother to answer, just turned on her heel and retreated into the school building, ignoring my braying protests.

Sean, who was waiting by the gate, didn't ask where Babs was. We headed out, shoulder to shoulder, toward Soldier's Field, a place we'd eventually take to visiting nearly every afternoon. There was a green hollow at the edge of the woods where we would sit, even in the winter, when the ground was hard and frozen. He was a great planner, Sean. If it was raining he brought plastic disposable ponchos; if it was cold, he gave me hand warmers, the kind that heat up after you shake them back and forth. What could they be made of, those chemical concoctions? The next day I'd find them in my pockets, formed into the shape of my inner fists, hard as ancient bits of chiseled stone.

My first thought, as I followed Sean to that field behind the post office, was that he wanted a touch of this or that. And he did, really. But he also fancied himself a poetry lover. He would arrange us comfortably, then pull out a book and start to read. I would sit there on the plastic tarp, smoothing the plaid skirt of my uniform over my wool stockings, rather at a loss. How is a girl supposed to react to Keats? Does she gaze at the reader adoringly? Lie back seductively on one arm?

*We will drink our fill*
*Of golden sunshine,*
*Till our brains intertwine*
*With the glory and grace of Apollo!*

"It's good, yeah?" he'd ask later.

"Yeah! Oh, *yes*." I'd try not to look bored, waiting for him to either kiss me or give me a Guinness out of his bag.

When I heard the other girls at school describe their first grapplings with sex—on the floors of garages, or pushed down on the hood of a car at thirteen—I knew that I was lucky. Sean was my first, and it was a truly lovely event, the details of which I would never share with anyone, even Babs. If I went over it, you'd probably think us just ordinary kids groping in a guest room. Yet in truth, there is never anything ordinary about the discovery of another sixteen-year-old's skin.

I was desperate for us to marry. I knew it was silly; we were much too young and no one stayed together from secondary to uni. Yet I rashly clung to the hope that we would. Surely Sean wouldn't leave me to navigate the world alone as my older sister did, with her one-night stands from pubs and bawdy talk of *cocks* and *balls* and dizzying lists of demands and frustrations. *Blew him for two hours, and not even a bloody text.* I was terrified of entering her arena and prayed Sean would protect me from it.

Yet my boyfriend—oh how I loved that word!—with his thoughtfully packed rucksacks and those wonderful ears, was a year ahead of me at school. This was a gap we eventually couldn't weather. He went away to Oxford, a place I could barely imagine visiting, much less attending. His going there only made me love him more, and when my mother dropped me off to visit, my mind fairly burst at the sight of those spires, those ancient corridors. It was a place, I knew, I was just being allowed a peek at. My grades weren't nearly good enough for me to even apply. I was no more than a frog trying to climb the lip of a bucket. And after just a few hours in that hallowed place, I began to feel physically ill.

"Hello, Beanie!" girl after girl cried all over campus as I walked beside him. These were college women, wild and free. They cruised the quads on bicycles with handlebar baskets loaded with impressive-looking books. One knobby-kneed brunette even stopped to talk. Gazing into his eyes, she chattered on, ignoring me completely.

"Have you read the Sophocles yet, Beanie? The last bit at the tomb—ugh! I was up all night in my jammies, weeping . . ."

Sean was sheepishly quiet after this one rode off. Sometimes first-years were given nicknames, he explained. *Beanie!* It was disgusting.

A few hours later, a serious talk on his bed after that last sad shag, followed by a heartache so acute I couldn't eat anything but broth and cocoa until the summer. *Beanie.* For years, the very word brought bile to my throat.

Sean rearranged me. Sometimes, in the months after it was all played out, I would look around and find myself able to pick out the other girls it had happened to, being left. You could *see* it—the slight dimming of the eyes, no matter how loud the laugh. Yet maybe the worst thing about it all was my mother's reaction. Leah Deacon had once had true passion: my father, an Irish doctor, who lured her from Tel Aviv after a series of research trips. But after children, his interest had waned, as had her faith and mental health. As a result, her absolute favorite pastime was hearing about the boyfriends she never had.

Sean she loved the most. When he stopped calling from Oxford, she grew so agitated I became afraid. *What* had I done? she demanded one afternoon, her Hebrew accent cutting into the words. She was a small woman, her once beautiful face shrunken into sharp angles. *Why* hadn't I managed to be more pleasing? Oh, it wasn't that she was a complete throwback—equal pay for women and all that, yes, of course. But in terms of male-female relationships, she hung on to traces of the customs and beliefs of her former household, so if something had gone wrong, clearly it was my fault.

No matter what they might say, the actual truth has no place in mothers' ears. They beg to hear, but they don't really want to know, do they? Not about how a boy might mash you up against a soda machine, scratching at your zipper. Not about an upperclassman who turns on a movie of bobble-breasted women spanking each other because he's so drunk that's what he needs. Yes, once university started, the stories for my mother had to turn to lies. But the first betrayal was this: her little jewel was no longer desired by this boy from Oxford. My mother was bereft, and I couldn't stand it. In desperation, I finally said it had turned out that Sean was homosexual.

Leah Deacon sat back, and then reached over and patted my hand. "It's a complication," she said. "But nothing we can't master."

"Mom! No, it's over. Really."

"Well. We will be more careful next time," she said, sighing.

Careful! I wanted to say. How? There was no manual for a girl like me. We were fondled, sucked, dropped, and we learned to do the same to the boys until we were all pliable and porous as old sponges. But for my mother, the story would be different. After all, I *wanted* something different. In her mind, I was taken to country inns, to long dinners in London, college dances, picnics in St. James's Park.

And now I was going to Italy. What fantasies I would create for her there! Or maybe the storytelling would end, and I really would meet someone we both thought was wonderful. Someone who wouldn't fall out of love with me the minute I was out of sight.

Once I arrived in Grifonia, I called my mother daily. She hung on to every word—about my classes, my friends, my new home.

"A *cottage*!" she cried. "How darling. And have you met any boys yet?"

Oh yes, I said. Many, many charming boys.

"Ahhhh. Can you send pictures?"

"I will, when I think of it."

"Ah! Sweetheart. You are dreaming. You are dreaming." She loved to say that. I think it was a bit of Hebrew that didn't quite translate properly. I never contradicted her. She hated it when we corrected her English, and anyway, she was somewhat right.

•

Those next few days, I saw Jenny only once. Well, that's not true. What I mean is, I *spoke* to her once. I saw her quite a few times, gliding across the main piazza, flanked by two other girls, a thin redhead and a tall black girl, all three dressed in long jewel-toned sundresses that flapped behind them in the late summer wind. They were an arresting threesome, promenading along the *via* there, and I watched as men and women alike turned to watch them as they passed. The scene reminded me of a bad painting my father had of the Greek Muses, holding their various instruments of art. It hung in his office at home, and as a little girl I used to stare at it, wondering who these women in the clouds could be, what their lives were like. And now, here they were, marching to Hotel Nysa for a Negroni.

The first time I spotted her I waved from the palace steps, but Jenny seemed not to see me, so from then on I kept to myself and simply followed the three girls' movements, which seemed focused and secretive. Sometimes they turned down a side alley, as if looking for something. Twice they stopped to speak with a small pod of Italians, but after a few words the three of them moved on just as quickly, their steps perfectly in sync. I couldn't help admiring how at ease they looked, as if they'd grown up striding through Italian squares, leaving cawing men in their wake, and I was filled with a flare of desperate envy.

My own social start in Grifonia was rather less easy. Other than directions and instructions on where to buy things, Gia and Alessandra, as warned, offered little help. There was a Welsh girl named Marcy who took an overly eager liking to me after singling me out at an Enteria orientation picnic, and, as I had little else to do, I obliged her by meeting her for drinks that night. But as soon as I approached the table my heart sank, as she had apparently put the call out to all the mousy girls in the program. I didn't like to think of myself as a wallflower, but I was, I suppose, the type who could go either way, and dear Marcy had picked that up about me. I had never seen so many eyeglasses or baggy cargo pants at one table. Amassed in the middle was a tower of guidebooks, in every language the Lonely Planet series had to offer.

"So what we do, everyone says, is have drinks here first. Then eat at Etrusco or get a kebab. Then to Malone's, then to the Red Lion. That's the track—every Thursday and Saturday night."

"How do you *know*?" asked a heavy German girl.

"My friend Cora told me. She did Enteria here last year. She knows everything."

"Or maybe we could try something different," I said. Marcy's ironclad, self-assured nature irked me. "Perhaps it would be better *not* to go where all the other students are going."

"No, no. Cora told me. Etrusco, Malone's, Red Lion. That's the drill."

And so we marched, from one mobbed student landmark to the other, ignored by the boys, who, seeing our practical, sturdy army advancing, instantly moved on. I had never witnessed a scene like that: thousands of people between the ages of eighteen and twenty-three spilling out into the street. I could barely hear for the chorus of voices ricocheting off the ancient stone—Italian, Spanish, French, English, Chinese. There were regular university girls in little dresses and Birkenstocks, boys in jeans and grubby shirts, and then the Italians themselves, dressed for a fashion runway, the girls walking with practiced ease on heels thin as needles. Our group seemed to pale even further among such plumage. Eventually we migrated to the steps of the cathedral, with at least five hundred other students and foreigners. Every ten minutes or so a thin, dusty man with red eyes would approach us.

"Ciao, *bellas. Spinello?* Hash? Zanopane?"

"What is that *last* one?" a Belgian girl asked. "Maybe we should get some."

*Zanopane.* The name sounded familiar to me.

"Don't even joke," hissed Marcy. "It's this new thing, makes you out of your mind, and then it's like, absolute *misery* the next day. And then you have to have more, or you'll absolutely die. No *thank* you."

The Belgian unsuccessfully tossed her frizzy chin-length curls. "It must be quite a high, then. *I* sort of think I want to try it."

"Well, at least wait for the Enteria connection. There's one every year, Cora says. But I'd stay off it if I were you. Cora told me the worst things about it."

After an hour of nodding at Marcy's readily crystallized opinions of Italian culture, I threw away my plastic cup and walked home, dejected. Surely there had to be more to my year abroad than this pantomime of discovery. In a fit of hope, I wrote an e-mail to Jenny offering help with her Italian, but after a couple of days of hearing nothing, I gave up and decided to make the best of things by joining the other students who chose to go on the Enteria orientation tours of key Grifonian sites.

Our guide, Loretta, was a plump, damp sort of person, perpetually perspiring even when we were in an air-conditioned room. I could not tell her age, though I guessed her to be ten years older than myself. Her brown eyes widened and snapped as she took us through our historical paces.

"All right. *Ragazzi*, look here. Here is an ancient monastery. In the nineteenth century, it became a psychiatric hospital."

"Is it still?"

"Of course!" The march continued. "Here, we come to an extraordinary building, see? Etruscan stones. Please look." We looked. "Above, this beautiful fresco of the Madonna, *con bambino*. See? Good. *Dai!*"

Loretta managed to show us little of interest to anyone unconsumed by a passion for the Madonna; by the end of her exhaustive tour of the cathedral, I'd begun to loathe the Blessed Virgin, with her superior stare, her resigned acceptance of her fate to look after a squawking baby she never asked for. Others must have felt the same way, for as the days wore on, the groups became smaller and smaller, until the only people left were myself, a French boy named Pascal, and an insular group of Germans I never got to know. I probably should have fallen off as well to do my own exploring, but then I'd always been almost constitutionally unable to shirk work. So I carried on, and at the end of those long, dull days I would look over my notes at the kitchen table, feeling bored and righteous. Hard as I tried to retain it all, most of the thin shell of information applied by Loretta fell away, leaving me more or less as ignorant as when I'd started.

But the griffin. The griffin I always remembered. The monster was everywhere: carved into rocks, staring at us from frescoes, leering down from marble buildings. Its head a screeching eagle, its body a lion—stone, overpowering chest and massive haunches straining to leap. Loretta insisted that it was a majestic animal. *Majestic*, she kept repeating, as if we didn't understand. Yet it didn't seem the right word to me. Sometimes on night walks I would visit a particular rendering in front of the palace, carved in the fourteenth century. This one had a neck so realistic the sculptor had captured its furious tendons; its beak and tongue were caught in stormy mid-hiss. A beast, I thought, forever waiting. I liked to stare at it, to run my hand along its cool ankle. As if I might be able to cause it to stir from its ancient sleep.

•

Two days after our orientation, I moved my things into Gia and Alessandra's cottage. Upon waking there my first morning, all I wanted to do was stay in my new little room and nest. Yet I was wary of giving the Italian girls the impression that I was some homebody who would crowd them. And so, tossing an apple and a bottle of water into my purse, I reluctantly set out into the late-August heat.

A girl in a strange city. At first, the thought of going out alone left me squeamish, but as Jenny wasn't answering and I didn't yet know anyone else well enough to call other than the less than appealing Marcy, there was nothing to do but make the best of it.

I wandered timidly at first, hesitant to venture away from the few streets I'd committed to memory. At one corner, I peered down a dark set of stairs seemingly leading nowhere. Suddenly a woman emerged from the shadows. I stepped back, for at first I thought she was a shadow herself. She looked black with soot, as if thickly painted from head to toe. Her stooped figure was wrapped in a black shawl and long skirt, despite the heat. Her eyes, too, were jet, glittering brightly as a bird's. I couldn't make out if she was young or old. She looked at me intently, gliding forward.

"*Perso?*" she rasped.

Her obsidian face cracked into a wide grin, showing red gums. Behind her I saw nothing but a dead end.

"You get lost, you go up."

She gestured to the sky, then vanished.

I squinted at where she had been standing, trembling at the thought that my dreams had extended themselves into the daylight hours. Yet what she said was true—the main piazza was, in fact, on the very top of the hill, meaning all roads sloping up would eventually lead to the correct place. Newly emboldened, I spent my morning darting back and forth into the city's cracks like a hungry sparrow.

By eleven o'clock the temperature gauge on my phone read 36°C. My mother used to speak of techniques to survive lethally hot weather—staying inside during the middle of the day or wearing a wet cloth on the back of the neck—but none of these sensible precautions had occurred to me that morning. I was just about to step into a restaurant to take a second breakfast just for the sake of sitting in the shade, when I saw a sign reading MUSEO ARCHEOLOGICO in front of a large stone building. Through the arched doorway, I could see a lovely green courtyard with twisting marble columns and a trickling fountain. Without further thought, I paid my four euros and slipped in.

The building, a former cloister, housed chamber after chamber of Etruscan urns, statues, tombs, and sarcophagi. Surprisingly, I was the only one there at the moment, and, as the guard appeared to be asleep, I took my leave to run my hand over the smooth stone of the displaced graves. The air inside was cool and delicious. I looked at the urns. The writing was indecipherable—Latin? No, Etruscan, according to the materials on the wall. I peered at the violent scenes depicted: a woman with a head of snakes, warriors tearing each other's limbs, and the griffin, its beak thrust forward, its great claws splayed in warning.

There was one subject that appeared again and again, the meaning of which I couldn't make out: a man carrying a struggling girl—sometimes small, sometimes a woman—to a rock. In one hand, he held a sort of bowl over her head. Around him, men and women were howling, their hands over their eyes. In one or two of the scenes, a knife was drawn.

I stared at the girl for a long time. After a while, I heard a group of heels clicking down the cloister behind me, as well as the voice of an Italian woman. I looked over and saw a rather efficient-looking signora in a navy summer suit, leading a wealthy-looking German couple who, I couldn't help thinking, seemed a bit overwhelmed by the amount of information raining down upon them.

"The Etruscans . . . a savage people . . . life cheap and extinguishable . . . yet unheard-of sophistication . . . mysterious, complete disappearance . . . an aqueduct we could use even today . . ."

"*Scusa*," I said after a while, hearing a pause in her commentary. The woman glanced over in that way only an Italian matron can, challenging, slightly annoyed, yet tolerant. She wore a large, expensive hat and looked pointedly at my grubby shorts.

"*Sì?*"

"Can you tell me what this image is?"

She turned to her charges. The husband, a stout man about ten years older than my father, was observing my legs with keen interest.

"Iphigenia," she said. "Stabbed as a sacrifice to Artemis."

"Why?"

The guide looked pleased at the opportunity. "Ah, this is a famous story. Agamemnon killed a deer in Artemis's sacred forest, so she stole his wind when he sailed to Troy. A prophet said the only way to start the wind again was to sacrifice his daughter Iphigenia. And so . . ."

"They slit her neck on the rock."

It was another voice—British, educated. Young, yet commanding. I turned around expecting to see a boy. But it wasn't a boy. He looked my age, but someone with so fierce a face—a beautiful, terrible face, with a nose proud as a hawk; wide, kind lips; and deep-set eyes that glittered in the shadows—could be nothing but a man. He was very tall. I wanted to go closer. It felt as though by being near him, I myself would grow more delicate.

"Agamemnon was being punished, and Iphigenia was his daughter. It was the greatest sacrifice."

The man was still looking at me intently, which left me feeling not altogether unpleasant.

"Yes, that's right," the guide said, beaming. She obviously liked the looks of this well-dressed, tall stranger much better than mine.

"So her father killed his daughter himself?" I asked. "To please the gods?"

"You are too interested in this gory story," the German said, catching my eye and winking.

His wife studied her guidebook, ignoring us both.

"This is a very prevalent image in Grifonia," the guide pressed, struggling to regain control of her charges. "You may see Iphigenia in several of the squares, in the base of the ruined temples, in the palace . . ."

"Why?" I asked.

"There's the theory that women were sacrificed in Grifonia," the

British man said, looking at the urn. "For fortune in war, or crops. Sacrificed to the gods."

"A theory based on nothing," the guide snapped. "What, you have credentials?" She lifted her badge, as if to show her superiority. "There is no proof. And certainly it would be pre-Etruscan. A tribal practice, if at all."

"It's all stories!" the German erupted. And then, almost pouting: "Though this is not a happy one."

"It's true," the wife said, finally looking up at him. I was surprised to see she was perhaps only three or four years older than I was. "It's a sad, complicated story. Much too complicated for you."

I turned to say something clever to the stranger, but he had retreated far down the hall now, rather deliberately alone, it seemed. I fought a pang of disappointment as he turned a corner and disappeared.

"No, not for me, these myths," the German said, pulling his tie, as if he had decided something important. "No one knows what they are for certain. And however they end, somebody dies."

The guide gave a tight smile, but I could see now that she liked him even less than she liked me. It hardly mattered. Siesta was approaching, and the museum, aside from us, was now completely empty. With a final half nod, the trio turned and graciously retreated; I was left in the cool unquiet alone with Iphigenia's ghost.

## *Adriana, 1st century BC*

Adriana Soevii, the daughter of a baker. The Soevii house was built in the shadows of an alleyway, so that no sun would ever fall near the already smoking ovens. It was Adriana's job to knead and bake the flat tablets of bread. Her brother pounded the grain. Her father made the purchases from the farmers and kept the accounts. Her mother, a pretty woman, went from house to house, taking the orders, although there were rumors that she performed other services as well.

The baker wasn't rich, but he had a good house, comfortable and clean. He was shrewd, and never gave away bread, even to needy soldiers during the beginning of the famine.

And then, the famine went on. Sometimes, at night, Adriana's father would come down to find thieves trying to break into the kitchen. He ordered a stronger bolt for the door from the ironsmith down the way.

It was a year free of rain. Dust filled in the sky and the grain seedlings withered in the ground. By the end of the winter, people were hungry, and the stores of grain were all but depleted.

On a hot spring day, Adriana propped the door open, waiting for a certain boy to visit, even though her father told her not to.

The boy didn't come, but a thief did. He was quick and thorough. He grabbed Adriana by the shoulder, then shoved a dagger in her side and turned it clockwise. She watched her blood pour onto the floor as she struggled for breath. She could feel the cold iron inside her, could see an organ spilling out. Finally blackness came and the man filled his bag.

Word traveled among the nobles, and money was raised for a proper sarcophagus. A girl like this did not deserve such a death. Carved into the stone, a relief of Iphigenia.

It was noted that there would be more deaths like this. The undeserved deaths of women in need of proper burials.

At this, a small Compagnia was formed. They gathered at various houses, planning, waiting for the next one.

*Adriana Soevii, fifteen years old, 1st century BC*

# 4

In the Etruscan Museum in Rome, one can see room after room of relics of a sophisticated, pleasure-loving society. Beautifully engraved plates and wine goblets, combs, pumice-holders, necklaces, bracelets, earrings. While the working class—for the classes were strictly divided—lived in comparative modesty, the wealthiest subjects surrounded themselves with luxury to the point of ostentation. They kept monkeys, dogs, and ferrets as pets. The men wore togas over tunics, bronze jewelry, high-topped boots. The women wore tunics with belts, often embroidered with gold.

And the parties, the parties. Banquets, sometimes two a day, were elaborate, served at huge tables heaped with meat, fruit, and wine. Men and women reclined on sumptuous sofas, their legs covered in blankets. They ate flatbread, fava beans, faro, eggs, pomegranates, grapes. The Etruscan wine cups were wide-mouthed, their platters long. Beneath the tables, animals rummaged for scraps. Sometimes, plied with wine and music, the guests would watch a wrestling match, followed by a fight to the death between gladiators. When one of the men was finally beaten, his bleeding carcass was dragged behind the gates of the arena, then fed to the waiting lions.

•

A few days after my trip to the museum, a thick cream envelope appeared in the hallway of our cottage. I'd been having my tea at the kitchen table, studiously using my Italian-American dictionary to look up the words I didn't understand in that day's local paper, when I heard a rustling and saw the letter shoot under the door. I'd only been in my new home four days, so, not expecting it to be for me, I didn't bother to look at it until some time later. When I saw my name, I hurriedly ripped it open, peering out the window. But by then, of course, the courier was long since gone.

*Dearest Tabitha Deacon:*

*You are cordially invited to be a part of the highly exclusive, top secret Brit Four Society. I'll explain later, but for now please trust that it's nothing weird or pervy. Really, we'll have loads of fun. Meet us at the corner table of Nido d'Aquila at seven o'clock tonight. Wear something nice but not too whorey.*

*xxoo*

I could hardly suppress my excitement. Obviously, the invitation couldn't be from anyone but Jenny Cole.

It takes being away from one's self to be a fair judge of one's own qualities. The truth is, while I was a friendly enough girl, I was never what you would have called "magnetic." I'd always done fine; I had some friends once I got to uni, I had my cousins and sister, and, of course, I always had Babs. But I was never exactly the center of things. Now, looking at the note again, my hands trembled with anticipation. Perhaps if I behaved properly, I wouldn't have to spend my year in Italy suffering through Marcy's company or shuffling about Grifonia alone. That afternoon, I showered and put on a rather prim shirt and jeans and some silver earrings my sister, Fiona, had passed down to me, and then I took the three-minute walk up to the pub.

It was a typical Enteria bar, Nido d'Aquila: a long, narrow space packed with loud foreign students. A bit nicer, perhaps, than the other expatriate establishments—cleaner and brighter, for one thing. But there was no pretense of its being a real Italian place. The walls were covered with photos of foreign students holding up shot glasses and brimming steins of Guinness, and there was no Italian anywhere on the menu. On Wednesday nights, the bar hosted a fully amped American karaoke night on the back veranda that was, by all accounts, the scourge of the entire north side of town.

The rest of the girls were already there, right out front at the bar's most coveted outside table. You could see everyone coming up the street from there, and, more to the point, everyone could see you. As a threesome, they were—as my mother would say—*certainly worth looking at.* Jenny had on a sundress that made the most of her ample chest and shoulders. She was at the head of the table, her ever-present designer bag beside her. On her left was the redhead, very thin, with skin the color of a marble bust and watery blue eyes. She was attractive but slightly sickly looking, as if she might be suffering from a permanent cold. To Jenny's right was the black girl I'd seen. She was the most classically beautiful girl of the group, body coiled and tight, with cheekbones that seemed to soar off either side of her face and amber eyes that scanned the street with detached interest. All three were dressed in lovely clothes, not the cheap frocks or tight pants I'd seen hanging on the doors of the shops on the smaller streets, but beautiful things—loose, knee-length tunics of silk and linen, glinting with embroidery and accented with delicate, expensive belts.

"Ladies, meet Tabitha," said Jenny, looking up with an efficient smile and sliding a glass to me. "Also a Nottingham girl. And our final member to arrive." She winked. "What you need to know about her is that she is always late."

"How do you know that?" I asked.

"It's in the dossier. Anyhow, it's a sin, one we'll have to beat out of you."

"That's right," the girl with the amber eyes said. "We killed the last girl who held us up."

She stood and extended her hand.

"I'm Luka, that's Anna. Don't remember seeing you back at school, but glad to know you."

"Thank you." We settled into our chairs. Now that I saw her up close, I realized that I had, in fact, seen Luka on campus, usually embedded in some exclusive, raucous group or another.

Anna's face, though, was new to me. She turned toward me now and smiled warmly. "I'm so glad you're here. We need a fresh opinion on Dottori. Luka says once a Fascist, always a Fascist, but I say just look at his work. After Mussolini's fall, the paintings are really *very* socially conscious."

Luka shrugged. "Murderers don't change their minds. Once you witness a killing, you can't go back."

"Jenny?"

"*I* think the things are hideous. Fascist, Statist, Socialist, whatever. The paintings give me a headache."

"I love you, Jenny," Luka said. "But I'd wager you're just saying that because you don't *have* an opinion." She turned my way and winked. "Fact is, doesn't matter who the artist is. It's the *work*. I don't care how many Jews his party murdered. I still bloody love the paintings."

"*Please* stop saying things about Jewish people," Anna said. "I'll have to leave."

"Anna had a Jewish boyfriend once," Jenny explained. "Old guy, of course. What, fifty or something, Annie? She says he was very funny. Damned good in bed, too."

Anna blushed. "I never told you that."

Jenny rolled her eyes. "Everyone *knows* it. They try harder. Taz, what do you think?"

"I'm Jewish," I said quickly, trying to stay calm. "Well, half. But my mother is—"

"What the hell. We don't care about that," Luka said. "So, seriously. What do you think of Dottori?"

"I'm so sorry to say, I haven't—"

"Don't let her make you uncomfortable," Anna said. "We only know him because we happened to go to a party at the contemporary museum last night."

"*I* bloody knew," Luka said. "And I'll be damned if I don't leave this town with one of his pieces."

"He's a local twentieth-century painter," Anna said to me. "You should have a look."

"Hell of a lot better than all of those damned pietàs. Virgin Mary, my ass. What a whore she was!"

"Really, Luka. *Must* you work so hard to shock?" Jenny said.

Luka sat back and drained her glass rather forcefully, as if making a point.

As they chattered on about the paintings, I sat there, my wineglass frozen in place, my face arranged in what I hoped was a knowing expression. It's not that they were ignoring me, exactly. In fact, they were rather pointedly inclusive, stopping from time to time to smile at me or shake their heads conspiratorially, yet they made no genuine effort to catch me up. It was as if I was expected to participate in this esoteric conversation because they had unanimously decided I *was* one of them already.

I felt a hand on my elbow. "I'm so glad you finally came out with us," Anna said to me softly. "We've been asking for you for quite a while."

What could she possibly mean, I wondered, thinking of the nights I'd spent dodging Marcy.

"Well," Jenny said. "We had to be certain."

"Please let the record stand that *I* was for you all along," Luka said. "These other girls were awful."

"I—"

"Luka, Luka," Anna pleaded.

"You're getting ahead of us as usual." Jenny made a drinking motion with her hands. "Do shut up."

"I can tell her," Luka said. "She'll laugh. Okay, so there was Libby, who shagged a German in the back of Club Lazar, right in front of us. Paula, dull as toast. And then that bulimic—"

"It's not like we're against handicaps," Jenny said. "We just can't have anyone slowing us down to throw up after every bloody meal."

"You all are so crass," Anna protested.

"But *you*," Jenny said. "You're perfect! So sweet, so funny. And besides—I've known you for years! More or less. Look, I'm sorry I had to look into other options, but we did only have the one spot."

"One?"

"It has to be four," Luka said. "Even. Two is too few—we're not lovers. And three . . . well, three's bad luck. Gets everything off-kilter."

"Right," I said, as agreeably as I could.

"Are you terribly shocked?" Anna asked, worried.

"She thinks we're *mad*," Luka said, clearly delighted by the notion.

"You'll understand everything soon," Jenny said. "And you'll see that this is the most reasonable thing in the world. We're not just anyone, you know. For instance, Anna here—she's the daughter of a fucking baron."

"He's dead," Anna said. "And the title jumped. So it's really nothing."

"And Luka's father is—" She named a singer I had vaguely remembered from my father's record collection. I couldn't remember anything but his one hit song, which was now the theme music to an overplayed Marks & Spencer television advert.

"Well. I don't even know what to say. Thank you for inviting me." I smiled at them. "I'm very flattered."

"Flattered?" Jenny's mouth pursed, as if she had just tasted something bad. "Tabitha, dear, we are offering you something very unusual."

"Oh, of course! I mean—no!—I'd love to be friends with you all. I haven't met anyone else but my Italian flatmates, and *they're* pretty busy, and—"

"Taz, let me explain." Jenny picked up her glass and swirled her wine pointedly before putting it down again. "We're not just some clique of Enteria girls—you know, the kind you see, stomping up and down the hill, lounging on the cathedral steps, chatting with every filthy backpack-ridden turtle with a fucking *guide*book."

My face grew hot as I remembered how she hadn't acknowledged my own presence on the steps just a few days earlier.

"Jenny says you speak fluent Italian."

"Maybe not completely fluent, but I'm not bad."

"Well, we're awful—all of us. We'll need you to translate some. We've been running into all sorts of trouble."

"Oh, I can certainly do that."

Jenny smiled approvingly. "Taz, you're going to have such a better year now," she said. "No more getting stuck at those awful student parties, downing purple drinks and dodging low-level gropes. No more getting lost in that damned crowd in the square on Thursdays. You won't be crammed into a student bar, yelling into a fucking *karaoke* machine."

"But they have karaoke here," I couldn't help pointing out, gesturing toward the back of the bar.

"Metaphor, Taz."

I felt an acute pang for Babs. What *was* this? Who outlined friendship in these . . . terms? And yet it was nice—being there at that table with those girls. People looked at us. Shouted over to us. One Italian boy took a picture with his phone.

"So it's official then." Jenny sat back in her chair, a smile on her face. "We're the B4."

"Must we put a name on it?" Anna whimpered. "I mean, really."

"Seems proper," said Jenny firmly. "It's not the worst thing for people to know we're different."

"Shall we have some shots?" Luka said.

"Damn right!"

A round of grappa was ordered. And then another. A digestif usually reserved for sipping after dinner while discussing love and politics, grappa would soon come to be something I downed like water. With us thus fueled, the night began to speed up, and soon Jenny was leading us in a game of "I Never."

Jenny leaned in, speaking in a charged, nefarious whisper.

"I never shagged in a car."

"This game is wicked," Anna giggled. We all looked at one another nervously, then drank.

*I never cheated on my boyfriend.*

*I never shoplifted.*

*I never had sex from behind.*

*I never had sex with two blokes in one night.*

The ugly truth quickly came pouring out. Again and again, Luka, Anna, and I found ourselves tossing back a shot. Not all of us every time, but enough that I was learning about my new acquaintances far too fast. Anna had slept with married men. Luka had once blacked out and woken up in bed with two strangers. I admitted things, too—mortifying secrets, namely how a boy at Nottingham had convinced me to try anal sex the year before in his dark, muggy dorm room. Actually, he hadn't so much asked as flipped me over and pinned me down, mashing my face in the pillow.

As soon as I took the drink, I regretted it. Would they think of me differently now? But how could they not, when they didn't even know me at all?

Too late, I realized that Jenny was abstaining most of the time. And of course it was she who asked the most lurid questions, only to smile and listen quietly, her glass sitting primly on the table.

"*Don't* tell me you haven't done *that*," Luka erupted when Jenny refrained from the *I never gave a blow job* question. "Come on!"

"A goddess never tells."

"What?" Anna cried, her thin voice wavering. "A goddess never *tells*? You—you bloody *started* this game!"

Jenny picked up a spoon, as if inspecting it for filth. "That's true enough, dearie. But I never said *I* was actually playing."

We stared at her, stupefied.

"Oh, don't be so shocked. See, you've already learned a lesson. An important one."

"I'm going," Anna said, rising.

"You don't really want to do that, do you?"

A look of dread came over Anna's pale face. She looked so fragile that, in my grappa-infused state, I wondered if she might break.

I glanced at Jenny. What could possibly have frightened Anna so?

"I was actually trying to make a point, girls. The thing is, you don't have to tell anyone what you've done. Ever. Fact, it's ever so much more powerful if you *don't*. We're the only ones who have to know our own secrets. If you drink too much, we're not going to get on you for it. If you go home with the wrong fellow, who cares? Blow an old codger, vomit into a plant. We have a pact, eh? *We keep these things to ourselves.*"

"It's true," Luka said.

"So come on, Anna," Jenny said, lighting a cigarette. "All right? Come around. Don't rip me a new arsehole over a stupid game. Or should I be saying that to Taz?"

Luka burst into laughter, while Anna looked at me to make sure I was all right, then smiled reluctantly. My face burned, but I managed to grin.

"I'm joking, Taz, darling. Girls. *Really.* Don't be upset. We are going to have *such* a lovely time here, the four of us. All right? We've been counting on it. And now I have a surprise."

"What now?" Luka drawled.

Jenny pulled four substantial, unfamiliar-looking coins out of her pocket. "These are passes to a private party in the country. *Very* insidery."

"How did you get those?" I asked.

"I get a lot of things. You'll see. All right. Luka, the bill?"

Luka signaled the waitress and handed over her card without looking.

"I'm sorry," I said. "Can't I chip in?"

"Luka will get it," Jenny said.

I glanced at Luka, who met my eyes with an impassive gaze.

"All right."

"Here we go then."

The cab ride took over an hour, jerking us through a tangle of steeply pitched streets and into the countryside. The other girls seemed perfectly calm, aloof even; Luka produced glasses and a bottle of wine from her bag, somehow nicely chilled. I knew nothing about wine, but even I could tell from the complex notes on my tongue that it was very good. These girls were not foodies, exactly, but they knew what was of value, and always insisted that we partake of it. Wines of the right year and month; crumbling white cheeses from the correct region, veined with sapphire; restaurants of the moment tucked away in stone basements with famous visiting chefs on sojourns away from Rome and Paris. I never quite knew how they'd learned such things, for I never saw any literature on the subjects, which, if not exactly complex, were certainly esoteric. It was as if people of the class they so obviously inhabited were simply born knowing the right way to do things, while the rest of us had to silently observe and study in order to catch up.

I stared out the window of the taxi, trying to look for markers in order to memorize where we were going. We went through several small towns, past a long, flat expanse of dead sunflowers, their burned shadows cast over the ground in the moonlight, and then up a steep mountain, lurching and spiraling onto a web of switch-backed dirt roads.

"If we don't get there soon I'll vomit," Anna whispered. Luka poured her another glass of wine. Finally we arrived in a tiny, nondescript town—less a town, really, than a grim string of damp, dimly lit houses, clinging to either side of the road.

"This can't be it," I said, but Luka elbowed me and pointed to the building reaching up before us toward the black sky.

Even in the dark, you could see that this cathedral had once really been something, and not simply because of its size. The face of it rose high into the night, formidable with its stained glass windows, which I now saw were lit from within. As we rolled down the car windows we could hear the muffled roar of music and voices—that intoxicating swell of a party that imparts both excitement and dread.

"It is," Jenny said. "Pay the man."

The fare was over eighty euros. Looking nervously at the meter, I ticked off in my head how much my share would affect the balance I had left for the semester. But once again, before I could produce my wallet, Luka paid. When I protested, she ignored me and got out of the car.

"But really—" I went on.

"Taz. No." Jenny's command was firm and businesslike, almost as if she were speaking to a spoiled dog.

Grasping at one another's arms, we approached the scene. I was trembling, and I caught myself thinking rather inappropriately of the war story of Oradour-sur-Glane—the women and children being locked in the church there and burned alive. The cathedral's great wooden door was shut, but seemed to visibly pulse with sound. I had to shake away the urge to run.

"Are you sure we're invited?" Anna said.

Jenny ignored her and pounded on the door in sharp, staccato bursts. After a moment, the door creaked open, revealing a woman with black hair pulled into a painful-looking bun and skin so pale I could see the blue at her temples. Jenny dropped the coins into her palm and the woman opened the door wider, revealing the inner world to us.

Jenny went first, her chin thrust forward. I was still clinging to Anna's hand, the tableau rendering me both elated and petrified. Candelabras big as trees lit the cavernous space with a flickering, ghostly glow. All the pews had been ripped away, leaving only the black-and-white marble floor, which someone had polished to a wet-looking shine. Everyone—young and old, male or female—was in black and white, as if utterly bled of color this night, the men's hair combed flat and glistening, the ladies' artfully arranged in chignons, bouffants, or glistening, wing-like sculptures. They clustered together in ever-changing groups, filling the air with the rolling syncopations of their chatter. Smooth, grim-faced waiters circled the room with precarious trays of Prosecco, served in delicate crystal glasses held miraculously aloft above the revelers. Some of the guests were dancing near an orchestra playing intricate, seductive music of a sort I'd never heard before, brimming with cymbals and a tight band of electric cellos and violins, while a small troupe of gymnasts in scarlet performed slightly lewd acrobatics in the middle of the floor. Elaborate as the party was, the room had a somber feeling, and I understood that this celebration was not just a frivolous gathering, but also an occasion that signified something.

"What is this party for?" I asked Jenny.

"A local club or whatever," she called out, and shrugged. "Patrick wasn't very clear about it."

"Jenny's flavor of the week," Luka whispered to me with a nudge.

I looked around to see if anyone else from Enteria was there, but of course they weren't. I looked silly in my jeans, yet the other three were dressed almost as casually as I.

"I wish I'd *known* it was a ball," Anna said. "I do hate being unprepared for these things."

"I'll get us some sauce," Jenny said, then disappeared into the crowd. The frenzy was rising, the great door swinging open and shut with a great *slam* twice a minute as more and more figures in black and white filed into the hall. The lights grew dimmer, the music louder, the dancing more feverish. Anna, Luka, and I stood so close our shoulders were touching.

"Taz," Luka said, "you're *gaping*."

"I know," I said, wondering only how they were managing not to. I'd never been to an event like this—a happening so clearly exclusive, so . . . desirable. Yes, that was the correct word. *Desirable.* You could feel it in the air, the privilege of being somewhere others would die to be.

"I once went to a wedding like this in Ibiza," Anna said.

Luka leaned into my ear. "The Jaggers, she means."

"Shut up, Luka."

"Odd, isn't it? How the *real* bluebloods are always the least discreet?"

I smiled, as if I had any idea what she might be talking about. Suddenly, I froze. There, just a few feet away, was the man from the Museo Archeologico. His figure jutted up through the crowd, his shoulders broad, his suit nice but a bit misshapen.

"Excuse me," I said to the girls, then, emboldened by the alcohol, made my way over. As I got closer, I felt an unreasonable chill, splitting me in two. His brown hair was soft, drifting over his collar. He held a glass of whiskey, neat, and was carefully looking at the faces in the crowd.

I tapped him on the shoulder.

"Hello," I said.

He turned and looked at me rather fiercely for a moment. Was he placing where he'd seen me before? And then he smiled—a smile broad as any girl would wish for. A surprisingly kind smile for a face so uneven and severe.

"Ah. Museum girl. The one after blood."

"What?"

"You were the one after that Agamemnon story."

"Oh, yes."

He looked down at my jeans. "Who invited you? You don't look Grifonian to me."

"Neither do you."

I thought he would smile, but the words fell flat. Before I could say anything else, my new friends were flanking me on both sides.

"Hello there," Luka said, elbowing me playfully. "Who are *you*? Glad to see a familiar. You know Taz from the Enteria class?"

"No," he said abruptly. My new friend (was he a friend?) then excused himself, disappearing pointedly into the crowd.

"Well, *that* won't do," Anna said. "What could he be on about?"

"I suppose that he . . . he doesn't like me very much."

"Impossible," Anna scoffed. "That's like not liking . . ."

She paused.

"Bread?" Luka offered.

"Cham*pagne*," Anna corrected. "Anyhow. Perhaps he's socially awkward."

"Perhaps he's a *bore*."

Just then, Jenny returned, followed by a waiter with four glasses of Prosecco. He presented them to us with a short, barely perceptible glance at our attire, and then moved on.

"Took a while to sort that out, I tell you. Christ. My Italian is inexcusably rotten."

We stood there, the four of us, in the middle of the throng. The other girls danced slowly with one another, and I followed suit, trying not to feel too awkward.

Surprisingly, Jenny knew a lot of people at the party. Every once in a while, someone would tap her on the shoulder, kiss her cheeks, and pull her aside. She would bend her head, nodding and listening.

Once she beckoned me over to translate to a twentysomething blond woman sheathed in white sequins.

"Tell her I'm going to the lake on Monday," Jenny instructed. I did, and the woman kissed both of us and wandered off, looking like a cat who had lapped up a cup of cream.

"Lake Trasimeno?" I asked.

She nodded. "I've got a friend with a house there."

*Of course you do*, I thought. What else to expect from a girl who got us invites to the most enchanting gathering I'd ever seen? Eventually the candelabras went completely out, and somehow the light transitioned to red lamps, bathing the room in a thick, smoky amber. Everyone was dancing now—it didn't seem to matter much who with—and even keeping off to the side, I was twice swept up in the sea of bodies. Round and round the room the four of us spun, finding and losing and finding one another again, until finally Jenny caught my arm and pulled me to a corner.

"What do these blokes want?" she asked, looking with annoyance at an intense little group of men in tuxedos gathered in a tight circle. "They keep talking to me."

Patting her arm, I turned to find out, only to see that the man from the museum was among them. Again, when I approached, he hurried away.

"My friend's Italian is very bad," I said. "May I help you?"

"You are no longer invited," an older man said curtly. "All nonmembers must go."

"Nonmembers of what?"

"You must go," he repeated, gesturing firmly toward the door.

I relayed the message to the others, feeling as if I'd somehow failed them.

"Fucking long way we've come, just to get kicked out at two-fucking-thirty," Luka said.

"It won't do to argue," Jenny said. "Lot of new friends here. Let's go while there are still cabs." She herded us toward the door, which was already clotted with other wilting female figures in black and white. Jenny wiggled out, cutting the line, and the rest of us followed with our heads down. In a moment we found ourselves—despite the jeers of those behind—in the very first car in the queue. The driver seemed hesitant, but once Luka presented a quick bundle of bills, he hurtled us down the mountain without further question.

"One last drink," Jenny said, popping a bottle. "Knicked it from the bar."

"Jenny, you are spectacular," Luka said. "Just has to be said."

"*We* are spectacular," Jenny corrected, handing me the bottle. "Say it," she commanded.

"You are spectacular." I took a drink.

"Nooooo," she said patiently, as if to a small, rather dim child. "The B4 is spectacular."

"Right." I wiped my mouth with the back of my hand.

"No. *Say* it, Taz." She leaned forward, pressing her forehead against mine. "Write it in fucking blood."

Anna let out a drunken giggle, her face covered by her lavender-tipped fingers.

I rolled down the window. "*The B4 is spectacular!*" I shouted, and we all laughed. We laughed all the way down the mountain, past the already waking lights of the farms, and across the dusty valley. At some point we must have stopped, because by the time the car was once again climbing the streets of old Grifonia, we were sleeping, our heads resting on one another's shoulders and pressed against the taxi's windows. Yet now, hard as I ponder it, I cannot remember at which point, exactly, our delirium ended and the slumber began.

# 5

The nights of early September steamed ahead with force and gaiety. Though we never found ourselves at another happening as strangely delightful as the cathedral affair, Jenny led us to all sorts of parties hidden throughout Grifonia, held in gilded pockets behind walls of stone where richly tapestried apartments and courtyards paved in glittering mosaics revealed themselves. We went to a private chamber music concert, a small fashion show, an art gallery opening, a particularly odd masked dance. Once she led us halfway down a narrow stairwell, turned in front of a wall, then pressed her hand against the stone relief of a rose. To my awe the wall opened to reveal a tunnel leading to an underground club. Sounds implausible, I know, but this was the sort of thing that happened to me all the time under Jenny's wing. The blurred faces, the candles flickering, the trays passed loaded heavy with glasses of Umbrian wine. Even when it was cold out, those enchanted chambers were always warm, almost murky, so that after a few hours the gossamer Italian dresses would wilt on their wearers' shoulders, the stays would loosen and buttons would come undone, to free up just a bit more skin.

We made no real friends at these gatherings, though Jenny always knew someone from her friend's house at Lake Trasimeno. *Going to the lake?* they'd ask, smiling. *When?* Jenny had most of her conversations through me. She kept them short and to the point, inevitably turning away when she was done. Mainly, we talked and danced among ourselves.

Back at home, Babs and I had waded meekly through uni parties. Yet Jenny, Anna, Luka, and I *were* the happening, and everything around us, the men, the chatter, the fashion, was just noise. People would stare as we arrived, as if someone had just switched on a light. Men often came to speak to us, but, following Jenny's lead, we'd brush them off until the end of the night. Then, once it was time to leave, if we didn't have another party to go to, we relented, letting them run to get us drinks or cigarettes.

I didn't go home with these men. They tended to be older, peering at us through half-closed eyes in a way that often made me want to run back to the cottage and pull on my lumpiest, thickest wool jumper. As for the more age-appropriate boys—the sorts at the dive bars where we'd make appearances late in the night—they were tourists or students, eager for quickie sex and nothing more. It's not that I wasn't mildly interested; it was just that, always pragmatic, I never saw the point.

Jenny, though, almost always said yes. Luka would sometimes sleep with women. Anna would more often than not walk home with me. But for Jenny, it was a new man every night. She would wave, smiling coolly as she walked out the door with Paolo from Florence or Barry from Atlanta or someone whose name no one really caught but who was tall and had decent teeth. It didn't seem to matter who these men were or how long she'd spoken to them. The range was wide: old, young, thin, fat, black, white, well-dressed, unshaven. By the end of the night, she always had someone.

I won't lie. I was shocked at first. But after a week or so, I came to accept that I was different from the others. Jenny, Luka, and Anna came from a world so distinct from my own . . . They were the kind of girls who would disappear for a day in another country with no reason for leaving but a party, or a shop. Luka, especially, was always jetting off on impulsive international jaunts. "Where's Luka?" I'd ask when it was only three of us, and the others would shrug. *Morocco, art bazaar. Portugal, polo match.* Luka just *went* to these places, the same way I might sometimes go to the sad little track at the bottom of the hill to get in a run.

I tried not to seem too impressed, but that was, frankly, the wrong word for my state. The truth was, I was deeply in love with each one of them, and when they took me aside to whisper their mesmerizing confidences—perhaps a night with a stranger in Trastevere, or a cocktail made of a strange liqueur one could get only in Belgium—I drank their words in greedily, savoring each syllable, each sweet breath of that new life.

•

Most mornings, I woke with a thick head. Our cottage was not a hundred feet from the bustle of the city center, but because of the position of the house, my room was hushed in the early part of the day and flooded with morning radiance. I could hear the birds in the sloped orchard, as well as the occasional rooster. I had always been a late sleeper, so generally, by the time I was awake, Gia and Alessandra were out of the house, at class or work or wherever their Grifonian lives led them in the course of a day. Sometimes, though, I'd hear them puttering about and lie in with a good mystery until they were gone, only then coming out to make my morning tea and read twenty more pages in the delicious peace, the sun streaming in the windows, the air heavy with the smell of the baked grass below.

One Wednesday, after a night out with the B4, I woke up paralyzed in bed, sick with sugar and rum. Determined to remain horizontal for as long as possible, I picked up Patricia Highsmith, then after a page or two tossed it aside for Ovid.

Anna had convinced me to join a monthlong seminar on Etruscan mythology. It took me a while to come around, but eventually I agreed. Due to the intensive nature of the course—six hours a week for the better part of a month—the class would count for as much credit as a semester-long one; also, the seminar happened to be taught by someone Anna knew, a family friend of some sort, and she promised he'd favor us with decent marks.

The syllabus, which Anna forwarded to me, was hard to make

out. There were no specific readings, only "expected working knowledge" of *The Homeric Hymns*, the *Iliad*, and the *Odyssey*, as well as all of Virgil and Ovid. I was hacking away at it the best I could, but it was crippling stuff:

> *The poet's limbs were strewn in different places: the head and the lyre you, Hebrus, received, and (a miracle!) floating in midstream, the lyre lamented mournfully; mournfully the lifeless tongue murmured; mournfully the banks echoed in reply.*

"Ugh," I cried through my hangover. "What does it *mean*?"

Just then, the door clattered open out front and someone stumbled in, dragging something huge over the rough tiles.

Even as I rose to see who was there, I faced a whole other wall of pain. *Rum.* I put on my robe and opened my bedroom door. A girl in a loose T-shirt, cargo pants, and Converse tennis shoes was dragging a huge, overstuffed duffel down the hall.

"Oh, hi." I took a moment. She was nice-looking but sloppy, this American. Unplucked eyebrows, ears pierced all the way up the sides, hair a curious, manufactured silver color, tied with the kind of elastic band you'd put around the newspaper.

But then she smiled, and everything changed. It was as if the delight of ten children shone from her face.

"I'm Claire."

Claire. Her loveliness grew fourfold by the end. Yet upon our first meeting, she was clumsy as a puppy, knocking into a lamp here, the counter there. She leapt over the bag and stuck out her hand, the loose flowered T-shirt she wore falling aside to reveal a soiled bra strap.

"Tabitha, right? They told me. But, you know what? I recognize you. I've seen you everywhere."

"Right," I said. It all came back to me now. She was the girl kissing the Italian on the steps my first day. "You do look—"

"Oh, shit, I didn't wake you up, did I?"

"Please. You saved me from Ovid."

"Nice. Amor makes an ass of Apollo. I remember. So you got the good room, huh?"

"Oh, well. I hope you don't mind."

"You kidding? If I'd gotten my stuff here first, I'd have done the same thing." She walked into my room rather brashly and stood at my window. "Wow."

"I know." Did the room smell stale, of sleep? And my underwear. It was lying on the floor next to the contents of my purse, which had spilled out onto the tile.

Claire seemed not to notice. She stood for a moment looking out at the Umbrian countryside, then trotted out into the hallway again. "And this fucking terrace," she said. "Can you believe it?"

"I just woke up . . ."

"I mean, mostly it's a view of the street, but if you turn *this* way . . ." She turned a plastic chair toward the hills and collapsed into it, propping her feet up, then took a pack of cigarettes out of her cargo pants. "You smoke?"

"No."

"Oh. I thought everyone in the house did." She tapped one out, lit it. "So you went out last night?"

"I did."

"Fun," Claire said with curiosity. When I didn't elaborate, she threw her barely lit cigarette into an earthen pot. "I'll make some coffee."

"Oh, yes."

The new girl shot up and began rifling through the cabinets. Gia's and Alessandra's doors were open, meaning they were out. Beds unmade, belongings everywhere. The Italian girls never shut their doors, nor did they seem to mind who happened to see their messes.

"This must be the coffeemaker," Claire went on. "I haven't quite gotten it yet but it looks pretty easy—wait, what about this one, though? See, I'm from Butte—totally weird, don't ask—and we need good coffee all the fucking time just to—wait, is this espresso or coffee? Too coarse to be . . . oh, fuck, a gas stove. Where's the lighter?

Oh, never mind—it's broken—no—oh fuck, the gas—shit! [*small explosion*] Okay! We're a go."

It was as if the filter between her brain and mouth was passable as air.

"I know, I can be a spaz. Anyway. You're pretty. Do people tell you?"

"Sometimes." The truth was, that statement was rarely made, and if so, it was by a boyfriend during sex or by my mother. I was not pretty; I was interesting-looking. My skin was smooth, my limbs thin, but my face was slightly off-kilter: eyes out of proportion with the nose, chin that ended too abruptly.

We were silent for a bit, waiting for the water to boil.

"Boyfriend?" I asked.

"Broke up. For the trip. We keep in touch, but really, it's better this way. You?"

"I recently got over something."

She took the coffee off the stove. "*That*'ll last, like, five seconds. You being single, I mean."

"Maybe." I watched her pour the coffee, spilling half on the counter.

"Have you met anyone here yet?"

"I have," I said. "It wasn't so hard."

"I hope not. Though I'm really hoping to meet Italians."

"Sure."

"Do you hang with Gia and Alessandra at all?"

"Not really. Not yet anyway."

"Well. We're going to have an awesome time."

"Absolutely."

She sipped her coffee, narrowing her eyes. "You remind me of someone."

"Yes. You, too."

"Really? Who?"

I blinked. I was just being polite. "I'll have to think of it."

"Well, *you* could be Winona Ryder. Before she got all fucked up."

I had to laugh. "Hardly."

"I probably remind you of the fucking Lorax. I dyed my hair this awesome purple color before I left, for shits and giggles, and also to piss off my mom. But now it's going back to blond, and it just looks weird."

"I like it."

She grinned and got up from the table.

"Rule number one, roommate," she said. "No more lying."

Claire threw her dishes into the sink and slid into her room to unpack. In her absence, the tiny living room stilled perceptively, almost sighing with the loss of life.

# 6

That month of September, my happiness was reaching a point of delirium. Young women of the sort I was are most content when they feel secure. Now that I had the B4—ridiculous and childish as the label sounded—I was bolstered. I wasn't naive enough to think that Jenny, Anna, and Luka were my good friends. They were sophisticated—vastly more than anyone I'd hung out with at Nottingham or at home, and I had every reason to suppose that, as soon as I got back, I'd be relegated to regular-girl status alongside Babs again. Yet just knowing that for now I had someone to call for lunches, night walks, and late-night pizzas . . . it was comforting. I had this group.

Perhaps because of my newfound social independence, Gia and Alessandra were getting nicer as well. The girls seemed to appreciate my studious attitude toward their language, and would bend over my shoulder, helping me translate the newspaper. Sometimes, if we all happened to be around together, they'd cook for me. Though tiny, our kitchen was properly outfitted with all the things any self-respecting Italian would bring to a house: a pan for sautéing, a deep pasta pot, a cheese grater, a baking dish, two separate knives, kept sharp, one for bread and fruit, one for meat. Alessandra had one pasta sauce she made every other day of tomatoes, something sweet I couldn't place, pitted olives, and hand-brined capers. She would cook fresh spaghetti, made that day at the grocery down the street, and top the strained and rinsed mound with curled shavings of aged cheese. Then, crowded next to it on our tiny, scrubbed counter: a bowl of insalata mista, sparkling with deep-purple balsamic; a plate of cold burrata, its wrinkled outer membrane straining to contain its succulent white insides; freshly sliced tomatoes, scarlet and bleeding; and thinly shaved prosciutto, transparent and rosy against the white china plate. I found myself getting up again and again, helping myself to seconds, thirds. I'd mop my plate shamelessly with bread and then, if there was none left, use my fingers.

One sultry night we dragged the little table outside. It didn't exactly fit, as our terrace was barely two feet wide and four feet long, but it made one feel romantic anyway, particularly if you were facing away from the busy street. Claire was out that night, presumably exploring.

"You are out every night, *bella*," Alessandra teased me, filling my glass. By this time I had taken to supplying my own wine, usually decent, three-euro bottles of Pinot Grigio, which, sipped out of the jelly glasses in the kitchen, tasted metallic and cold.

"No boys yet?"

I shrugged, my mind lurching immediately to the man from the museum.

"She hasn't met the ones downstairs," Gia said. "Or they haven't seen *her*. Soon enough they'll come sniffing up."

"Are they nice?"

"Nice!" Gia laughed, showing a mouthful of bread. "No. Well, Marcello, he's okay. Alfonso is an ass."

"Don't listen to her, *bella*," Alessandra said. "None of those boys are nice. I can barely walk down there, it stinks so much from *spinello*."

"I hate nice boys," Gia said, tearing her bread.

Alessandra stood to clear the plates. "These guys buy drugs, probably they sell them, too, for all I know. That Alfonso was bragging about a gun once. I don't like them at all."

Gia shrugged. "Like I said, Alfonso's an ass. So what do you think of the new girl? Claire?"

"She's sweet," I said.

Gia nodded. "Very beautiful."

The words stung, somehow.

"I think she likes to party," she added.

"I hope not too much," Alessandra said. "Not here."

"*You* are a good flatmate, Taz," Gia said.

"Yes," Alessandra said. The two women gazed at me thoughtfully, as if I were an object they were thinking of buying.

As sweet as my flatmates were to me, I had yet to go out with them. They had their own full lives, and while I believe they genuinely liked me, taking me along to their parties and gatherings would have, as my sister would say, sandbagged them. Most nights they spent at their boyfriends' apartments. And when they did bring their boys home, they were utterly silent. No amorous groans, not even the inadvertent smack of a kiss. Certainly sex happened; that I knew from the strewn lingerie and condom boxes. Yet they kept their passions silent.

Night after night I went out with some combination of the B4. Sometimes, at twilight, Jenny and I would take a blanket and a picnic basket to a lawn in front of one of the smaller churches, where we would drink Prosecco and eat fruit and various cheeses she'd picked up from a shop she liked behind the university. Jenny paid special attention to me. Whenever the four of us had plans, she would come by and pick me up first, linking arms with me as we walked down the street. Despite the unlikely nature of it, I couldn't help wondering if I was her favorite.

By this time I had quietly used some of my father's money to buy a long blue dress and silver sandals more in keeping with what the others so often wore. Anna, spotting the ensemble the first afternoon I wore it, remarked on it as she joined Jenny and me on the grass to polish off a bottle of Orvieto white.

"Taz, is that new?"

"Yes," I said. "There's this very nice shop near the university where—"

"Look, there's no reason to buy new clothes. I've got loads. We all borrow one another's things. I'll bring some over."

"Oh, I couldn't—"

"You're not allowed to buy anything more," Jenny said in a final tone. "We can't let you waste your money."

"I've got money. I mean, I'm not as rich as all of you, not by a long shot. But my father gave me four thousand pounds, and I made two thousand at my job this summer. I have six hundred euros right here in my purse."

I don't know why I said it. I suppose I was tired of feeling like the beggar girl. But the silence that followed was clear. The words hovered and spun, waiting to be waved away.

"Nevertheless," Anna finally said, mercifully. "You oughtn't spend that on something we already have."

As promised, there was a bag left inside my door the next day. When I shut myself in my room and tried on the contents in front of the mirror—jewel-toned frocks and tunics of finely wrought silk and wool—I couldn't help the girlish, giddy feeling that a hidden door to a secret garden had been opened just for me.

One night, Luka suggested that she and I go to an outdoor movie. I met her at her apartment—a charming, luxurious flat with a brick floor, vaulted ceilings, a fireplace, ferociously clean linens, and a view of the grand fountain in the main piazza. Jenny loved to have us gather there. She called it "the Club" and had taken to using Luka's marble bathroom instead of the crowded shared shower at her residence hall. Most of her clothes were in a cardboard box on Luka's floor.

The apartment was filled with odd pieces of art from Luka's travels. There was a painting of a factory rising above a beach in Réunion; a few rubbings of some particularly sexual bits of the walls of Angkor Wat, done in fluorescent paint; a collage of South African soda and beer labels, compiled to form a vast, intricate landscape. I was impressed that Luka had brought all this to Italy, but when I asked her about lugging the stuff around, she shrugged. "I like to have my art around me."

"Are you a collector?"

"Hardly. I mean, look at this stuff. It's mostly crap."

But it wasn't. Even my untrained eye could see that these pieces would be expensive and difficult to find.

"You doing art history, then? That's why Enteria?"

Luka shrugged. "Modern Italian painting, that's my main thing."

"Then why not Rome? Or Florence? There's not a lot going on in Grifonia art-wise after the fourteenth century, is there?"

She turned away from me. "You need a drink."

Luka made a show of fixing us both large martinis at a polished wood bar cart complete with a silver mixer and a collection of tools I didn't recognize.

"I had them shipped over," she explained as she wielded the shaker with an expert hand. "The Italians aren't much for cocktails."

"And where is this one from?" I persisted. It was a portrait of a young woman in a slip hugging her legs on a bathroom floor. It was a startling work, extraordinary in its realism and color.

"I did that," she said, so quietly I almost didn't hear her.

I turned the corner to the bedroom. There were more watercolors and sketches of the same model, a plain young woman with light-brown hair. In some she lay on the floor, in others on a bed. In all of them, her face was lifeless, her gaze off into the distance. She looked familiar in a couple of them, but her features were so blurred in others she could have been a thousand different girls.

"I didn't know you painted, Luka."

"Come on, bottoms up," she said. "Movie's in just a few." I sipped my drink, the vodka burning my throat. On our way out, seeing I'd had only a few sips, she downed the rest of my martini in one swallow before swinging the door shut.

At the film—*Amarcord*, an ambitious choice, given our poor mastery of the language—she pulled out an engraved silver flask and two matching small silver cups.

"Aquavit," she said loudly, drawing irritated looks from the Italian girls sitting near us. "Ever had it?"

"No."

"Well, cheers," she said, handing me my cup. Better than the vodka, but it was much too strong, and by the fantasy scenes at the Grand Hotel, I was passed out on Luka's shoulder. We struggled back to Luka's apartment, and I woke at dawn on her sofa to the sound of her snoring loudly. She was in an expensive-looking slip, sprawled out with a silk eye mask over her face. Scratching out a thank-you note, I slipped out, wondering whether I should ever mention the evening again.

Passing time with Anna was a different sort of beast. Most of the time she seemed genuinely kind, possibly the nicest of the three. She loved to walk arm in arm on the promenade and talk about her childhood home: the horses, the teas, the tiresome, charming droves of cousins. She never specified when this life had ended, or why she was out of contact with her mother; indeed, the memories seemed quite alive to her.

Yet often, my new friend would veer wildly from her genteel manner. Particularly while shopping. For Anna Grafton was a vicious bargainer. Not a bargain *hunter*—Anna took no pleasure in finding knockoffs or cheap things. She shopped at the most expensive stores, and wouldn't leave happy unless she had cut the salesperson down some notches. This habit, Jenny told me, she picked up having watched her mother abuse servants and salespeople throughout her childhood in a variety of cities and countries. It was only natural for her to do the same.

"Get me the green pants!" she'd say from the fitting room of the most expensive shop off the main piazza. "No, no, *no*, the ones on the left!" Sniffing, the Italians would serve her, obviously impressed.

"How much?"

"Four hundred euros."

"For *these*?" Anna would scoff. "The thread is coming off. Look!"

"I—"

"It's dreadful. Four *hundred*? I thought Italians were all about quality!"

"Signora—"

"Very disappointing. All right, hand me that red dress. Yes, the Dolce! What did I just *say*?"

Anna never actually bought anything, usually storming out instead in a cloud of feigned fury. It was a lesson in human nature, really. The worse she treated these people, the better they treated her. I would watch, fascinated, as the terrifyingly chic shop women slashed their prices more and more in an effort to please this impossible young woman.

"One hundred," one salesman practically begged, holding up a two-hundred-euro dress. It was exquisite—a close-fitting floor-length black skirt and sleeveless top embroidered in gold and jet beads.

"Maybe you should actually buy this one," I whispered. The salesman—compact, over-sunned—raised his eyebrows. Anna paused, then looked at me and smiled.

"I will buy it for my *friend* for ninety euros," she said.

"No, no, I—"

Anna held up her palm, silencing me. The man's shoulders sagged a bit, and she smiled.

This is how I came to own the only truly beautiful dress I ever had. I was mortified that she bought it for me; but, then, she insisted, and terrified as I was of running through my father's cash, I was quietly thankful. Afterward, I said goodbye and rushed to the cottage, the dress thrillingly heavy in my bag. When I came in, Claire was sitting on the terrace, strumming the guitar in messy, loud strokes.

"Hey!" she said. "Finally I have you all to myself."

I smiled politely, wishing just then that the other girls were home, and then feeling guilty for it. I had only been alone with Claire a few times, and though I liked her, I found her air overly familiar. She was a girl who rushed in, without giving a damn if you were ready for the intimacy or not.

"What's in the bag?"

"Oh, I—I got a dress."

"Just a dress? Let's see it."

I drew it out and held it up carefully to my body.

"Oh my God, Taz. You'll look like a princess in that. Seriously. Try it on."

"Oh, we don't have to—"

"Come on, hottie. Let's have some wine. Here." She rose, stepped into the kitchen, pulled out a bottle of white, and poured us both large jars full, plopping ice in for good measure—a move that truly would have made Alessandra faint. "I have a dress, too, that I bought in Germany." She pulled off her shirt, throwing it on the floor. "It's in here somewhere."

I took a long sip and retreated to my room. The truth was, I was afraid to put the dress on, as I hadn't actually tried it on in the store. I'd only seen it on Anna, who was so thin she looked consumptive. I pulled off my jeans and shirt and looked at the dress, which I'd laid carefully on my bed.

The door opened. Claire was in an ill-fitting electric-blue strapless dress that was too tight on her hips and had a terrible fringe at the knee. Yet on her, it looked charming, slipping dangerously off her shoulders, pouring over her curves.

I was only in my underwear. I covered my chest with my hands.

"That is a truly horrible dress," I said. "But of course it looks terrific on you."

"I'll take that as Irish humor." She reached over and pinched my naked waist. "Come on."

"Just give me a minute, please."

She pushed her way into my room and sat on the bed, watching. Flushing, I grabbed the dress and pulled it over my head.

"Lemme zip it," she said, shooting up again. Turning me a little roughly toward the mirror, she kept her hands on my hips. She had a smell to her, clean but mysteriously masculine, as if perhaps she used her father's aftershave.

"Damn," she said.

I looked in the mirror. The black silk grazed my hips and flowed along my body to the floor. A band of gold-and-black beading accentuated my waist, which, despite the recent influx of pasta and gelato, remained respectably narrow. I thought of what my sister, Fiona, would say, seeing me dressed up like this. And Babs. And my mother, who, I knew, would beam and ask me to twirl in front of her.

"It's a little tight," I said, moving away a bit.

"It's *hot*. Like, really hot." She gazed at my image, then looked at my face. "But you don't look that comfortable."

"Well, it's for . . . a ball or something."

"Your new friends told you to get it?"

"Something like that."

Claire paused, her hands still on my waist. "Hey, take it off. Let's go outside." She moved away to the window, looking down at the ravine. "There's an old shed down there, I want to check it out."

Quickly, I took off the gown, stepping back into my shorts and T-shirt.

"Come on," she said.

We walked out into the garden, then hopped the wall into the grove. Music was playing from the apartment below. The sun was bearing down, and I could see Claire's shoulders were burned. On her left tricep, a large and hideous tattoo of a moose. It was as if her beauty overwhelmed all the things she did to herself, defeating the piercings all the way up the lobe, the dirty nails, the lavender hair now fading to gray, the worn, soiled clothes.

We descended farther into the thicket of olive trees. Claire was still holding her wine. "There," she said, pointing to a crumbled pile of stones and faded tiles.

"It's nothing anymore, is it?"

"No, but think of what it used to be. Maybe a family lived here. Or an outlaw."

"Maybe."

"Oh, definitely." Claire sat on the slope in the shade, looking at the valley. I sat next to her. Above us, the traffic throbbed on.

"So why did you come to Italy, Taz?" Claire asked, handing me her jar of wine.

"Oh, to get away. Out of Nottingham. And Ireland. My family can be . . . well, I'm the youngest. I suppose I needed air."

"Air." Claire nodded. "Yeah." She crossed her arms over her knees. "You know why I came?"

I shook my head.

"Because here, I can be anyone I fucking *feel* like."

She rocked back and forth, her hands playing with the dead grass.

"No one knows me. No one's heard of me. It's fucking fun. It's more than fun. It's . . ." She stopped. "I can't think of the word."

"Freeing?"

"*Liberating.*"

"Isn't that the same?"

"I mean, I *like* sex, you know? I've liked it since junior high school. It made me a freak. And everyone knew. Butte's not exactly a huge town. So all through high school—*boom.* Claire the slut."

"I see."

She grabbed the wine jar, took a greedy gulp, then wiped her lips.

"I don't know. And when I moved to Missoula to go to the U, it was still the same. It's like, if I sleep with a guy, everyone knows. I'm a slut. I'm easy. I can't just *enjoy* sex, or experiment. It means there's something wrong with me. Not that sex is all there is to it. Here, I can be a bitch. Who's going to care? Or I can try . . . I don't know. The guitar. I can play in the square, like, for money. Made seven euros yesterday."

I burst out laughing. "I hate to tell you this . . ."

"I suck. I know."

"Maybe."

She kissed me on the cheek and pressed her forehead to mine.

"I've gotta go," she said.

And then she stood and disappeared. There was no other word for it—I must have turned my head just three seconds later, and she was gone. She had a way of doing that when she left places. I could only guess that growing up in the wilds of far-off Montana, she knew how to avoid making sounds or footprints. As if she were a hunter, born knowing how to track.

## *Thainia, 1st century AD*

A short girl, stout with dark hair and olive skin, a nose that hooked out and down. In the spring, she went for a walk outside of the city walls with her brother. He was her twin, and it was his wedding day. They were to slaughter a lamb for the feast in the family's fields.

Thainia was starting to do work in the kitchen now, as women in the house, if they were not brides, had to make themselves useful. Thainia's hands were already rough with cuts, but she didn't complain. She was a loud girl, brassy, with a wine-fed sense of humor. Her father didn't care for her much, but her mother liked having her at banquets.

Just as they neared the low stone wall that marked their land, some thieves came upon the brother and sister. Thrusting out their daggers, they moved to pull Thainia away.

The scene of what was to come unfolded quickly in Thainia's mind.

Her father would never come look for her—to do so would start a war with the barbarians, and he would have no interest in losing men on her behalf. Her mother would cry, resigned, for if Thainia was raped, the girl would not be allowed back into the Volsinii house. It was against common law. If she didn't end up a slave to these brutes, Thainia would end up wandering the streets and dying there.

"Help," she said, looking at her brother.

Her twin didn't have to ask what she meant. He put his knife to her throat. When the men charged forward, he slashed as hard as he could, struggling with the tendons and bone. Still she breathed, so he pierced her heart.

Thainia, the first entry in the Compagnia's ledger. The first Good Death.

*Thainia Volsinii, eighteen years old, 1st century AD*

# 7

Registration was long over for all classes, including Intensive Etruscan Mythology. But since Anna knew the professor, I was sure I wouldn't have a problem.

I was wrong.

"No," the administrator behind the desk said when I went to register. He was sleek as a whippet, with a tan shaved head that made his age impossible to gauge. "You are too late."

"But this class hasn't even started yet." I opened my eyes wide, trying to channel Jenny's sex appeal and Anna's bargaining powers.

"It is forbidden. I am telling you. You cannot enroll. Enrollment was last Monday."

"Oh. I see."

I stood there for a moment, but he didn't look up again.

All right, I thought. So, then, no seminar. I started to turn away.

"*Scusa! Ragazza!* Where are you going?"

"I'm sorry. Perhaps I don't understand. You said I couldn't enroll."

"Well, yes, I *said* no, but not *always*." He sighed, as if I were maddening him. "Ah! All right. For you, we make an exception."

"Oh! Well, you don't have to—"

"Here is your paper. You show this to the professor, and then if—*IF!*—if he wants you, he will let you in."

"I—"

"This is very unusual, what I am doing."

"Yes . . . I . . . thank you?" I ventured. He stroked his chin, clearly pleased. The transaction was, somehow, complete. This would not be the last time, of course; again and again, this happened. On trains. At the grocery store. We don't usually sell just a hundred grams of this porchetta, but for *you* . . . because it is *me* . . .

Italy, I found, is full of exceptions.

As I ran out of the college with my paper in my pocket, my excitement was so acute it had a taste to it—a metal pole on a winter's day. Still, every time I looked at that syllabus my stomach turned. Ovid I gave up on after a good three hundred pages; now I was giving Homer my best shot. But e-mails kept coming from the professor, adding texts he'd forgotten. Apuleius, Euripides, Hesiod, "and, of course, Pindar."

*And, of course, Pindar.* My belly grew cold, my mouth prickly and dry. Who in God's name was Pindar? Nor did Anna particularly quell my fear the next time I met the B4 for drinks at Hotel Nysa.

"Well, of *course* I know Pindar," she said. "I'm a classics major. But don't worry. All you really need is the *Iliad* and the *Odyssey*."

An uncomfortable silence followed.

"Oh, girls, don't tell me. Doesn't *everyone* have to read those? You know, to get a diploma?"

"Not in psychology," Jenny said.

"Well, there is that terrific painting of Circe by Waterhouse in the Oldham," Luka said. "So I've always assumed I got the gist of the thing."

"I'll try to get through it," I said.

"Can we get some more drinks here?" Luka called.

"Tabitha, look. It's very simple. Just read those two, all right? And *not* the SparkNotes, the *books.* Okay, if you're lost, you can read the Graves supplement. At least you'll be covered in an emergency. But be as quiet as you can in class. Arthur's a genius, so he'll know in about five seconds that you're . . ."

"Illiterate?" Luka said.

"Call it under-read," Anna said.

"Anna, you do get so dull when you're pretentious," Jenny said.

"Hear hear," Luka said, picking distastefully at a tray of olives.

"Christ," Anna said, almost to herself. "You know, it really is appalling, how I'm wasting—"

"What?" Jenny asked. "Your life?"

Anna grabbed her bag, squirreling around for something. Lip gloss, it turned out.

"I'm interested, Anna," I said. "I am. I'm really looking forward to the class."

"Kiss ass," Luka muttered.

But Jenny wasn't through yet. "Do tell us, Anna, are you blowing this professor of yours?"

"Don't be disgusting." Carefully, she slicked her thin lips.

"It's just that you seem terribly knowledgeable of his every bloody word. And of course, we *know* about you and older blokes, don't we? Major weakness, that's the word."

"Jenny—"

"Oh, skip it. Anyway, tell us. What *else* does Arthur say?"

Anna drew herself up in her chair. "Well. That without knowing mythology, we're doomed to make the same mistakes over and over again. And he's right. Look at Persephone. She was having a laugh, not paying any sort of attention, hanging about with her mates, and then she was dragged off by Hades—"

"Now we're getting somewhere!"

"—and taken to the Underworld because she *wasn't* careful. Sound like something that could happen to you?"

"Oh, I wish it would," Luka said. "I'd like to be dragged and tied. Sex is so boring in uni."

"You're all hopeless and sick. Taz is the only one of this lot with even the slightest curiosity and sense at all."

"You just want to be dragged and tied up by Arthur," said Jenny. "You bloody well love old men, the crustier the better, and you know it. You want him. Admit it."

"Please. He is my *professor.*"

"Well, I don't like this at all," Jenny said. "It makes me cross, actually, not knowing what this is all about."

"We can have interests outside of parties, Jenny," Luka said.

"Can you?"

"Look, I'm not excluding you from anything," Anna said. "You can take the class."

"Not interested. Too busy."

"Then what's the problem?" Luka asked.

"The problem is Anna's propensity toward old codgers, and we don't want the bother."

"Arthur Korloff was a close friend of my father's," Anna said. "They met in New York in their twenties. He's my godfather."

"All right. I'll trust Taz to keep you in line," Jenny said. "Won't you, Taz?" She turned and patted my arm. "I want a full report, eh?"

Just then, the waitress set four large Camparis in front of us: cherry red, topped with thin slices of oranges. Beads of moisture dripped down each glass.

"Oh, thank God," Jenny cried, suddenly peaceable. "Right then, you fucking nerds. Here's to . . . mythology. I choose Bacchus, all right? Please, let's get drunk."

•

The next day, Jenny came by to see me. More and more, she seemed to take a particular liking to having tea with me in the afternoon, often popping around unannounced.

"It's important that we get our *alone* time, Taz," she said, sitting on the terrace, smoking. Her purse was at her feet. It seemed to grow larger and shinier each time I saw it.

Jenny wore it well, her class. She was extremely good at getting people to serve her. For her visits, I'd drag the real teapot from the top shelf. Not that she would have said anything if I'd just handed her a mug with a bag, as I was used to, but I just knew it wouldn't do.

"Remember, just a little dip in the water," she said. "I can't take that builder's tea."

"No, of course."

I handed her a cup. She sighed happily. "Anna and Luka are lovely—they are. But you're my only friend here."

I knew, of course, my former hall mate was saying that very same thing to Anna and Luka, but I didn't care. It made me feel special, being singled out, however disingenuously. That day, I remember, I lit a cigarette because she had, and sat at the edge of my plastic chair, my legs positioned tensely in front of me, as if I were about to leap.

"I mean, Anna's a little snobby, don't you think?"

"Oh, I don't know," I said. "No."

"Oh but she *is*. Trust me. Those girls with titles. It's a handicap. I'm surprised she isn't *more* that way, actually."

"Well, I don't—"

"And Luka! Total show-business kid. They're always 'artists,' aren't they?"

"I think her paintings are rather good."

"Maybe. Still, she's such a lush. Not that I don't love them both. I absolutely do. Absolutely. It's just . . . they're not like *you*. Solid. Such a good head on your shoulders."

"Well—"

"It's true! Look—you were just completely unwilling to give away your compatriots. I love that. I do." She leaned over and, squeezing my hand, spoke in that low, intimate tone she had. "I'd *die* without you. Really, I'm not joking." She held my gaze for a moment, but I wasn't sure what to do with any of it. My head felt muddled, my cheeks, hot.

"Now," she said, leaning back again and picking up her tea with a brisk smile, "you *might* think about wearing that white sweater tonight."

"Really? But I just got that blue peasant thing from the square."

"I know, I know. Still, I'd wear the white."

"Maybe."

"Here's the thing, darling," Jenny said. "I—well, *we're*—a bit worried about you."

I shifted in my seat. "What do you mean?"

"We are a group, of course. Of friends. But we're also . . . we're more than that. We're an *alliance*."

"And?"

"Well, I've been watching you. And I've been watching others watch you. And what I see is a little alarming." She looked at me, wrinkling her eyes at the corners. "You're much too breakable. I'm—we're—worried that some man . . . that some man is going to come along and just *crush* you. That you'll have one horrible affair with an arsehole and end up a pile of dust."

"Look," I said, smiling with what I hoped read as composure. "I've *been* dumped before. I've *been* a pile of dust. If I ever do meet someone I halfway like, I'll be all right."

"You won't, though. I can see that you won't."

"Oh, I don't see that."

"Listen," she said. "Can you imagine *me* being screwed over by some man?"

I had to admit, nothing seemed less likely.

"I've learned to be this way, you see. The thing is, I play the men before they play me."

I smiled. "So you're some sort of X-treme courtesan, then?"

"No! Sadly for my wallet. I'd never pull it off. Besides, the girls from Belarus have that whole Grifonia whore angle rather cornered."

"So that's what all the sex you're having is about? Playing?"

"*All*? Well, yes, silly. The more sex the less I care about it. It's scientific, really."

"I see."

"You don't, though, do you? I wish you did. The way to avoid it is to get out in front of it."

"Avoid what?"

"It. The pile of dust."

"So you've been a pile."

Jenny smiled. Her eye makeup was running, and in the afternoon light she looked almost ghoulish.

"Oh, a huge pile."

"And what's the solution? Take a lover?"

"Take *ten* lovers. That's how it's done."

I shrugged without conviction.

"It's just . . . your time here's been so *chaste*. I just wonder . . ." She leaned forward. "Are you holding back? I mean, is something wrong?"

"Wrong?"

"Like a health thing? Or something?"

"What?"

"It's just that you told us about your past, Taz. That first night during the game, remember? So I just thought . . ."

"Are you joking? No. Nothing's wrong."

Jenny put her tea and saucer on the little plastic table beside her, then leaned forward, lowering her throaty voice. "There was this girl from Manchester back at Nottingham, Susan Dunhill? And she did that with a guy, and then she spent the rest of the semester in the infirmary with—"

"Zanopane," I said.

"What?" Her voice betrayed an almost inaudible note of alarm.

"I'm just remembering," I said. "Susan Dunhill's roommate—she died from taking that stuff. Zanopane. Someone mentioned it—the drug—and I was trying to remember what it was."

Jenny rose, taking her teacup and cigarette to the counter.

"Her name was Eleanor Peterfield," she said, still standing. "Did you know her?"

"Not at all. I just remember the story. Everyone was so . . . surprised. I heard she wasn't even the type."

"She wasn't."

"So you knew her? Eleanor Peterfield?"

"From around. It was all very sad." Jenny took a long, thoughtful drag and sat down again and looked at me. "Listen, Taz. I want to tell you something. Something I've never told anyone."

"About Eleanor?"

"What? No, no. Don't be dull. About what we were talking about before. Men."

"Right. Men."

She paused, crushing her cigarette. "My first year at Nottingham, I was completely plowed over by this upperclassman named Marshall Chapman. Know him?"

"No."

"Complete wanker. Big rubgy player, rich as hell. No?"

"I'm sorry. I don't—"

"Anyway, I followed him all over the place. A bloody puppy, I was. We were shagging for a few weeks, and one night he gets me stupid drunk. Next thing I know I'm upstairs at some party at a club in a room full of his arsehole teammates. A stranger has my knickers and my legs are over my head."

"Oh God, Jenny."

"Chapman *gave* me to them." She shook her head. "It's the worst thing that can happen to a girl. And you know? It was my fault."

"I'd say not."

"It was. Because I didn't stay in front of it. You see? I let myself get . . . I don't know. Weighed down."

She looked away. A tear rolled down her powdered cheek.

"Oh, Jenny. Oh, God. I can't believe you really think that. Of course it's not your fault. Look, they have support groups for this. I'll go with you."

"Fuck your support groups." Jenny patted her face delicately with the back of her hand. "I'm a realist. You get into a fix like that, it's because you're not watching out. You're not in *front* of it."

I put my fingers to my temples. "I don't think—"

"Oh, we all know you're not the type of girl to get herself into a situation like that. I can see that. But just don't let anyone fuck you over. Literally or otherwise. Stay in front of it. That's the key. Do you see?"

I was unable to move. *Jenny Cole had cried.* I waited for the sky to go black, for day to turn into night. Yet when I glanced over, she was already toggling through her phone, smiling slightly at a message.

"And you only have this once, you know," she continued.

"What once?"

"*This.* We get to be this happy *now*, don't you see? Before the awful things happen."

"Yes."

"And if they don't happen, well, that's almost worse. Then we'll just be *old.* Skulking about, eating too much, complaining about . . .

I don't know. Babies? Work? I mean, look at the *Eat, Pray, Love* ladies. You've seen them, right?"

I knew exactly what she was talking about. They were all over. Forty and up, solo, filmy dresses, clutching guidebooks, nursing glasses of wine alone in public cafés waiting for their lothario to materialize.

"It's pathetic. Life is going to get so horrible someday. For all of us. But it doesn't have to be dreary *now.* We're in a magical place, don't you see? I want you to enjoy it. Because someday you may very well be miserable, or sick, or chained to a desk and living with a cat."

She stood up abruptly and smiled. "All right then. Enough of this talk—it's giving me a bloody headache. Let's have a look at your closet. I'm so sick of everything . . . Maybe if you wear the white top, *I'll* wear the peasant."

She left soon after with a bag full of my clothes, but her words lingered, leaving me dizzy.

I went to my room and pulled out the white top. But it wasn't just white. You see, without the details, every story is a lie. The top was, in fact, a sweater of some soft synthetic material. It was cream, and tight, showing the outline of my breasts. There were little ridges in the fabric at the edges. It was freshly washed and smelled of a little bit of cinnamon lotion I knew boys liked.

I pulled it on and looked at myself.

We get to be this happy now.

Was it a promise, I wondered? Or a threat?

# 8

The day before I left, my father and I had lunch in Dublin at Botecelli, his favorite Italian restaurant. It wasn't very pleasant at first—he was pissed, and with good reason: I was an hour late. He'd been phoning me but I'd ignored his calls; my plane for Rome was leaving at seven the next morning, so I had loads to do. I mean, really, I thought—who makes their daughter go to lunch the day before she's leaving for Italy? I'd offered other days, but he'd had too many patients, which was really *always* his line, during the whole of my life.

Of all of us, I was the most tolerant of my father. My sister, Fiona, barely spoke to him, and my mother mourned. But me, I cashed in on a dinner at least once a month. It had been fifteen years since he left us and moved to the city. He was a bastard, we all agreed. But for whatever reason, I always possessed, at least in some measure, the ability to forgive.

Not that in my way I didn't punish him regularly for leaving us. That afternoon, for instance: my supposed reason for not rushing to lunch was . . . a shopping crisis. What if they didn't have Zara in Italy? What if there was no Topshop? So I was in the shoe department, unable to decide which boots to buy, brown suede or black, brown suede or black—a monumental decision at the time. Fiona said I was gone in the head to buy boots in Dublin at all. I was going to *Italy*, for fuck's sake.

And so, slightly aware of my tardiness yet not particularly sorry, I breezed into the restaurant with my shopping bags.

"Taz!" my father bellowed, looking up from his laptop. "An *hour*? Jesus fucking *Christ*!"

"Sorry, Da," I said, using the name I called him as a baby for good measure. "I just—"

"—have no respect for fucking time?"

He wasn't wrong. All my life I ran on my own schedule. "Taz Time," my friends always called it. It wasn't that I didn't *respect* time; it's that I didn't understand it, really. I'd linger with friends for hours on the street. Minutes would go by as I stared at something pretty in a shop window. When it came to schedules and me, it was like trying to trap air.

"I got the brown ones," I said, giving him my biggest, most dazzling smile.

"Brown?"

I opened the box and put the boots on the table. My beautiful, beautiful new brown suede boots.

"Tabitha, I've got people waiting."

"Who? Someone who needs a nose job?"

"You know perfectly well—"

"Deviated septums. Yes."

My father shook a finger at me, simultaneously signaling the waitress.

"It's the deviated septums, and ear canal work, and throat cancer surgeries, that're going toward your Italian rent, if you must know."

"Perhaps I should thank these patients personally. Since you see them so much more than us."

"Can we just have a nice lunch?"

"All right," I said. "All right."

We ordered pasta, wine, and a chocolate torte. He asked idly after my mother's health.

"Not great," I said. "Still depressed."

"I'm sorry," he said, fingering the tablecloth. "She taking her meds on time?"

I bristled. What he really cared about was her ability to keep taking care of us. Because what if she stopped? What then?

"Of course."

"Good." He took a sip of wine. "Boots. What the hell. You know it's crazy to—"

"*Buy shoes before going to Italy.* I know. Fiona already said the same thing." They were identical, those two, the way they thought. And yet they scratched at each other, like angry cats.

"I bet she did. She never did any Enteria, I can tell you."

I shrugged.

"You living with friends?"

"I'd like to find a flat with Italians."

"That's right," he said. "Finally breaking out on your own, eh?"

"I guess, yeah."

"You've been in your sister's shadow for too long, that's for bloody sure."

"That's not what it's like," I said, secretly pleased, because in truth that was exactly what it was like.

Our food came, platters of bland pasta.

"How're the lads?"

"Good, good."

"The studies?"

"Good."

"Anything that's not?"

"Other than my mum barely getting out of bed? And Fiona shagging everyone in Dublin but never finding a good boyfriend? Not much."

My father sighed. "Yes, your sister's a mess. I know you think it's my fault."

"She could use some fatherly guidance."

"She could use a bloody whip, Tabitha. At some point you have to take responsibility for your own problems. Everyone has some sort of awful thing happen. I couldn't be happy at the house in Lucan. Your mother and I—"

"Agh. Da, I don't want to talk about it."

"The point is, it's your sister's turn to take care of herself. She's twenty-six. She gets plenty of money from me. Speaking of which." He slid over an envelope. "I already had it changed over from pounds."

"What?" I peeked in to see euros, lots of them. "Dad, I've got plenty from my summer job at the movie theater. And I have the Enteria scholarship."

"I get it, brainy. We're proud as hell, yeah. But your scholarship's not going to pay for the next thing you want to buy over there. Or a trip to Florence. You can't miss Florence, you know."

Humbled, I twirled my pasta into a spoon.

"I'm proud of you, Taz," my dad said.

"Thanks."

"Oh, what a life." He patted my hand. "It'll pass in the blink of an eye, though—mark my words—and then you'll be an old codger like me."

"Daaa*aaad*." I hated it when he got sentimental. Not just because it was cringy, but because he didn't deserve to be sappy as hell. You can't just swoop in once a month with all of these feelings, I wanted to say. You can't just ask about the "lads." You have to be there. I mean, don't cry over my leaving when you never really see me to begin with.

But I didn't say that. And you know what? I'm glad.

"I know, I'm awful. All I'm saying is, make sure to make the most of it. You know? *Enjoy* it." He took out his wallet to pay. Just then the sun hit the window, momentarily blinding me. "Look at you. An angel. How could I ever have created anything so beautiful?"

"Ew. *Dad*."

He laughed and waved at the waiter. "Right you are, my darling. Shall we go?"

He had a surgery waiting; residents were scrubbing in, and just then his cell rang and beeped with a text at the same time. My father kissed me hurriedly, barely grazing my cheek as he focused on the glowing numbers in his hand. I reached for my phone as well, not wanting to be bested. And in this way, we parted: him looking elsewhere, me slipping into the streets, sure as a trout in a late summer river.

Goodbye, Da.

•

The night Jenny asked me to wear the white top was a different sort of evening. Jenny had suggested we slum it at the Red Lion, a basement bar always crowded with a particularly vicious blend of students and tourists. Having grown used to a more elegant scene, I was disappointed at the idea, but the others seemed keen enough. Luka was on a weekend trip to Athens, but we still met up at the Club before heading out in order to drink and preen. Anna brought a special curling iron, so all of us wore our hair in goddess ringlets. We smelled nice, wore clothes that sparkled and underwear that coyly showed through our shirts or peeped over the tops of our jeans. Delectable; that was the general idea.

Thanks to the social frenzy at Nottingham, I had come up in pubs and gone home with men; I was plenty used to that sort of slippery, shoulder-to-shoulder club scene. Though I was a good soldier, I never enjoyed these nights. The heat, the crowded floors, the shouting. The more of it a girl managed to survive, it seemed, the harder she became.

We took a table and watched the floor. Jenny was keenly aware of our competition, and just as she predicted, they began arriving from all over. It was amazing how much the other groups looked just like us—best friends of a few weeks, coy, an air of game if entirely unearned confidence. There was a German group, and then a pack of French girls. And the Israelis, breathtaking in their brief clothing. Jenny cut her eyes at them and proceeded to order another round of special Enteria shots, which that night were something sweet and green.

"It's so *cheap* here!" she cried, delighted. "A true shithole. He gave me two of these ghastly things for *free*."

By eleven, I'd had three shots. We migrated to the dance floor in a circle. It passes the time, dancing. Grifonia was a place, musically, that signaled no era: the DJ played Gnarls Barkley, Gem, Madonna, the Rolling Stones, the Birds, Wham!, Morcheeba. I'd drifted to the side to watch how the Italian boys patrolled the floor, always in pairs, turned out in pressed shirts. Never endearingly awkward like the English and American boys, but instead smooth and treacherous as rising water.

Jenny was getting a little sloppy. She tripped, fell, got up again, yelped.

"Whatever happened to dance cards?" I yelled.

"What?"

"You know—Jane Austen? Romance? Balls?"

"Did you just say *balls*?"

A man approached, cocking his head. He was tall, with tan skin, heavy eyebrows, and hair tipped in blond dye. I'd seen him often, standing outside the Albanian bar on a small street that bled down to the university. Up close he smelled heavily of bad cologne, but I didn't want to stand by myself anymore. He drew close, moved my curls from my ear, and yelled that his name was Ervin.

I followed him to the dance floor, feeling the eyes of my friends on my back. Ervin began to move in a natural, graceful manner. His clothes—a Spanish football jersey and baggy jeans—were reassuringly familiar. He tried to talk again, but it was impossible to hear anything, so he shrugged and danced on, and I copied.

Given more time, I think, I might eventually have become a truly great dancer. The kind that mesmerizes. Like my sister, for instance. On the street, she's far from beautiful, but when she dances, she hovers inches from her partner, looking into his (or her) eyes with just the right sort of challenge and promise. But at that point in life, it was all too intimate for me. I could do the moves, sure. I had even inherited a certain sort of grace. My mother, years before, had spun barefoot on a dance floor in Jaffa, catching my father's eye. He had never seen anyone so alive, he once told me. So yes, I knew how to dance. I just wasn't able to look at the person I was dancing with. A sort of glass cage fell over me, in the form of a distant, distracted smile.

Ervin grabbed my hand, then pressed into me. *There*, I thought. *See, Jenny? I'm with someone.* But good Lord, this song was lasting years. How long could I keep this up? His face was so *close* to mine. Did my breath smell? What if he saw the clogged state of my pores?

Suddenly, Anna was beside me, tugging my arm.

"Taz," she said. "Jenny's bought us some drinks."

I looked at Ervin apologetically. "I'll be back."

He shrugged, turning away. I followed Anna, a bit deflated that he'd been so passive at my departure.

"Don't want to dance with an Albanian wanker for too long," Anna said.

"He wasn't so bad," I said, my voice lost in the din.

"Taz!" Jenny shouted. "Shots!" She handed me another Enteria special, which turned out to be vodka, blood orange juice, and a dash of absinthe. "Good Lord, look at that girl's skirt. I can see her fucking Brazilian."

Anna moaned in disgust.

"I told you girls all to get them," Jenny said sternly. According to her, that was yet another B4 requirement. "Taz, have you gone yet?"

"Not—"

"Jenny, stop it," Anna said. "Here, Taz. Have a drink." I obeyed, relishing the burning in my throat. "Don't worry. You can't be expected to succumb to every one of Jenny's ridiculous whims."

I smiled gratefully and followed her back to the dance floor. Within minutes, another group of boys had enveloped us. I moved side to side, letting the alcohol numb whatever self-conscious thoughts were left. Then, an unmistakable wave came over me, and a web of thick saliva began to form in my mouth.

I broke away from the new boy and moved to Jenny, who was dancing nearest to me with a large dreadlocked white guy.

"I've got to get out of here," I shouted.

Jenny ignored me. I yanked her arm, causing her to whirl around in annoyance.

"Taz, come *on*, don't be a killjoy. It's early."

My entire body cramped. Anna was far away in the crowd. I

struggled to make myself heard over the music. "Please. Can you just get me to—"

"*Tab*itha!" I turned at my name. It was Claire. Unlike the rest of young Grifonia, she hadn't dressed up at all for the evening. In fact, she seemed to be wearing what I'd seen her in the day before—baggy jeans, a T-shirt, and Converse tennis shoes. "What's up?"

Just then a second wave of nausea hit, only this time I actually felt the bile in my throat, tasted it. I gripped Claire's arms and stumbled into her.

"Claire, can you—I'm . . ."

My American flatmate understood instantly. Moving behind me, she took me by the shoulders and steered me at a sure pace through the crowd.

"*Scusa!*" she called. "Move please. *Scusa! Move!*"

Once we reached the bathroom—a revolting, overused cell—she moved us right to the head of the line and banged on the door. "Sick girl here! Out, okay? I'm serious—get out!"

For you to understand how grateful I was to Claire at this moment, you'd have to know that I'd never been sick in public before. And that while I often drank to quiet my nerves, I'd never actually seen the room spin. You'd have to know that my mother regularly cleaned the house with bleach due to a slight obsessive compulsive disorder. That, due to this, I often had nightmares about being attacked by germs and bacteria. And so, when Claire held me away from the urine-slicked floor, cleaned my face, found soap to wash my hands, pulled me outside, and found me a bottle of water, it was all I could do not to cry as we walked down the sloped alleys toward home.

•

The next morning, I woke with the poisonous remorse that is often alcohol's parting gift. The very air in my room felt acidic. Claire was strumming the guitar in the living room, and though there was a door between us, it sounded as if her fingernails were raking my head.

"Made you breakfast," Claire said when I came out.

I shuffled to the counter, where she had set out a bowl of fruit and some yogurt. In my diminished state, the colors looked positively radioactive.

"Thank you."

"Time-tested U of M recipe. Yogurt to calm down your stomach. Fruit for detox. Juice for sugar. And the most important food group? Advil." She pointed to two pills she'd laid by my plate.

"This is so . . . kind." I poked the yogurt with the spoon, knowing I'd never be able to get it down.

"No worries."

"I'm so sorry about—"

"Please. You know how many times I've puked my guts out from drinking? God." She sipped her coffee. I sat near her, setting the food on the table. "I'm just glad I was there. Did your friends not hear you or something?"

"No. I guess not."

"Pretty insane in there, I guess." She looked at me over her coffee. "Taz, can I say something to you?"

"I can't pretend to be coherent. But yes, of course."

"Just because we're away from home doesn't mean you have to be something you don't *want* to be."

I pushed the yogurt around. "I'm not following you."

"The clothes. The drinking until you can't fucking stand up. It's not . . . you."

"How do you know what's me?" I said, my face flushing. "You just met me. And anyway, you're the one who was talking all that liberation rubbish."

"I'm not saying I'm a guru. Half of what I say is bullshit. You have to figure out what makes *you* happy. You're different."

"Different?"

"I'm saying don't push yourself into being slutty because your friends want you to."

"Well. Maybe I'm trying this freedom thing, too."

"All right, okay." Claire held up her hands in surrender.

"Who were you with, anyway?" I asked. "It was really nice of you to leave on my account. Did you get a chance to say goodbye?"

Claire shrugged. "I was just by myself."

"At a club? Really?"

"I go out by myself all the time."

"Seems lonely." I tried to picture going to the Red Lion alone, without the promise of a single familiar face inside. "What for?"

"Oh, I like it, actually. I like to be able to come and go when I want. You know. If I meet a guy. Or get sick or something."

She winked. I sipped my juice wanly.

"Kidding. So what are you doing today?"

"Dunno. I was planning on lying down, mainly."

"And miss the festival?"

"Ugh—I can't."

"Come on. Come with me. It's, like, the Capulet versus Montague parade, or some shit. It's a big fucking deal."

I looked out the window. The sky was an achingly clear blue. I could hear it now: the music from the square was already ricocheting off the hills.

*You get to be this happy now.*

"All right."

I went back to my room and pulled on jeans and my Nottingham jacket. Too tired to shower, I rinsed my face and brushed my teeth, then froze when I saw my reflection in the mirror. My skin had a green cast to it, and there were dark smudges under my eyes. My teeth looked yellowish in the bathroom light.

"God," I cried. "I look thirty."

"You look great," Claire said, crowding in beside me, her face right next to mine. Her cheekbones slanted upward whereas my cheeks were full. Next to my dark eyes, hers were a shocking hue of green. There was something otherworldy about her beauty. It made one blind to anything else in the room. I moved back, afraid I would disappear.

"Well, we both look kinda tired," Claire said, nudging me. "But who cares, right?"

We stepped into the garden, through the gate, and made our way up to the main piazza. The air was thick with the smell of cooked sugar. The alley we took was narrow and steep; the sun was blocked on three sides by the high walls, so that the only light fell from the opening between the houses hundreds of feet above. Every balcony was crammed with herb pots and laundry. All around us students and families pressed upward toward the festival. Claire grabbed my hand, so as not to lose me. Then, just as the little street was too crowded to bear, we were tossed into the wide main square, punctuated by the huge fountain. We dropped hands and took a breath, looking around. A band was set up on a stage in front of the palace steps, and well-dressed children ran back and forth, darting by our legs.

Festive as it was, the crush of people was weakening my resolve. There was still too much alcohol in my system. My head felt caught in a vise grip, my vision blurred; it occurred to me I was still a little drunk.

"I really think a nap—"

"Wait here," Claire said, parking me on the edge of the stone steps of the cathedral. "I'll get us whatever it is they're rioting over." She muscled her way through a small crowd out of sight for a moment, before appearing a minute later with two paper cups. "Chocolate brandy, I think?"

"Claire, I can't drink this."

"No, it's exactly what you need. Here—just try it."

We put the limp paper cups to our lips and tasted it. The concoction was bitter, yet sweet and spicy. She was right—the warmth in my throat and stomach helped. She took my wrist and led me to the steps of the cathedral, where I'd first seen Claire just weeks before. We sipped our brandies and looked out at the throngs.

"Did your friends call yet?"

"No."

Claire rolled her eyes.

"What?" I said.

She paused. "Taz, look. You disappeared from a club at like, four a.m., drunk. Don't you think they should have called before now?" She looked at her empty cup. "Oh, fuck it. Never mind. That's exactly why I don't go out with swarms of girls like that."

"What do you mean?"

"Girls in groups have no qualms about stabbing one another in the back. Friend on friend? There's some loyalty. Groups? Forget it."

"Seems a bit of a generalization."

"I really don't think so. I mean, I get it. Women in a foreign country, blah, blah. It's good to go out together so you can have, you know, someone to walk *in* with. Also so you don't get fucking roofied. But then, after that, everyone's just going for the same guys. Right? And by the end, no one can even keep track of anyone anyway."

"Very modern of you."

She shrugged. "Or stupid. Who knows? Maybe I'll go out with you guys one night," she said, standing too quickly for me to tell her she wouldn't be welcome because of Jenny's laws.

I bought some olive oil for my mother (found later under my bed, wrapped), then we wandered over to a less crowded pocket of the festival. There was a puppet show in the little square in front of the Irish pub, a rendition of *Peter and the Wolf*. Parents stood around as their children strayed in and out of the crowd. Their voices rose, melded, and spiraled around us, caught by the stone walls of the square.

Suddenly, to my left, I heard a roar. I looked around the corner and saw a Fiat—its driver obviously uninformed of the festival—hurtling up the tiny street. I grabbed Claire's arm. Just a few feet from us, a little boy was playing with a ball directly in the path of the car.

"*Riccardo!*" a man shouted.

Claire shook me off and lurched forward, though there was no possible way for her to get to the child in time. A few yards ahead, a man—perhaps the father—launched his body in front of the car. He flew through the air, as if in a stop-motion movie, then bounced off the hood and rolled into the street. The impact didn't stop the car, but it did slow it down, and an older man reached out and snatched the boy out of the way.

The little boy screamed, as did the women around him. The man in the street groaned in pain.

"Water!"

"Ambulance!"

"Get back!"

"Maria! Get the mother—"

"Fuck! What should we do?" Claire cried.

"Get out of the way."

"No. No. We should—"

"Really." I tugged her arm. "They're not going to want outsiders here. Come on."

It was hard to pull her out of there, but after a minute or so, she finally relented. We retreated down the alley back toward the fountain and the cathedral steps.

"Well, I guess they'll be okay."

"Yes." The festival was pulsing harder now. Revelers swelled around us, jostling our shoulders, spilling glasses of beer. Another band had started—tinny Italian rock—and the sound was deafening.

"Please. Can we go home now?" I begged.

"Sure." Claire hooked her arm in mine and steered me on a roundabout path to our cottage. We passed beneath an Etruscan arch into a small stone stairway, and, as if a cruel spell had been lifted, the music diminished. I concentrated on the steep, narrow steps, coated in dust and gum. Two black dogs darted back and forth in front of us, searching for scraps in the bins.

"Well," I said after a while. "You got right in there."

"What do you mean?"

"All I did was stand aside. Of course there was no way to . . . But you were actually running to save that tyke."

"Eh, it was just instinctual."

My head was pounding again from the hangover.

"Yes. I suppose that's what I'm talking about. I'm impressed by you."

"Taz, it was nothing. Stupidity, if anything. You know, like, if you see a baby going for a socket with a fork, you don't just sit there and do nothing. You run for it. It's called being a human. It's just your gut."

Looking back on this now, it's hard for me to believe this conversation really happened. That, after coming so close to witnessing a death, she and I spoke these words, as if the day were scripted to give us hints of what was to come.

For this is not just a memory selectively shaped by the things a girl is willing to admit and remember. I can't tell you much about where I am, but I can say this: Later, you can hear your life again. Word for word, unbiased. As though recorded by an invisible hand. And you know, it's the silly things that become extraordinary. When you're going on and on, thinking you're being meaningful, it's all just garbage. It's the throwaways that count in the end.

"You have a stronger gut than I do," I told her.

"Oh, come on. You'd come after *me* if *I* were the baby. With the fork, I mean. Right?"

"Sure. I suppose."

"Oh, I'd fork anyone for you," she said.

She said that. She did.

"Mother forker."

"Shut it, Claire," I said, laughing.

"Fork it," she said.

## *Althea, 6th century AD*

While Grifonia was under siege by the king of the Ostrogoths, Althea was put in charge of catching and killing pigeons. She hated the task, but was frightened of starving, so she stalked the alleys with a net and a knife.

After two years, the Porta Sole was opened by a traitor. The Goths rained over the city, stabbing children with their swords, pulling women to the ground and raping them, striking down the old men who pleaded for their daughters.

In the great square where the fountain now stands, the soldiers dragged the city's bishop to a platform. Behind him, looking on in horror, was a line of faithful soldiers, and at the end of that doomed line, Althea.

Using daggers freshly sharpened for the purpose, the Goths cut long slits circumventing the bishop's arms, legs, and torso, and peeled the skin from his limbs. Afterward, they started on the soldiers, flaying them one by one.

By the time the executioners had finally gotten to Althea, a small band of the Compagnia had formed next to that stack of skinless bodies. Before the Goths could flay the girl, the rebels grabbed her from the platform.

*Buona morte. Buona morte*, they murmured. They were now trained to slit throats quickly. Cleany. In the same manner as a butcher killing a sow.

The Goths executed them all immediately, and split open the girl's chest as a lesson. The crowd cried out in wonder. When the soldier held it up, the young girl's harvested heart was still beating in his hand.

*Althea Francisco, fifteen years old, 6th century AD*

# 9

I went back to the cottage, took some aspirin, and slept, waking after three hours in a pool of alcohol-tinged sweat. The clock read four p.m., and the house was eerily silent. I sat up gingerly, pulling on my clothes. Shuffling into the living room, I saw that everyone's doors were open, as if they had rushed out to see something in the street. The front door was ajar. Gia's underwear was drying on a rack on the terrace; Alessandra had a pot of bean soup on the stove that was still warm. The table was hidden by newspapers, magazines, and espresso cups. The air had a pungent smell that begged for the rubbish to be taken out.

Glancing out the front window, I walked into Claire's room. Not that she would have minded; she looked in my bureau all the time for clean socks. Still, the intrusion. I opened her drawers, looking at her mismatched bras and panties, tangled with balled-up shirts. Jeans, shorts, one yellow sundress dress presumably for special occasions, all stuffed in. That electric blue frock, dangling from a wire hanger. Beaten-up American paperbacks: Kerouac. Grace Paley. An impossible-looking tome by Bolaño. There was a blue journal I didn't touch. Some condoms in a plastic bag shoved under the bed.

I stood there for a few minutes, feeling the oddness of quiet in a place that usually is not. Finally, I returned to my room, brushed my hair, and went out.

In the last few weeks, my favorite stroll had become a narrow yet lovely road that led from the university to a quiet pocket of town, ending at one of the city's seven ancient gates. Despite the neighborhood's charm, in places it was quite seedy, simmering with bad ideas. Locals spilled into the street from cafés, sitting on the sidewalk, smoking *spinellos*, shouting to one another through the windows and doors. Dogs ran back and forth, most without collars. Girls who must have been five years younger than me leaned against the thick walls in torn dresses. Socks and underwear hung to dry above, from huge stained jockeys that billowed dreadfully to the briefest slips of gossamer lace.

That was the way it was in Grifonia's old town: if you lived there, your life was flung onto the sidewalk for anyone to sift through with a stick. Though the wooden shutters were often closed to block the sun, the inner panes would gape wide to encourage cross-ventilation such that, at any hour, shouting, ecstatic moans, or sobs seeped out of the flats, in an endless drama available to any passerby who cared to listen. I had always been rather squeamish, yet the frank, almost sexual squalor of it all fascinated me. *Who were these people*, I wondered, *letting out their sounds with such abandon?* The screaming, the bodily squawks. It couldn't be real, the way these people lived. None of it, it seemed, was real.

At the end of the road, past the antique shops, the notary, a mosque, and the world's shabbiest gym, the businesses thinned out and the neighborhood became blissfully quiet. In the shadow of the outer gate, I came across a small stone courtyard planted with wilted flowers. I sat down, thinking of the day's strange events. So thick was my haze that I didn't notice another figure standing near the far wall—a stooped old woman, dressed head to toe in white and covered in a white shawl. She was running her blue fingers over what appeared to be an inscription.

"*Buon giorno,*" I mumbled, just to let her know I was there. She didn't acknowledge me, and before I could say anything else she was making her way out. I saw, as she passed, that she wasn't old at all, but a lovely young woman, with a face so pale it was blue, body hunched as if from the cold. As soon as she stepped into the sun, she vanished.

I poked my head out after her, searching for her apparition. She wasn't there, but I forgot her quickly, as the man from the museum was, just then, ambling around the corner toward me.

"Oh," I said, blocking his path. "Hello there. Hi."

I never would have been so bold even two weeks before. *I can be anything I fucking feel like*, Claire had said. I didn't know who I was trying to be, but certainly I desired to be different from the shy, slightly jaded girl who had arrived on the train.

We stood there for a moment. Up close he was paler than I remembered, and bigger. He was at least six feet tall, large shoulders and hands but not heavy. He had dark, straight hair that needed a cut. There was an academic air about him. Again, he was carrying his notebook. And oddly, he seemed not at all surprised to see me on this abandoned street corner on the outside of town.

"Here we are again!" I said, my voice cracking.

He nodded.

"I'm Tabitha."

"Colin," he said. Then, after a pause, "Nice to meet you."

"It is." A car tore up the street. He lightly pushed me farther inward on the sidewalk. "So did you have a good time at the party?"

"Not particularly," he said.

"No?" A group of girls was coming up the street, presumably to sun in the park by the gate. Colin's eyes flicked over toward them, then back at me.

"There's one every year. I've been going with my father since I was thirteen."

"So you're Italian, then?"

"Yes. Half. My mother's back in Surrey, but my father's Grifonian. He lives here with his second family, down near the San Francesco church."

"That's why the British accent."

"*E l'italiano perfetto*," he said, smiling.

"Sorry you had a rotten time at the party. I thought it was grand."

"Well, there were all these crashers," he said, tipping his head back a bit.

I blushed. "Oh, right. That was my friend's idea." Behind the wall across the street, some children were shrieking. "It wasn't so bad, was it?"

"You ought to be careful. Some of these Grifonians can get territorial."

"Actually, we had invites," I said, remembering. "These coin things."

"You shouldn't have been given those."

"What was the party for?"

"Just a local organization. Sort of a Masonic thing."

We regarded each other. Or rather, he regarded me. Because of the difference in our size he had to bend down to speak to me, the same way a gardener stoops to tend to a flower on a shelf.

"How old are you?" he asked.

"Twenty-one," I said. "You?"

"Older than you."

"Too old?"

He cocked his head, as if trying to make me out. "It depends on how old a twenty-one-year-old can act."

My face had become hot. I knew I couldn't keep this up.

"There are a lot of uni kids here." He pushed his glasses up his nose. "A lot of brats from London."

"I'm Irish," I said, quickly.

"That I discerned," he said.

"I just go to school in the U.K. I'm on an Enteria scholarship."

"Yes, that's what I thought." He nodded. "And your friends, too."

He said this as though perhaps Enteria was not something he particularly liked.

"What do you do here?" I asked.

"My history dissertation. I'm getting a PhD."

"Wow. Well, then maybe you can tell me something," I said.

"Maybe."

"I was looking at that garden there. There's this plaque . . . my Italian is pretty good, but I can't quite make it out."

He straightened, pleased. "That's Nicolai, the martyred bishop. Another gory story." Colin smiled again. I felt as if I'd earned a prize. "You like those, it seems."

"I do, I guess."

"All right. Well. The city was under siege. For two years. There was no food, and the Grifonians were dying of starvation, on the verge of defeat. So the bishop—Nicolai—he had an idea. He took the very last goat out to the hills where the Goths could see him, then slaughtered it so that they'd think we had all the food in the world. He thought if they presumed we had enough supplies to last through winter, they'd give up."

"Did it work?" I asked.

Colin raised his eyebrows. "Suppose you haven't gotten to the history section of your classes yet? No, it didn't. A traitor let them in, and what followed was a period of bloody Goth rule."

"Ah. Right. Goth rule. I'll look into that."

He crossed his arms and looked at me, amused. I felt a fluttering I hadn't experienced for some time.

"Well . . . I better be going," I said, hoping he'd think I had things to do. "Maybe I'll see you soon."

"Maybe," he said, heading toward the gate.

Well, when? I wanted to ask. I should have. I should have said so many things.

Instead I watched Colin walk through the city gate until he disappeared from view around the corner. I stood there for a moment, hoping he'd come back. He didn't. To my left, the woman in white hurried back into the courtyard. I glanced inside again to see her crouched there, her finger out, tracing the stone.

•

Just as Claire had predicted, Jenny, Luka, and Anna seemed less than contrite about not following up on my disappearance from the bar. As I climbed the brick stairs to the Club, I experienced a distinct air of foreboding. It was the first time I'd been truly angry with any of them. I could hear their laughter trickling down from two stories above, which only provoked me further.

"*We* thought you'd gone off with some guy, finally," Jenny said offhandedly when I presented my complaint. She got up to refresh her glass. They were sitting on the floor with two bottles of Orvieto and a large platter of pasta tossed with oil and shaved truffles. Luka had asked her housekeeper to make it that afternoon.

"I told you I had to go. That I was sick. Remember?"

"Must not have heard you. Anyway, I met a lovely bloke," Jenny said. "In fact, I seem to be the only one out of all of you able to hook up with an Italian."

"A hippie," Luka said. "I'm not into that."

"He was an artist. Like you, Luka dear."

"How *did* you get home then, Taz?" Anna asked.

"My flatmate."

"The American?" Jenny asked. "The strange one?"

"I never said she was strange."

"You said she was a tomboy."

"Oh, I don't like that," Luka said. "Dykes are always so touchy."

"*You* are a dyke," Jenny said.

"Recreationally," Luka retorted. "Not the sort that wears work boots and stomps around making little cakes for her girlfriends."

"What are you even talking about?" I asked. "I never said Claire was gay."

"So which is it then?"

"She's just, I don't know—American. Your outdoorsy type. Independent. Goes to pubs alone."

"Alone?" Luka scoffed. "Don't get me wrong—I love a drink, as we all know. But even *I* don't go out alone."

"It is whorey," Jenny said. "I'm actually intrigued."

My frustration was building. "She's a good friend, all right? And she was really nice to me last night, unlike some of you, so I'd rather you all shut up about her."

Luka poured herself another glass of wine.

"Sorry, Tazzie," Jenny said. "We'll give her a chance. You know her better than we do."

"I do."

"Just remember, though—she's an American," Luka said, looking at herself in the mirror.

"So?"

"It's more than an ocean. That's the phrase, isn't it? She'll never really get you."

"Bull."

"Wait and see," said Jenny, patiently twirling her fettuccini into a plump bite.

"I'm going to go."

Jenny chewed delicately. She took a sip of wine and swallowed. "Won't you just come up for a smoke first?"

"I don't think so. I'm feeling—"

"Just one. Keep me company, yeah?"

I gave a little sigh for show, then left the others and followed her up the stairs to Luka's roof deck, an intimate spot with a whitewashed trellis struggling under a massive tangle of trumpet vines and clematis.

"Look, I'm really sorry about last night. I really thought you were off with someone. We all did."

"Only I *told* you I was sick."

"I didn't hear you. I swear it."

I picked off a leaf, pressing it with my nail.

"We do look after one another. It's just . . . not in a girls' school way. We can't be expected to know where everyone is at all times. That would be impossible. People need space, after all."

"I just think sometimes you act quite strange. I mean, why don't you ever ask me to this lake house of yours? We're supposed to be so damned close, but you seem to go off to Trasimeno with every other girl in Enteria."

"Taz, I'm so glad you asked," she said. "That's what I wanted to talk to you about."

"Oh?"

"Well, where to start?" She took a breath. "You've probably been wondering how we're so connected here."

I shook my head, a little embarrassed. "No. I just—"

"You just thought I was invited to every good party in town? Me, a college girl from Nottingham?"

"Well." I paused. "You are posh."

She tipped her head back and laughed. "Posh. Please, Taz. You're so dated. We've got a little business going on here, you see. Nothing serious."

"A business?" God bless me, I couldn't even begin to imagine what she was talking about.

"I'm sure you've guessed it."

"I'm sorry?" I said softly, as if she had said something I couldn't quite hear.

"Oh, you're making me spell it out. Christ, I hope you're not wearing a wire! We're the Enteria connection. You've heard of that, at least?"

I thought back to the conversation I'd had on that horrible night with Marcy at the beginning of the program. *At least wait for the Enteria connection*, she'd said to the Belgian girl wanting to get high.

"It's drugs!" I said triumphantly. "You all are selling drugs?"

"Taz, don't be disappointing. It's not as tawdry and simple as that."

"So you don't sell drugs?"

"We *are* the drug." Jenny ran her fingers through her hair, yanking girlishly at a tangle. "We provide an image. Yes, you can buy coke from us, or hash, or zanopane, or whatever you want. But by doing business with us, what you really get is the privilege of having us in your life."

"Do other people know?"

"*Everyone* knows, Tazzie. I honestly can't fathom how you didn't."

"But how does it even work? Where do you get it?"

"Luka does it. She goes in a car to pick it up in different spots every week. Anna houses it. And I sell it."

"In England, too?"

"No. Well, a little, just before we came. Just to try it out. It's why we came together, you see. After this year, it's to be over. And then we'll pass the baton along to someone else."

"How did you think it all up?"

"We didn't. No, no. There's an Enteria connection every year. I just happened to meet someone who knew about the last one. Told me how much money we were going to make. It was all incredibly easy to get into, actually."

"And you do it at your friend's lake house?"

"Oh, Taz," Jenny sighed. "There's no lake house. It's a little thing called a code. If I'm going to the lake, it means I have inventory. Didn't you ever notice I never actually *go* anywhere?"

"But why do the Italians come to you? Why isn't it just the Enteria students?"

"The Grifonians love us. Why would they want to buy coke from the seedy guys down on Via Saint Elisabetta when they can invite some pretty girls to a party?"

"What's going on?" Anna asked, emerging on the roof.

"I've told Taz about our arrangement. Didn't want her blundering on about going up to the bloody lake house."

"I see," Anna said, looking even paler than normal. "I hope you don't think of us differently now."

"No," I said. "I don't. I'm just surprised."

"Why?" Jenny asked.

"I thought you all came from money."

Jenny laughed. "Luka's dad has three ex-wives. All his royalties go to their plastic surgery. And I don't believe he's had a hit since what, 1991?"

"And my father spent all ours," Anna said.

I looked at Jenny. "And you?"

She turned toward the square. "Me. No. I most certainly am not wealthy."

"Well." I hurried to cover the blunder. "Nor am I."

"Compared to me, you are," she said. "My father is a science teacher, Taz. A *teacher*." Her lips curled around the words with distaste. "My mother sits around all day, doing God knows what. Making us disgusting roasts. We were stuffed in a one-floor flat, furniture from bloody IKEA. They think it's fancy." She leaned on the railing. "Don't get me wrong. It's not that my parents aren't good, sweet people. I love them, sure. They just don't fucking care about the world. Not a fucking iota of ambition in that house except for me. My mother'd be happy if I worked at the grocer's and got fat and had a baby at twenty-three like the other girls in my class. And, well, people like me, they don't just *go* to Italy. Even if I worked all the bloody time, I couldn't afford to be here."

"But at Nottingham, you—"

"I figured it out," she said. "That's what smart people do, Taz. We stay in front of it." She continued to survey the action below. Whining strains of the theme to the movie *Amelie* were bubbling through the air. "Oh, that damned accordion player! What sort of sin did he commit to deserve such hell? Anyhow Tazzie, welcome to the fold. It's no big thing, really. Let's go back down before this music drives me batty."

She disappeared down the stairwell. I turned to follow her, but Anna's boney fingers held my arm.

"Don't let Jenny romanticize it, Taz. We're just a tiny drug ring."

"Sure."

"You won't tell anyone, will you Taz? It's a small thing. All I do is keep a satchel in my room, but if Arthur found out somehow, I'd just . . ."

"It really doesn't matter to me," I said. I was telling the truth. They were still the B4. And to me, that meant they were spectacular. "I love all of you. Even if I found out you were a lot of cult murderers, I wouldn't tell."

"And it's not such a horrible thing, is it?"

"Absolutely not," I said. "And I'll tell you again if you need me to."

I thought Anna would smile at my reassurance. Instead she seemed to wince, I supposed in deference to the accordion player's hopeless wails.

# 10

Heeding Anna's commands, I arrived only one minute late for our first class on September 15—for me, practically early, really—panting after sprinting up four flights of stairs. Despite my apologies, Anna was incredulous.

"Taz! You live five hundred yards *away*," she hissed.

I gave her a sheepish grin and looked around. Etruscan Mythology was held in a building on my block, in what seemed to be an ex-palace of a noble. Ours was an unexpectedly exquisite little chamber at the very top of the building, boasting hand-painted murals on the ceiling and views to the borders of Lake Trasimeno. The walls, painted light blue, gave the illusion almost of being suspended in the sky. In the middle sat one large, ancient wooden table, surrounded by well-used library chairs.

Arthur, known to the rest of us as Professor Korloff, did not arrive until fifteen minutes after five o'clock. It was the earliest he would arrive during the class's monthlong duration. When the door finally burst open, we all turned, and the conversation instantly hushed. Professor Korloff threw his bag down onto a desk and stood in front of us, arms folded over his chest, rocking slightly back and forth on his feet.

"Hello," he said, idly surveying the names written out in front of us, as was the custom on the first day of classes. I looked at Anna in surprise. Well, at least some of Jenny's questions could be put to rest. There was no way Anna could be in love with Arthur Korloff, I planned to report. He was old. Not as in "father" old, but *old* old, with skin like crushed tissue and hair the color and texture of the first falling of snow. Also, he was hideously dressed—a rumpled blue shirt, worn pants with all sorts of pockets, dirty old trainers. He was at the stage of life where the primary parts of his body seemed to have shrunk, even as his appendages were still growing, so that his ears and nose were out of proportion with his face. To say nothing of his eyebrows. And then there was the clincher: Professor Korloff was American. New York American, to be specific. A girl like Anna—Anna *Grafton*—could never be attracted to a man like this.

I was vastly unprepared for the class. I had waded through the *Iliad* and the *Odyssey*, but most helpful, unexpectedly, were my memories of *d'Aulaire's Book of Greek Myths*, an oversized, brilliantly illustrated children's book that Babs had in her room growing up. We used to pore over it, the exquisite illustrations spilling over our small laps, engrossed by the images of angry Athena springing from her father's head and Icarus falling in flames from the sky. So from that book alone, I had a reference to at least a third of what we discussed in that lovely little room, if not in any particular depth. As for the other gods, I took dutiful notes on them with every intention of looking them up later.

What Professor Korloff lacked in charm, he made up for in exuberance. He was a mesmerizing orator—the sort of person who could speak about used coffee grounds and manage to hold his audience. I spent much of class nodding thoughtfully as if my silence were not simple ignorance. Yet it was painfully clear, once discussion got going, that I was by far the least versed in the classics among the group.

"Let's talk about Minerva," Professor Korloff said, his cigarette poised. "The Etruscans revered her—put her on urns, mirrors. Her statue guards tombs. Why?"

"Goddess of war," said Pascal, a tiny older French student who sat in the very front, without missing a beat. Since the first day, he had been vying with Anna for Arthur's highest esteem. Word had it that a recommendation from Arthur was a platinum ticket to a graduate program with a healthy fellowship, though personally, I couldn't imagine anything worse than a life of studying the words of the dead.

"The Etruscans were in a constant state of battle against the Romans," Pascal continued.

"And one another," Anna added.

"Of course," Arthur said. "All right, then, thank you. But *let's* delve deeper, shall we? The Etruscans revered women more than any other ancient society. The Greeks, as you may by now have gleaned, were complete misogynists—everyone always getting raped and carried away. An entire war waged because of a petty fight over something as ephemeral as beauty. Beauty as a good, that is—as chattel—something you stole. But to the Etruscans, goddesses had more power, more agency. To the Etruscans, goddesses were every bit as important as the male gods. From what we can find, men and women were nearly equals. Equal burial rights, equal representation in their artistic renderings. Women, in Etruria, were—how should I say this? The shit."

The class laughed.

"But now I want to get to the mystery. One that even after studying this stuff for fifty years still keeps me awake. The Etruscans' reign was as mighty as that of the Romans and the Greeks. Their territories were vaster, reaching as far up as France. A network of twelve great cities. Yet there are no written texts—no historical documents, no hymns, no poems. *Why?*"

"The texts were destroyed by the Romans," said Pascal.

"A complete eradication," Arthur said, nodding. "A literary genocide more thorough than that of the Nazis, say, or the Stalinists."

"Or else—"

The class turned and looked at me. I looked back at them, waiting for whomever it was to keep talking, only to realize with a start that the voice had been my own.

Anna turned and peered at me.

"Well?" Arthur said, stepping closer. "Go on?"

"I was just saying . . . maybe they did it themselves."

"Aha. And how so? Magic? From the grave?"

"Well, if the literature had been destroyed by their enemies . . . I just think someone would have been able to find *something*. Some poet would have buried a manuscript, I don't know. A manuscript under his bed. But you say there was nothing. I just feel that—"

"You *feel*?" Arthur said, raising his eyebrows.

Anna put her face in her hands.

"I *believe* the destruction of their history had to have been, you know, a concerted effort. Maybe there was, um, something they didn't want to share. Something they didn't want the Romans . . . to know."

"The secret to eternal youth?" Arthur said, smiling.

I shrugged.

"Well, my dear, convoluted as that was, it was, in fact, my eventual point. So brava. Now let's be clear—no theorist has ever proven this, no artifact has ever backed me up. But what Tabitha Deacon *supposes*—oh yes, dear, I *do* see your name—is basic human nature. *No one* can bear the thought of being unremembered once they vanish, and the Etruscans would have fought to keep their history alive; they would have buried it, written it on scrolls and tucked it into the ceilings of their worshipping places. Really. Think about it. If you knew you were going to die, wouldn't you have done the same?"

We were silent for a moment.

"Yes," Pascal finally allowed.

"Now think of it *this* way. What if your society had great secrets that others did not? Plumbing, crop rotation, God knows what else? These people—the Romans—were raping old women and killing children. The worst thing the Etruscans could *do* to their conquerors was . . . tell them nothing."

"But how would they get their message across the entire kingdom?"

"Yes, that would have been an amazing feat. Impossible, for any kingdom to have people so loyal they would submit to such an effort. But we are forgetting something. The Etruscans, unlike the Greeks and the Romans, were great believers in the afterlife. They built tomb palaces, remember? Lined their graves with tools they would need later. There was great emphasis on the grace of death, you see. So maybe they didn't worry about leaving their history for the next generation. Because they expected to die a good death, and then to pass comfortably with their beloved things into the next world."

"And did they?" Anna finally asked.

I looked around. We were all leaning forward over the table.

"Die and find out," our professor said, putting out his cigarette.

•

After a few days of class, Professor Korloff grew restless—even in our blessed azure garret.

"Learning doesn't take place in rooms," he grumbled, after delivering a mind-bending lecture that lasted until ten at night on the heroic search for Eurydice. "Well, it does in England. But how am I supposed to lecture when Romulus himself lies in wait under the ground? No, no, no. Tomorrow, we go."

"Where?" I asked.

"Wear walking clothes and come with trust," he said. "Be out in front of the building at five o'clock sharp. We're going to visit the Etruscans."

And with that, he waved us off. Anna and I descended the stairs slowly, followed by Pascal. He had recently taken to shadowing her after class. Perhaps inevitably, their sparring had developed into a full-fledged crush on Pascal's side, and watching Anna's studious, silent denial of the situation, I couldn't help but take pity on him.

"Come for a drink?" I asked in English, as Pascal's Italian was as bad as Anna's and my French.

"Yes, thank you. Yes." I cringed; there was something so terrifyingly eager about Pascal—he almost exactly matched the desperation I'd exhibited just weeks before.

No matter what the angle, Pascal was just not attractive. He only came up to my shoulder, and had a distinct penchant for ugly printed shirts. An odd threesome we were: the fragile daughter of a baron, the everyday schoolgirl from Lucan, the jittery scholar from France.

Without discussion, we went to a popular garden bar behind the *enoteca*. It was already crowded. We squeezed into a table next to some Russian students, who sized us up briefly before turning back to one another again.

"Hard to make an impression without Jenny, isn't it?" I said.

"That's what she's hoping." Anna turned to Pascal. "So, you're enjoying the class?"

Pascal jumped a little, then smiled. "Yes, I feel very lucky. It is wonderful to study with the professor. I've used his articles for my thesis, and when it was clear he was going to be here . . ." He rolled his eyes to the heavens and took a drink. "And I'm so happy, Anna, to have in the class someone who loves Homer."

"I certainly *don't* love Homer. Not all of it. You know what they say, Homer wrote the *Iliad* while he was asleep."

"*Oui?*"

The two plowed into a conversation about the third book of hymns I couldn't follow. I looked around the bar, studying the different groups of students who milled about, shouting and laughing. I thought about how wonderful it was to be there, and how just three weeks ago, this scene would have inspired in me a sort of dread.

"And you, Tabitha?" I suddenly heard Pascal asked me. "You all right in the class?"

"Oh, sure."

"Only you are very quiet."

"I'm okay. Hopefully I'll be able to hack through the final paper."

Just then Pascal knocked over his glass. He shot up to fetch napkins. When he returned, his attempts to clean made things even worse, as he pushed the ruby liquid into our laps.

"Oh!" Anna cried.

"Excuse . . ." Pascal mumbled. Jumping up, he threw a ball of euros onto the table. "Here. To pay for the cleaning. I'm very, very sorry." And then he darted off too quickly for us to even attempt to stop him.

"Poor Pascal," I sighed, watching his retreat. "He really likes you."

"I like him, too. But not enough to sacrifice this silk. Damn." She dabbed at the spot hopelessly. "Besides, he's not my type at all."

"Oh, you liked talking to someone smart. I could tell. You get bored with us sometimes. Admit it."

"Never." By her tone, I could tell this was truer than I'd have liked.

"Look, someone needs to unearth the fifth Homeric hymn with you."

"Aphrodite *is* such a flighty tramp." She waved for the waitress to refill her glass.

"Why don't you start a reading group or something? An intellectual salon. With that guy Ethan in class, and Pascal, and maybe a couple of others. You could . . . go on trips and things. I'm sure there are plenty of classics students here. It *is* Italy."

"It is," Anna said, a bit grimly.

"Well?"

"I just . . . couldn't do something like that. I'm too busy."

"With what? You're not so terribly involved in the thing, are you? Don't you just keep it under your bed?"

Anna looked at me a bit fiercely. "Tabitha, do us both a favor and drop it. All right, love?"

I searched for something else to say.

"So Arthur lived with your family?"

"For a little while. My father was quite a bit older than my mother. When he died, Arthur took us under his wing."

"Well, not to be cynical—"

"Oh, *you* couldn't be cynical if you tried. You're much too sweet. But go on."

"Well. Just—it's not like it can have been too big of a chore, coming to stay with his friend's beautiful wife and daughter in their enormous country seat."

"Oh, but Taz. My mother isn't beautiful."

"No?"

"She looks like . . . well, we're in a row just at the moment, so it's hard for me to judge. But she's a haughty old skeleton, really. And the country seat? Mum sold it as soon as Dad died. A mountain of debt to pay. Now she lives in Kensington, clinging to the title."

"Well, at least that's still legit?"

"Sort of. I mean, he's dead of course. Has been since I was six. But still, it gets her into terrific parties."

I took a sip, thinking.

"So, why *are* you in a row?"

"She said I got in the way of a relationship she was having."

"A boyfriend?"

"Sort of."

"You didn't like him?"

"It was complicated." She cleared her throat. "There was a man who used to date my mother. For years, actually. And then I came home from Nottingham last summer and we realized it wasn't my mother he was in love with."

The silence that followed was impenetrable, even by me.

"Anna," I tried. "Is that what Jenny has over you? Why she keeps you and Luka so tight?"

"I don't want to talk about it anymore." Anna had a way of shutting things off so completely. There was no getting through the door once Anna had closed it.

"But speaking of Arthur . . . ," she said.

"Yes?"

"He's asked if we might like to join him at his friend's castle."

"A castle?" I blinked. "Us? When?"

"The second weekend in October. The place belongs to some sort of patron of his. Someone who funds his research. Apparently he—the patron—would like to meet some local students to get a sense of . . . of . . . Arthur's teaching."

"A castle!"

"You really are a simple little thing," Anna said.

"I'm not. So what's he up to?"

"Pascal's been invited, too. So it's not scandalous or anything. Anyhow, I asked if Jenny and Luka could come. It'll be the four of us—a proper country weekend. What do you think?"

"A castle!"

"Now, aren't you glad I swindled that dress for you?" She pulled out her cigarettes. She made a point of keeping them in a silver case, a trait I found wonderful. "I have to admit I'm bloody nervous about bringing Jenny," she said, almost to herself.

"Why? She certainly won't say anything about your arrangement."

She looked up, as if startled that I was there. "Well. Arthur, he can be very . . . judgmental. Just makes me nervous is all. Hey, now. Isn't that your flatmate?"

I glanced over. Claire was sitting at a table across the garden. It had been so crowded I hadn't noticed her. She was with a man I'd never seen, a tall Swedish-looking person with so many tattoos that his skin was unavailable to the eye. His hand ran up and down her thigh frantically, as if he were fluffing the hair of a dog.

"Claire!" I called out. She didn't hear me over the music. The man said something, and she looked up with that brilliant smile, leaned over, and kissed his neck.

"*Who* is that thing she's with?" Anna trilled.

"Never seen him."

"I hate to say it, but I wouldn't let that bloke in the house to fix my drain."

We watched, mesmerized, as his hand moved between her legs over her jeans.

"Is this normal American behavior?"

"It's like she doesn't care about anything," I whispered.

"Oh, everyone cares about something," Anna said. "Me, it's trying like hell to get into a graduate program. Luka, it's—well, we've got to get past the drink first to find out. Though she falls in love with girls she can't have a lot. Your roomie, I'm guessing it's to get shagged by a foreign skank for kicks. As for you . . ."

She rested her chin on her hand and looked at me.

"For you, I believe it's to be part of a group."

My face grew hot, giving me away.

"I thought so! Don't worry, your secret's safe with me. And, you know what? We *all* like being in a group. Anyhow. Jenny, she's all power. In fact, she's sort of the most honest of all of us."

"I suppose so."

"I *know* so," Anna said. "Luka . . . me . . . you can't trust us a mite. But Jenny says what she means. She's very honest, with her business and everything. If there's something you need to know, she tells you."

"I'm sorry. I don't—understand you. What do you mean about you and Luka?"

The Russians at the next table had started singing. One of them put his arm around Anna's shoulder, indicating she should join them. My friend drew away sharply, as if stung.

"Oh, this place is tired," she said, swiveling off the bench. "Shall we go?"

# 11

The next day was our Etruscan outing. It was insufferably hot, even at five in the afternoon. Not knowing exactly what "walking clothes" meant, I wore shorts and trainers; Anna looked flawless in a short, loose dress and gladiator sandals, and Pascal followed close behind her in an impractical outfit of chinos, a long-sleeved button-down, and a ridiculous straw hat. As for Professor Korloff, he looked almost athletic in army shorts, sandals, and a T-shirt.

"Okay, here we go," Professor Korloff yelled. "If you get lost, ask the locals where that American ass is who's looking for the old hole in the ground."

We followed somewhat sluggishly; there were thirteen of us, and none of us wanted to look like a tourist group. But Professor Korloff marched ahead with determination, so after a block or two, we broke up into twos and threes. Following in his footsteps, we walked out of the gate of the old city, then we reached a highway.

"Don't get killed," Professor Korloff cried before darting in front of a bus. "Can't have you expiring on my watch." We crossed successfully after a few minutes, then continued down a hill to what must have quite recently been a country road, making a right on another dusty avenue until we reached a small valley. It was a strange neighborhood, a mix of old houses flanked by flat-roofed postwar apartment blocks, now as dilapidated as their three-hundred-year-old neighbors. A few people poked their heads out as we passed—mostly mischievous children, and behind them perhaps the shadowy face of a grandmother. Some of the shutters slammed shut, the sharp sound mocking us from the slope of the hill.

Finally, Professor Korloff led us down a narrow dirt path to a stone farmhouse hemmed in by a well-tended vegetable garden. Instantly, we were surrounded, all thirteen of us, by a lively population of chickens. I tried not to laugh as Anna kicked the animals away with her silver sandals; when Pascal attempted to shoo them away for her, they pecked angrily at his feet. After a few long minutes a farmer ambled out of his small stone cottage, looking at us through half-closed eyes, a handsome rifle held loosely in his left hand.

"*Buon giorno*, Cesare," Arthur said pleasantly.

"*Buon giorno.*"

"We came to see the caves."

"Professor, you know there are no caves," the farmer said. The rest of us shifted back and forth on our feet, afraid to make a sound.

"Don't tease me, Cesare. You've been with me yourself."

"Not with a crowd." He gestured at us with his gun. Arthur reached into his back pocket, pulled out a billfold, and waved a twenty-euro note back and forth.

"Put that away," Cesare said.

"These are Enteria students, Cesare. Very serious."

Cesare peered at us. "Students."

"Actually, no. *Scholars.*" Arthur held out forty euros this time.

Cesare put up his hand. "Just twenty. Only twenty."

"For your trouble."

"All right. There *is* one cave. But it is just dirt now. Your scholars will be disappointed."

Professor Korloff gave us a sly look.

"All right, all right," said the farmer. "Behind the old stable. You'll see it. It's just a little hole, and the cave is very small. They will think it's nothing."

"Perhaps."

"Did you bring a lantern?"

"Yes."

"Well, don't touch anything."

"Of course not, Cesare."

"Tell them, too?"

"As I said, these are Enteria scholars."

Cesare frowned. "The students are loud in Grifonia."

"Not these students. These are serious people."

The farmer laughed shortly. "Very young people. I know all about it. Well. The caves are in the back. I will bring some wine to the table under the trellis."

Cesare disappeared back into the house.

"Such service," Professor Korloff said. "Despises you all, but he gives you wine. Get it? It's not the money, it's the dance."

"We're not that bad, are we?" Anna asked.

"Not *you*, in particular, no—though I know nothing of your nightly activities." Anna and I exchanged a quick glance. "But he's not wrong. The student population has grown completely out of control. Grifonia, when Cesare was young, was a beautiful town. A quiet town. Mussolini had built the great University to show off Italian culture, and there wasn't too much damage from the war. But, of course, it was poor, and students from other countries have, well, money. Get it? Now the place is clogged with jerks. It's loud, too many drugs. A lot of the families moved out here. No, the old Grifonians are never going to like you. But being in Enteria sometimes helps."

He took a final drag of his cigarette and flicked it away.

"All right. Let's find that stable." We followed Professor Korloff around the cottage across a small yard to a crumbling building out back. Ancient tools and sacks were visible through the holes in the walls. Behind it stretched a bare field, in the middle of which jutted a grassy mound, roughly fifteen feet in diameter.

"Our tomb, children," he said, gesturing toward it.

Pascal and Anna instinctively took the lead. As we got closer, we saw what looked like a large, dark mouth, gaping into the ground. The opening, about eight feet below the level of where we were standing, was supported on three sides by girders, each made of a single, huge stone. From far away, because of the blond grass jutting off the top, the tomb almost looked like the head of a huge, yawning baby.

"This, believe it or not, is the site of one of the greatest recent discoveries in Grifonia," Professor Korloff said. He kicked a stone down the path; it rolled down into the darkness as if guided by a magnetic field.

"A hundred and eighty-two years ago, an Italian excavator stumbled across this tomb here while looking for some urns. The Etruscans, we know, were great preparers for the afterlife—as extravagant as the Egyptians, nearly—building entire houses to live in once they died."

He paused and looked up at the trees. It was the last day of September, and most of the leaves had turned, though the air was thick and hot as July. Sweat ran in rivulets down all our faces, save Anna's. She remained mysteriously cool, her clothes spotless.

"Fortune hunters illegally gutted the thing and sold everything inside. Augusto Castellani bought most of it and put it in the Etruscan Museum, after picking off all the things he liked best. Nothing categorized, of course. It was a really rotten time for archaeologists. But the structure is still here, and I wanted you all to see it. To see how these people built houses that bloomed underground."

He switched on his lantern and twitched his head toward the hole, indicating that we should follow. No one seemed eager. The pitch-black mouth looked less than inviting.

"Believe it or not, we'll all fit. So, okay, come on."

Single file, we followed Professor Korloff into the tunnel, which was about four feet wide and eight feet tall. The slope went down and down and down, until we were at least fifteen feet below ground. I was the last, behind Anna, or so I thought—when I turned after going a good ways down the underground path, I saw a figure in the opening, standing in the light.

"Hello?" I called. My voice produced a horrible echo, not of my words but a low monotonous boom that coiled ominously down the passageway.

"You all right?" asked Anna.

"I thought we left someone."

"What?" She went back a few feet and looked, then turned again. "No, there's no one there. Probably just the farmer."

"What if we get stuck down here?"

Our mixed speech intensified the low reverberation, which was now almost deafening.

"Taz, don't be silly. Come on, it opens up ahead."

She took my hand and pulled me about ten more feet forward to where Professor Korloff was standing with the others, shining his lantern so we could see. Anna was right. There, the tunnel gave way to a large hall about thirty feet long and wide, with four smaller rooms branching off its sides. My claustrophobia subsided as I stepped away from the group, exploring the space. The ceiling in the chamber was approximately fifteen feet high, allowing an air of spaciousness. The walls were stone—perhaps there had been paintings on them at one time, but they had been either rubbed off or worn away. There were benches carved into the walls, and at the front of the room was a large, bare altar, with the blurred stone remnants of some sort of creature staring down.

It was dark. I suppose that's obvious, but it was a different kind of darkness from when a light is turned out in a closet, a bedroom, or even a cellar. Those places, at least at one time, were touched by the sun. No part of this tomb had ever been exposed, even once, and it never, ever would be. There was a constant dripping of something thick. A sucking of air in one of the corners. And of course the absence of all sounds from the outside—breeze, birds, cars, voices. Life.

"Here we are," our professor said. "The Soeviis' final home." The echo had ceased, I assumed because of the shape of the room. "Not too bad. And it was a lot nicer. The walls would have been covered in frescoes and carvings of the family's favorite items. Tools, pets. Things they wanted to take to the next life. Which, by the way, they were banking on. Obviously, this house wasn't cheap to build."

"How were they buried?" Pascal asked. "Are they in here somewhere?"

"No, Elvis has left the building, unfortunately. They were in sarcophagi, probably, though some may have been embalmed and laid out. The slaves were in urns in the smaller rooms. Everything, of course, was taken and sold. When I first came down here twenty years ago, I was really hoping I'd discover something—a miniature Tarquinia. But it's not always about what you find, when you're a scholar, but what's possible."

I made my way into one of the smaller chambers. Even this space seemed comfortably large to me. I ran my palms against the cold wall, resting my cheek there for a moment. I pressed my ear against the stone, as if an answer might come as to why anyone would build such a place. To prepare for death with such fervor. Closing my eyes, I pictured the place exactly as it had been—the shining walls, the coffins studded with jewels and glittering mosaics.

"You okay, Taz?" Anna said, stepping in behind me.

"Yes," I said, embarrassed.

"A bit frightening, isn't it?"

"Not to me." Indeed, I felt the odd sensation of having been there many times before.

"Come on out," Anna said. "He's starting to talk."

Professor Korloff lectured for a while on Etruscan death practices, and then brought us back above ground. I was the last out, leaving somewhat reluctantly, but when we emerged the farmer had some bottles of wine open on a plastic table. After a half bottle of wine each in the sun, the tomb was all but forgotten, and we trudged painfully up the hill. By the time we reached the gate to the city, any thought of the strange familiarity of the place had diminished to some pale shadow in a midnight dream. The sort that pricks you awake at the time, only to sink to the very lowest priority in the light of day.

## *Lucia, 12th century AD*

Lucia Baglioni, daughter of noblemen. The Baglionis were a venomous family, everyone struggling for power. Lucia was proud of her clan, but the politics made her tired. Her father had promised her to her cousin Paolo, in exchange for a palace on the central *via*. But Lucia was sixteen, and she hated Paolo, with his oily skin and fat haunches.

She waited a few weeks, wondering what to do. Then, as the union grew nearer, she took her fiercest brother aside.

I want you to kill Paolo, she said. While you are hunting. Make it look like an accident. For me.

Lucia's brother was torn. He was fond of his sister, but his alliance with Paolo gave him great power. While they were hunting, instead of fulfilling his sister's request, he told Paolo of her plan.

Both men, as noblemen, were members of the Compagnia. Additions to the ledger were now quite precious. A truly good death meant the highest prestige.

Three days later, in the earliest hours of the morning, Lucia's brother came into her bedroom. He grabbed her wrists. Still half-asleep, she didn't fight. He kicked open her shutters and threw her three stories down into the street.

Intruders! Paolo screamed behind her, waving the phantom murderers away.

The next day Paolo made the entry. Lucia's brother witnessed.

*Lucia Baglioni, served a good death by her brother Diego Baglioni. Saved from eternal loss of virtue by raping thieves.*

*Lucia Baglioni, sixteen years old, 12th century AD*

# 12

Friendships, and marriages for that matter, are often a simple result of geography. Babs and I, for instance. We were lifelong friends only because she lived around the corner from me in Lucan. Our parents, before my father left for Dublin and my mother slipped into self-created illness, were weekend friends, the type who take their babies to the pub together to pass the long Sunday afternoons. Babs was the type of girl who constantly had a fuzzy nest on the back of her head, as she only thought to brush the hair she could see in the mirror. Her palette consisted of all the colors of the rainbow: green-and-red Christmas tights with a bright-blue spring dress, red pants with a dung-colored sweater. She could have hardly been more different from my tight-lipped, hair-bow-matching-the-ankle-socks youthful form.

As we grew to plotting age, I was the one with all the plans. I always played the queen, while she was the hired help. So when she burst into my room breathless one morning when we were nine, her cheeks burning red, I sat up in my magazine-littered bed in mild alarm.

"I have an *idea*," she said, plopping down on my bed.

"What?"

"We'll make a *time* capsule. I saw it on the telly. You put things in a box, toys and notes and candy and things, and then you close it and—"

"Who's it for?"

Babs stopped, confused. "For?"

"The candy. Is it a present?"

Babs's face broke into a crooked smile.

"It's for you, silly!"

"Babs." I patted her shoulder, trying not to be too condescending. "That is so . . . I don't know. Okay, it's stupid. Why would I give myself candy I already *have*?"

"Taz! We'll bury it somewhere. Or put it somewhere safe. Then in, like, fifty years, we go get it again."

"The candy will go bad, you daff."

"Fine. Twenty years."

"I'll be twenty-*nine*." It was utterly unimaginable.

"Well, even if you forgot about it, I'll be there to tell you to go open it."

"Yeah, but what if we're not friends?"

Babs's face fell. She actually looked like she might cry. I felt a bit of a thrill.

"You think we might not be?"

"I don't know. It's a long time from now."

"I'll *find* you," Babs cried. "We'll *be* best friends. I'll *tell* you to open the box."

There was no arguing with her. We spent the next hour trying to decide what to give to ourselves at twenty-nine. In Babs's box: four Cadbury bars, a Sinead O'Connor CD, a copy of *Go Ask Alice* (we'd shared it and hid it from our parents), and a picture of her dog, Barth. In mine: a shell from our summer trip to the sea, a bag of pickle-flavored crisps (I wasn't certain they'd still exist when I was twenty-nine), and that day's *Lucan Times*. We both also wrote letters to ourselves on my purple lined stationery.

*Dear Me: (meaning Ms. (Mrs.????!!) Tabitha M. Deacon)*

*Hi. I can't believe you are twenty-nine. But you are me, so I guess you can believe it. I hope you are married, because you are really really old. I also hope you have a cat because Mum would never let us have pets. She can be really awful sometimes but it's just because of stupid Da. Do you still love*

*Leonardo? Maybe he's who you are married to. Anyway, this is dumb. This was all Babs's idea. Have a good day, and give everyone my love. If Fiona is still being mean, tell her she still looks like an arse pillow. Also, I hid ten pounds behind the bookshelf. If you need it.*

*Love always, Taz*
*October 16, 1994*

The papered box was, thirteen years later, found by the police. They came to search my room at home, thinking perhaps the reason for my murder had to do with a stalker or a spurned lover, someone who came all the way from the green hills of Lucan.

You can imagine how the Irish cooperation with the Italians went. The officers were vaguely excited, as it was a famous case—in the tabloids and all that. But the drive from Dublin to Lucan backed up, it was raining, and my mother, who was still heavily in shock, forced them to sit down to an incredibly awkward cup of tea.

Apologetically, the officers came into the room, opening drawers with gloved hands, looking for letters, notebooks, anything that might give them a hint as to who might have wanted me dead.

"I've got something," the younger one said finally. He was standing on a chair, looking on top of the closet. Carefully, he slid it off the shelf. Sitting together on the bed, just as Babs and I had all those years ago, they bent their heads over the papered box.

"Boyfriend notes?"

The other shook his head. They lifted the lid and sifted carefully through the candy and rocks. The elder picked up the two envelopes, marked:

*To Tabitha Deacon, from Tabitha Deacon, to be opened in 2014.*

and

*A note for the future from Babs. Open in 2014!!!*

Neither officer said anything for a moment.

"Might as well—"

"Yeah."

My mother had come up the stairs and was silently watching them through the doorway. They read my note, then put it down. Then they read the other.

Another pause.

"Mrs. Deacon . . ." the elder officer said.

"Yes?"

"Who is Babs?"

"A friend. They are—were—friends."

The officer handed her the note.

*Dear Tabitha,*

*You are a real arse sometimes. Remember how you didn't want to do this time capsule? Now you're glad, see? Arse. Love you anyway.*

*Babs*

My mother stared at the note for a full minute. The officers shifted on their feet. Finally she put the letter back in the envelope.

"So this is nothing . . ." the younger officer said.

"They were nine."

"Yes . . ."

"*Please.*" My mother's voice was low. "I'm still here, do you understand?"

The men just stared at her.

"It's not supposed to be this way. It's *never* supposed to be this way. We go first. Do you see? But I'm the mother and I'm still *here.*"

•

We were still best friends, Babs and I, even after all those years. She had grown somewhat pretty, in an off-kilter sort of way and morphed into a hipster, even, wearing black horn-rimmed glasses. She had been in New York for a science conference, and had bought them there. She had never visited Italy and couldn't relate at all to my stories of Jenny and the B4. It was the first time we'd faced a real distance between us, and it was becoming a problem.

"Why does it matter if you sleep with men or not?" she asked when she called the day after the hike to the tomb. "It sounds like you're having a nice time with them, but this advice is very odd."

"It's about power," I said, parroting Jenny. "It's about staying ahead of feelings."

"No, that doesn't really make sense either. There's nothing powerful about being . . . a . . ."

"Slut?" I said.

"Taz!" Babs's tone was disapproving, and it irritated me.

"I just think you're not understanding the situation."

There was a silence on the other end of the line. "Maybe," she said. "I just worry about you. Are you certain you're all right?"

"Why wouldn't I be?"

"Maybe Mum'll give me some Christmas money to come over. It's only the first of October. I can ask. I'll try. I really will."

I hung up, an odd feeling in my belly. The cold truth was, I didn't *want* Babs to visit. For one thing, I was certain Jenny wouldn't like her. For another, I knew what she would bring with her—the baggage from my past. And what if she happened upon the fact that my new friend was a drug dealer? One who passed herself off as "small time," but who now had me translating for her either in person or on the phone at least three times a day?

But the very thought of not wanting Babs around was a betrayal. I certainly didn't like Jenny and the girls better. It was just that, at the moment, they seemed to understand me more.

I sighed, restless, and tried to work. As I sat there, thumbing through my book on Etruscan stone reliefs, Claire came out of her room, fresh from an afternoon nap. Due to her increasingly frequent absences, this sort of meeting was becoming more and more rare.

"Oh, good! You're here. I never see you." She rubbed her eyes. She had a waitressing job that often had her out late. "Hey, I need a coffee. Let's go to our place."

It bothered me, the way she ordered me around sometimes, but I was glad for distraction that day. "Our place" was a little café just steps from the cottage, an unexpectedly pleasant spot with a lovely patio looking out at the busy street and the basketball court. Grifonia had surprisingly few good cafés like this; even the Italian spots were usually filled with loud foreign students looking for "authenticity" who took the tables and forced the locals to the sides. But the owner ran a tight ship, shooing out loud and disrespectful clients. The bar gleamed; the espresso maker hissed with cheerful resilience; glasses clinked with the confidence of an expert barman doing his job.

We were sitting outside. It was British weather—the air was crisp and smelled of burning wood; the sky was sharp blue. "Isn't this coffee like no other coffee in the world?" she asked.

"Yes," I said. "Well. I hear the coffee is also pretty good in Turkey. Finland maybe."

"Taz. You're so fucking *literal*." She picked up the tiny cup, sniffed it, and put it down again. "It's hell on the stomach, isn't it? I'm so jonesing for a latte right now, but the Italians say it's disgusting to drink milk after noon."

I looked down at my cappuccino. Claire loved to proclaim herself an expert on Italian culture, even, sometimes, to our Italian flatmates.

"Now." She leaned forward, stirring her espresso. "Tell me again about your home. I want to know all about it. Like, *everything*."

I smiled politely, a bit disheartened. I often felt, when fielding Claire's questions, that she was looking for a specific answer I was never going to be able to give.

"What is your house like? Is Lucan one of those cute Irish villages with leprechauns and crap?"

"It is rather cute. But it's just a suburb. We're getting swallowed by the malls and the sprawl."

"And your house?"

"Oh, a very normal house. Four bedrooms. Fuzzy carpets."

"Taz, come on."

"What?"

"Is it a *happy* house?"

I looked out at the square. The same woman was always there:

thick but small, dusty, visibly strung out. Her outfits varied—today she wore a too-short yellow dress. She could have been anywhere from twenty-five to fifty. At one point in her life she had probably been what Jenny would call "a shag-worthy girl."

"A happy house? You're very American, aren't you? Raised on sitcoms."

"Well?"

I shrugged. "Of course. Why wouldn't it be?"

She shook her head, annoyed. "*Plenty* of people live in unhappy houses. Like my house before my parents divorced. We had this big fancy place, with, like, these stupid remote-control fireplaces. That's what I remember most. You'd press these buttons and then, boom! I thought it was the most awesome thing in the world. But my parents used to tear into each other. It was a fucking battlefield in there."

"That's too bad."

"It's cool. It made me who I am. Now my mom lives in, like, a tiny bungalow in a shitty area near the train tracks, while my dad's still in his fucking disgusting McMansion. But she's happy."

"That's wonderful."

"Whatever. But your house is perfect, huh?"

"I wouldn't say that. I mean, my father doesn't live there anymore."

"He left?"

"He lives in Dublin. Left when I was six."

"Shit. I'm sorry."

"Don't be. Everything's for the best. I'm sorry to disappoint you, but I just don't have anything to complain about."

"God, Taz." She'd finished her coffee by now and had moved on to mine.

"What?"

"You just never give anything. You're so . . . *serene*. How the fuck am I supposed to get to know you?"

"With time, I suppose."

"Just give me one thing. Something to go on."

"All right." I looked out at the park again. It was hard and ugly, with just a few trees struggling for light. The woman in yellow was now sitting with the woman in white I'd seen the other day. She was even thinner than I remembered, really nothing more than a skeleton covered in skin. The two were leaning over an old book of some kind.

"Taz?" Claire prompted. I turned back to her.

"Sometimes I picture . . . dying. What it would be like. You know."

"I totally *don't* know. Like suicide?"

"No," I said. "I'd never do that. Too scared."

"Fuck yeah."

"But I feel like maybe I know . . . what it's like. I don't know."

Claire looked at me carefully. "So? What's it like?"

"Well, I read a lot of Sylvia Plath in school—"

"Oh, man. A Plath freak?"

"I suppose. Well, no. I just read. And when she attempted suicide, she wrote . . . well . . . something like, 'I succumbed with bliss to the whirling blackness.'"

"'With bliss'?"

"Or 'blissfully.' Something like that."

"Death is not fucking blissful," Claire said, lighting a cigarette. "If anything, *sex* is blissful. Sometimes. But fucking death?"

"Oh, I didn't mean—"

"Let me tell you something," she said. "I've got this uncle, and he has a ranch. Like, in the rolling plains, you know? Sea to fucking shining sea. Mountains, rivers, whatever. Looks like a movie. But the point of the place is to slaughter these cows, right?"

"Right."

"Okay. So I watch sometimes. It's seriously screwed up. And the most fucked up thing is they—my uncle and his partners—have these *hugging* machines so the cows don't get scared. They smell the blood, they see the blade, but this . . . electronic hugger holds them until they bleed out, and they never shake. Like, at all. My uncle says it's humane."

"God."

"You might trick yourself into thinking whatever the hell Sylvia

Plath said, but it's bullshit. Or else my uncle wouldn't spend three hundred thousand on an electric cow hugger."

She looked at me over her cigarette.

"Do I have to worry about you, Taz?"

"Absolutely not. I was just conversing. A thought. You know."

Something caught my eye. The women I'd been looking at before were walking slowly, arms linked, down the dark alley that led to our house.

"Perhaps we should—"

Then, with a sudden jerk Claire lurched over and embraced me. Her iron café chair knocked to the stone ground with a clatter. I wriggled a bit, but she was strong, and held me fast. Her hair brushed my face. She smelled of soap and coffee.

"Just had to do that," she said, finally releasing me.

"So you're my electric cow hugger, eh?"

Claire laughed, righting her chair. I stood to go, and she reached over and squeezed my hand. When we got back to the house, Gia and Alessandra were sitting at the table. The sharp scent of marijuana hung in the air.

"*Bellas!*" Alessandra said. She stood up and kissed us both. I was getting more used to this. Claire, of course, loved the custom and took the opportunity to kiss anyone she could. "How are you?"

"We picked some figs from the orchard," Gia said, nodding to the basket on the table. She wore a crooked, stoned grin.

"That's amazing!" Claire gushed.

And here, the afternoon briefly varies from what I know happened to what I know didn't. Because in truth, I know that Claire dumped the fruit in the sink, and then all of us went to our respective rooms to get ready for the evening. That we soon called out farewells and drifted to different corners of the city: Claire to a tavern, me to a party with Jenny, the Italians to dinner in the home of yet another friend they wouldn't introduce us to.

But soon blood would flow, and the others would, knowingly or not, change the truth. Their lies were out of fear, I suppose. Though it could have been something else. Didn't I, who had in the past weeks transformed myself from the mouse I'd been, know the power of changing reality? Or perhaps it had something to do with the geography of the house itself, its precarious position on the edge of that hill. A strong wind, or an earthquake, and we'd topple downward. How could any memory in such a house be trusted?

So I, too, feel I may create one tiny scene that I deeply wish had happened. A lovely false memory we'd all have to hang on to, if we had been closer, or the hour had not been so late.

You see, it was a Friday. The four of us sat down at the small table, talking and laughing. We were still innocent, all of us. Our elbows knocked, and the air smelled of fresh coffee. Claire washed the figs while Gia told us stories about her family's small farm outside Florence. Alessandra told us, shyly, about the first time she'd been in love back in Milan. Bringing the knife and a slab of wood over, Claire put a row of green figs in front of us.

Yes, I know what happened to that knife.

But I can tell you we'd never seen such fruit, none of us. Once sliced, those lumps of chlorophyll revealed their gleaming, bruised hearts. The seeds clung to our teeth. Juice streamed down our wrists.

Four almost-women, sitting at a table.

We tore into the fruit and ate.

# 13

Tuesday, the second of October. I was on my way back from Arthur's class, in my usual intellectually humbled state, wearing my boots over jeans and a jumper that I had purchased on a whim during an evening shop with Anna. (She had bargained it down to forty euros from ninety.) I scuttled down the alley steps, across the busy street and into our garden. The gate clanked behind me. As I neared the door, I saw that a figure was coming up from behind the cottage.

"Ciao," he said.

He was a strong, short boy, a little heavy, with black curls and small dark eyes. Perhaps my age, perhaps a year older. He wore jeans and a leather jacket, unzipped. He had a Vespa helmet in his hand. As soon as he saw me, he smiled widely. His lips, for some reason, reminded me of salt.

Despite my flatmates' warnings about the boys below, I'd never seen them. I could often hear their stabbing shouts of laughter through the floor. Male smells—sweat, fried food, the sharp, strong scent of marijuana—often drifted into our kitchen.

"You one of the new girls?" he asked in Italian.

"I guess."

"You must be the pretty one."

"That's the other one, actually," I said.

He laughed. "No. Well. You're here now. And so am I. I'm Marcello. Where are you going?"

"Home," I said.

He smiled and rocked back and forth on his feet.

"No you're not. You're coming for a coffee with me."

"I can't," I said. "Really. I've got to be somewhere."

The B4 was getting together in forty minutes at the Club.

"Where?"

"I'm meeting friends."

"Aren't we friends?"

I gave a small laugh and leaned against the gate.

"You like it here?" he asked. "In this house?"

"Of course," I said. "It's so cute."

"Gia and Alessandra?"

"They're lovely."

"They're okay," he said. "They get pissy when we get loud."

"Well, you are quite loud."

"Oh-ho! The new girl is pissy, too."

"I never said anything. Just that you make a lot of noise."

"You know what else about Gia?"

"What?"

"She and my flatmate, they had a thing last winter. Alfonso. That's why she never comes down."

"So?"

"Right. Who cares? I'm just trying to gossip with you."

"I don't know anything."

"Sure you do," he said. "We'll talk. You're my new best friend."

"Well, I've got to—"

"Come down Thursday night. We're having a little party."

"What time?"

"After ten."

"Maybe."

"Stop teasing, beautiful," he said. "You're driving me crazy."

"Can I bring my friends?"

"It's boring, the way you foreign girls always travel in herds. Like goats. Are you a goat?"

"It's safer," I said.

"Don't bring them. I only want you to come. We'll all be there. Alfonso, Ervin. Everyone. Come on."

"All right," I said. "I guess. I mean, I know you, you're my neighbor."

"Yes." He nodded. "You know me. So we'll see you?"

"Okay."

A final smile raced across his face. Marcello kissed me on both cheeks, holding my arms a bit roughly. He smelled as if he had recently eaten something delicious. Then he slipped out the gate.

•

The next day, the sky turned black and wet. October squalls were coming from the south. I was so used to seeing Grifonia beaten by sun, the rain seemed an unexpected and highly unwelcome visitor.

"Apocalyptic," Claire said, peering through the shut door of the terrace.

"Well. There's no need to be dramatic."

I'd been drinking too much, three nights in a row at the bars with the B4. My translation duties were getting irritatingly frequent, sometimes requiring conversations at three a.m. The night before, Jenny had led us to the Red Lion again and I ended up kissing a pudgy American out of nothing more than boredom. Now I was to meet the girls for a pizza to rehash it all, but the prospect of getting to the restaurant in the rain seemed a grim task. Meanwhile, our cozy cottage had shrunk drastically in the horrid weather. Gia and Alessandra had abandoned the place after snapping at each other all morning, and now Claire was pacing back and forth as if caged.

"Taz, what are you doing tonight?"

"Dinner out, if I manage it."

"Can I come?"

She looked over at me, catching my obvious pause.

"I'm just so bored, and I don't feel like eating alone."

I closed my book, smoothing the cover with my fingers. I'd been dreading this moment. Compared with me and my highly organized semester that was paved and paid for by Enteria, Claire was a lone wolf. Her university's program was sloppy and unstructured. She'd met a couple of older girls, but she rarely saw them. Sometimes she met them for one drink and then roamed about alone. She had never said she was envious of the B4, but until now I'd kept them away from her, for fear that she would ask to join.

"Sure," I said. "Come with us. Come get a pizza." I didn't want to tell her about Jenny's rule of no extra girls at B4 dinners.

"Great! Thanks. Let me just shower," she said, disappearing into our tiny bathroom. When I heard a burst of water, I picked up my phone to call Anna.

"Alloooo?" I could hear music and laughter in the background.

"Hey."

"Taz! Luka and I came to that horrid Malone's place to pass this rain. But you know? It's much nicer than I thought. We're a little out of our heads. You should come."

She sounded more cheerful than usual; since her godfather's arrival in Grifonia, she had been acting almost happy.

"We have that art history paper due tomorrow. Doesn't anyone in Enteria but me do any work?"

Anna laughed. "Not really. Except in Arthur's class."

"Listen, I have to bring my flatmate to dinner. Do you think Jenny will mind?"

"Yes," she said. "Of course she'll mind. Can't you get out of it?"

"I can't. Not without being a bitch."

"This is the American flatmate?"

"Yes."

There was a pause and a bout of murmuring, during which she conferred with Luka. "Okay. Text her. Jenny. Tell her you're bringing your flatmate like she asked."

"Asked?"

"The other night at the Club."

"It's not a fucking club!" Luka yelled into the phone. "It's my fucking apartment!" Behind her some boys bellowed.

"Jenny *said* that she was curious to meet her. Just pretend you took her literally."

"That's sort of brilliant."

"Text her and then turn your phone off."

"Okay. Seven?"

"Seven. Though you'd both better have a drink first. Jenny can be prickly."

"Oh, God. I don't know if I'm up for this."

"Up for what?"

I whirled around. The water was still running, but Claire was standing behind me, naked.

"The rain. I don't know if I'm up for the rain," I said, hanging up on Anna. "What are you doing? Where are your clothes?"

"I came out for my razor," she said. "You're not ready, are you?"

"No, no. I'm not going for a while. Take your time."

She didn't move, instead continuing to stare at me.

"Taz."

"Hmmm?"

"You're okay with me going, aren't you? Because I can really stay home if you're not into it."

"Of course I want you," I said. "Don't be silly."

"You're not lying?"

Again, that stare. I felt a flip in my chest I was surprised to recognize as fear.

"Of course not."

Seemingly satisfied, Claire padded back into the shower. I texted Jenny and turned off my phone as Anna had instructed, then poured myself a large glass of wine.

Yet the remorse was seeping in. The only thing my flatmate wanted was to meet new friends. Was I so stingy that I couldn't share? And I knew about being lonely, didn't I?

You see, that was the thing about Claire. I *knew* her. She and I wanted the same thing. Later, she was painted a hundred different ways: insane, sexy, volatile, brilliant, stupid, insatiable. But the Claire I knew was just a girl with the same simple desire I had—to be loved by as many people as possible.

"I'll have a glass with you," she said, coming out. I resisted the urge to advise her to change. She was wearing her ripped baggy jeans, which were stained with something yellow, and a large brown sweatshirt emblazoned with the word RINGO.

"Claire, you're the only twenty-year-old in the world who is obsessed with the Beatles. Even the Brits are over it."

"Oh, they're pure genius. The lyrics!" She grabbed the guitar and strummed. "*She came in throooough the bathroom window . . .*"

"Oh, God."

"Protected?" She pointed at me.

"Protected by a silver spoon."

"Right." Claire strummed, the key a bit off. "*Didn't anybody tell her?*"

"Didn't anybody see." I said it flatly.

Claire finally gave mercy and rested the guitar on the floor. "I could listen to that a million times."

"And if you listen to 'Revolution 9' backwards . . ."

"Turn me on, dead man! Oh, I love that you know that." She put her arm around me and squeezed. "Nobody *ever* knows that."

Have you ever been close to a truly beautiful person? Experienced the sensory disorientation, the racing of the brain? Her shirts always too loose, her breasts free, her hair slipping into her eyes as she looked at you, full of questions.

"I have two boy cousins," I said hurriedly. "They know all of that rubbish. I heard it's actually true. I think they tried it on my dad's old record player."

"Hilarious," Claire said, picking up my wine. "I think I heard it once, too, but I was super high."

We were somewhat drunk by the time we got out of the house, huddled under my pink umbrella. As we tripped up the stairs to the square, she held on to my arm, laughing.

"Aren't you glad we're roommates?"

"Yes." I tried to hold her upright. She stumbled again, embracing me.

"Oh, Taz. I just feel like everything here is . . . destiny. You know?"

"Yes."

"Hug me back, Taz," she commanded.

I patted her back weakly.

"I could totally kiss you right now, you know. In Italy, friends kiss."

She drew back, peering at me with that challenging look she had. It was exactly like being dared by a small, naughty child.

"Do you want to?" she whispered.

"Well, I—"

"Oh, I'm starving." She pulled away. "Where *is* this place?"

Even in the rain, there was a crowd waiting outside the door. Pizza Bella was the most popular pizzeria in the old town. We were in the habit of going often, as it was close to the Club. The space was cozy, at best. There were few tables, and always a long queue outside. Diners were not welcome to linger—the management wanted the customers to order pizza, eat, and get out. But when we went there, which was often, Luka would come early and bribe the management for a table. As usual, I was the last one to arrive.

As we walked into the place—bustling, bright, thick with the smell of baked bread and garlic and cooked cheese—I felt a surge of panic. Jenny was sitting at the far end of the room, whispering to Luka with a sour look on her face.

"Come on," I said rather harshly, forging ahead through the clot of tables. Claire trailed behind me. I felt a wave of embarrassment and shame at bringing her.

"Hello!" Jenny said. To my relief, she looked pleased to see us. I looked at Luka and Anna, who smiled reassuringly. "We've been waiting for you."

"Oh! This is—"

Jenny held up her hand to stop me.

"I got your text, but you didn't respond to mine."

"Sorry. Phone was off."

"Hmmm. T'sall right."

"This is Claire."

Slowly, Jenny turned her head in my flatmate's direction.

"Hi!" Anna said. Luka raised her hand in greeting.

"I didn't know they sat tables before the whole party got here," Claire said, glancing at the line outside. "This place is popular."

"Well, Luka gave them enough to let us stay until tomorrow if we want."

"Gave who what?" Claire asked, taking off her jacket.

"Never mind. So you're Taz's flatmate! We've heard so much about you. Have some wine."

Jenny nodded at Anna, who poured Claire a glass. It was going to be all right, probably, I thought to myself. I leaned back in my chair, beginning to relax.

"Thanks."

"So you're doing an independent study?"

"Yes," Claire said. She folded her arms and put her elbows on the table. For some reason it made her seem manly. I wondered if the others noticed.

"How do you like it?"

"I love it."

Anna beamed generously. Luka drained her glass.

"But it's hard to meet people."

"That's too bad." Jenny gathered her heavy hair and put it over one shoulder. "It's hard, of course, when people already have their friends. Hard to crack it."

"I guess." Claire smiled. That smile! Jenny turned away, as if the glare of it were too much to take.

"Of course, I have Taz."

"Do you really?" Jenny raised her eyebrows.

"How do you guys like Enteria?"

"Fine, fine," Jenny said, waving her hand, as if bored. "It's brilliant. Other than the lack of decent men. We need to go to Rome or something."

"Lack of men?" Claire looked around the restaurant, filled with men of all ages. "Seriously?"

"Real Italian men. With good taste and class. The Grifonians are complete roughnecks. Haven't you noticed? It's like the Liverpool of Italy."

"Doesn't stop you from shagging them," Luka said.

"I want to meet an Italian gentleman. With a villa or something. Maybe from a political family."

Claire looked over at me.

*Just go with it*, I prayed.

"Wait until that thing at the castle," Luka said.

"Castle?" Claire asked.

"She's joking. So where are you from?"

"Butte."

"No idea."

"It's in Montana. Near—"

"Ah, here's the pizza," Jenny said, abruptly cutting her off. "We ordered already." The bedraggled waiter threw down the platter and ran away again. "I hope you eat meat? I know a lot of Americans don't."

"Yup," Claire said. To my horror, she reached over and took three pieces at once. The B4 were in the habit of taking just one, in case Jenny—a more enthusiastic eater than the rest of us—wanted seconds.

Anna, who apparently couldn't take the silence that followed, turned to Claire politely. "So what are you studying?"

"Italian. Politics. Lit. You?"

"Same, same," Jenny said impatiently. "We're all studying the Italians. Obviously. What I want to know is, are there any nice lads?"

"Sure," Claire said.

"Maybe you could bring some around for Taz. She's having rather a dry spell."

I studied my plate, as if the patterns of basil held a secret message for me.

Claire paused, her pizza midair. "Taz doesn't need my help."

"Speaking of lads, are you recovered from last night, Taz?" Anna asked.

"That was fun," Jenny said. "Those people we met were *hilarious.*"

I looked at her. We had only gone to the ghastly Red Lion. And it hadn't been particularly fun, which is why I kissed the fat boy from New Jersey.

"Where did you go?" Claire asked.

"Just a place," Jenny said coldly.

I expected Claire to look confused, but instead she just smiled again.

"But it sounds like *you've* met a lot of guys."

"Yes, here and there," Jenny said. "When in Rome, or Grifonia. You know. No one I really like."

"Now that's where we differ," Claire said, finishing her wine and pouring another glass. "Because I fuck every night, too. But I actually *like* them all."

Everyone else at the table froze. Claire crammed more pizza into her mouth with her fingers.

"Every night?" Anna asked.

"Oh, sure," she said with her mouth full. "Hang on." She swallowed. "First, I totally fucked a guy on the train from Germany. In the bathroom."

"What?" Jenny said, recovering. She gave a merry laugh. "You little slut!"

"Oh, I'm from Montana. Nothing to do but screw in barns. They give out condoms in kindergarten."

"Taz, did you know this?" Jenny asked.

"I—"

"She doesn't know, 'cause I don't bring the guys home." Claire licked the cheese off her fingers. "That would be rude. I just screw them where I can. Outside. In alleys, or work. You know."

"You've got to be lying," Luka said. Anna just stared.

Claire shrugged.

"Well," Jenny pressed, "if only you could rub some of your . . . *mojo* off on poor Taz."

"Oh, I fuck Taz all the time," Claire said, smiling.

I leapt up from the table. "Bathroom!" I cried, rushing off. Miraculously, it was empty. I locked the door, splashed water on my face, then put my head down. How bad would it be if I left? Could I say I was sick? Or faint?

The knocking started after four minutes. When the all-out banging began, I relented.

"Sorry," I said to a stormy-faced Umbrian woman holding two children. When I spotted our table, I stopped in horror. Claire's head was thrown back, and she was . . . *singing* while clutching a glass of wine.

*"OOONLY to find Gideon's BIIIIIble . . ."*

I wove through the tables. Even the impossible din of the pizzeria was beginning to fade in surprise.

"She's drunk," I whispered to the others.

"No I'm not. I just fucking love to sing." Her eyes were like two chips of green glass.

Most likely not by coincidence, the bill came an instant later. Luka grabbed it.

"What do I owe?" Claire asked.

"We've got it," Jenny said.

"What? Why? No, I can—"

"Just drop it. We've got it."

Claire slowly turned and looked at Jenny. "I'm sorry, but why should I drop it?"

Jenny rolled her eyes. "Fine. Give us ten fucking euros, if you're going to be that way about it."

"I guess I just don't get it."

"No, you wouldn't," said Jenny. "British tradition and manners and all that. Well, we've got to shove off. Taz, we'll see you later at the Club. Allie, we'll . . . see you."

"Claire."

Jenny stood and looked down at her. Before, I had thought of

Jenny as a pretty girl, but I could see why she was threatened. Claire flattened Jenny's advantages. She seemed, for the first time since I'd known her, ordinary.

My friend from Nottingham smiled and picked up her formidable purse.

"Oh, right," Jenny said. "Claire. Well, don't worry. If I see you again, I won't forget."

•

On the way home, Claire started talking. I'd expected as much. Even when silence was earned, she couldn't ever stand to be quiet.

"Crikey," she said.

"What?"

"What? Seriously?"

I didn't answer.

"Did you want to fucking go with them? To that Club place?"

"It's not a club. It's just an apartment. Where Luka lives."

"You can totally go, you know. I can walk by myself."

"No, I'm tired. Thanks."

"Look, Taz, let's air this out. Those other two seem all okay, but that Jenny girl—"

"She's my friend, Claire. I've known her since my first year at Nottingham."

"She's so *mean* to you. Why would you want to be around somebody like that?"

I looked at her, blinking. How could she not see why I would want to be with them? How smart, funny, and amazing they were?

"You just don't understand the British sense of humor. It sounds cutting to Americans."

"Come on. I'm not an idiot, okay? I mean, personally, I hate this word. But she's a serious cunt. Why would you spend time with someone who treats you like that?"

I bit my lip, thinking of the other side of Jenny, the confessions she'd made to me.

"I think you just don't get her."

"I get that you're better than that Eurotrash. You're a nice person, Taz. A smart person. Don't let yourself get . . . I don't know. Fucking pulled *under*."

We had wandered in the opposite direction from our cottage. Claire stopped at the city wall, looking at the vast valley below. The holy city of Assisi twinkled in the distance, its cathedral jutting out from the mountain. In that moment, I wanted to go there and never come back.

"Look, it doesn't matter to me at all. But you matter. Is it worth feeling like crap just to be able to hang out with her? Is that what you're looking for?"

I shrugged. "I don't know. I guess I'm looking for a lot of things."

She laughed a bit too hard. The unbalanced nature of it frightened me. I stepped away.

"What?"

"We're *all* looking for a lot of things, Taz."

Drunk as I was, an unfamiliar sense of agitation rose in my chest. I felt the surprising urge to slap her face. I was the youngest in a loud Irish family. If there was one thing I hated, it was unsolicited advice.

"Should we go back?" I said, stopping at the top of a stairway leading toward our house.

"Nah," she said. "I think I want to go out for a little."

"You have friends in the square?"

"No. I'm just going to see what's going on."

The rain had thickened from a fine mist to large, sloppy drops.

"I'm sorry if you're angry," I said. It was true. It made me nervous, seeing her upset.

"I'm not pissed at you," she said. "I'm pissed *for* you."

"Don't be."

She nodded and played with a button on my coat for a moment.

"I'm going on, I think," I finally said.

"So am I. Hitting the Red Lion. Those girls made me want a serious drink." She reached into her pocket and pulled out a cigarette. "See you later, yeah?"

"Yeah," I said, starting down. "Bye." As I descended, I looked ahead to make sure the streetlamp was lit. I longed for bed, or one last healthy swallow of wine.

"*You're fucking better than they are*," Claire yelled, suddenly. I was halfway down the staircase now, and she stood at the top, looming, backlit by the spotlights above. I couldn't see her face, but her voice was shaking. Before I could speak, she turned and, in that quiet way of hers, sauntered away.

# 14

Sometimes on my walks, if the square was crowded or if I took a quick turn down an alleyway, I'd bump into a couple, disturbing the cloying sweetness of their connection. Perhaps the woman would be looking at a scarf while her lover waited, or the man would be studying the menu in front of a restaurant. They might glance at me briefly—not in a rude way, just, *What are you doing here?* I'd hurry away, feeling dirty and cheated, a cold panic creeping through. What if I was never loved, I wondered? It happened, surely to some people. You just never knew.

The night of Marcello's party came slowly. Even Professor Korloff's class crawled by that day. My neighbor had said ten, but I didn't dare go down before eleven. By nine-thirty, I could hear the stirrings of a party below me. Music pounded through the floor. I fluttered about in preparation. I was a neat person, almost obsessively so, but that night my room was wrecked with clothes and makeup. Feist on the stereo, "1234." Butterflies in my stomach over a boy.

I hated all my clothes, but when I gingerly poked through Claire's closet, I found that the most feminine thing she had other than the horrible blue frock was that yellow dress, which was stained. I decided on my own shortish black skirt—*A skirt? Should I really?*—with tights and a modest sweater, then settled on the couch with a book and a drink to pass the time.

I'd told the B4 I was too tired to go out. They hadn't tried very hard to convince me otherwise; since Jenny's showdown with Claire, our own friendship had chilled. It wasn't that she was angry with me, exactly. She didn't even mention it. Yet she hadn't been over for tea, and twice I'd heard her and Luka talk about a particularly randy party to which I hadn't been invited.

I stood, finishing my Campari. It was what I had taken to drinking before I went out. It had a nice lift, different from wine, somehow, though two made my head ache. Straightening my skirt for the last time in the mirror, I contemplated texting Claire to see if she'd been let off early, then didn't. I knew it was stupid, but it was my first time without the B4, and I wanted to keep the boys downstairs to myself.

Finally, I descended the dark path behind our house and knocked at what I thought to be an appropriately late hour of eleven-thirty. Voices seeped through the walls. I wiped my clammy hands on my skirt.

It was a different boy who opened the door. His eyes widened hungrily. I crossed my arms over my chest.

"Hi. I'm Taz."

"Alfonso. Ciao."

I hovered in the threshold. "Marcello invited me . . ."

"Ah." Alfonso flung the door open for me, almost spitting his words. "Marcello! The neighbor girl is here."

There was a brief rise of voices and laughter. I peered into the apartment, almost completely dark, lit only with candles. Trance music was playing. I could see a group of Italians on the sofa, bare limbs tangled. A bong was on the coffee table.

I could get out of this, I thought. I could say I was sick, run back upstairs, have one more Campari, and go to sleep.

"You know . . . ," I said to Alfonso.

"You know what?" asked Marcello, emerging.

I had forgotten about his skin. It was almost velvety. Marcello's heaviness wouldn't have suited many men, but on him it lent an air of permanent joviality. The right side of his face was marked by a deep dimple that hovered even when he wasn't smiling.

I liked him.

"Hi," I said.

Marcello took me by the shoulders. He kissed me on both cheeks and then kissed my mouth, in front of everyone.

"Ciao," he said. "You came. I thought you might not. You're late."

"I was out," I said.

"No you weren't."

"No?"

"No. I came up and looked through the window. You were reading."

"You're right. I'm sorry."

He tipped his head back and looked at me. We were still standing in the doorway. He wore jeans and a jumper. I tugged at my hem.

"I shouldn't have dressed up."

"What?" Marcello moved his hand through the air, as if brushing away a fly. Grifonians didn't talk about appropriate dress. If you pulled it off, you were appropriate.

"You don't want to come in, do you?"

"Of course I do."

"You don't. You're shy. It's okay. It's dead here anyway. Let's go out." He stepped out, closing the door abruptly. He gazed at my short skirt. "You'll need a coat."

"Yes. I guess I thought I was just coming here."

"Let's get it."

He put his hand on the small of my back and steered me back up the hill to our apartment. My Italian was still less than perfect, but I could comprehend almost everything said directly to me now, and I could make myself understood. I was proud he wasn't trying out his English on me, which was what most Italians did at first.

"You don't lock the door?" he asked as we entered.

"Never."

"You need to," he said. "Really. Grifonia isn't safe."

"It feels safe. I don't even know where my key is. And anyway, all of you are downstairs."

"It's not." He put his hands in the front pockets of his jeans and walked around, inspecting. He opened the refrigerator, looked in, and closed it again. He opened the cabinets, poked his head in our rooms.

"Your house is much nicer than ours."

"Well. We're girls."

"It's not very clean though," he said, looking at the mud on the floor. "This your room?" He pushed the door open and went in. I rested my hands on the back of one of the dining chairs. I couldn't go in there. It's where my coat was, but we'd only spoken a few words. I couldn't be alone with him in my room.

"Do you want some Campari?"

"Never."

"Wine?"

"Good."

To my relief, he emerged again into the living room and sat on the sofa. I quickly grabbed my coat from the vacated room and threw it on the table.

"Here," I said, handing him his drink and sitting in a chair opposite. He smiled, as if laughing at my sitting so far away.

"Where are you from?" I asked. "I don't even know."

"Naples."

"Ah." I knew nothing about Naples.

"You'd like it. Probably. It's rough. My family doesn't live in the best area. But it's the best food you'll ever eat."

"The food here is good."

"The food here is all bread and pork. It's hard. Umbrians die early."

"And in Naples?"

"Fish. Olive oil." He took a long drink of wine.

"I'm from Lucan. Near Dublin. Have you ever been to Dublin?"

He smiled and got up again, looking at a sparsely populated bookshelf. "I will never go to Dublin."

"Why?"

"Guys like me don't go other places. I'm happy in Italy. I have what I need. Why go to Dublin?"

"To see the world."

"I went to Paris. It was nothing. The people were ugly. If we marry, you'll move here."

"Do you even know my name?" I asked.

"Elizabeth."

"Tabitha," I said.

"Tabitha?"

"Taz."

"Like the devil. Tasmania."

"Tabitha," I said again.

"Do you know," he said, settling on the arm of the sofa, "that this city is ten thousand years old?"

"It is not. Even I know it's not."

"Sure. We probably had cavemen living here, under this house."

"You're crazy."

"There are graves back there. Alfonso found a skull."

"Liar."

"Maybe." He kicked me lightly with his foot. "Let's go out."

The air outside was cold and wet. Pneumonia weather, my mother would have called it. She always overdressed us in layers of coats and sweaters, wrapping us in scarves and hats until the only bit of us that was visible was our eyes. I put up my hood as we walked. Marcello led me up a side alley I'd never taken that opened into a wide *via* behind the palace.

"All right, Devil. Look here." He pointed at an ornate building studded with gargoyles. "Sophia Loren used to own this house."

"I don't believe you."

"You're right. It was Anita Ekberg. She came to Grifonia to sleep with Fellini in secret."

"I didn't know it was a secret."

"Sure. We'll get you in the fountain later."

"I'd say not."

"I'll tell you this. Here is the best bar in Grifonia. This is where your Prince Harry drinks when he visits."

"I'm Irish. Don't care about the royals."

"Well, this is the place." He led us into a tacky café, video-poker machines glowing in the corner. "Best beer on this street."

"Marcello!" the barman shouted. "You pig."

"Beer for us both. Me and the beautiful lady."

The barman put our drinks down, insisting they were free, then topped us off with glasses of fernet. When we were finished, Marcello guided me to two more bars. Everywhere, the drinks were free.

"I'm not sure about your tour-guide abilities," I said, "but you certainly know the bars."

"I know everyone," Marcello said. "I've been here four years."

He was studying engineering, he told me. In the end, he said, he would design and build ships.

"Then I can be in Naples and make money," he said. "It's hard to be rich there. I want my family to do better."

"I can see you on the high seas."

"Sure you can, Devil. Sure you can."

Marcello put his hand on my back.

"You should go to the church with me one day."

"I'm Jewish."

"Really?" he asked. "Don't know many. Anyway, I didn't mean for services. I've got a key. My friend does restoration, and we go there sometimes, make a little fun."

"In a *church*?"

"So shocked, Devil."

He put his nose to my cheek. *We get to be this happy now.* I turned my head and kissed him, pressed my body into his, put my tongue to his lips.

"Okay, okay," he said, laughing. "Hey. Let's go back to the party." We finished our drinks. Marcello left the barman three euros and then took my hand to lead me out. He stroked my fingers up and down with his rough thumb. I felt dizzy, as if a small balloon were inflating in my head.

When we got toward home, a group of boys called out to Marcello. He yelled back and abruptly dropped my hand. There were three of them, talking rapidly in a dialect I barely understood. One of them said the word *powder.*

"*Sì,*" Marcello said. "*Sì.*"

The boys followed us down the steps to the house. There was a light on in our flat, but I couldn't see anyone through the window. It was one a.m. by now, and I wondered if Claire was at home.

"I'll meet you inside," I said to Marcello.

The door of the flat was, as usual, open, but when I called no one was there. I poured a bit more Campari for courage and brushed my hair, lingering a bit. When I came down, the party had become more crowded. The music had been upgraded to rap, and there was a dance party happening in someone's cramped bedroom.

"Taz!" Claire yelled. She was sitting next to Marcello on the sofa, holding her guitar, her flannel shirt unbuttoned low.

"Hi," I said, walking over. Everything was turning over inside me. Marcello got up and kissed my cheek again, then pulled me to the couch and placed me next to Claire.

"I'll be back," he said.

"How are you?" Claire whispered.

"Fine. I just looked for you. I didn't know you knew about this party."

"Sure. Marcello and I met yesterday, and I came down to play guitar."

"Oh. Yesterday."

"You?"

"A couple of days ago. I guess I didn't know," I said, looking for him. When I spotted him, he was bent over the dining room table. For a moment, I thought he was looking at a map, until I saw him put a straw to his nose.

Claire was saying something.

"What?" I tore my eyes away.

"I said, we haven't hooked up, if that's what you're wondering."

I stared at her. I believe I blinked, but I can't be sure.

"We might, though," she said.

"Okay."

"But you can have him if you want him."

I paused. I had no practice at fighting. My sister and cousins were all within fourteen months of one another, and they scratched and clawed for attention, fighting violently among themselves. My cousin Julian's ear is, to this day, deformed because my sister bit it so hard that a piece of it actually came off. However, by the time I came along they were too spent to pick on me. I was spared, and spoiled, and therefore was left in the world to fend for myself without claws.

"Are you mad at me about the other night with Jenny or something?" I asked.

"Why would you say that?"

"I don't know. It's just, I've never heard you be this way."

"Taz!" Claire engulfed me in an embrace and put her face in my hair. "I'm just *kidding* you! You really are so literal. I don't give a shit about this guy. *You're* the important one."

"Of course," I said, delicately extricating myself.

She drew back, still grinning.

"This place is a dump, huh?"

I glanced around. Their flat was as small as ours, but it suffered from a lack of windows. In the candlelight I could see mounds of books and clothes in every corner. The air was heavy with the smell of pot and cigarettes.

"It's all right."

"It's not as nice as our house."

"No. Not as nice as ours."

"And these guys are cokeheads. I guess I should have known it."

Alfonso handed me a jelly glass of wine. As soon as I took a sip, I recognized the vinegary red from the *enoteca* nearby. Marcello was talking to some Italian girls across the room, whom I instantly hated. I took a large gulp and put the glass down.

"This wine is gross," Claire said. "Let's have something else."

Alfonso handed her a green liquor bottle. She unscrewed the cap and took a gulp, to the boys' delight, then screwed up her face and shut her eyes.

"God. What is that?"

"It's Bechorovka. From Prague. It's for sipping."

"L'Americana doesn't sip."

The boys exchanged a joke I couldn't understand, and the way they laughed I was fairly certain I didn't want to.

We all got drunk. It was as if we were on a mission, Claire and I. She filled my glass, then I filled hers. We were drinking quickly, hungrily, dare I say competitively. By three a.m. the room was tilting. Claire put her arm around me and drew me protectively to her. I was too drunk to move. My face was flushed red, my equilibrium off-kilter, and the boys were beginning to notice that the girls from upstairs were cuddling on the couch.

"Beautiful," Alfonso said, gesturing at us.

"What's beautiful?" A voice said from the door.

"Hey," Marcello said. "We were wondering when you'd show up."

It was Ervin, the boy I'd danced with at the Red Lion.

"Hello," I said. He nodded, barely.

"Taaaaz," Claire said, elbowing me. "How do you know *him*?"

Ervin pulled out a bag of cocaine. The kids fell on him as pigeons fall on bread.

"I just met him out one night."

"Hi, Claire," Ervin said.

"Hey," she said, rather coldly. Then, to me: "He's a big dealer. Bought pot from him and he wouldn't leave me alone one night. I'm beginning to get ideas about you."

"No, no," I said quickly. "I met him once. Barely."

On the other side of me, Marcello was saying he'd take me upstairs.

"You're not touching her," Claire said. "Not while she's this drunk."

"I'm fine," I protested. I wanted to kiss Marcello again. His bulk seemed comforting. I wanted him in my bed. But when I sat up, the floor rose. I sank down again. "Fine-*ish*, anyway."

"Nope," Claire said. "You'll get your chance another night, O."

*O.* So they already had nicknames for each other? The new stranger gave a laugh. Short, loud, a bit violent.

Marcello shrugged. "Sure. I'll see you tomorrow, Elizabeth."

"Tabitha," Claire corrected.

"*Taz*," I said.

"Goodnight, everyone," Claire said, guiding me by the arm. "Goodnight."

On the way up, I behaved badly.

"I want to stay."

"You really don't. You'd be embarrassed, Taz."

"You just want to go out with him yourself."

Claire stopped on the stairs and looked at me squarely.

"Taz."

"Mmmm."

"Remember what I said about fucking every night?"

"Mmmm-hmmm."

"I wasn't completely lying, okay? I do screw around. A lot."

"A lot?"

"It's not a big deal. I'm safe about it. And you were right, I did sort of want to fool around with Marcello. He's cool. There's just something about him. But I never would now, because you're into him."

"Mmmm-hmmm. Yeah."

"Plus, druggies. Not my scene."

I didn't want to hear any more. I wanted to pass out.

"You don't believe me," she said, hauling me up the stairs.

"No."

"But you will."

# 15

We were invited, the four of us, for three nights. The house was owned by an English couple who sponsored Professor Korloff's work; he and his wife had a hobby of collecting Etruscan and ancient Roman art. People who had houses like this, Jenny informed me, liked to use any excuse to invite people over to show off, which is likely why he'd asked Professor Korloff to bring us. Anna, who had been to one of Arthur's gatherings before, said it would be more of a salon atmosphere. She imagined there would be some academic Italians, some high society Brits—"I *know* I'll know *someone*," Jenny kept saying—and us, the students.

The night before we left, B4 came over for dinner and to talk about the weekend. My mother phoned in a baba ghanoush recipe for me to make, which, due to the limited ingredients in Grifonia and my awful cooking skills, was cheerfully acknowledged as a disaster.

"So will I need my long dress?" I asked.

"Most definitely," Anna said. "There'll be at least one formal dinner. Not to the *letter* formal, but these people will appreciate it if you make an effort."

"Girls, what can I borrow?" Jenny asked.

"Something from me," Anna said. "I've got five good ones. Even after Dad died, my mother dragged me to weekend things so it looked like the family still had it going on."

"Which you do," Jenny said. "Obviously."

"Well, I *will* have my doctorate someday. So that's something."

"For what? Working?"

"I'd be the first woman in my family with a job. It's sort of a nice idea."

Jenny snorted. "Until you're thirty-eight and an assistant living with a cat. No thank you. I'd snap up one of your mother's lords if I were you. Or how about an Italian count? After all, if we can't find rich Italian boyfriends at this thing this weekend, we don't deserve to live."

"You're such a modern girl, Jenny," Luka said.

"I'm beyond modern. Haven't you heard? We're all done with that dreary women's movement. Everyone's snapping back again."

"It's not like you *don't* have a job," Anna said.

The silence was deep but quick; if I hadn't been used to the girls' rhythms, I would have missed the beat of fear.

"I'm going to be a detective," I said. "Like in books. Always wanted to do that."

"What?" Jenny asked. "Really?"

"Sure. I've told you that."

"You haven't."

"Oh. Well, yes."

"Taz, you would be the worst detective in the world," Luka said. "No offense. But you didn't pick up on the drug thing for weeks."

"People find me easy to talk to. I'm good at interviews."

"It's actually true," Anna said. "You'd be the perfect spy, because no one would ever suspect that a girl as nice as you had anything but sweet intentions."

I looked at Jenny and smiled. She didn't say anything.

"She does have one of those blank faces," Luka said. "Impossible to read. I'd wager she's a plotter though. The quiet types always are."

"Well, God forbid you actually follow your tawdry career dreams," Jenny said. "And what about your flatmate? What's she going to do, be in a cover band that plays at casinos?"

I picked at my all-but-inedible eggplant.

"She's a bit odd, isn't she?" Jenny persisted, putting out her cigarette and taking the chair next to mine. She smelled of ashes and wine.

I shook my head, feeling the danger. "She's fine."

"Taz," Anna said, "I hate to mention it, but I was just in your bathroom and noticed, in a clear plastic bag on the floor . . . well . . . a vibrator."

"Oh God! It's not mine!"

"You see?" Jenny said, leaning closer. "The roomie's a sex maniac."

"Nothing wrong with a vibrator," Luka said. "Though Taz *did* say the American doesn't know how to use the loo brush."

Jenny swiveled her head at me. She put her hand on my arm, pressing a bit.

"Tell us."

"I know I can be a prig about these things," I stammered, remembering, with shame, talking about this when I was drunk with Luka at the movie. "But she doesn't understand . . . with the loo . . ."

"Leaves crap in the toilet? She *doesn't*."

"It's on the sides there . . ."

The girls burst into laughter. Part of me felt bad. But *I* was making them laugh. It wasn't something that happened often.

"You *need* to tell her to use the brush. It's your duty."

"Your *doodie*!" I said.

Another round of delicious giggles.

"And does she Skype naked with that boyfriend she was talking about? I bet she does."

"No." We didn't have wireless in the house, so Claire spent who knows how many euros a week Skyping with her "on hold" boyfriend from home at the Internet café around the corner. The place offered two computers from Maggie Thatcher's time and a sad variety of panini. I doubted very much that naked Skyping could happen there, no matter how much the B4 wanted to imagine that it did.

"She's bizarre, Taz. Face it. Your American loony."

"I *like* her."

"She's too pretty," Jenny said decisively, pouring herself more wine. There was a somewhat pained silence. Because that was it, wasn't it? That would always be Claire's exposed heel, the piece of flesh that, once the deed was done, everyone would rush to pierce. She was just too beautiful. It made everything somehow unbearable.

I looked around. The rest of us had begun to wither. I thought of Marcello, how he looked at Claire. How he was obviously deciding which of us to choose. How he hadn't called since the party. It made my throat close, made my heart go dark.

Jenny cleared her throat, demanding loyalty.

"You know, maybe she does Skype naked," I said, leaning over and filling my glass with Campari. "I wouldn't be surprised. She is a bit strange." The girls murmured appreciatively. Jenny patted my arm.

"Good girl," Jenny whispered. Only then did she take her hand away.

•

We left for the weekend at noon the next day. I didn't get to say goodbye to Claire—she'd been out until late, and then left in the morning. She left a note on my door that said, *Yo, T. Have fun storming the castle. Miss you already. xoxo, C.*

My Italian flatmates hovered over me as I finished packing. Gia was impressed by the coming trip, but Alessandra was fretting.

"The house is owned by an Italian?"

"I think so. Or the wife is and the husband is British. Or something."

"You *think* so? Whose house *is* this?"

"My professor's friend."

"You cannot go to a house if you don't know who owns it," Alessandra said, crossing her arms.

"Where is this place?" Gia asked.

"Gubbio."

"Well, there are many foreigners in Gubbio," Gia said.

"I think you should know where you are going," Alessandra said.

"All right."

"You write down the *name*."

"All right."

"Here." Alessandra pointed to the refrigerator, which was crowded with messages.

"Yes. Oh, and speaking of safety . . ."

"Yes?"

"Marcello thinks we should lock the door."

"Marcello?" Gia raised her eyebrows. "See what I told you, Alessandra. The fox already figured out how to get to the hen. Tell Marcello maybe those boys should lock their own door, keep the whores out."

There was a honk out front as Luka pulled up in the car. I kissed Gia and Alessandra and dragged my suitcase—ridiculously overpacked—across the gravel to the gate. Anna was in the front seat.

"Where's Jenny?"

"Running late. Too many potential wardrobe changes."

"Ciao."

I turned. Marcello had just come around the bend. He smiled lazily, and looked heavier than normal in a thick down coat.

"Where are you going?" he asked.

"To a party," Luka said in English through the window. The girls were both leaning forward, looking Marcello up and down.

"What party?" Marcello switched to English, too.

"In a castle. No boys allowed," Luka said.

"Your friend's a liar, Devil," he said in Italian. "When will you be back?"

"Oh . . . a couple of days." I averted my eyes, wondering what the girls must think of him. Luka popped the boot of the car open, which was already stuffed with the other girls' suitcases, along with extra bags of hair tools and wine.

"When you come back, I'll take you on another tour."

"A bar tour?"

"Of course."

"Maybe," I said.

"Or I can make you dinner."

"Naples food."

"Sure."

"Just us?" I asked. "Or Claire, too?"

"Be nice, Devil," he said, waving his finger at me.

"Let's go, Taz," Luka interrupted. "Jenny'll throw a fit."

I got into the car. Marcello was still standing there, watching, his gaze following us as we drove away.

"Who was that?" Luka asked.

"My neighbor."

"He's very sexy," Anna said. "In a hearty way."

"I like a big man," Luka said. "Though he's a bit Manchester-y. Drunken fights at the football game and all that." We stopped in front of Jenny's rooming house. As soon as she got into the car, the seating was rearranged, with her in the front next to Luka, while Anna and I were wedged in the back with a cooler.

"Oh, girls, I'm so excited. God, it'll be nice to meet some good people."

"I can't promise good people," Anna said. "It may be a bit of an academic crowd."

"Even academics like a good time," Jenny said. "And don't tell me there'll be no one worth meeting. It's a castle, for God's sake."

"A *castello*," Luka said. "And Jenny, no more worrying about Taz. She's got a gorgeous."

"Bring him out, for God's sake."

"He likes Claire, too," I said.

"Oh, God. *Claire*. Better give it up. I'm sure she's shagged him by now."

"She said she wouldn't."

Jenny turned. "She *said* she wouldn't? She actually had to say it?"

"It came up."

"I bet it did. What were her words exactly?"

My face colored. "She said . . . I could have him if I wanted him."

"You've got to be bloody kidding me. And you actually like this girl?"

"It's true," Anna said. "That doesn't sound very good."

"Forget her," Jenny said. "It's just as Luka said. We can never really be friends with Americans. It's a different language."

"Where's the wine?" Luka said. "I put a cold bottle in a cooler by your feet."

"Oh, Luka!" Anna's voice was tinged with disapproval. "You always have a drink ready."

"That's the wonderful thing about drunkards," Jenny said. "They're so damn fun to drink with." She poured the wine into glasses and passed them around. Luka grabbed the bottle from her hand.

"So, before we get there . . . ," Anna said, almost timidly. "I just want to reiterate, Arthur is my most important family friend. So if we can just . . ."

"Don't worry, Anna," Jenny said. "I promise we'll behave. We've got manners, haven't we, Luka?"

"Not me." Luka took a long draw, then put the bottle in her lap.

Gubbio is generally a straight shot from Grifonia, but the road to our *castello* was a treacherous, winding drive. I looked out the window at the land. The harvested fields were brown and used. The hills and mountains rose up dramatically behind the flat plains, as if carved out on purpose. On top of almost every hill was an old fortress, castle, or tower, left over from the days when villages plundered one another for food, power, and God.

After a while, our chatter died down. Luka put on *Nashville Skyline.* As if consciously countering her father's cheesy songs, she had excellent taste in music. The morning started out chilly and windy, but the sun had broken through with forgiving arms. I rolled down the window to let the air touch my cheeks and hair. I've already said this, but I must again—it's these throw-away things that are extraordinary. A ride to Gubbio. I wonder if the other girls know that now. Because I can tell you with authority: there is no better place to be at twenty-one than in the backseat of a car, driving to a party in autumn.

Gubbio is a spectacular little town of polished stone with a fine cathedral. We didn't stop, but looked at the structures in awe as they rose on our right from the bottom of the valley.

"We should probably see more sights," Luka mumbled, finally breaking the peace. "You'd think we were a bunch of fucking ignorant mucks."

"Keep up that classy talk," Anna said. "My professor will love that."

"Look, I grew up working class and I'm proud of it."

"Not me," Anna said. "I'm just letting you chauffeur me around."

"Are you serious? So you're finally bringing up the black thing, you has-been elitist snob?"

"Please, I wasn't talking about *that*," Anna said.

"You were."

"Oh, go to hell."

"I was hoping someone would."

"What? Go to hell? Or bring up the black thing?"

"Girls, don't be so middle class," Jenny said. "*I'll* bring up the black thing. Our club is diverse because *I* made it that way."

"I suppose I'm happy," Luka drawled. "Now that we've got a Jew. It used to be so stacked against me. Especially with three other white—"

"Shut *up*, Luka," Jenny hissed.

I stiffened. "My mother is Sephardic, not that you even know what that means. And if you think I'm not proud of it—"

"Lovelies," Jenny said. "We're all friends. And we're about to have this fabulous time together. Can we stop fighting?"

"I'm not fighting," I said.

"No," Jenny said, looking at herself in the rearview mirror. "That's the wonderful thing about you, Taz. You never fight."

"I don't think—"

"Here's the turnoff," Luka said. "Can you see the house?"

"No."

"I see a tower," I said.

"A tower?"

"A spiked gate."

"Holy . . ."

As soon as we pulled up to the front, it became clear that Professor Korloff had not exaggerated at all to Anna when he told her about where we'd be staying. The place was, indeed, a medieval castle. We were on top of a large green hill, fortified by our weekend's lodging. The walls soared above us, gray and thick, with only slits allowing glimpses of light inside.

We got out of the car, looking up in quiet awe.

"What is this place?" I breathed.

"This would be a very impressive ancestral home," Anna said. "An exceptionally grim-looking one. It was likely recently bought from some Italian count who needed bailing out and completely refurbished with ghastly fixtures."

"Not too ghastly, I hope," a voice said.

We turned to see a man, roughly my father's age. He was tan and rangy, wearing fine chino pants and a close-fitting burgundy sweater. A camel-colored scarf was wound round his neck, lending him an air of delicacy, as if he needed to be tended. Yet his voice was strong and his eyes, from where I was standing, were almost a black color, like jet beads. When looking at him, I couldn't help thinking of the crabs my sister and I caught on our infrequent childhood trips to the seashore.

"I'm Samuel."

"Hello," Anna said. She put out her hand. "I'm Anna Grafton. Is Arthur here yet?"

"Fabrizio's just bringing him from the station now."

"Ah." We stood quietly, regarding one another. To everyone's relief, less than a minute passed before we heard the welcome crackle of car wheels on gravel. Anna waved a bit frantically as the car made its way up the drive.

"The girls!" Professor Korloff cried, alighting from the sedan, followed by Pascal, looking carsick. "Samuel! Ladies!" He embraced the man in the camel scarf. "Where's Elena?"

"Had an appointment in Lazio. There's some sort of private auction. She feels horrible, but there were tables to buy."

I was surprised to see a look of distress cross Professor Korloff's face.

"And she knew I was coming? With students?"

"I'm certain I mentioned it. She feels horrible to miss you." He gave the professor a hearty pat on the back.

"Well, let me introduce you. This is Anna, my goddaughter."

"You're wonderful for having us," Anna said.

"You're wonderful for coming," Professor Korloff said abruptly. "All right. So. Samuel. This is Tabitha. This young man here is Pascal. And who are these fine additions?"

"This is Luka, and Jenny," Anna said.

"Fabrizio," Samuel barked without acknowledging them. In a moment, an old man, gnarled and stooping, emerged from the car. "Take the ladies' things up first."

"Should we help?" I asked, eyeing the old man as he began to unfold our bags from the trunk. Jenny rolled her eyes at me.

"Come," Samuel said. He pressed a button and the black gate creaked open, revealing our first glimpse of the inside. Before us lay a velvety, obsessively trimmed lawn cut in a neat, large V by two white gravel paths that led to either side of the building. And what a building it was. A castle—a real, live castle—its medieval walls and towers shooting toward the sky. Ivy clambered up the lower walls, and from an upper turret, a curtain fluttered in and out in time with the wind. On either side of us, bordering the lawn, stretched two one-story buildings; one was the kitchen, in which I could see people dressed in uniforms moving back and forth in front of a stove, and the other appeared to be bedchambers. Through the arched gates, I could see expansive views of miles and miles of Umbrian countryside. Though not beautiful, exactly, it was the most imposing private house I'd ever seen.

"So just one family owns this?" I asked.

Samuel looked pained. "Yes."

"May I ask who else is here?" Anna asked.

"My son, Ben, and a couple of his friends from school. A business associate of mine named Roberto. He's quite a jolly one. As I said, my wife, unfortunately, is in Lazio."

He paused for a moment, regarding us as if we should say something to this fact.

"I'm sorry," I said. "I would have liked to have met her."

Samuel looked at me as if he hadn't noticed me before, which was probably true. "Would you have, dear? I'm sure the feeling is mutual. My Elena simply loves ingénues, as do all middle-aged women."

Professor Korloff shouted with uneasy laughter. "Jesus, Samuel! Don't terrify us."

"Ah, yes. Still young enough to be properly frightened."

"I was talking about *me*," the professor said.

Samuel laughed shortly. "How wonderful you are. That New York sense of humor. I'd almost forgotten. All right, let's get you little chickens settled."

Samuel led us to the right of the castle, then up a white stone pathway that threaded through a stone arch. Here, we found another lawn, where there was a charming, long wooden table for dining alfresco. "The dining hall is through there," he said, pointing to one of the low buildings. "It used to be in the main castle, but now we've moved it to be near the kitchen. The castle itself is dreadfully uncomfortable. But you'll see. Fabrizio!"

The old man emerged, his face purple.

"For God's sake, get the cook to help you," Samuel said. "I can't have you dead during a house party. Take the girls up, will you? Make yourselves at home, if you can. We'll have drinks in the main hall at five, though the boys will start earlier. Dinner dress, I'm afraid. You have something?"

"Yes," Anna said.

"My wife insists on the tradition, and even though she's abdicated, she'll be livid if she hears otherwise. All right, Arthur, let's look at those pieces."

"I'll be right there. Anna, a moment?"

Samuel gave a jaunty wave and disappeared through one of the doors in the old stable. Anna stayed behind with Arthur, while the rest of us followed Fabrizio around the side of the building, then through another thick archway and into the castle's dark belly, pausing on the landing to study the coat of arms.

"Ask how long the Websters have owned it," Jenny instructed me.

"Eight years," Fabrizio answered when I translated. "But really, of course, the city of Gubbio owns it. The viscount built it for Italy, not to own. Hundreds of people lived here then, a whole town."

"Any ghosts?"

Fabrizio sighed, as if tired of being irritated by tourists. "There is a story of a dead nun."

He took us up the wide, cold stairs, pointing out the main hall—large, dark, and grim, with twenty-foot ceilings, red polished stone floors, and a dusty chandelier that threatened to fall at any moment. The music room, housing a neglected piano and harp. A library, also with walls that climbed seemingly impossible heights to the ceiling, with bookshelves so tall they required long ladders to access. Down a long, unassuming hall was a chapel—the only cheerful room in the fortress. We could look at it from the bell balcony, but could not enter because of the danger from earthquake damage. A cat had crawled behind the altar last year and been crushed, Fabrizio said.

We climbed higher and higher, past the ladies' salon, the men's salon, the upper kitchen (added for the last owner, who did not like to go all the way outside for snacks), the "television room"—surprisingly opulent, with gilded, French rococo furniture, mirrors and sofas with high backs. Then we pressed on even more, up a winding narrow staircase to a covered outdoor passageway on the very top of the long walls, once patrolled by guards in case of attack.

"Here we are," he said, opening two locked doors with the keys attached to his belt. Each chamber was the same: two hard-looking single beds, one window facing the inner courtyard, a dresser, a sink, and a writing desk.

"What are we, fucking monks?" Jenny said, throwing her purse down.

"Maybe this is where that nun died," Luka said.

"Thank you so much, Fabrizio," I managed. The Italian retreated; as soon as the door closed Luka unzipped her suitcase and pulled out a bottle of scotch.

"So what then?" Jenny said. "Why've they stuck us up here in the servants' hall? And do you think Mr. Webster is looking for a girlfriend?"

"Ew, Jenny," Luka said. "He's ancient."

"He's not bad, and think of the private planes to Paris and Rome."

"Please," Anna said, entering the room. "This is serious. Arthur is my mentor. No preying on the married host. And absolutely no sales. To anyone."

"What did Professor Korloff want?" I asked.

"He's worried one of us will tempt Samuel to . . . misbehave. Apparently without his wife he's a bit of a drinker. Arthur asks that we keep our heads."

"Scotch me, Luka," Jenny said. "Well, the quarters are Spartan, but the place is interesting. You can't laugh at all those centuries of rich people. I'm glad to have to dress for dinner, anyway. It's a good sign."

"I think I'll go down to that library," Anna said. "And later, Arthur said Samuel might let us look at his Etruscan pieces."

"Sexy," Luka said. Jenny laughed.

"I'm serious about what he said." Anna gave Jenny a pleading look. "It was embarrassing for him to bring it up. Please let's behave."

"Of course, of course."

Anna took a breath. "Taz? You want to come to the library?"

"I'm going for a walk." Since we'd stepped into the castle's walls, I'd felt trapped, as if the very air were crowded with souls.

The others declined to join, so I hurriedly slipped on my trainers and made my way down through the gloomy hallways. I ran down the stairs to the courtyard, giving in to an impulse to jump down the stairs into the gravel. Tiny stones sprayed out from my feet. I had the sudden feeling of being watched, and looked up. There, in the window, was the crow-faced woman in black I'd seen in Grifonia while wandering the streets in the heat. When I glimpsed her, I had that feeling of recognition, the same sort as when I'd see a friend at school with another acquaintance, without previously understanding their connection.

*Of course you're here.*

I blinked and squinted, trying to get a clearer look, but my efforts were futile: the woman had either moved from view or vanished altogether.

## *Lucretia, 13th century AD*

Lucretia wasn't a nun. She was a servant. Her duties were to clean the church after Sunday Mass. The *castello* wasn't a convent, so no nuns ever lived there, but there were services every Sunday, for which a cardinal would ride up on his horse. He would arrive on Saturday, attend dinner in the great hall, then perform the Mass in the morning. The cardinal's weekly visit was an important mark of status to the Rivaldis; as a token, they had a portrait commissioned of the clergyman holding his favorite horse in his hand.

The cardinal's name was Ignatio. Lucretia was the daughter of the cobbler. She was a pale creature, meek with pleasant gold hair and papery skin. Her father had many children, some by his dead wife, some by her replacement. Lucretia was quiet. She faded into the din.

One day after the service, while Lucretia was wiping the mud from the pews left by the boots of the horsemen, the cardinal grabbed her by the hair. She didn't fight. She told herself she was doing it for God. She didn't fight the next time, or the next time either.

Eventually she started to swell. She told no one, but the cardinal noticed. No one else did. She was nothing in the castle to anyone and she knew it. Even her family had trouble keeping track of her.

The cardinal didn't say anything on the last day. He took her as he usually did, but would not look at her during it. Afterward, he slapped her and hurried out.

A servant impregnated by a cardinal. There was only one way this could end. She would be cast out. She would die alone in the snow.

The Compagnia was contacted. A nameless noble came in the night with a sharpened dagger. When Lucretia saw the blade at her neck, to her surprise she was flooded with relief.

Her body was carried out in the dark morning. She wasn't missed in the castle for days.

In the ledger, the death was noted but no one claimed the privilege. The act was simply credited as a service to God.

*Lucretia di Bologna, seventeen years old, 13th century AD*

# 16

I took my time getting back. It was cool but sunny—almost mid-October. Winter was approaching; these were the last days of walking without a jumper or a coat. As I made my way back toward the castle on the dirt road, I could hear what sounded like bottled laughter. Staying close to the wall, I went closer and peeked around the garden gate.

A group of men lounged under the awning in cycling gear on the lawn. There were five of them, only one of whom looked especially correct in spandex. Not wanting to meet them alone, I darted into the courtyard and ran up the stairs, where Anna was reading a booklet about the castle, and Luka and Jenny were napping next to empty glasses rimmed on the bottom with the brown sticky remnants of scotch.

"Do you know, this place is eight hundred years old," she said, not looking up. "I tried to call my cousin to see about the Italian royal registry, but there's no service up here. Samuel seems to be nobody special; I only know that because no self-respecting Englishman of class would buy a whole castle these days. It's just a thing Internet people do."

"Can you imagine being that rich?" I asked.

"Two hundred families lived here in the 1400s. They were attacked all the bloody time. There was a blacksmith, a stable, farming, a clergy staff . . . up to a thousand people right in these walls, it says. Pretty incredible. We must be in the servants' quarters, or the soldiers' barracks." She glanced around. "They *could* have given us better rooms."

"I suppose they wanted to keep us together."

"Who is the son, I wonder?"

"I saw him, I think. And his friends. They were downstairs on the lawn in cycling clothes."

"And?"

"I don't know. They seemed all right."

"Taz, come on. Were they attractive? Old? Rich?" I shrugged. "Did they look like the sort to show a girl a good time?"

"They seemed a little drunk."

"Well, that's something, anyway."

We were late to cocktails, a move calculated by Jenny and, in the end, all wrong. At six, we entered, shimmering in our long dresses: Luka in gray backless satin, Anna in a somber column of black, Jenny in dark red, and me in my gold-and-black dress. Samuel and Professor Korloff were alone in the main hall with Pascal, who was lingering idly under a painting. The professor was sitting in a large leather chair with a glass of wine, clearly annoyed, and didn't bother to rise when we came in. Fabrizio stood behind the bar, equally peeved.

"I know it seems strange, ducklings. But when I ask students to a party, I mean for people to show *up*."

"I'm so sorry," Anna said. She truly looked as if she might cry.

"We got so caught up in our preparations," Jenny said grandly. "It's Tabitha's fault, actually. We were doing her hair."

This was clearly a lie, as my hair was curly and loose, the same as it had been in the morning. In fact, the bathroom had been so thoroughly occupied I hadn't even taken a shower.

"Which one of you is Tabitha?" Samuel asked.

"Me," I said. Samuel looked at me for a long time, his eyes traveling up and down my body. I had never felt like a whore before that, even when my college boyfriend had treated me like one. I crossed my arms over my chest.

"Well, you look very nice," he said finally.

"Yes, very respectable," Professor Korloff said coolly. "You *all* look nice. Pascal! Come over here. Now, then. What can Fabrizio get you girls to drink?"

We anxiously accepted glasses of Lillet. After a few painful minutes, the voices I'd heard from the lawn traveled up the stairs, growing louder. The boys burst in, a glad sight to me in their dinner jackets, carrying with them that enviable, boisterous air of having just come from the most amusing party on earth.

"Where have you been?" Samuel asked.

"Down in Gubbio, then we had to dress." He introduced himself cordially but disinterestedly as Ben, Samuel's son. He was twenty-four and at university in Rome. He had three friends: Jean, Marc, and Raffie. There was also Roberto, who was older and portly, with a tan, likable face.

As soon as we spoke to these specimens of the opposite sex, it was instantly understood among Anna, Luka, Jenny, and me that Ben and his friends were gay. That Samuel seemed oblivious to this fact—the rest of the evening, he made references to our pairing off—could be nothing other than stubborn denial. The men other than Roberto talked of going on holiday together, of going to clubs, of their boyfriends. Ben was the most aloof, and, it must be said, he never himself admitted to having a gay lover. But it was more than understood, which is why, with much of the pressure off, we females began drinking with abandon—even Anna—and having rather a good time.

The night was unseasonably warm, so at Ben's insistence we ate on the lawn, as the dining hall was "an absolute crypt." The table had been dressed with a starched cloth and set with silver, an assortment of crystal, and several bouquets of herbs. The trellis had been strung with white lights, and tall candles flickered on silver candelabras. Someone had even taken the trouble to put out place cards, ensuring that the company was properly mixed. Anna was next to the professor. Jenny and Luka were placed in the center of the men. I was near the end, next to Samuel, who headed the table with solemn duty.

The servers came out immediately, silent and quick, averting their eyes from ours. Our wineglasses were filled to the brim with a sharp white. Samuel gave a grim toast to the legacy of academia and the common man. And then, before we could even put down our glasses, the food started to come.

There was an antipasti course of four different types of shaved ham, surrounded by carved melon so sweet its curves pooled with juice; bufala mozzarella made that morning; pecorino, slightly oily, with cold fresh fig compote. Fried zucchini flowers, still hot and spilling over with fresh ricotta. Goose pâté laced with pine nuts. After that: large trays of fresh fettuccini in oil topped with shaved truffles and cream. A fillet of beef so rare it bled, served with a trio of pink, white, and black salts. A salad of arugula tossed with virgin olive oil, toasted hazelnuts, and vinegar. Another platter of cheeses, shot through with blue mold and truffles, served with fresh figs, pears, and plums. And finally, a panna cotta, cold and quivering, topped with sap-colored honey from the castle's hive. Each course was served with its own wine, so that by the third course, the lot of us were not only full, but pleasantly drunk.

Anna was holding back, terrified as she was of Professor Korloff, but Luka was quite cozy with her new friends from Rome, who were thrilled by her intimate knowledge—real or not—of the private life of Rupert Everett, a "close personal friend of her father's." Next to them, Jenny was letting old Roberto lean in cozily, affording a generous view of her ample bosom.

As I watched them, I had the acute feeling that I didn't fit in. I did know some of the celebrity gossip from Luka, but I didn't want to sound distasteful, so I tried to switch the topic to the politics I'd been studying in the paper.

"And what about Berlusconi? When he runs again, will he have a chance?"

"Tabitha is one of my brightest," Professor Korloff said. "Though she doesn't know that politics aren't always fodder for parties."

"Not at mine," Samuel said. I would later learn that Samuel was a personal friend of the prime minister. Still, the gentle reprimand reinforced the feeling that I was a fly caught on the wrong side of a pane of glass.

I was seated next to Samuel, who did not bother to talk, but glanced up from time to time at the table with a sad, rather hopeless expression, then turned his attentions back to his dinner. It was an awkward place, sandwiched in between Jenny and Roberto's obvious oncoming affair and the sullen proprietor. Finally, when the limoncello bottle was empty and all that was left of the panna cotta were sticky plates, I broke the silence.

"Do you miss your wife?"

"No."

I nodded, and looked desperately down the table.

"Poor lamb, that was not what you were counting on."

"Oh, no. I—"

"There was a time when I would have said yes. I bought this place for her, you know. She is an ace of a woman. Legendary, really."

"I saw pictures. When I was looking around."

"And there's Ben, of course. But she and I are so sick of each other now, I'm afraid. It's a hazard of long marriages. We'd divorce, but it's so tiresome."

"My parents are the same way. Apart but not divorced."

"Are they? How interesting." He said this as if it were the least interesting thing he'd ever heard. "We'll get around to it, I suppose. Eventually. Luckily my life affords us much time apart."

"I see."

"No you don't. You're all of . . . what? Eighteen?"

In the candlelight, his face was gray and waxy. I couldn't begin to guess how old he was. Younger than the professor, but not by much.

"Twenty-one. I'm nearly graduated."

"Congratulations." He turned away, dismissing me. "Ben, what now? Are you children going to town?"

"I suppose so."

"I'll get our things," Anna said quickly, and disappeared, I suspected for a cigarette out of sight of the professor.

"Ben promised us a ghost," Raffie said. "You can hear her walk in the dark."

"How wonderful," Professor Korloff said.

"Oh, you don't want to take these girls poking about the dank rooms. It's morbid."

"No, we'll love it," Jenny said, who was now practically sitting in Roberto's lap. "Really."

"It *would* be fun," Pascal said.

"Don't you want to take them into Gubbio, Ben? Fabrizio can drive you."

"I don't think the girls want to go where we tend to go, Father." Ben poured himself a drink from the grappa bottle, which had mysteriously appeared while I wasn't looking.

"Here, let's let this one decide," Raffie said, nodding to Anna, who had returned with our purses. "Mediocre club in Gubbio, or a private ghost tour in a haunted castle?"

"Is there even a question?" Anna asked.

"Excellent!" Professor Korloff bellowed, beaming at his protégée. Samuel pulled out a cigar and waved us on. The rest of us trotted after Ben, leaving the remnants of our dinner—smears of cream, pools of bloodred balsamic on white plates, the pits and stems of sucked brandied cherries.

Anna, Luka, Professor Korloff, and Pascal were at the front, engaged in lively conversation about trapped spirits. They were followed by Jenny and Roberto, who were now holding hands. Fraught with unreasonable melancholy, I trailed behind, looking idly into the different chambers. After a while the others disappeared around a corner, but I could still hear them, so I stepped into the music room to look at the portraits there.

There were eight of them, oils at least ten feet tall, of what appeared to be the family in the eighteenth century. There was a small boy in a powdered wig, posing proudly by his mother, a romantic background of trees and sky behind them. There was a woman in her thirties, sumptuously dressed in red-and-silver brocade, her shoulders white and sloped, her face limited by an incongruous nose and close-set eyes, even under the kind brush of the commissioned artist. There was a severe-looking cardinal, dressed in black, bald with a long gray rather sharp-looking beard, inexplicably holding a tiny horse in his hand. And there was a pretty little girl, again in a powdered wig, in an intensely uncomfortable-looking, elegant dress of blue silk. At her feet was a little dog, jumping up on her hem.

*So they had dogs*, I thought. *Were they pets? Or were—*

And then, everything went dark.

I gasped and stumbled toward the door. The lights, as far as I could tell, had been turned out throughout the castle. There was no moon, though some sort of dim light was coming from the hallway. An emergency light. I made my way to it, clutching the wall. My hand brushed a ceramic vase and it crashed to the ground, shattering. I could hear my friends' laughter, but it was very far away now, and I was too frightened to try to find the stairs to get out. I thought about those portraits, those dead faces on the wall, and slid down to the floor, put my head on my knees, and waited.

"Ben!" Samuel's voice, angry, burst up the stairs. Thinking of the vase, I pushed myself away from it. "Ben, that's enough of this foolishness! Turn on the breaker!" He was on the landing now, marching forward. His foot crunched the shards of pottery.

"Damnit! Ben—is someone there?"

He turned on his torch and shined it into my face.

"Ah. The Indian princess." He laughed a bit scornfully. "Well. Are you all right?"

"Yes," I said, embarrassed. I got up, brushing off my skirt. "I just got a little scared, is all."

"Ah." He softened a bit. "You're all right. Why aren't you with Ben?"

"I just stopped to look at the portraits."

"Hmmm." Samuel sighed. "They aren't very good, but they're interesting. Well. My charming son and his friends appear to have switched off the fuse for effect." He swung his light toward the center of the castle, but the weak light made only a feeble attempt to fend off the darkness. "Are you having fun?"

"I'm not Indian," I said.

"Pardon?"

"My mother is Israeli."

"You're nice-looking, whatever you are. That's what's important."

"It is?"

"In your current situation, yes."

I was drunker than I thought. "That's—I don't know what you mean."

"I mean that you, and your compatriots, are here to offer charm and beauty to the party. Arthur brought Elena and me some young things to make us feel relevant. She donates an exorbitant amount of money to his research, so it's certainly fair. You are part of that decoration committee, my dear. As it happens, you are the most interesting of the four."

"I don't think so."

"There's no question, actually. Not a classic beauty, but interesting. There are channels in there to be tapped."

We stood there in the dark, that fading man and I, breathing together in the bowels of his house. We could hear the others giggling in the rooms above. Jenny's shriek ricocheted down a stairwell.

"Let's go somewhere with lights," he said. "I'm too old for this. Come to my study, it's on a different breaker. We'll wait out their idiocy and get my ass of a son to turn the lights back on."

I paused. It wasn't appealing, following this man to his private rooms. But neither was waiting in the dark.

"This way," he said, stepping ahead.

•

Samuel led me to a living room behind a closed door, more sumptuous than the rest, with velvet wallpaper and deep sofas. He walked to a sideboard, took two crystal glasses, and poured us both some brandy. I took it tentatively and stood by the window, afraid to sit down.

"They should be down soon," he said. "Don't worry."

"I'm not worried."

"You are, and it's fine."

He took a book from the shelf and began to read, not seeming to mind that I was standing there, doing nothing. After a few minutes of pretending to stare out the window, I sat on the sofa and took a large swallow.

"She sits," Samuel said, looking up. "Progress."

"Sure."

"So tell me a little about yourself. Tabitha."

*Tell me about yourself.* So few people ever said that to me, or cared. There was Fiona, so loud and vibrant. My athletic cousins, rugby champions both. At home I was drowned out by their voices. *Are you fine?* my mother would ask. *Yes, Ma, I'm fine.*

"I'm a student. At Nottingham. Third year."

"Nottingham . . . no wonder you wanted to get out."

"It's a good school."

"It's a factory," he said. He took another sip of scotch. "And what are you studying?"

"Forensics."

He laughed. My cheeks flushed uncomfortably.

"What?"

"I can't see that. I'm sorry, but you're much too ladylike."

"Everyone keeps saying that. But you don't know me."

"Yes I do. Let me see. You have siblings—sisters, I suppose. You were one of the youngest."

"One sister," I said, looking at my drink. "I am the youngest. Yes."

"Ah. What else? Italy is your first trip abroad."

"I've been to Germany with my father."

"When you were a child. But Italy is the first place you've traveled to as a woman. Am I right? There's no shame in it. Italy is the very best first trip. You're young. It will color the rest of your life."

"I'm not that young. A lot of people have jobs by twenty-one."

Samuel got up. He leaned over and took away my glass, then walked back to the sideboard. My hands fluttered nervously as his fingers brushed mine. When he came back he sat on the sofa—not close enough to be threatening, but not far enough to be disengaged.

"So what have you learned? From Arthur?"

"Oh, a lot. We mostly talk about the Etruscans."

"The Etruscans. Yes. Arthur's favorite mystery."

"What do you think happened to them?"

"I think they were wiped out by the Romans. That's what everyone thinks."

"And their writings?"

"Please don't tell me you've fallen prey to his little fantasy. Oh, he's gotten far on that, believe me. What scholarly conference doesn't want a lecturer with a theory that good? A *cooperative* effort to destroy the art . . . to save it for the next life. It would be impossible. There would be no way an empire of that size—we're talking twelve cities, my dear. Hundreds of thousands of people."

"But—"

"The great professor certainly has woken you up, though."

"What do you mean?"

"When you walked in here this afternoon, you were just a shy thing. A slip, as they say. Following your friends. But you've actually got a mind in there."

I inhaled sharply.

"Please don't take it the wrong way. I don't like it when young women are too bold. It makes them foolish. That blond one will burn out by twenty-five. You're more cautious, I can see that. I was just happy to see there was something there."

"Of course there is," I said. "Goodness. You must be very mean-spirited to think there couldn't be."

Samuel laughed. "I'm much less mean-spirited than I'd like to be."

I took a long sip and looked at him closely. He was older than my father, there was no doubt. His lines were deeper; the whites of his eyes were almost yellow. His hands bore large brown spots, making me think of two sad toads.

"So what else about you then? Where are you from?"

"Outside Dublin."

"What do you like to read?"

"Mysteries, murder, that kind of thing."

"Christie?"

"Patricia Highsmith."

"Mmmm-hmmm. And what do you think of Italy?"

"I can't say."

"Why?"

"You can't think one way of an entire country." I took another sip. "It's not a person. I could live here my whole life and not know what I think of it."

"That's right," he said. "The rest of us are too simplistic. We say, oh, the wine! The food! But that's insulting, really."

"It is," I pronounced, feeling rather proud of myself. I was in a black-and-gold dress. I was sitting in a castle sipping brandy, chatting with a distinguished man. My mother would swoon.

Then I felt it, light but insistent. Samuel's index finger was on my knee. It wasn't moving back and forth, or fumbling, the way a boy back at Nottingham might do. But he had no intention of removing it. It was a possessive gesture, and, God help me, it wasn't altogether unpleasant.

"I'd tell you what to do," he said quietly, after what seemed a very long while.

I looked at the candle, thinking about what it would mean, to be Samuel's lover. Dresses arriving in blue tissue paper. Maybe some jewels. Mornings in hotels in Rome, espresso and pastries on the terrace. Making love with my head turned, eyes on the ceiling. Skin that would surely feel like that of an elephant, wrinkled, gray.

"You see—"

"There you are!" Arthur said, walking in. He was smiling, very hard, at me.

Samuel moved his hand away ever so slightly. "Any ghosts?"

"Not that I could see. Though Ben is asking for you. Can't seem to turn the breaker on, now that he's shut it off."

"Idiot. I hate to phone Fabrizio in the middle of the night. All right, I'll go look at it."

He left. The professor sat in a worn leather club chair and looked at me.

"Callisto," he said. "Europa."

"I'm sorry?"

"Leda. Alcmene. Danae. Are you getting my point?"

"Are you supposed to be Zeus?"

"I'm talking about Zeus, yes. I'm talking about young girls taken advantage of by the all-powerful. In the form of swans and showers of gold. Samuel is not your shower of gold, is what I'm saying. He is no swan, no eagle. Not even a fucking bull."

"Professor Korloff, I think you have the wrong impression."

"I have eyes. My patron was about to have you for a snack."

"I wouldn't have done that."

"He's an old man. You're a young minx."

"Minx?"

"All right, I'm a bit sauced. Here's the deal. You're a lovely young thing, and Samuel has taken to you. Saw it the moment I walked in the door. So I'm going to do the nice thing and save you from yourselves."

The professor reached over for Samuel's glass.

"I don't need saving."

"Well, I do, sweetheart. If Elena catches any wind of this crush, I'm screwed. Let me be straight. I need these people. I need their money."

"I'm not—"

"It's a shitty position they've put me in. The goddamned rich. They want the young smart kids at their fancy castle. What good's a castle without the kids? But if something goes wrong, I'm out. And I can't be out. No one will give me grants for my research, it's too out there. My theories are completely unsupported, get it? Private donors are my bread and butter."

"I still don't understand what I did."

"Nothing. You were just sitting there. A nymph waiting to be taken. You're right, you're completely innocent. But I need you to keep us all out of trouble and leave in the morning."

"Leave?" All breath left my body.

"Just say you're sick or that you have a family emergency. No, sick . . . it's better. I'll pay for your taxi, sweetheart. And I'll not only pass you, I'll give you an A."

"You really have this wrong," I said. "I didn't start this."

"I know, I know. But it's started."

I took my glass, finished the brandy, and coughed a little. "I really loved your class, Professor Korloff."

"Thank you. You're a smart kid. You'll do okay."

Suddenly, a sort of calm came over me. It was as if I were looking at myself from far away, above.

"Well, if I leave, I don't want to have to write the final paper."

Professor Korloff smiled. "Fair enough. Particularly since I don't want to *read* your final paper. Or anyone's, honestly."

"Okay." I rose, smoothing down my dress.

"All right, well, you'd better get to bed."

"Wait," I said.

"Yes?"

"You never told us what happened."

"What do you mean?"

"To the Etruscans. When they died. What they thought—where they went."

"Oh." He tilted his head, pleased. "See? I knew you were listening."

"Yes."

He cleared his throat.

"Well, the truth is, there's never been a firm stance on the thing. How the Etruscans—before Rome, I mean—viewed death. Was it a battle, or a party? Some scholars believe that they prepared for monsters and battles. The other idea is that the Etruscans—at least, the Grifonian Etruscans—prepared themselves for a journey to a faraway land. A journey that they packed for. But there's not enough evidence of this."

"What would evidence be?"

"Tombs filled with items. *Optimistic* items. In Grifonia, most of the tombs have been robbed, and what are left are sarcophagi with images to ward off the evil spirits. To appeal to Roman gods. You see, the Roman view on death was pretty grim. You were pulled down into that dark hole and a dog decided where your soul would go. The theory—my theory—is that the Etruscan view was more benevolent. That they built a house for the next life, where they would just keep on existing. But other than in Tarquinia, there aren't many artifacts as evidence of that theory. So it's just an idea. One I like. The Etruscans looked forward to death, whereas the Romans feared it. From what we know, the Etruscans killed one another more freely. They really didn't fear death, because they were just going somewhere else."

"And the Romans?"

"The Etruscans didn't particularly *like* the Romans. The Romans took their power. So their revenge was not to tell them how to prepare for the journey. On *purpose*. They didn't want the Romans around, get it? They wanted the next life all to themselves."

He looked at me expectantly.

"I see."

He laughed. "I doubt that, sweetheart. Girls like you don't spend much time thinking about death. But you will someday. So hopefully I've added something to that mind of yours."

I tried to smile, but the expression disintegrated.

"All right. I hope you continue your studies, Tabitha. You're bright, you just need to read more. But I think you should go to bed now. Get up early, call that cab. And don't worry too much about it. Don't get upset. This has happened before. Why do you think his marriage is so fucked?"

I got up to leave. "So I'll count on that A, then."

"Sure," Professor Korloff said. "A plus."

"All right."

"I'll come down late in the morning so it's not awkward," he said.

"I'll be gone."

"Okay, then," Professor Korloff said, holding Samuel's drink. "Good luck, honey. Good luck."

I walked out into the black hallway. I could hear private moans coming from a room somewhere above. How much time had passed?

My eyes were now used to the dark enough for me to see shapes. I'd never make it up to my room, I knew, but I could get down to the garden, if I was careful. Keeping my hand on the stone wall, I made my way down the steps. I was drunker than I'd been before, so the lack of light seemed less frightening. After what seemed like years, I was in the courtyard. The gravel glowed white in the darkness. The windows stared down at me. I ran through the archway to the garden, where our table still lay in ruin. The lawn was silent. Something was glowing on the table. I saw that it was my phone. It had one bar of connectivity, and, at 12:47 a.m., Claire had called.

The sound that came out of me—a sob of joy. There was no use waiting until morning. In the dark I'd never find our room. I pressed her number, my hands shaking as I waited for it to connect. After a tense moment, the other end rang.

"Hey!" she answered. I could hear voices behind her. "How's royalty?"

"Claire . . . I can't explain now, but I need a favor. Do you think you could find a car and pick me up here?"

"What? Wait a second." I could hear a scuffle, and then a door slam. "Okay. What happened?"

"Nothing horrible. I just need to get back."

"Yeah, my boss has one. Or someone does. Where are you?"

"Gubbio. I have the exact address." I told it to her, glad that Alessandra had insisted I get it before leaving.

"Cool. I'll map it. Okay, I think I can get out of here. It's dead anyway. But yeah. Go wait outside in about an hour. I'll swing it."

"I can't tell you what this means to me," I said.

"We're friends," she said. "Of course I'm coming."

The phone cut out before I could answer. Using the dim screen as a flashlight, I searched the ravaged table until I found Ben's matches. There was one left in the book. Hands shaking, I lit it, guarding the flame closely with my hand, and lit one of the half-destroyed candles on the table, and then another, then took them into the kitchen and found a piece of paper and a stub of a pencil.

*Girls*, I scribbled.

*I'm so sorry, but I had to leave. Something came up. Please don't worry, it's nothing to trouble about. Mr. Webster, thank you for your hospitality.*

I paused.

*Professor Korloff, thank you for a stimulating class.*
*Sincerely,*
*Tabitha Deacon*
*P.S. Anna, would you mind terribly bringing my things?*

I read the note twice, left it on the kitchen counter under a meat cleaver, then made my way back to the garden. The castle was quiet now, other than the occasional trickle of laughter. Taking one of the throw blankets from a garden chair and wrapping it around my bare shoulders, I crept to the entrance. Just as I pressed the release to open the outer gate, the lights went back on. There was a cheer and a bit of shrieking. I clanged the gate behind me and slipped down the path to wait.

It was one-thirty by the time I settled there in the dirt, my back against the cold stone of the gatepost. The road was as dark as the garden had been before Ben put the lights back on; we were too far from town for streetlights of any sort. I was tired but too scared to sleep. I could hear the forest's small animals singing in the woods; or I hoped they were small.

As I waited there, later and later, I thought that perhaps I had made a mistake. I was being childish to leave this dramatically. After all, Professor Korloff hadn't demanded that I leave that instant. I could just get the note off the counter, sneak upstairs, and play it off with a smile in the morning. I stood up, no doubt looking like a ghost myself in my long silk dress and white blanket. But the thought of Samuel's face in the morning kept me there. Even though I was guilty of nothing, I had, for a moment, considered his offer.

It was three o'clock before a car came crawling up the bottom of the hill, stopping every few hundred feet as if its driver were looking for an address. Claire. But I was still frightened, so I remained behind the post, peeking out only when the car was close enough for me to see the driver, who actually wasn't Claire at all.

Marcello looked at me through the open window.

"Devil," he said. "You look like a drunk angel."

"You came!" I ran to the passenger's side. "Where's Claire?"

"I was with her at her bar. And she told me you needed help. Alfonso has a car."

"I'm so glad."

"Dirty man?"

"Not so dirty. Just old and sad. Not Italian."

"Get in."

I opened the door and settled in, fastening the seatbelt over the blanket. I felt shy, suddenly.

"Thank you for coming," I mumbled.

"Anything for you, Devil. But now you're Angel. Here." He leaned over, took a beer from the backseat, and handed it to me.

Suddenly, my phone rang with a text. It was from Claire.

*Liking the switch?*

"What was that place?" Marcello asked.

"It was a castle. I was with my friends."

"And they let you run away?"

"I left them a note."

"Strange friend you are, Angel," he said. "They'll be worried about you."

"No they won't." There was no question—they wouldn't worry at all. I could just see it. *Oh well*, Jenny would say, with a somewhat annoyed frown. Anna might worry about Arthur's feelings, only to find him grimly approving. And Luka . . . would drink.

"Then you need better friends, Tasmania. Like me. Look at me, I came all the way just to kiss you."

"But you haven't kissed me."

"No!" Marcello stopped the car, veering onto the shoulder. He leaned over and snapped off my seatbelt, then covered my lips with his.

I wonder, listener, if you have ever been kissed by an Italian. It's different somehow. Marcello knew he had the right to kiss a woman, whereas the English and Irish boys of my youth, they were always wondering.

"All right then," he said, starting the car again.

Marcello fiddled with the radio, singing along to songs he knew. He was the sort of person who didn't like silence. He told stories in fast Italian. I tried to laugh in the correct places, while looking out the window at the dark houses, the sleeping families, the people who had only a few hours before it was time to get up and work.

"Where should we go?" Marcello asked, drumming his fingers on the wheel. "Alfonso's a lazy shit. Doesn't need his car. Florence? Rome?"

"I have class—" I stopped myself. "Sure. Rome."

"No. Rome is too far. I know where to take you. You'll like this better."

We were on the outskirts of Grifonia now. I wanted to ask, but kept silent as the car climbed up the steep hills of the old city. Marcello drove fast; I gripped the door handle as we whipped around curves. We went around the square, and back down again. I breathed a sigh of disappointment as we neared the cottage, but at the last minute, he veered toward one of the outer gates, stopping just short of the walls of the old city.

"What are we doing here?"

"My friend is doing restoration there. Remember? I told you. I have a key."

"Ah!" I said *ah* a lot when I was speaking Italian, even though it wasn't an Italian expression, as far as I knew.

"Finish your beer."

I put the empty bottle by my feet and got out. Marcello came around the car and looked at me.

"Angel. Let me see under the blanket."

I dropped it from my shoulders.

"The rich dress looks good."

"Thank you."

"You're wrong. You are the pretty one. You know that?"

"Stop it."

He took my hand. I felt something like a bird fly up my throat. It was trapped, hovering there. Together, we walked to the front of the church. It was a round stone building with a lovely park where I liked to read sometimes. During the late afternoon, after siesta, it could get rowdy with lovers and pot-smokers, but tonight the place was silent. As we stood, looking at the ancient stone, I thought about loneliness. The sweet, sickening nature of it. How it tugged one downward so insistently, even when the day was sunny or your grades were good or everyone in your family was healthy. Then, just like that, you had someone with you, and it became inconceivable that you could ever experience the affliction again.

"How do we get in? You can't open that door, can you?"

"Of course." He pulled out a huge key, the sort that clanged on the belts of monks. Looking around quickly to see if anyone was watching, he unlocked the door. With a loud crack and whine, it opened.

We stepped inside. The church was completely dark, save a few candles burning at one of the altars. I imagined I could hear whispering and clutched his hand harder.

"It's just the wind," he said.

"Of course."

"This used to be the Temple of the Sun," Marcello said.

"I don't believe you. Now you'll say cavemen were here."

"No, it's true. This was an Etruscan temple. You see, there are the old stones. And then, the Church rebuilt it."

"Are you Catholic?" I asked him, looking at the shrine.

"I am nothing. But my mother is Catholic. So I know it, I understand."

He put his arms around me from behind, then drew my hair away and put his lips on the place on the spine just below the hairline.

"You okay, Tasmania?"

"Marcello, what is my name?"

"Shhhhhh."

I felt faint; my knees buckled. Things progressed in that fashion until I pulled away, my dress falling from my waist.

"Wait," I said. "We can't do this here."

"Why? You're Jewish."

"There's still God."

"He doesn't care."

Marcello put his lips to my ear. A sound came from my chest that I didn't realize I was making, a sort of soft keen. I thought, inappropriately, of Colin.

*Will I always hunger for the thing I don't have?* I wondered.

Yet the thought died as soon as it came. Marcello led me to a spot near the door where there were no pietas in view. Before I could talk, he kissed me again and arched his body into mine. His waist was thick, but I liked it. It made me feel small.

How to explain those hours with Marcello? I have already spoken of darkness in the tomb, the carnal, cold satisfaction of it, the way it permeated the body, swallowing me whole. Now it was happening again. My thoughts of the other man—of everything in the world—were completely blotted away.

Marcello, for all his charm, didn't love me. I knew he didn't. And I didn't love him. He was rough, and not truly looking at my face. But his lips did, indeed, taste of salt. And when that essence was released behind my teeth, something permanent changed in me. A sort of breaking. I yowled; I bit and bucked against the stone floor. *No one can take this away from me.* The last, cloying tendrils of childhood receded. I was, quite simply, more awake.

# 17

During the days I've described so far, I was mainly quite happy. Yes, there had been a small rift with my new friends, some homesickness, some melancholy that resulted from too much alcohol, lack of sleep, and the yawning emotional range of a girl just out of her teens. But I was comfortable in my new life. Just the physical space from home was heartening. Yet the day after I returned from the castle, everything shifted. There wasn't one singular event that caused it. Instead, it was an all-encompassing weather change, one that affected our harmonious little house slightly but lethally, the same way a deep freeze and thaw will lead to a permanent crack in a foundation, causing the whole place to list.

It was nine in the morning when I finally came in the door of our cottage. The other girls were up: Gia draped in her underwear on the sofa, Alessandra in a robe mixing something in a bowl, Claire on the terrace despite the cold weather. When I walked in, there was an appreciative round of cheering and laughter.

"Big night, *bella*? Still in the dress!"

I knew I should be laughing, too, given my strange evening. But for some reason the cheer had the opposite effect on me, and I began to cry.

"Oh no!" Alessandra cried in English. She put her bowl down and rushed over. "*Bella, bella.* We were joking. You just look fun in your beautiful dress."

"Funny," Claire corrected.

Alessandra gave her a look and switched to Italian. "A long dress in the morning! You understand. Are you all right?"

"Yes."

Gia crawled to the edge of the couch, perching like a cat. "So the kings of the castle were bastards after all?"

"I suppose."

"And the house?"

"It really was a castle. With towers and stone and everything."

"I do not like these places," Alessandra sniffed. "Always cold."

"You've never stayed in a castle," Gia said.

"I have. It was a hotel in Turin. Very cold."

Claire smiled. "So . . . Marcello came and picked you up like I told him to?"

"Yes."

Gia whistled. "All the way in Gubbio!"

"Yes. Claire sent him."

"It was no problem," Claire said. "He was at my bar anyway."

"And your friends?" Alessandra said impatiently.

"They stayed."

"So this party is still happening?" Gia said. "Maybe I'll go."

"And Marcello?" Alessandra said.

"We had a very nice time. He was . . ."

"Nice," Gia said. "Right?"

"Yes."

"Well, I'm glad you're back," Alessandra said. "It never sounded like a good idea."

"I'll just shower." I slipped into my room and closed the door, then stood looking out my window. The landscape seemed darker, the colors tarnished. After a moment, Claire came in.

"So what *really* happened, Taz?"

"Nothing."

"Did you get in a fight with Jenny?"

"Jenny! No. Not at all. It was . . . there was just an awkward situation that came up."

"Yeah?"

I sat on my bed. "The owner of the house came on to me, and . . . my professor—"

"The mythology guy?"

"Yes. He thought something inappropriate was happening, so he asked me to go."

Claire was quiet for a moment. She played with the makeup on my dresser. I tried not to flinch when she touched my earrings, which were neatly arranged in an ivory inlaid box.

"So was it?"

"No. Samuel—the host—was old. I was lost, and there was a ghost hunt, and there was this dead nun."

"What?" Claire asked.

"Oh, no one will believe me."

"You can fucking sue about this kind of stuff," she said. "Your professor should be looking out for you."

"Oh, he was, in a way."

"By kicking you out of the house he invited you to? You've got to tell the Enteria people. This guy is a class-A dickhead."

"He's a good teacher, actually. And I couldn't do that to Anna."

"Why? Is she blowing him?"

"Claire! No, he's her mentor. It'll cool down. Besides, Marcello came, and it was . . ."

"Nice."

"Yes."

"Did you hook up?" She plopped down next to me on the bed and poked me in the ribs.

"Claire."

She dug in a bit harder, then smiled and crossed her arms.

"Come on! I *gave* you that guy."

My face reddened. "It seems that he drove quite a long way of his own accord."

"Oh my fucking God, don't be so Jenny. I just want a little credit. Details."

"But I don't want to tell you," I said. "I'm different from you."

Claire pressed her lips together and stood up. "I'm sorry I'm such a perv. The truth is, I liked him a little, but I didn't want to step on your toes. Like I said the other night. You're more important to me than he is."

"As are you," I said, trying my hardest to mean it.

"I'll let you take your shower." She stopped at the door. "Hey, I have the night off. Going to hear some classical music at the college. It's free. No booze, no creepy old men. Come?"

"Maybe." I paused, thinking. It *would* be good to get out of the house, to let Marcello know that I wasn't just waiting around for him. The perfect way to stay in front of things.

"Well, yes. That would be nice. Thank you."

"We can wear our dresses."

"I think I've had enough of this dress."

Claire put her hand on the door handle as if to go. Then, in a swift, impulsive moment, my flatmate turned and sprung forward, crouching in front of me. She grabbed my shoulders and put her lips to mine, then slid her tongue onto my teeth. Our tongues flickered there. For long? Five seconds? Ten? Finally, my mind took over and I pulled away.

Claire didn't let go. Cupping my ears, she pressed her forehead to mine.

"See?" she whispered. "Friends."

I had no idea what to say or do. After a long pause, I nodded.

"All right," she said. "See you."

And then an odd thing happened. Claire . . . disappeared. There still is no other word for it. As I've said, she moved like a hunter, as if she were made of smoke. Yet on my tongue, the taste of someone else's cigarettes. And in my chest, the feeling of something enormous turning and turning again.

•

We went to the concert as planned. If Claire felt strange about the morning's events, she didn't act so. Perhaps this was an everyday occurrence for her, kissing girls. Following her cue, I pretended all was normal.

When we walked through the great doorway of the university concert hall, I was met with an unexpected wave of nostalgia for Professor Korloff's class. This room—the Aula Magna—was just as beautiful as our classroom had been. It was a magnificent place, with gilded fixtures and a Socialist mural of men toiling with rocks by the great Gerardo Dottori, the artist Luka and Anna were deconstructing the evening we met.

The concert hall wasn't nearly full. Claire and I took seats near the back. I looked around, half expecting to see Anna or Jenny, who hadn't bothered to call. I wondered if they were angry with me. If they thought I'd caused a scene, or was a slut. And, of course, Marcello hadn't called either. I had a vaguely nauseous feeling, as if my very center were hollow.

"You all right?" Claire asked.

"Sure."

"We can bail if this is boring."

"No," I said. "It's fine. I'm just tired."

The music began, Bach. As I listened, my mind wandered shamelessly. I thought of Marcello, how his palms had felt on my body, how I could feel the bruises on my lower back from the church's hard floor.

After a while, I had the feeling of being looked at. I jerked my head, thinking it must be Marcello. But the walls seemed to fall as I saw that it was, instead, Colin, who nodded slightly and waved.

"Hey, who's that?" Claire whispered. "He's totally hot. You know him?"

"Ahhhh," I said slowly. "Barely."

"How?"

"Uh, we met at the museum. He's British."

"Can you introduce me?"

"Well, as I've said, I barely . . ."

The music stopped. There was a smattering of applause. The intermission was announced.

"Hey," Claire called out.

Colin turned his eyes to her and rose from his seat. I could feel a shadow settling over me.

"Hello," he said to Claire. Then, turning toward me: "Hello, Tabitha, how are you?"

"I'm doing all right," I said, my hands sprouting rivers.

"Oh, she's super," Claire said.

"Oh?" Colin raised his eyebrows.

"Oh sure. New boyfriend. The cool guy downstairs."

I looked down, away, at the stage—I don't remember. Just anywhere but his face.

"I'm Claire," my flatmate said.

"Hello," Colin said.

"Your name?"

"Colin."

"And I'm Claire."

He smiled. That rare and wondrous phenomenon. Only this time it wasn't for me.

"Right, Claire."

She laughed, and he did, too, and as they looked at each other I saw everything happening, and felt a pin going ever so slowly into the taut balloon of my heart.

Claire laughed. "So you know Taz?"

Colin shrugged. "We've met."

"Well, we should all go out after this," Claire said. "New friends always welcome."

"I'm actually feeling rotten." I got up hastily, knocking my bag to the floor. The sound of coins dropping echoed throughout the hall. "Do you mind if we go home?"

Claire looked at me and—maddeningly—winked.

"Actually, I'll stay for the second act. I like Baroque."

"Yes, these musicians aren't bad," Colin said.

"Oh," I said, as everything in the room grew smaller. "Oh yes. All right."

"Are you okay to walk home?"

"It's a block," I said, recovering. "Of course."

I waited for them to talk me out of it. Colin stared at the stage, and Claire gave me a horrid, blank grin.

"Goodnight, Tabitha," Colin said.

Claire kissed my cheek. "See you, Taz."

I walked out with what I hoped was an aloof manner, looking back only once to see their heads bent together in conversation. I hated them both. And then I hated myself even more. What was I hoping? For everyone in the world to be in love with me?

Eventually I reached the gate to our little house. Standing on the steps for a while, I listened to the traffic and the wind. I knew I should just go inside, but instead I crept down to the boys' apartment. I could hear Marcello playing the guitar. The door was unlocked. I cracked it open, and was greeted by the smell of cigarette smoke, garlic, old beer.

"Marcello," I said. "Hi."

He looked up and saw me. His face was wan, and he had dark smudges under each eye.

"Ciao."

"Can you come up?"

"I'm very tired, Devil. Last night, you know."

"What happened to Angel?"

"Good question."

I smiled, blushing.

"Tasmania. Go up. I'll see you tomorrow."

"What about now?"

He tipped his head back. "All right. Just a minute."

Marcello put his guitar down and went into the bathroom. I could hear something clinking against the sink. The water ran for a moment, and then he came out, drying his face and rubbing his nose.

"Devil, you are trouble. Another night of no rest."

"I'll let you rest."

"No. I won't rest now. No. All right, a party. I'll bring the guitar up."

"No."

"Some beer."

". . . No."

"Just me then?"

"Yes. Just you."

Marcello laughed and took a step toward me, then stopped. He had this way of smiling sometimes that made me want to run and hide under the covers.

"Well, I don't know, Devil. Tell me why I should come."

"Why?"

"I'm very busy, you see."

"Oh. Well. I don't know. I . . ."

He was still smiling at me in that way. I looked at the floor.

"If you have time, I'd like you to please come upstairs to visit me."

"What?"

"I'd like you to come up please. If you want to."

"So I can fuck you?"

I backed away, putting my hand on the doorknob.

"I'm sorry. I think I should probably—"

"You want me to fuck you now? Is that it?"

Breath, suddenly, escaped me.

"Tabitha?"

"Yes," I whispered.

Swiftly, the Italian rushed forward and pushed me into the door with all his weight. My shoulders and head slammed against the wood. I cried out, pressed flat between the door and his body, chest airless, pelvis crushed.

"Now?"

"Marcello, my head—"

"Say it."

"Yes. Yes. Please. Now."

# 18

The B4 came back with something in between a bang and a whimper. A whine, perhaps. The girls were tired, and grumpy, and cross with one another. None of them seemed especially curious about why I'd gone. They were too busy complaining about the others.

Luka came by first, around noon on Monday. All three had texted individually, saying we should get together. I replied vaguely, as I always did, waiting for the others to make plans. It wasn't that I didn't have ideas, but the other voices were so loud, I'd long ago stopped bothering to make any suggestions. Now Luka was at my door, knocking insistently.

"Don't you have class?" I asked. Since I'd received a full credit for the mythology seminar debacle, I had no class on Mondays, but I knew that Luka and Jenny did.

"Fuck class," she said, sweeping in. "Christ. I forgot how small your little house is."

"Yes, when the terrace door is closed, it is quite cozy."

"Let's go to lunch. I feel like that Argentinean place, the one with the good steak."

"All right. Can you wait a minute?"

"Sure."

I opened the door to my room, where Marcello was still sleeping. We'd woken earlier, but after a long morning in my room, he'd fallen asleep again. Seeing him gave me a sense of satisfaction. It wasn't the giddy happiness I'd experienced with Sean, but instead as if I'd acquired something coveted. I kissed his shoulder, then went out and pulled the door closed again.

"Tabitha Deacon, do you have someone *in* there?"

"No. Well, yes. My neighbor—the one you met."

"Oh, good for you."

"Thanks, Luka," I said.

Just then Anna stepped in, wrapped in a real fox fur.

"God," Luka said. "Even I am offended by that thing."

"I see Luka's gotten here first."

"We're about to have lunch," Luka said.

"Lovely—I'll come along, then. Dress warmly, though, little Tabitha," Anna said, squeezing my arm. "It's absolutely freezing."

"I'm all right."

"Doesn't want to go back into her room," Luka said, grabbing a scarf of Gia's off a hook and throwing it to me. "She's got a bloke."

"Really?"

"The neighbor," Luka crooned.

"Asses, stop doing that. I'm standing *right here*. Come on." I ushered them out the door, before Marcello woke and got forced into conversation. "He came and got me Friday night."

"So that's why you left?" Luka asked, leading us up the hill. "Whisked off your feet by the hot something?"

I looked down at the slick cobblestones, as if trying to keep my footing. "Yes."

"How romantic!" Anna said with unconvincing enthusiasm.

She stopped in a doorway to light herself a cigarette.

"We're almost there," Luka said, impatience coloring her voice.

"Oh, I forgot. It's noon! Go have your drink, Luka. I'll just finish my smoke."

"You invited *yourself* to lunch," Luka said. "So don't be a royal bitch about it."

"Just . . . look—don't worry. You lot go on. I'm not in the mood anymore. I'm actually not even hungry."

"Come on, Anna," I urged. "In fact, I'll call Jenny and we'll make it a B4 thing."

"Do that, Taz, and I'll *never* speak to you again," Anna cried, her voice close to tears.

"We'll meet you at the restaurant," Luka said, steering me away. "Come," she called over her shoulder to Anna. "I'll buy you a steak. You need it."

We left her in the doorway, a tiny girl in a fox coat.

"What *happened*?"

"Drink first." Luka glanced at me. "The fact is, we're in a bit of trouble."

Mendoza was a long, narrow restaurant with a cathedral ceiling and a large, well-tended hearth. The room opened out to a wide terrace with a modern outdoor sitting area below that was popular on warm nights. The smell of meat was so strong I stepped backward as we entered, a little dizzy. We took a table by the fireplace, and Luka ordered a bottle of Montefalco, her favorite Umbrian red. The waiter, a pleasant, older Italian, opened the bottle with a flourish—it was that kind of a place—and the wine poured thick and meaty into our glasses. It occurred to me that I hadn't even had coffee yet, but after a morning of sex, good red wine seemed just the thing.

Luka took a long drink, stopping just short of finishing it.

"Jenny fucked up," she said, putting her glass down carefully.

"How?"

"She slept with that Samuel person."

Fear, cold and persistent, curled its fingers around my chest.

"I thought she was with Roberto."

"She *was*, and that would have been okay. Not great, but okay. But he left Saturday, and it seems she got bored. So she threw herself on the host."

"And he was interested?"

"Of course. She's twenty-one and he's—I don't know. A hundred?"

"What did Professor Korloff do?"

"That's the problem. He got furious. Quite a flip from the kind professor I'd seen. Burst into our room in the morning, yelling at Anna. Said something about how first you tried—"

"I didn't, though!" My voice rose, shriller than I'd have liked. "He thought so but I really didn't."

Luka finished her wine and signaled the waiter to fill her glass again, then ordered loudly in English. "Two steaks, rare, potatoes, salad, Worcestershire sauce if you've got it." He raised his eyebrows, obviously a little impressed by her irreverence toward his country and language.

"What about Anna?"

"Absolutely devastated. Her dad died when she was a little girl, you know. So she's got quite the daddy complex. Completely idolizes Arthur."

"He's very sweet to her," I said.

"Oh?" Luka said. "I think he's a fucking sponge."

"Why?"

"A bloke like him needs money, Taz. Like we all do."

"Sure. For his research. It's hard for him to get grants."

"I'd say it's for his flats in London and New York and for his extravagant trips, living like the aristocrat that he's not. I think Professor Korloff likes the finer things."

"You mean the way Jenny does?"

"The way all of us do. You included. I didn't see you turning down our dresses or the dinners."

"You all never let me pay. I try every—"

"Nevermind. I'm happy to treat," she said, cutting me off. "Anyway. Teaching gigs pay him some, but *Samuel* pays him hundreds of thousands of pounds to hunt down pieces for him. Or his wife does. He was telling us all about it the second night before everything went south. But you see, Samuel's wife's the one with the money. And Samuel is just itching to leave her."

"This is . . . too complicated."

"It might not have been, if Jenny hadn't fucked up like she did. Of course, she was just thinking, here's a bloke to add to the bank."

"She does go over on that empowerment thing. Staying in front of it, she says."

"Empowerment? Oh, Taz. Please. You know perfectly well Jenny Cole is about *money*."

I tasted my meat, the texture of which just then felt revolting.

"So she and Samuel got together."

"Yes. I think the professor tried to intervene, but he didn't have any power over her."

"Poor Anna."

Luka inspected a piece of steak meticulously, then popped it in her mouth. "Jenny doesn't give a fuck about Anna. Not really. She's just a prop for her ego. We all are."

"Luka, don't say that. She has her faults—we all do. But she's—" The word so often used in our cottage, *nice*, wasn't quite correct. ". . . a strong, loyal person."

"Not to Anna."

"It's complicated. She must have felt it wasn't Anna's place—"

"Anna *begged* her, Taz. Begged. Jenny sleeps with a new bloke every two days. Did she really need Samuel? And the fact is, Arthur practically threw us out yesterday. He told Anna he was disgusted. Bloke's the closest thing she has to a father. I think she's going to have a nervous breakdown."

"Did Jenny come home with you?"

"That's the worst part." Luka pushed her plate away. "No."

"Where *is* she?"

"Dunno. She stayed there with Samuel. Arthur left the same time we did, barely even waved. God, what a mess."

"I'm so sorry."

"And let me guess: she's already tried to get to you to tell you her side first?"

"She did text. Yes."

"Just be careful. The drama factor is high right now. She's going to lean on you, now that Anna's all pissed."

"For what?"

"Running mate. You know Jenny. She's got to look a certain way."

"What about you? You don't have allegiances, do you? I mean, Jenny messed up, but you'll still go out with her, even if Anna won't. Right?"

Luka shook her head. "I could never be her number one."

I looked at my half-empty glass. Luka had consumed almost the whole bottle.

"Luka, why *do* you drink so much?"

She shrugged. "I like it."

"But don't you . . . you know. Worry?"

She picked up her glass, examining the color of the trace of wine at the bottom. "I don't know why I do it. Maybe I like the taste. Or maybe I can't commit to the thing about liking girls. Maybe there's someone I'm trying to get over. Or maybe I just don't like myself very much."

"Luka!" I put my hand on hers. She waved it off.

"No, no. I'm not going to have a scene. I drink too much, it's true. But I'll worry about it later. Italy is not exactly a time for personal cleansing. Thank you, though, for your prudent mothering." She lit a cigarette.

"Can I have one of those?"

"You don't like smoking."

"I do today."

She tossed me the pack.

"Well, *I* like you," I said.

Luka looked away. "Fine. I like you too. Not in the sexy way, no offense. You'd be a cold fish in bed, I think."

"Am not."

"Should I ask the neighbor?"

I blushed.

"That flatmate of yours, though. Hallelujah."

"She's taken too. Most interesting guy in town."

"Naturally. All right, now. Where are you going to stand on this Anna thing?"

"I'm not going to choose sides if I can avoid it."

"Grand idea," Luka said, holding the lighter in front of me. "Impossible, but very smart."

"Or perhaps I'll just lay low for a couple days, until they stop clawing each other. Turn off my phone, hang out with my flatmate."

"Just go back to bed with that big neighbor of yours." Luka signaled for the check.

"Well, thanks for lunch."

"It's from the pot. Better use it up before everything gets fucked up."

"What do you mean?"

"I mean our arrangement doesn't have a provision for bickering. Jenny's sort of going rogue on us. And I'm sure you've picked up that Anna can be fragile. I wouldn't be shocked if she pulled out."

"I suppose. Anyway, thank you for letting me know about all of this. You're a good friend."

"I'm not, particularly. But I do hate watching the slaughter of innocents."

The waiter came with the bill. Luka, as usual, paid without looking at it.

"Anna never came in."

"No," Luka said, standing. "She didn't."

•

When I went home, I did exactly as Luka told me. I turned off my phone and got back in bed with Marcello, who was still asleep, his face resting on his arm, his black curls so deceivingly cherubic against the pillow. I kissed him, but he waved me off, so after reading a bit I left to study at the library. I might not have any more work for Etruscan Mythology, but this was hardly the case for my other courses, and I was, by now, wildly behind.

The University of Grifonia's library was a refreshingly sleek glass building, filled with quiet cubbies and modern wooden tables to work at. Still, I couldn't concentrate. It wasn't just Marcello that drove me to distraction now, though my mind did trip into carnal memory of our bed at least every three minutes or so. But who were these girls? I was attracted to them; I wanted to be part of them. But something was off. I knew it, even as I also didn't want to know.

I'd never in my life had such Byzantine relationships. The boys I'd loved either loved me back or plainly wanted sex—no subterfuge involved. And Babs and I just loved each other, period. I could be domineering, she could be consciously naive, but we knew that we would never do anything to hurt each other. If one of us tripped, the other would catch her elbow, and if we weren't in time for that, we'd run off for Band-Aids and disinfectant lotion and cake. We fought, of course. I blamed Babs constantly for our isolation from the other girls. Yet our fondness for each other—or perhaps our need for each other's company—drummed the tension away.

And now, Luka, Jenny, Anna, with their champagne and swirls of smoke and cars to Milan! Even there in my library cubby thinking of them, it was as if I were drowning in my desires. Distracted to the point of unproductivity, I picked up my books and my purse and walked to the café next door—a loud, cheerful little place—ordered an espresso and called Babs.

"What's wrong?" she asked immediately upon hearing my tone.

"Oh, Babs." I stirred my coffee.

"Oh, Taz."

We laughed.

"Won't you visit? I *miss* you!"

"It's not nearly Christmas yet. Anyway, I'm working on Dad for a ticket. How are you? What's wrong?"

"I went to a party . . . and this old man hit on me."

"Ugh."

"And this other old man—my professor—thought . . . you know, it's too confusing."

"But are you *all right?*"

"Yes. I miss home. Isn't that funny? I went on and on about coming, and now I miss Lucan."

"It's nice. You like us."

"My friends here are all so strange. I never know what they're on about. They're—" I paused, once again deciding to keep their activities from her. "As I said. Strange."

"What about the American?"

"Claire? Odd, but sweet. Sleeps around a lot."

"Oh!" Babs laughed. "That reminds me. I have something to tell you."

"What?"

"George asked me to marry him."

"'That *reminds* me'!" I shouted, jumping up and running outside. "'That reminds me.' How could you not tell me straightaway?"

"You had things to tell me."

"Babs, you're maddening. Engaged!"

"Yeah. I mean, we won't get married for a while, not for years, probably. But he wanted to ask."

"It's just so . . ."

"Early?"

"*Sweet.*" Oh, God. How could we be there already? Babs would be married, taken away from me. "It's wonderfully sweet. He's such a solid bloke."

"I know." Babs had met George their first year of uni. They were a good-looking, solid, dull couple whom I'd always been a little envious of.

"Well now you *have* to come. If George gets you forever, then I should get you for a few days."

"All right. I promise I'll come. Have to get a look at this neighbor, anyway, don't I?"

"He's—" I paused. "Terrible. No, wonderful."

"Oh, Taz!"

"Oh, Babs!"

We hung up laughing. When we ended conversations, we never bothered with goodbye.

# 19

Within a week, the inevitable happened. Claire and Colin melded into one spectacular body. And in order to hide my unreasonable jealousy, I became the American's main confidante.

When Claire wasn't with Colin, which was practically always, she walked about in a sort of dream state, staring out a window for minutes, saying nothing. She had an air of desperation when he wasn't near. Yet, at least in the beginning, Colin seldom left her unaccompanied; he even sat at her bar with his research for her entire shift.

Sometime after the middle of October, Claire stopped sleeping at our cottage. Her clothes disappeared from the living room; the same balled up dress remained on her bed for a week; the guitar was left neglected behind the sofa; the vegetables on her shelf withered and turned curious colors of yellow and white.

It brought a change in chemistry to our little house, this new bout of love. I was rabidly envious, but the feeling was so unacceptable I hid it with every ounce of concentration I had. I often asked after her happiness, how everything was for them. And the truth was, I really missed her.

Still, it was a relief not to be around her so much, around that strange intensity. Now that the cold weather had set in, it became clear that our home truly was too small for four young women; the place was bursting with our possessions, our emotions, our more and more frequent arguments. Claire was, without question, the loudest and messiest. It wasn't that she was lazy—she wasn't. She just seemed rushed, as if life outside were beckoning so forcefully there simply wasn't *time* for something as mundane as, say, cleaning a dish. So with her gone more, things got tidier, quieter.

Sometimes Colin would come to our house, and she'd make him lunch. These interludes were inevitably uncomfortable. He would avoid looking at me, which I began to consider ridiculous, as we had no connection. Claire would insist on touching him all the time, which he seemed to like. He would just smile and let her climb all over him as he annotated his large, dusty texts.

"Pesto?" she'd ask. "It's just from the jar."

Colin was always quiet, working. Yet he often stopped to gaze at her as she moved about the house.

"Whatever you want," he said. "It doesn't matter."

"I want pesto."

"Then I do, too."

"What are you looking at today?" Claire rested her chin on his shoulder. An ancient, large script was spread over our counter.

"A list of families on Via Bartolo in 1614. How many children, yearly deaths, things like that."

"Because that's who the order helped? Children?"

"Sometimes."

"What order?" Gia asked.

"An old Masonic health order. I'm writing my thesis on it."

"What's the name?"

"Misericordia."

"Never heard of it."

"Not many people have. It was small, but provides an interesting window into the era. That's why it's a good thesis. No one's done it before."

"Those orders, were they always men?" Claire asked.

"Yes," Gia said. "Always."

"It's fascinating," Claire said, kissing him. "I love it, what you're doing."

"What is he doing?" Gia asked.

Claire kissed him again.

"It is difficult," Alessandra said once after they left. "They are so passionate, I feel I should give them privacy. But it is the kitchen! So."

Claire, being Claire, wanted to share everything about the experience she was having. "I feel amazing," she said, tossing herself on my bed one afternoon. "Is that how you feel about Marcello? Amazing?"

I hesitated. I hated it when Claire compared Colin to Marcello. I had never felt more frustrated by men, the having of one, the wanting of another. Lately, Marcello seemed barely interested. He had a habit of not calling for days, even if I did. Also, he only appeared late at night.

"I don't know. Sure. I feel good about him."

"Well, I feel *amazing*. Colin says all these things. Whatever. He likes to speak Italian to me. I have no idea what he's talking about. But it's like, I understand him, totally. He's so . . ."

"Romantic?" I asked, a tad longingly. "Sweet?"

"Yeah." She giggled happily, a sound that made me involuntarily wince. "Do you want to hear how we did it?"

I did, actually.

"He ties up my hands sometimes. Not in a bad way. And then he kisses, like, every part of my body. And one time we took this olive oil and—"

"Oh, don't say more."

"Sorry. I had to tell someone. Anyway, we should all go out. The four of us. Could we?"

"Maybe."

"Taz." She grabbed my hand and looked at me rather desperately. "I want you to be as happy as I am. Every bit as happy. You know? You *deserve* it."

"I'm happy, Claire."

"But why not let yourself go a little. With Marcello, you know?"

"I let myself go exactly as much as I like to. We—we're going just fine."

She looked at me thoughtfully. "Hey, why don't we go underwear shopping? Now. You know, to spice things up."

"I don't know. I—"

"Come on," she said, grabbing her pack. "We need it. Well, I do. Mine look like they've been in some kind of war zone."

I relented, because when Claire wanted something, it was impossible to refuse her. We climbed up to the piazza, stopping first in a very fine store I'd been to with Anna. The proprietor, who recognized me, greeted me with something between enthusiasm and fear.

"She knows you?"

"I've come here with friends."

"*Oh* my God," Claire said, fingering the bras. "Ninety euros? Jesus. Your friends are seriously loaded."

"Let's go somewhere else."

We walked outside and she linked her arm with mine. "You know, I think I might actually be in love," she said.

"It's been a week and a half, Claire."

"So?" She squeezed my arm harder. "I'm twenty. I'm supposed to fall in love in a week. So are you. Haven't you read Daisy Miller?"

"Sure. She ended up dead of fever."

"Yeah, but she was in *love*. I mean, Taz, I think about Colin all the time. It's sort of torture. It's like, I'm not really *here* in between the times I see him. I mean, I'm here, but I'm totally distracted, just waiting for him to call. This *can't* be the way it's supposed to be."

"It is, unfortunately," I said, remembering my misery over Sean. "There's lots written about that, too."

"Nerd."

"Just keep your head."

"Oh my *God*, Taz. 'Keep your head.' That is so *you*. The whole point is to lose our minds."

"But you just said—"

"You can't trust what I say. I'm a complete psycho. Here, this place is cheap. Let's go in here for a thong. A hot-pink one."

"I—"

"I'll *buy* it for you, prude. Come on." She grabbed my hand. "Let's get you into some danger."

•

One night, after attending an oddly grim cocktail party on the north side of town with Jenny, I came home to find Claire on our tiny sofa, poring over an Italian grammar book. There was a bottle of wine on the floor next to her, three-quarters empty. The ashtray, still smoldering, was brimming over.

I took off my coat and sat at the table.

"Why aren't you at Colin's?"

"Because I'm allowed to take a fucking night off."

"Yes, it's just—"

"Also I'm failing Italian."

I laughed. "Because your boyfriend is half British?"

"Because I'm an idiot." She threw the book on the floor, then brought her knees to her chest and dropped her head into her folded arms.

"Claire?"

"What?" Now she was crying.

"What could be the matter?"

"He's fucking other people. Colin. I'm, like, doing everything for him, and then he's—*fuck*. I can't even talk about it."

"Claire. That can't be true. He's with you every single night. How could he possibly have the time?"

"During the day. He never tells me where he's going."

"Isn't he working on his dissertation? It's a huge thing."

"Right. No. I mean, that's what I said. You going to the library? *No*. Where are you going, then? I said. And he looked at me like I was the most annoying bug in the world. Like I was a *roach*."

"You're not a roach."

"He said I didn't have to know where he was all the time."

"Well . . ."

"Well, what? I tell him where *I* am all the time. I could be fucking all of Grifonia if I wanted to."

"Absolutely. You did."

"What's that supposed to mean?"

"Just that—"

"Screw it. I know what you mean. I like sex. Fine. But I gave that up after Colin."

"Claire." I got up, fetched a jelly glass, and poured myself some of her wine. "It's only been three weeks. What, exactly, have you given him?"

"I told him I loved him."

The recklessness of the notion—admitting such a thing so quickly—both thrilled and sickened me at the same time.

"Oh."

"Bad idea, right?"

"It is soon."

"So fucking what?"

"I just mean . . . Claire. Can you really love someone that soon? Look, you don't know anything about him. Here you are, saying so. You may be feeling this way now, but just a month ago you didn't know he existed."

"But now I do," she said.

"It's too fast."

"It's not. There aren't fucking rules about this, Taz. I know what I feel."

"Miserable?"

"Go to hell." She put her face in her arms again.

"Claire. It'll be all right. We're just foreigners. This is all temporary. We're just having a good time."

Even as I said the words, they sounded weak. I wanted to tell her that she'd forget the man from the museum. That if he was sleeping with someone else—if that was even possible—she'd get over it, be as carefree as she was before. But I still felt the sharp edge each time I thought of Sean, my boyfriend from long ago. And, of course, I still longed for Colin myself.

"Look," I said. "Let's have some more wine. We can go out if you want. And I'll help you with your Italian. It's really not so hard."

"You know what I want?" she said suddenly, looking up. Her perfectly symmetrical features were mottled, her cheeks pink, like a child's. "For you to arrange that date. With you and Marcello. Will you come out with us, to see what you think?"

"Why would that help?"

"It would. See, he likes you. Said it's funny that you like gory history stories."

*Was that all he thought of me?* I wondered.

"Claire."

"Can you do it?"

I got up again, opening another bottle. "I'll try."

"I knew you would," she said, wiping her face and smiling. That perfect skin, those slanted cheekbones, that ready mouth. Her hair had lost all its previous lavender color and was now caramel blond. She was a real, live siren. It was the fatal problem that ran silent beneath it all.

•

A few days later, Colin came over while no one was home but me.

Claire was sleeping at his apartment again. I hadn't yet arranged the date she'd asked for, because I hadn't seen Marcello. He'd gone out of town. It was a rainy Tuesday afternoon, and I was napping on the couch under a musty blanket, having put in a valiant forty-five minutes on my art history paper, something about the medieval perspective on horses. There was a polite knock on the door, and Colin poked his head in.

"She's not here," I said, sitting up.

He looked at me in that serious way he had, leaning against the doorjamb and polishing his glasses. Obviously he had come over to slowly pleasure my flatmate with cooking oils and whatnot, and was disappointed to find only me.

I cleared my throat.

"I know she's not," he said. I caught my breath at the hope that he might have actually come to see *me*. But then he reached into his bag, taking out what I recognized to be her green rain jacket. "It's just that she needs this today."

"Of course." In the last week we had gone over autumn's precipice, sliding headfirst into Umbria's months of gray sleet.

"How are you?" Colin asked. He drew closer, placing the jacket on the couch.

"Oh, good. Napping. I don't know." I shook my head at my stupidity. Colin smiled slightly. It wasn't the same with him as with Marcello. With Marcello, everything crackled. I never knew exactly what to say or do, or even if he understood me. Colin was the opposite. With him, even saying nothing was exactly the right thing. He was comfortable in life's pauses.

"What are you studying?" he asked, nodding at my books.

"Art history. Horses."

"War?" he asked.

"What? Oh, no. I'm writing about perspective."

"How dull." He gazed at me for another long moment, then looked at his watch. "Anyway, I have a meeting."

"With a professor?"

"No." I studied his face to get a clue as to whether he was, as Claire feared, sleeping with someone else. But his face was hard and blank as she'd described. "Give her the jacket?"

I nodded. Colin went back outside. I ran to the window, watching him go out the garden gate, then grabbed my own coat and left.

Even now, I can't clearly pinpoint all my motives for following Colin through the rain that afternoon. Or I can, but don't want to. I told myself I was doing it for Claire. That if this man was indeed sleeping with another grad student, she should know. I would help her through it, like the friend that I was. I would end it with Marcello, even. Let her have him.

It was easy to follow someone in Grifonia, just as it would be easy to hide. The narrow streets are long and sloped, so as to lend a view of the person at least a hundred yards ahead. And with the constant activity, it was easy to blend in. Colin went up toward the main piazza, then took a left into a smaller square, then another right. He never looked behind him, and certainly didn't seem nervous or act as if there was anything nefarious at all about his activity.

A ways down the hill, he stopped in front of an old but nicely renovated stone building and went in. It was a narrow town house, same as all the others on the *via* except that there was no laundry hanging from the window. The house was tall, with freshly painted shutters. There was no sign, simply a number on the building. I waited for a few minutes, then tried the door, which was open. I could hear voices upstairs.

I climbed up the stairs slowly and silently, looking behind me every few seconds. The second landing consisted of only a closed door. When I reached the third, I could see a plain white room through an open doorway, lit with fluorescent lights. There was a large circle of plain wooden chairs, all occupied by men—perhaps thirty or so, of all ages. They all held what looked like cheaply printed booklets in their hands and laps. One man was speaking, but then, he wasn't . . . it was more of a chant in a language I couldn't understand.

Latin, I realized after a moment.

Someone sneezed; another man was yawning. I spotted Colin not far away, his back to me, his coat tossed over a chair. The men continued to chant for a few minutes, then stopped. At the far end of the room, another man walked to the podium and opened a sheaf of old parchment. I thought something might happen, but again, he spoke monotonously in Latin. The men picked up their booklets again.

After a few more minutes the enormity of my intrusion overtook me. What if Colin found me spying on his Latin class? I turned and went down the stairs as quietly as I could. When I hit the second landing I began running. I didn't stop until I was blocks away, my crime safely behind me.

## *Agnese, 16th century AD*

Agnese was twenty-six and unmarried by choice. During her childhood, a bout of plague had struck Grifonia, and after losing a brother and cousins, she was no longer interested in forming an attachment.

With her father's money, Agnese started an apothecary particularly popular with the ladies. Throughout the day servants were sent to procure tinctures for monthly pains, ointments for aging skin, herbs for fertility. Even, it was said, for cutting pregnancies short.

In 1588, the papacy fueled an Inquisition, already rampant in Siena. In Rome, it was said, a witch had confessed without torture to the murder of thirty children and to sucking their blood. In Florence, fifteen witches had been tried and burned.

The Compagnia had been weakened by the plague. Many members were lost. The charter was now more than a thousand years old, and the mission was in question. Though some mercy killings were performed during the great illness, the practice grew too dangerous, as many of the Brothers contracted the disease themselves, only to be sequestered. The dead were too many in number to provide proper burials. Many of the members were wondering as to the point of the order at all.

Yet now, the witch hunt. Grifonia had a history of distrusting the papacy. The Compagnia, after several meetings, concurred that this hysteria was fueled solely by fools. They were rising again.

Agnese was the first turned over. The Compagnia would not be able to service the nine other girls burned in the next weeks, but Agnese's father was part of the order. With bribes, they got into her cell. She herself instructed the men in the mixing of the poison.

*Agnese Gagliardi, twenty-six years old, 16th century AD*

# 20

Claire's insistence on a double date continued. So, with some coaxing, an outing with Marcello and me was arranged.

I decided not to tell her about following Colin to his meeting. For one thing, I was embarrassed, and for another, all I had found out was that he was taking some sort of community seminar in Latin. She continued to complain about his odd absences, and I continued to reassure her with a certainty I didn't explain.

"But you'll come out?" she said. "You'll see if he's acting strange around me?"

"Of course."

Yet when I brought up the idea with Marcello, my own Italian boyfriend—or whatever I was supposed to call him—was less than enthusiastic.

"Why?" I asked, with somewhat guilty relish. "Don't you like her?"

We were naked in my bed, hiding from the dripping afternoon weather.

"Claire? Sure. Of course I like Claire."

"Because she's beautiful?"

"Devil, don't be crazy. Pretty, not pretty. It's all you talk about. We're all pretty."

"Well, then—"

"She's funny, that's it. Funny."

In the past weeks, our sex had become rougher. I was fairly sure Marcello still liked me, but in bed he was impersonal. Almost pornographic.

I'd made him milk tea, which he pushed away. Now I gripped the pillow I was holding over my chest.

"What does that mean, funny?"

"Devil, don't get jealous. She's a great girl. She comes down, you come down, we're all friends. You're funny, too."

"No I'm not."

"Oh you are. You don't know it. But trust me. Trust Marcello."

I scrunched down beneath the covers.

"I've barely even seen you lately."

"Devil, are we married? I'm busy. I have school. So do you. Anyway, I've seen you, out with your girls. Not Claire, the other girls."

"You did? Where?"

"I don't know about them. You know they are the drug girls, yes?"

"I'm just friends with them."

"Careful, Devil. They might be fooling you."

"They're not."

"How do you know?"

"I know them."

"All right." He put his arm around me. "Listen to this story, Angel. Okay?"

"Fine."

"My father. He always wanted to screw girls from America."

"What?"

"Just listen. I'm telling you a story."

"This is not starting well."

"Just listen. My father and his friends, they liked American girls. But the girls who came to Naples, they only wanted rich guys. Imagine it. Blondes from California. They drove my father crazy. He dreamed about their skin. Those girls, they'd taste like Coca-Cola. He knew it, Angel. Like those big lollipops swirled with pink. And they'd only sleep with assholes with money. It wasn't fair."

"Marcello . . ."

"So listen to what they did. Alone, they were poor. But they got together, six of them, and bought a Spider. The Fiat Spider, you know it? They got it used, fixed it up. Painted it. And they would take turns. They would go to the train station, one by one, maybe two at a time. They dressed up, looking rich. I think they even shared the clothes. These were guys who worked at the docks. They had nothing."

He looked at me. I waited.

"So at the station, they'd find a pretty American girl, or two. They'd go up to them on the platform and grab their bags. They'd say, 'Hey, don't take the train. I'll give you a ride. You and your friend.' "

"Would they now? And the girls said yes?"

"They were American," he said.

I shook my head.

"So the girls would go. They'd get into the car, with the top down, their hair blowing. And they would think, here I am with a rich Italian. And they would sleep with my father, or his friends. Whoever had the car that night. They all chipped in on hotel rooms, too, I think. And then in the morning, back to the train station. Boom. Goodbye girl. And then it was another boy's turn."

"That's so terrible, I can't even talk about it."

"Oh, Devil, don't be so shocked. Everyone had a good time."

"What is the point of this story, Marcello?"

"I forget." He blinked, thinking for a moment. "Oh, yes. I was talking about these girls. These friends of yours. I think they are pretending to be something they're not."

"I already know all about that. And I still like them."

"All right. Fine. Here's another point of the story: those girls who went with my father, they had a good time. They had a nice night in a hotel room in Italy. They went back to the train and kissed the Italian boy goodbye and thought, I just had a big adventure."

"But it was all lies."

"Why was it a lie, if they believed it? They went home to America, had babies, grew old. Told their daughters all about it."

I was silent for a moment, thinking of those blondes, their hair blowing in the wind from the sea.

"What happened to the car?" I asked.

"Tasmania, who the hell cares about the car?"

He hoisted himself out of bed, looking out the window. There was something decadent about looking at Marcello. His smooth belly, still brown from the sun, hanging above his hips; his penis, still somewhat erect, dangling from the dark sleek hair between his legs. He didn't crouch the way I did when I was naked. He just stood there, proud as a well-fed nobleman.

"It's a good story."

"It is."

"But, I have to ask. Why don't you want to go out with Claire and Colin?"

Marcello inspected his nails. "The guy is odd."

"You know him?"

"I've seen him. I know people who know him. His father is from a very old Grifonian family, and he is strange. Everyone knows it."

"Claire doesn't seem to."

"Well, *Claire*."

"Yes?"

"She likes everyone." He pulled on his jeans.

"Well, she really wants this, so let's do it."

"All right, Tabitha. For you."

I rested my head on my arm. I liked it when he said my name. And it felt nice, to be wrapped in a white sheet like that, watching my lover leave.

"Marcello, what color was the Spider?" I asked.

My neighbor leaned down and kissed my ear. "You're the girl in the car now, Devil," he whispered. "What color do you want it to be?"

•

Our outing was set for the last Saturday in October. We were to go to a concert. Before, this would have been a night reserved, without question, by Jenny. But now the B4 had all but fallen apart. Jenny was still the center of my social life, but we mostly went out alone. She made references to outings with Luka, yet as far as I knew, she and Anna were no longer speaking. Though going out with Jenny was akin to boarding the lead float of a parade, I missed our foursome. My afternoons, which before had brimmed with invitations and meetings, were now unbearably hollow. And it seemed unnecessary, the break. Jenny never mentioned Samuel, which meant, I assumed, that she had dropped him, too. And with class officially over, Professor Korloff had left town—after awarding me my A.

The day of our outing, Claire dragged me around town to assemble the perfect picnic. Bread from the baker near the university. Salami from the alley across from the cathedral. Two bottles of wine procured from two different *enotecas*, at least a mile away from each other.

"Claire, this is insane," I grumbled.

"And whiskey," she said. "I bet he'd like whiskey."

They were dizzying, her preparations, not to mention costly. When it came time, I helped her load the food into her backpack and walked with her through the winding alleys to the terraced park listed on the flyer she clutched in her hand.

Arriving before the boys, we spread out the blanket and waited. Once the music started, Claire smoked and scanned the park for Colin. He still hadn't arrived by the time the first song began, nor the second. She checked her phone, frowned, lit another cigarette. Marcello arrived, plopping down between us in his leather jacket, setting down a few beers. Claire gladly took the first one, drinking steadily until Colin finally came, unrepentant, swathed in a cashmere coat.

Claire couldn't stop touching her lover; she kissed him over and over, she played with his hair. Sometimes Colin winced a bit when she threw her arms around him. He didn't always respond to her, and once, when we were spreading out the blanket, he lightly shook her off. The expression on her face was so pained I had to look away. If she could have, I think she would have turned to smoke and poured herself into his body.

It was cold for an outdoor concert, but we soldiered on, huddling up under our blankets. I tried to concentrate on the music but my fingers were too frigid. Marcello, who hated silences, began teasing Claire about her Italian and about the bad music. She laughed, and I felt a rush of gratefulness as it was the first time I'd heard her giggle all day. Colin remained silent, watching the band.

After a while, I felt Claire elbow me.

"Taz," she said. "Are you going to try it?"

"Try what?"

She smiled and held forth what looked like a Communion wafer in her hand.

"Where'd you get that?"

"Ervin," Marcello said. "So?"

It was zanopane, that mysterious substance. I hesitated. The few drugs I had tried—marijuana, hash, a stray mushroom with one of my boyfriends back at Nottingham—had mostly just left me dizzy and nauseated. Claire liked to smoke marijuana in the house, always announcing, rather irritatingly, that she was about to smoke a *spinello.* Gia and Alessandra also indulged, but as far as I knew, the B4 avoided any of these drugs. They were all for alcohol, but drugs seemed not to fit in with their lifestyle, other than healthy sales.

Marcello turned to me.

"It'll be fine, Angel," he said, then parted my lips and put the wafer on my tongue.

As the bread dissolved in my mouth, I thought of how, one night, Professor Korloff spent the better part of an hour in our cozy little classroom musing about the drug use of the Greeks, Romans, and Etruscans. "Homer was all about opium," the professor told us. "What do you think nepenthe *was*? Drug of forgetfulness, my ass. Look at Telemachus when he visits Menelaus in Sparta. Helen doesn't want him to know what happened to Odysseus, so—boom! A little nepenthe, and he forgets his dad altogether. Oh sure, they were all into it. Marijuana, hash, mushrooms. Scholars don't like to dwell on it, but where do you think all those visions came from? Oh, I'm for it. Yes, yes. The more visions the better."

With zanopane there was no waiting for something to happen. The chemical seemed to travel immediately from the mouth to the rest of the body, then shot through from the top of the head to the ends of the feet. I can only describe it as a warm rush of absolute delight. My heart was bursting with the knowledge that everything in the world would eventually be all right—wars, politics, sickness, everything. Hunger would be solved, disease cured. I was surrounded by the best people in the world, people who utterly loved me and whom I loved back.

And the music! Before, the band had seemed irritatingly twangy, but now I understood that there was a great method to it, and that if I just listened, I mean, really *listened*, I would understand not only its patterns but also the patterns of the forbidden history in this place, of Arthur's precious Etruscans and the fallen lovers and magistrates and the rest of the secrets the dead had to offer.

We sat there, the four of us, holding hands, lost in our own thoughts for days. But it couldn't have been, because the music was still playing, and the other people were still around us on their own blankets. Finally Colin turned to the rest of us and said, in that authoritative way he had, "Let's go home."

And how did we *get* home? I couldn't tell you. Or I could tell you too much. Because this drug was not like the liquor constantly filtering through my bloodstream that fall, soaking my synapses, clouding my judgment. With zanopane, everything is sharper. Life's little confusions pulled away. I remember rising, being helped up by Colin while Marcello looked on. I gathered the blankets. In my hands, they turned into a handful of rabbits. Colin led us outside the park gate and put up his hand. In a moment, a chariot arrived, driven by my father, pulled by two sad-looking horses.

"I'm so happy to see you," I said.

He looked at me and smiled, the same smile he would give me when I was a little girl and we would all go together to the park. My mother, my aunt, Fiona, our cousins, and I. They were older, five, six, and horribly tempered. I would hang back with my parents while the others ran ahead, knocking things over and making trouble, and my father would pick me up and whisper: *Never tell anyone, little Tabitha, but you are the dearest, and I love you best.*

We all got in and he drove us up and up to our cottage, which someone had cleaned and decorated in a very fine manner, the way the Little Princess's cold garret had been transformed in that book about the orphan, which had always been Babs's favorite. Babs! There she was, handing me tea. She told me not to worry and went into the other room. Which was silly, because I wasn't worried—quite the opposite, in fact. But I was a bit tired, so I went to lie down on my bed, only it wasn't my bed but a bed in an apartment, which must have been Colin's. It was very spare and neat, with a map of ancient Grifonia, shelves and shelves of books, and a small set of knives in a glass case set into the wall.

"I hope you don't mind if I rest," I said to Colin, who was in the kitchen.

"We'll all rest," he said, bringing me water. "It was a long walk."

And then they got in bed beside me, all three of them, which was quite cozy, really, because even if you have a lot of money, it is hard to find a large bed in Umbria. No one told me that, it was just something I suddenly knew. I told Claire this and she laughed.

"Taz, you're the funniest person I know," she said.

"I'm not funny at all. I keep telling you all that."

She smiled and rubbed my foot. For some reason she was down at the bottom of the bed. Then Marcello kissed me. I was a bit embarrassed, having him kiss me right there in front of the others, but Claire was still rubbing my foot, so I supposed it was all right. But it wasn't my foot anymore, and was it Claire? I opened my eyes and I was kissing her, not Marcello, though he was there, next to me, watching, smiling.

This kiss was different from the other one, back in my bedroom. Freed by the zanopane, I pulled her close until we were matching—leg to leg, waist to waist, breast to breast. Perhaps it was supposed to be this way all along, Claire and I. *At last, at last.* Certainly I could begin to see how these things could be possible.

"You are a very nice person," I told her. Marcello laughed, because now he was the one I was kissing, and the balance was correct again. And then, growing tired, I rolled away to let the inevitable happen. This was my job; it was how I would come to understand. And I did. I did understand. It was all about balance, really. Love, friendship, life—all of it. Sometimes you are balanced, and everything is all right with the world. Other times you're not and everything goes off-kilter. When you're not balanced, you just have to wait it out, and the person you are kissing will move on and the right one will come back. It was about waiting. I knew that now.

We were moving toward something else, too—that warm, comforting blackness I'd happened upon on our trip to the tomb. I was there, running my hands over those walls, pressing my body against the sides of that magnificent underground palace, only it was all just the way it had been originally built. The murals on the walls were still bright, the carvings were still sharp, free of erosion and time. There were stone beds with pillows and blankets carved into each wall, along with wine pitchers, flutes, cups, even robes hanging next to the beds and slippers on the floor. The ceiling was grandly arched, and columns were carved into each corner. Chariots. Wrestling. On the far wall, a scene of a lively banquet, complete with music, men and women toasting, and cheetahs lounging on the floor. High above us all, near the ceiling, two griffins reared back, their lion's paws out, their beaks open to announce that this place was everything we needed, all of us. The Etruscans had built it, and now I would lead us. I would show us all how to travel unhindered to the next world.

# 21

I woke early the next day in my own bed, alone, fully clothed, the covers up to my chin, as if someone had tucked me in there. My phone was blinking with texts from Luka and Jenny and a message from my mother. For some reason, I couldn't read the clock. As I swung my feet to the ground, I was hit with a black wave of dread so enormous I fell back down again. Tentatively, I allowed myself to remember the evening before, and all at once the mood in the room changed into something evil. There was a roar, and the guilt took the shape of water, rising and dark. It came under the door, oozing. I shuddered, climbing to the head of the bed, but the slime continued to rise, until finally I called out for Marcello, Claire, Colin, anyone to help me.

The door flew open. It was Jenny, looking resplendent and chagrined.

"What on *earth*?"

"Oh!"

"What are you doing in bed? It's time for my cuppa, four-thirty. Though from the looks of things perhaps we should skip right to brandy."

I began to sob.

"What is it? Good Lord, Taz, I never thought I'd see tears out of you. Always so stoic. It isn't the neighbor? I told you not to put all your eggs into one cart."

"Basket."

"*You* are a basket. What the hell is going on?"

"We took zanopane last night and now I feel shitty beyond belief."

"You did what?" Jenny's voice was sharp with alarm.

"Zanopane. Marcello had it."

"I didn't sell to Marcello," Jenny said.

"No, no. It was someone named Ervin."

"Come on," she said, pulling me up. The movement caused the room to whirl. "Obviously he gave you the cheap stuff. You can die from that."

"I think I might vomit."

"Oh, you should. Into the shower," she said. "Go."

"I can't."

"You're shaking all over. Hasn't anyone told you about this stuff?" She grabbed my hand and led me to the living room, then with both hands placed me on the sofa, as if I were a rag doll. With great authority, she began bustling about the kitchen, boiling water and cutting bread.

"No food," I moaned. "I'm serious."

"Tabitha Deacon, listen to me. You have broken the B4 rules. You *know* that we never take drugs. It's our law."

I blinked. "Actually, I never heard that one."

"I know I've mentioned it. My God, between you and Anna, this is getting truly exhausting." Jenny slammed the teapot down. "Profiting from zanopane, or whatever, is one thing, That's just *smart*. Once you start dabbling in it, you're right in there with the rest of the idiots. Especially when you don't know if it's *decent*."

"I'm sorry, Jenny. All I can see right now are giant black ants crawling up the wall."

The toaster rang. She took the bread out, buttered it, and handed me a piece. "All right. Eat. Now."

"I can't."

"Do it."

Tentatively I nibbled at it, then gagged. It tasted like a mouthful of sand. When I started choking, she handed me a glass of water.

"All right, dearie, all right."

She sat down next to me and rubbed my back.

"You mean to tell me," I finally managed, "that you sell the stuff, but you've never taken it?"

"Of course we have," she said. "But I decided it was detrimental to us. Too many unfortunate incidents."

I moved away from her slightly. Something was flickering behind my left eye, a candle I'd forgotten to blow out.

"Jenny, why do we have to follow your rules?"

"You don't obviously. And look at Anna. She and I are in a huge row."

"I know. She's very angry with you."

Jenny sat next to me on the sofa, tucking her feet under her.

"Oh dear," she said. "You *do* look green. Now, Taz. It's best that you don't tell anyone—and I mean anyone—about your little experience."

"But I did it with three other people."

"Talk to them. They'll understand. It's for your safety."

"What is?" Claire said, emerging from her room. She was wearing only a towel, and her hair was a mass of tangles.

"Hello," Jenny said, barely looking over.

"Jenny! Long time. I'd hug you, but . . . you hate me. Also, I feel like I'm dying. Been puking all fucking day."

"Ugh." The vision brought bile to my own throat.

"I was just telling Taz here it would probably be best if you didn't spread it around—about your experience last night."

"Which one?"

Jenny raised her eyebrows and cleared her throat. "The zanopane, dear."

"Oh." Claire shuffled to the window, looking at the rain. "Why?"

"It's very easy to get a reputation as a user. If you're not careful you'll get all sorts of North Africans knocking on your door."

"Oh my God, you are the worst," Claire said. "A racist, too? Taz, are you kidding me?"

"I'm not a racist. I happen to know that there is a large population here of North Africans, Syrians, and Albanians who immigrate here from their . . . unfortunate situations. As you ought to know, people in unfortunate situations can get very, very desperate. If they find out you do drugs, they will do their best to *sell* you drugs. And frankly, girls, your neighborhood is not exactly the best."

"First of all, fuck you for making me argue with you while I'm in this state," Claire said, pouring herself some tea. "*But*. I stand by the fact that you *are* a fucking racist."

"You're missing the point, dear. You don't want the other dealers to know you."

"*Other* dealers?" Claire asked.

Jenny glared at Claire and pressed on. "Just do me this *one* favor and ask your boyfriends to keep it down about your night."

"Weird," Claire said. "But fine."

"And don't take it again. At least you, Taz. Look at you. You're a mess."

It was true. I couldn't even move.

"Do you promise?"

"I do," I said.

"Good," Jenny said. She sighed. "Then I'm going to find you something decent to wear. We're going for a walk."

"I—"

"No protesting." With that, she marched back to my room.

"I'm sorry," Claire said once she'd gone. "I didn't know Marcello brought it along. We'd been talking about taking it a few weeks ago, but I didn't know it would be last night."

"It's okay."

"Seems like Jenny's watching out for you. I still think she's a bitch, but at least she's doing that. About this drug thing, anyway."

"Oh, she always looks out for me."

"Taz, my friend," Claire said, resting her chin on my head. "When I believe that, I'll grow a pair of wings."

•

It took a day for my narcotic hangover to dissipate. By the next morning the hallucinations had subsided, but the feeling of unease remained. It was all I could do to lie flat and wade through my yet-unfinished novel of Ripley.

Once Tom had off'd Murchison, I decided to get out of the house. Anna wasn't answering my calls, but I expected that if I showed up, she'd talk to me. I missed her, especially in the wake of these very strange past few days. She was mercurial, but I liked her, possibly the best out of all the B4. It was sort of exciting, never knowing where one stood.

Though Luka had the most expensive flat, Anna's was the most interesting: a decrepit, dank palazzo cut up into high-ceilinged rooms with loft beds. Her bedroom was huge and grim, with exposed-stone walls, six-foot-tall windows, a brown tile floor, and a tiny, added-on bathroom with a drain that smelled of something beyond dead. A leak in the plumbing added a constant, ominous dripping sound. It was exactly the sort of room, in fact, where you'd expect a disgraced, penniless noblewoman to languish.

The palazzo had at least ten other rooms like Anna's and, at the end of a long, dark hallway, a bunker-like communal kitchen. The front door was locked, but all you had to do to enter was buzz or wait for someone to come in or out. No one ever asked me who I was or whom I was seeing. That morning, the heavy wooden door was pushed open by someone I actually knew— Ervin, the boy who sold Marcello the bad zanopane. I didn't respond when he greeted me, and continued on into the gloomy front hall. I was about to call Anna's name when I heard Luka's voice; her tone caused me to pause out of sight.

"You can't just *stop*. You know what she'll do."

"I don't believe it. If other people knew, she would face it all as well."

"No, Anna. She wasn't *there*, remember? We were the only ones—"

Just then, the sound of something clattering to the floor. "Fuck it!" I blinked in surprise. I'd never heard Anna swear before.

"You have to be reasonable, all right? It's not so very terrible, is it?"

"It *is*. It is. I'd rather die than keep on like this."

"Ah, the dramatics. You know, *I'm* the one who loved her."

"Which makes it all the more sick."

"Anna."

"It's true. That . . . *bitch* is ruining my *life*. Without Arthur I've got no one."

"You have us."

"God! I don't like *any* of you. I'm sick to death of you. Don't you know I'm a different sort of person? I sit in libraries, I pore over the minutiae of what Orpheus's last song to Eurydice might have sounded like. I hate your parties, your constant bloody boozing, your insipid conversations. No, I'm ending this. I'd rather just face it all than live this way."

"Anna—"

A door slammed behind me. I tiptoed backward into the flatmate who had just come in.

"Ciao!" I shouted too loudly, then, to the girl's confusion, turned around and stomped back toward Anna's room. "Anna!" I cried. "Annnnnna! Oh, *there* you are. Hello!"

Luka was standing over Anna, who was lying on the couch with her hand over her forehead. Both gave me looks of pure irritation.

"Please stop shouting," Luka grumbled.

I smiled brightly and pressed on.

"Listen, there's this guy who just came out of here who's quite sketchy. He must be dating one of your flatmates. I thought he was nice myself at first, but Jenny says he's no good."

"Dunno. Could be anyone," Luka said. "This place is a fucking brothel."

"Anyway. I was just walking this way, and I saw that pastry shop we like, and I thought—"

"I'm sorry, Taz," Anna said. Her face was a frightening shade of white. "I cannot possibly fathom going out today."

"I think it might lift your spirits. Besides, I want to talk to you. I had such an insane night with Claire. Did Jenny tell you?"

"If Jenny told me anything right now I'd—"

"She's in a bit of a mood," Luka said, cutting her off. "Better maybe to just leave her alone, Taz."

"You, too, Luka," Anna said. "I want you both to go."

"Just please don't do anything stupid," Luka said. "You know this affects both of us."

"What?" I asked. "I'm tired of being in the dark. What are you on about?"

"Just talking about the thing with Samuel and the idiot professor again," Luka said. "She's still upset."

"Will you both just *go*?" Anna exclaimed.

Luka turned and left, with me close on her heel. When we hit the street, she began walking so fast I practically had to jog to keep up with her.

"Luka! Can't you tell me what's wrong?"

Luka kept walking. "You don't want to know. If you're smart, you'll go have an adventure with your weird flatmate and forget this entire incident."

"I want to help."

"No you don't," Luka said. "You want to *know*."

"I—"

"That's what you've always wanted. To know what it's like on the inside. Because even though you are, you know you're *not*."

"I don't believe that," I said. "It's just that Anna is my friend, and she's in a bad way."

Luka pulled a chocolate bar out of her purse and handed me a piece. "Here's what you do, Taz," she said. "And I'm sorry I didn't tell you this before. You should cut us all off. Cozy up with that shady neighbor boy. Have a good time."

"What do you mean?"

"We're a bad lot, Tabitha. A nice girl like you doesn't need us around."

"I don't think you're a bad lot," I said. "I know all about you and I really don't. We're friends."

"You don't know anything," Luka said. "You see, we're just using you. You're basically just our translator. That's why Jenny always has you with her, why she sought you out. *We don't bloody speak Italian.*"

"But I'm not even that good at it."

"That's the best part. Keeps you in the dark. Also keeps it from being so obvious to the Grifonians."

"You *said* you liked me." The words sounded so forlorn, so pathetic.

Luka bit off another square.

"Yeah, well. Not really."

"You're lying. Something happened."

"None of us do, Tabitha. We *laugh* at you. The Irish poseur, trying to fit in. But you're just a weak little thing, aren't you? Following us around like a bloody shadow."

"Look, I'm going to walk on," I said. "But I have to say, you're being very strange. If there is something bothering you, I wish you'd just tell me. Perhaps I've hurt your feelings somehow."

"My feelings?" She looked at me, her big eyes barely open. Then she turned and, weaving slightly, disappeared down the street.

# 22

The next day—and years—was filled with clues that made themselves known, rearranged themselves, and faded in time with whomever was being accused at the moment. Almost as if we had all been playing a game in order to lead the police and the world down an endless array of paths. The answers were, in fact, there in the initial police report, though the story was infinitely complicated. The police wanted a snapshot, whereas the truth, as it often is, was more of a shadowy, ever-changing tableau.

But the belly of it, the real cause, was never mentioned or even asked about later. The thing I'm speaking of is hysteria. *Hysteria*, a condition diagnosed for thousands of years as a malfunction of the uterus. *Hysteria*, a word eventually used to describe the phenomenon of female sexual dysfunction. *Hysteria*, a term later morphing into a sort of split consciousness causing women to become unknowable. *Hysteria*, the sudden lack of reason that drives a person, or a group, to lose control over their actions. The medieval Catholic Inquisition and murder of witches—hysteria. And then, there was the hysteria I knew firsthand: a terrible, relentless tugging at the heart and mind that denies all reason.

I wish I had another word for it, but I don't. It's what it was. We were very young and the ground beneath our feet was shifting; the violence of our emotions was palpable. We didn't know our boundaries anymore, and the hysteria was building at an alarming speed. We all felt it and moved among one another in those last days warily as cats, knowing, I think, that soon one of us would, inevitably, be torn limb from limb.

•

All Hallows' Eve. A night Jenny and I prepared for with a keen eye for detail. We decided, after a Campari-soaked discussion, to be witches. Italians don't usually dress up on their own, but local entrepreneurs had long since been catering to the students by setting up makeshift costume shops. We bought pointy hats, capes, red dye, black eyeliner, green makeup. She'd boasted of a party at an Italian diplomat's apartment on the north side of the old city. Apparently, there was an indoor pool.

During the afternoon, I'd gone for a rare run down at the track, which was clogged with other students, mostly American. It was nearly dusk when I returned to the cottage. Upon opening the door, I paused: Gia was dressed in a lace bra, a long, tight white skirt, and a large white sunhat with a huge brim. Bright red blood dripped in lines down her face, her neck, and her chest. I turned to Alessandra for explanation, but her costume—an ancient granny nightgown, also splattered with blood—was no clearer.

Both of them were laughing.

"*Bella!* You must dress!"

"I am, I am. But what are *you*?"

"Bloody sexy," Gia said in English, clearly delighted by her own cleverness.

"That's very good, actually. And you?" I nodded at Alessandra.

"Bloody *nice*."

"Nice!" We all burst into giggles. "I think you've got it down."

Gia switched back to Italian. "It's not an Italian holiday, so we decided on English costumes."

"They're terrific."

"And you, *bella*? What are you? Sexy or nice?"

"Both?"

"The worst kind," Alessandra said. "You want to come out with us?"

I was honored: it was the first time they'd asked me to do anything social. "I have plans, actually, but I'll call you."

"Ah," Gia said, looking a bit relieved. "Good, good. With Marcello?"

"Partly." I hadn't actually seen him since our zanopane experience four days before. "Do we have any wine?"

"Too much," Gia said, pointing to the floor. Indeed, below the table was a plastic two-liter jug filled with red from around the corner. As sour as it was, I poured myself a tumbler and drank it down.

"Halloween!" Gia cried, delighted.

I went into my room to dress: black jeans, a tight black top, a long black cape. I painted my face green, rimmed my eyes with black, and lined my mouth and neck with fake blood.

The girls were still getting ready when I came out, listening to loud music, a mashup of Michael Jackson and the theme to *The Munsters*. I waved at them through the cigarette smoke and slipped out to go downstairs.

I stepped into the fresh air, pausing. The gate was wide open. There appeared to be a figure hunched by the lemon tree, but when I looked closer, I saw that it was just a bag of trash the boys had been too lazy to put in the bin. I could hear music and voices drifting up the garden.

I rolled my shoulders back and went down. Marcello hadn't called or even texted, despite leaving me in a drug-addled state alone in my bed. I opened the door with what I rather desperately hoped looked like confidence. The smoke was thick. A trio of Italian girls on the sofa, drinking and giggling, paused to give me a collective glance of appraisal. Alfonso was on a chair, a plump redhead with a welcoming set of breasts in his lap. To my great surprise, he was holding a pistol. The two of them were inspecting the barrel.

Marcello was in the corner, playing the guitar with what I now knew to be drug-induced intensity.

"Hi," I said, standing in front of him. He looked up, seeming genuinely frightened to see me.

"Devil," he said. "You look terrible."

"It's the point. Halloween."

"I don't believe in these costumes. But most of the girls are sexy witches, no? In bras and things. Garters. But you are a real green witch."

"It's just Jenny's idea."

"Oh yes. The girl who fools you."

"Oh, I don't think so." I sat on the arm of his chair. With his bearlike arms, he pulled me into his lap. "Marcello, why does Alfonso have a gun?"

"He's going to shoot Gia later."

"What?"

"Kidding. No bullets. He's just an idiot, trying to impress that girl. Did you hear that, Alfonso?" He shouted.

Alfonso ignored him.

"Idiot!" he repeated.

"It's creepy," I whispered.

"So is this green face."

"So are you coming out?"

"I don't think so. This night, it's just for foreigners. I don't like it much."

"You should come."

He looked at me. "I thought you might be feeling strange," he said.

"Why?"

"The other night, Tasmania."

"Oh. No. I mean, it was a stupid thing. I don't think we should do it again."

"Devil." He took my hand. "You know, we are not married."

A cold, familiar feeling began creeping through my chest. "You've said that before."

"So just because you won't do that again, doesn't mean I won't. Do you understand?"

"I know that. I guess. I mean, sure. You do what you want." I moved away slightly. There was a new distance between us. I could feel it.

"Because I thought it was fun. I thought we all thought it was fun."

"I got a little sick."

"I'm sorry." Marcello leaned over to grab the bong. "Don't drink too much tonight, then. Sometimes you girls drink too much."

"Isn't that what your father counted on? When he got the girls into the car?"

"All he needed was that car, Devil." He inhaled, then blew out the smoke. "You have fun tonight. You and those girls. Dance with some new boys, maybe."

"Dance?"

"And more, if you want. I'm trying to be nice to you. To tell you that I don't care. That it's all right for us to do these things."

"Well of course it's all right. It's more than all right. What did you think, you were my boyfriend?"

"Come on, Tabitha."

"It's just my year abroad, Marcello. You're acting like this means something to me. It doesn't. It's just a bit of fun. I'm seeing a lot of people. I have a lot of friends. I almost shagged a bloke in that castle. Really. You should know that."

Marcello shook his head. "Don't be angry, Taz. You are a nice girl. You live upstairs, I live down here. I will see you."

I looked over at the girls on the sofa. How silly I was. How silly we all were. Here I was, getting blown off again. And I'd thought, because of Sean and everything else, I'd be all right with it. That I'd be in front of it. But of course, you're never in front of the heart.

"I'm off," I said. "Oh, and also, fuck off."

"Devil, come on. We were all there. Devil?"

I was already out the door. As it closed, I could hear the redhead laughing at me.

## *Maria, 17th century AD*

Maria Mencaroni, twenty-four, a midwife much in demand. In order to cut pain, she sometimes used strong poppy tea, a secret kept between herself and her patients. Opiates had been popular and accepted among the Etruscans and the Greeks, but by 1647, this practice was long over, and it was frowned upon for women to use wine and liquor, much less opium. When one of Maria's patients remained drugged for a full day after the birth of her child, the baby went hungry for nursing. The father, a wealthy merchant, blamed Maria, a stonemason's daughter from the edge of the city. There was a swift trial for witchcraft overseen by a tired and hungry magistrate. Within twenty minutes, she was condemned to the cages that hung from the Palazzo di Priori, where criminals starved to death in plain sight.

It took a week for Maria to die. Her sisters visited every day, crying and praying. She shouted to them when she had the strength, but after the fifth day, she accepted her fate and merely lay there, suspended above the square. On the sixth day, the prisoners were checked on by the guards through lovely windows at the top of the Palazzo. If the prisoners failed to stir when poked with a barbed spear, they were taken down; if they were still breathing, the soldiers would finish the job.

Maria died on her own, her eyes open, her face turned up toward St. Francis of Assisi. Her body was then turned over to the Compagnia, which took it along with three others and, after saying a sacrament, placed the dead prisoners in the crypt under the church. When the crypts became full, the skeletons were moved to another, neighboring chamber, and when that, too, overflowed, the mixed bones and dust were taken to a field outside the town, thirty feet behind a restaurant on the road to Ripa, six miles from Grifonia.

*Maria Mencaroni, twenty-four years old, 17th century AD*

# 23

I didn't keep a journal in those days, but Claire did, one that was later grossly misinterpreted and pored over for clues that weren't there. In it, she wrote of me, and Alessandra, and Gia, and Colin, and Marcello. She wrote of our cottage, of the Swede she slept with "on a dare with myself." She wrote of being unable to concentrate on her homework because of her obsession with Colin's "eyes like endless sparkling pools." She never wrote anything negative, never a word about people she didn't like. Jenny, for instance, was never mentioned. And a few times, next to my name, she drew a heart and a flower with a purple pen, just as Babs and I had done when we were little girls.

Those who read the diary during her interrogations tried to find something sinister in those hearts, something dark and sexual. *Killed out of obsession*, the Italians wrote in their spectacular tabloids about me. *Killed out of revenge.* The journal, of course, was good as smoke. Claire was in love with the same person as I was. This was true. And we were doubtlessly in love with each other. But she wasn't a killer. Or she could have been, I suppose. But not without help.

•

Heeding Jenny's last-minute text invitation, I met her at Pizza Bella. I could have told her about Marcello, but I didn't want to talk about it. Anyway, somewhat appropriately, the mood was a somber one. Jenny wasn't at a table drinking wine, but instead outside, shivering in line. Luka was also there, a fact that made me less than thrilled after our last conversation.

"No inside track tonight?" I asked.

"Different bloke than usual," Luka said, though to me, he looked like the same man she'd always bribed before with perfect success.

"All right."

"Listen—sorry about the other day. What I said. I was bloody hungover and in a pissy mood."

"It's okay."

"What are you talking about?" Jenny asked. "You're sorry about what?"

"I was a bit of a bitch. What else is new?"

"Luka, you must watch yourself," Jenny said.

Everything felt off. I longed for a glass of wine.

"And, Taz, what's with this blood on your face?"

"I was trying to be scary."

Jenny laughed, looking anything but in the low-cut black dress she wore under her cape. Her hair was blown out to perfection and she had forgone the green paint we'd bought together for a full face of proper makeup. "The point's to *attract* men, not frighten them away."

"Fine. I messed up. Again. Are we still going to this party, then? With the indoor pool?"

"'Fraid not. Lost the connection I had to the host."

"How?" This had never happened before.

"The guy just isn't going," she said impatiently.

The line moved quickly, but being a regular customer wasn't nearly so pleasant as our former VIP status. We were served as slowly as anyone else in the place, and the waiter seemed to hover ominously throughout the meal, ready to shove us out as soon as the plates were cleared. Finishing too early to move on to the Red Lion properly, we sat on the cathedral steps, taking sips from Luka's flask in the cold. I kept waiting for Jenny to make a joke about slumming it with the other students, but she was uncharacteristically silent. Or perhaps it was Luka's mood, grim to the point of suffocation, keeping any sense of lightness at bay.

"Any news of Samuel?" I asked, for want of anything else to talk about.

"Over it. Bored me stiff."

"Oh. That's too bad."

"From what I heard, the boredom was all his," Luka said. "Did he ever call?"

Jenny swiveled sharply. "You know, you and Anna are really trying my patience, Luka."

"Oh, *I'm* sorry."

"What is it, love? Might as well get it out."

"I'm fucking bored, is it," she said. "Same as Anna. We've *served* our time on this ridiculous venture, Jenny. We don't need to go out together all the time. Or anymore, period, since you're stopping things."

"I'm not stopping forever. Just until she calms down."

"I'm just sick of it. I want to do what *I* want. I need to go to Rome, take a painting class. I need to meet some new people. We're here, in the most amazing place in the world, but we're stuck being your window dressing. You know, Ben and his friends at Samuel's were fun. Smart. We could have had a hell of a time in Rome with those blokes, but you mucked it up. You said it was all going to be fabulous, but you know what? It's a prison."

"You can go to Rome," Jenny said. "I don't need you." She twirled a piece of wheat-colored hair around her finger. "You're just sitting on me, that's all. To make sure I won't say certain things. Because if I did, what would happen, Luka?"

Luka didn't reply.

"That's right. If I talk about what happened to your girlfriend, it wouldn't go so well, would it? Not that I would. I'm not usually like that. But I get sloppy, don't I? Talky. That's what you and Anna are worried about, isn't it?"

"Of course it's what we're fucking worried about."

I sat hunkered in my cape, still as a stone.

"I never would. But then, I couldn't live with it either. Not with what you lot did."

"We didn't do anything."

"That's right. And it's the worst part. That's not staying in front of it. That's just . . . meanness. Or is it murder? I can't decide."

Luka looked at me. "Jenny, stop it."

"Oh Taz doesn't know. She doesn't care. She's sweet as pie. No, I think it's your guilt keeping you here, Luka. After it all happened I said I was still going, and you both rushed over to Italy to be with me. Not because it would be fun. Not that. You came to keep me quiet. You think I don't know that? I never said I would tell. Never. But I do like to have a drink and talk. Yes I do."

I glanced at Luka, who was crying, big tears hitting the ground.

"It's Anna you have to worry about, right now. Not me."

"I know."

"Why don't you go home, love. You look terrible. We'll talk about it all later."

"Yeah."

Luka looked at me again, her eyes red and lost, then retreated into the crowd. Jenny and I remained there for a while, sipping from the flask. After half an hour, I finally got up the gumption to talk.

"Can I ask?"

"It's not important."

"You said murder," I said, carefully.

"Figure of speech, love. Just an old girlfriend of hers. You know how she can be about it. She's fucking gay, and can't just go with it."

I knew Jenny was lying. She was never sloppy. Ever. Never said a word she hadn't calculated and planned. But I was freezing and knew she wouldn't tell me anything else.

"Shall we go?"

"Why not?" I said.

We marched together, arm in arm. I tried to shake off the heaviness of Luka's outburst, but something was just different—I could tell as soon as we entered the bar. Usually when we walked in there was a feeling of the seas parting. Now people just looked at us and then went back to their conversations. We were ordinary now, simply two girls in trampy costumes swallowed by the crowd.

"Know anyone here?"

"No."

Just then the Belgian girl with the frizzy curls who I'd met at the start of the semester spotted us. I almost didn't recognize her; she was pale as a sheet and must have lost upwards of fifteen pounds. Who loses weight *in Italy*? I wondered. To my surprise, she tapped Jenny's bare, glitter-painted shoulder.

"Hey," she said. "You going to the lake soon?"

"Certainly not," Jenny said. "The weather's rotten. Probably not for a couple of weeks."

"A couple of *weeks*?" The girl's bloodshot eyes darted back and forth. "Is anyone *else* going?"

"I don't know."

"That's total bullshit. I paid you and you said—"

"Calm. Down." Jenny spit out the words.

"Sorry," she said, glancing at me. "Well, if you *do* go, will you call me? Right away? All right?"

Jenny gave the girl a final glare that sent her scuttling away.

"Jenny, what is going on?"

Jenny raised her hand to hail the barman. "I'm taking a break from the business until I see what happens with Anna. She's a live wire right now, and personally, I don't want to go to Italian prison."

"That girl seemed pretty keen on getting her supply, I suppose."

"Well, she's paid for it." The barman slid Jenny a drink over the bar. "Liston, I hate to ask, but do you have any money for that pizza?"

"Of course." I tried not to sound surprised, though I almost never carried much money with me anymore, as everything was always taken care of. I reached into my pocket and pulled out twenty euros.

"Wouldn't mind a bit extra if you can spare it."

"Sure." I handed her another twenty.

"Thanks," she said. "God, this is a miserable place. Let's make the best of it, then. Have some shots and dance."

I obliged. There was something particularly awful about the Red Lion that evening. Perhaps it was the crush of girls baring too much cleavage in their cat and barmaid costumes, or the ghoulish rubber masks the boys had bought in haste from the makeshift Halloween shops lining the piazza. The dancing was savage, the music grating, the stink of bodies thick in the pillowy air.

"I'm going to stand on the side for a while," I shouted at Jenny, who had surrendered to dancing with some fat werewolves. She pointed to her ear to indicate that there was no way she could hear me. I moved to the bar to watch.

"Hey." Claire was standing beside me, in jeans and a T-shirt, and a spider drawn on her face with black eyeliner, smudged. "You look awesomely terrifying."

"Yes, I mistook the point of the evening, I'm afraid."

"No, it's great. All the zombies will want you, bad."

"Where's Colin?" I asked.

Claire shook her head, unable to speak for a moment. "Home," she finally muttered. "He hates this place."

"I sort of do, too, really."

"Oh, it's okay. Cheap drinks, music. I kind of like it. Are your girls here?"

"Jenny's over there. With some wolves."

"Appropriate." Claire crossed her arms, looking at the dancers. "What a shitty night."

"Why?"

"Colin. He's doing . . . that thing. Pulling a fade. Not that he's not always aloof. He's quiet, you know. But he's shutting me out."

"Marcello isn't being so terrific either. Just told me I could go make out with someone else. Thanks a lot."

"There's nothing worse," Claire said, as if she hadn't heard me. "You think you have someone, you know? You really have them. That you're on the same page with each other. That you like each other the same amount."

"You said love the other day."

"That was stupid of me." Claire gave me a look and took a drink. "I guess he's just a little freaked out about the other night."

"Oh? I thought the two of you might have done that before."

"Why the hell would you think that?" Claire's tone was sharp. I turned to study her face.

"Well, because you had no qualms taking it, Claire."

"Oh, the *zanopane*."

It happened in a single instant, a fluid chain of expressions moving like quicksilver over her features. Her complete openness—it was always her downfall. That clean, lovely face transmitted what she was thinking with such precision and vitality, she may as well have been an artist's canvas, waiting to be colored and shaped.

"Why?" I asked slowly. "What did you think I meant?"

She looked back at the churning dance floor. "That. The zanopane is what I thought you meant."

"You know, the first day you said it. You made the rule, when I said your bloody hair looked nice. *No lying*, you said. So what is it?"

She looked at me, stricken. "Oh, fuck. Taz."

"What?"

"I knew you were being too easy about it. I told Marcello so yesterday."

"Why did you see Marcello yesterday?"

"He came to see me at the bar. He—well. He wanted to talk to me."

"About?"

"So you really don't remember."

"Remember?"

"Shit, Taz, you were right fucking *there*."

I stepped back. She was wrong—of course I remembered. My ear ringing where my hand was pressing against it, propped up as I was on my elbow. Colin in a white shirt and khaki corduroys, sitting up with his arms wrapped loosely around his knees. I remember the texture of the pants. I wanted to touch them, but I couldn't because of the legs between us. We were watching them, Claire and Marcello. Her ankles around his large brown back. Both of them naked, their skin pressed together, the smacking of their hips. Claire's head turned toward Colin, Marcello's eyes rolled upward in pleasure, the whites almost blue.

"Taz—"

Claire could not, *could not stop talking.*

"I'm so so fucking sorry. It wasn't even that—well. I only did it because I thought Colin wanted me to. I thought it might get him interested again, so he'd let me *in* a little. It sounds weird, to do that for someone, but he's been so . . ."

"He's been *what*?"

"The afternoons. I told you. He sees someone else. I just wanted him to like me enough to—"

"It's just Latin class!" I shouted.

"How do you—"

"You wanted to make him *like* you?"

She grabbed my arms, pleading. "You know what it's like, don't you, Taz? When the other person just makes you . . . I don't know. *Insane*. Colin was so into me at first, but he's been distracted, and it kills me. It really does. I can't even *sleep*, Taz. You know? I feel like I'm going fucking nuts."

"Don't." I pulled away from her. I didn't want her touching me.

"Taz! I mean, it's not like you didn't know. Or I *thought* you did. I mean, you were there, just . . . smiling at us . . ."

I was physically hit only once in my life. When I was six, I put on a velvet top that my sister had gotten as a present. It was a white off-the-shoulder thing. Then I got into her makeup and painted my face. Bronzer dripped all over the shirt, staining it a muddy color. When my sister walked in, she didn't say anything; she just balled up her fist and hit me in the stomach as hard as she could. This felt the same way: a fistful of knuckles in a six-year-old gut.

"You don't even seem to like him, Taz. Marcello. Really, it's impossible to know *what* you like. If I'd thought you really would have been hurt, I wouldn't have . . . Oh, Taz. I love you so much, I really do. I'm so sorry. *You're* the one who really fucking matters to me. I'd tell them *both* to fuck off if you wanted me to. Taz, say something. Taz?"

"I'm surprised," I said finally. "That's all, all right? I didn't remember, and I'm a little surprised."

"Do you remember the other things that happened?" Claire asked.

I paused. "I remember kissing you."

"Yeah, you did." Her hands were still on my elbows. She released them. "But that's all we did."

"And then?"

"And then you rolled over and watched, and Marcello started to take off my clothes and I looked at Colin and . . . whatever. You and Colin watched. Both of you did. I guess I thought you were into it."

"I don't think so."

"But maybe you were, though." She stepped closer to me. I could smell the rum on her breath.

I shook my head. "Don't be sick, Claire. This isn't my fault. No wonder Colin isn't with you today."

"That's pretty bitchy, Taz."

"It could be true, though."

"So you are pissed."

"I guess I am." I wasn't certain if this was true. Now that I remembered it, Claire and Marcello writhing there, anger wasn't the exact emotion that came to mind.

"Fuck," Claire said. "I'm sorry, Taz. I don't give a shit about Marcello. This all went the wrong way. I just—"

"What's happening?" Jenny had glided up through the shadows. "Oh, hello Claire. What sort of costume is that? A Graham Greene thing? The Ugly American? Oh, I'm hilarious. Hold up. Tabitha, why are you crying?"

I didn't answer. Instead I left them both and ran outside.

It was happening, after all. Change. A new need sprung forth that night, honest and bleeding. The desire to feel everything, no matter how awful. And so, despite Claire and Jenny's cries from the bar doorway, I ran straight into the middle of the piazza. I joined the great warriors there, looking skyward.

*You want me to fuck you now?*

*Finally, finally.*

It was raining, coming down in sheets, and for once I stood right in it. For the first time in my life, I allowed myself to get truly drenched.

# 24

The last morning, I woke clear-minded and rested at eleven. A hangover eluded me. I was tired, but nothing more. My phone was blinking with voice mails and texts; all of those voices closing in, yet the one person I wanted to hear from was missing.

Anna. Where *was* she? If anyone could make sense of all these silly, girlish emotions, I thought, certainly she could.

Thankfully, the house was empty. Alessandra and Gia had left in the early morning for their parents' for the holiday; both left sweet notes saying goodbye. Claire, no doubt, was hiding from me at Colin's house. Or perhaps she was downstairs at Marcello's? I didn't care. Or I did, but . . . what the hell.

I showered, scrubbing the green makeup off my face, then dressed warmly in a wool jumper and jeans. After a quick scramble up the stairs to the café, I had a cappuccino, then another, and climbed up the hill to Anna's flat.

The double dose of caffeine had unfortunate effects. By the time I got to Anna's, I was dripping with sweat. I waited for ten minutes, but it was apparently too early for any front door comings or goings, so finally I pressed my finger on the bell.

There was still no answer even after a full minute, so I buzzed again. Nothing. Finally, on the fifth ring, a cautious "*Sì?*"

"Is Anna here?"

I was answered with only a blank crackle over the intercom. I buzzed again, then knocked. When ten more minutes passed, I pounded relentlessly, slapping the door. By the time someone finally came—an Italian flatmate I recognized but whose name I didn't know—my hands were bloodless and smarting.

"Anna is not here," the girl said. "The old man took her."

"The old man? Who?"

"The man. The English man."

"What are you talking about?" I felt like shaking her. A roar rose in my ears.

"I told you, the English—"

In my pocket, my phone began vibrating. I picked it up and saw it was a London number.

"He said she wouldn't be back," the girl said. "That they are going to England. Do you think we can have her clothes?"

"No! Just a moment . . ." I turned away. "Hello?"

"Tabitha Deacon?"

"Yes?"

"This is Arthur Korloff."

"Oh!" The flatmate shut the door and locked it again. "I'm so glad you called. Anna's—"

"With me."

"Ah." The panic receded. "I see."

"I need to meet with you."

"In London?"

"Of course not. I flew in to Grifonia last night."

"What? Why?"

"I received a call that Anna was in trouble. So I came."

"A call? What sort of call?"

"Meet me at the main university building, in that concert hall. It's usually open at this hour for kids who want to practice, but no one ever goes."

"When?"

"Right away. We'll be taking a train as soon as possible. As soon as she's fit to travel."

The pounding was back. "All right."

"Come now, Tabitha. As in, *right* now."

He hung up. I left Anna's house, walking quickly down the street, past the building I'd followed Colin into that day, then down to the school. The college was crawling with students headed to their midday classes; I thought sheepishly of the ones I'd been skipping. The main concert hall was open. I sat in front of the mural, looking at the stony faces of those noble laborers carrying those huge blocks of stone. After a few minutes, the door slammed behind me. Professor Korloff walked to the very front of the concert hall with his satchel, took a seat on the stage, feet dangling off the side, and lit up.

"Hello again," I said.

"Tabitha." Professor Korloff was dressed up today in a blue suit, though he still wore trainers. "Well. I knew you girls were bad for Anna, but this is a whole new level."

"I'm sorry?"

He looked at me over his glasses and blew out the smoke. "Jenny called me yesterday. Not that I'm her biggest fan, after what she pulled at Samuel's house."

"And?"

"She said . . ." The professor took a breath. "She said that Anna was selling drugs. And using them. And on the verge of getting herself either arrested or killed."

I sat down heavily in one of the wooden seats. "I'm sorry, but I just don't know how that could be true."

"No?"

"I've never seen Anna take anything. Ever."

"Well. She was out of her mind this morning on something. How do you explain that?"

"I—"

"And all the bags of coke? And heroin? And those wafers? Don't think I don't know acid when I see it. Found them all under her bed. Explain that."

"Look, why would you think I have something to do with all of this?"

"Because," he said, "you're the Persephone."

"What?"

"You have those eyes. As if you were *meant* for . . . I don't know. Subterfuge. You seem sweet, but it's impossible to know what's going on in there. Has anyone ever told you that?"

"No," I lied. Lots of people had told me that.

"Jenny called me yesterday, saying she was worried. Anna had been acting erratically, she said. Getting high, disappearing to other countries for weekends."

"Look, I'm sorry. I've just never seen Anna high. And she never goes *anywhere*. Our other friend Luka does, but—"

"Well, Jenny went through Anna's things because she wanted to know what the hell was going on. And boom, a huge stash."

"Professor Korloff " I paused, shaken by the enormity of Jenny's lies. "Maybe it's not hers."

"That, frankly, is very hard for me to believe." Seized all of a sudden by a wracking cough, he sat back for a moment, recovering, then threw his cigarette onto the floor.

"All right. This meeting has been amazingly useless. Tomorrow, as soon as she's sober, or as sober as she can be, I'm taking her by train to Rome and then to London. I'll check her into a quiet, low-profile rehab facility and she can forget about all of this."

"But she's not a drug addict."

"Really? Because she told me she's ready to go. *Get me the hell out of here* were her exact words. And when I found the . . . products, she admitted the whole thing. She's been selling."

"With who?"

"She didn't say. But I have a guess."

"I swear it's not me."

"Well, of course. If you swear."

I sighed. "Where is she? I need to talk to her."

"I don't think that's particularly wise."

"Professor Korloff, Anna really is my friend. I would like to at least say goodbye."

The professor looked at me. "I put her in a room at the Nysa. It's expensive but I needed discretion. Also, coming down from whatever she's on will be uncomfortable, so I thought the nice room would help."

I picked up my bag and started for the door.

"One moment," Professor Korloff said.

"Yes?"

"I need you to deal with these drugs."

"Deal with them?"

"Get rid of them."

"I'm sorry. I—I wouldn't know the first thing about how to do that."

Professor Korloff looked at me for a moment, then got up and rushed toward me. He leaned over and shook me roughly by the shoulders.

"Stop lying to me!" he growled. "Grow up, Tabitha! All right? Fix your fucking mess!"

"I'm not lying. This whole time, I've never lied."

The professor released me. He paused, straightened his clothes, then walked to the satchel he'd brought in and held it up. "It's all in here. Take it somewhere."

I took the bag. It was heavy, significant. As if there were a head inside. Reluctantly, I pulled the strap over my shoulder.

"You know, this all used to mean something," he said, gesturing with disgust at the sack. "Girls who went abroad, they were breaking out. It was a sexual revolution. They were . . . tearing at ropes tied by their brothers and fathers. When a girl fucked you, she was fucking the *system*." He ran his hand over his thin, delicate hair. "The Italian girls had to cover themselves all the time, you know, for religious reasons. So you know what they did? They wore these long white dresses, and then put on these black bras and panties, so we could see them through their clothes. Jesus, it *killed* us." He shook his head. "And the drugs! They were a symbol. By getting high, you were getting away from the establishment. You girls, you have no idea why you're in Italy or what you're doing. You could be in your own living room. You just like that the colors on the walls are different."

"That's not true."

"Is it? Why are you here? Why did you even come here at all?"

I hesitated. "To be someone . . . different from who I was."

"Different." He looked at me. "You girls have everything. Education. Money. Study and work, and you'll get any job you want. We *smashed* those glass ceilings for you, baby. And you want to be something different?"

I looked at the professor. His used-up face, his withered hands.

"I think it's the wanting," I said, finally. "It doesn't matter when it is or who we are. The wanting never stops."

Professor Korloff had no reply to this.

"All right," he said, after a moment. "So now, voilà, you got what you wanted. You're *different*. Just get this crap away from my goddaughter."

"Okay." I felt myself physically drain, as if someone had pulled out a stopper in a tub. "But I'm going to the hotel to say goodbye. You don't believe me, but I didn't have anything to do with her trouble."

"Then who did?"

I hesitated. The answer was obvious, but the fact was that I was still in love with the idea of Jenny and Luka. "I don't know."

Professor Korloff waved his arm at me, as if shooing me away. "You know what? I don't give a shit. I just need to get Anna out of here."

"Where is she?"

"Room 406." He looked so tired then. And sad. "Just knock. She's completely fried. Jesus, she'll probably let you right in."

•

Given the staggeringly high prices of its rooms, the security at Hotel Nysa isn't exactly top-notch. I breezed past the front desk, took the elevator to the fourth floor, and knocked. When there was no answer, I went back downstairs and told them, in Italian, that I was Anna Grafton's sister. Without comment, they handed me a key.

I opened the door slowly. Anna was on the bed, eyes wide, watching television. She didn't even look over at me.

"Anna?"

She nodded, her eyes still on the screen. Encouraged, I stepped into the room.

"Are you all right?"

Another nod.

"How are you? I haven't seen you in forever."

Anna swiveled her head at me, her eyes loose.

"Oh, Mum," she said. "I'm so sorry."

"What?"

"I'm feeling under the weather, and Ginger's foot is off. Can't we ride another day?"

"Anna. It's Taz."

"Oh!" She got up and beamed, as if I had just come in. "Where have *you* been?"

"At home. Well, around. Listen, how high are you?"

She laughed. "Kiss me, you fool."

"Zanopane?"

"What? Never. Jenny would never let us."

"You sure?"

"Nasty stuff. And the thing with Eleanor was so *frightful*."

I looked at her closely. Maybe she was sober after all?

"Would you like to—"

"I told you, I don't *want* to go riding. Stop making me do these things I don't want to *do*." She threw herself on the bed again.

"Okay, Anna. Who gave you the—"

"I'm sorry about Julian, Mummy. It just started happening, you see. For a long time. And then one night I climbed into his bed, you see, and . . ."

"Stop," I said. "Don't tell me."

She nodded, frowning as if perplexed. "Luka was right. We should have done this ages ago."

"Luka? Did Luka take it, too?"

"Of course. Coffee and wafers. She came over this morning. She's over there." Anna gestured at the empty corner. "Oh. I suppose not."

"Anna." I sat on the bed. "It's going to be okay."

"Of course it is. Arthur's rescuing me. King Arthur! He went out for the banquet meat. Hunting the boar."

"He says he's taking you away."

"Yes, getting me *out* of this mess. Messy messy, messy mess." She laughed, then looked at me and paled.

"Eleanor?"

"No, Anna. No. See? I'm Taz."

Anna shot up off the bed, looking down at me with terror. "Eleanor, I'm so sorry. We didn't know how . . . how bad off you *were*."

"Anna—"

"I would have called the doctor. I thought you were sleeping. Eleanor—"

I rushed over and grabbed her arms. "Anna, calm down."

She screamed now and jerked wildly. "Oh, *God*. The shades. Shit. *Shit*. I'm so sorry, Eleanor."

I backed away, unable to speak. She looked up at me and grabbed my hands.

"El, you must tell me."

"Tell you what?"

"Tantalus. Is he *there*?"

"I can't—"

"Is he?"

"I . . ." There was no reasoning with her.

"Is he desperate?"

"Wouldn't *you* be?" I asked.

Anna put her head in her hands. "I don't know. What's going to happen?"

"Anna, I've got to go." I didn't really have to leave, but she was scaring me. "I'll call you tonight. I promise."

"You do? You swear it?"

"I swear."

I led her to the bed and tucked her in tightly. Then I took the bag, tiptoed out, and shut the door.

## *Eleanor, 21st century AD*

The others weren't tempted to try it. They knew what it was, where it came from. But Eleanor always prided herself on her democratic sensibility. Before she got involved, it only seemed right, sampling the product.

She didn't know that she'd been born with only three heart chambers. She'd always breathed a little heavily, but it was . . . nice, really. It gave her voice a throaty quality that boys adored. Killed any interest in athletics. Anyway, she was slight, so she attributed it to that. "Eleanor!" the other girls trilled admiringly. The waif with a hollow leg. She loved her drink, and had no trouble keeping up with the others in that sport. Jenny Cole said she was the best weekend companion she knew.

When assembling her group, Jenny forbade them all to take it, ever. But Eleanor wasn't going to take orders like the others did. Anna was all over the place. She needed managing. And though Eleanor was enjoying the fling she was having with Luka, the girl was a drunk. No, Eleanor had a mind of her own, which is why before going out one night, she took a wafer alone in her room.

Anna and Luka came into the room a little while after. It could have been minutes, it could have been hours. The high was maddening. Eleanor knew something was wrong. Her heart was crawling out of her chest. Still she could hear them. She knew they were there. She heard Luka shout.

Darling, did you—

Of course she did. Bloody idiot.

Anna, she's blue! Call an ambulance!

We've got to get it all out of here first. They'll look everywhere.

But—

She hardly wants to go to prison, Luka. Whatever her state.

Their voices faded. The organ, which she could feel swelling against her skin, strained and burst. She heard the sick popping sound, felt it go limp, felt the air whistle out of her body. Eleanor was drowning. She reached for the others, but they weren't there, weren't there.

The girls came back in, panting.
Oh my God, oh God, is she—
No no no no no—

*Eleanor Peterfield, twenty-one years old, 21st century AD*

# 25

When I walked outside, the afternoon was already waning. Even though the satchel weighed at least a stone, I ran the entire way to the farm. A couple of cars passed me, but no one looked twice, as I must have looked like a schoolgirl returning home for her mother's evening meal. The windows in the houses were all shut; I could see slices of light glowing inside the latched shutters.

The farmer's house was dark, and his truck was gone. My hands were trembling, but I didn't slow down until I was at the tomb behind the old stable. Taking baby steps, I inched down the ramp until I was in the main chamber. The darkness was, if possible, even more all-encompassing than before. Strangely, though, I wasn't frightened.

*Perhaps that zanopane is still in my system after all*, I thought.

I thought I heard something scuffle in one of the corners. Certainly just a drip of moisture from the weather outside, but it was enough to remind me that I was sitting alone in a tomb that almost no one knew about. The fear that was missing before now flooded in, filling my belly with panic. I dropped the bag onto the ground and pushed it under the stone bench in one of the old side chambers, then turned and ran out of that desecrated place, back into the comparatively blinding light of the late afternoon.

It was four-thirty when I arrived home, and, to my relief, no one was there. I was filthy, so I took a quick shower and changed into jeans, an athletic jacket, and trainers, then picked up the phone and called Luka, who, of course, didn't answer. I tried Jenny as well but she, too, failed to pick up. I had class to attend at five-thirty, but knew I was too worked up to sit in front of my art history professor's slide projector. Instead, I wrapped my scarf around my neck and rushed outside, then threw myself into a search of Jenny's usual haunts.

Most of the bars were empty, save for students drinking the late afternoon hours away. Had they skipped town, I wondered? Fleeing to Rome, Paris, or home? Finally, as a last effort, I went to the Club and leaned on the bell. To my surprise, Luka greeted me politely over the crackling speakerphone and an instant later, buzzed me in.

I slipped into the room, ruddy and damp. Jenny was sipping a glass of white wine; Luka had draped herself over the couch, an empty tumbler perched on her knee. Neither looked surprised or pleased to see me.

"Hello, dearest," Jenny said wearily. "We've got a pizza in the oven. Looks fairly disgusting, but we're trying to budget."

"Drink?" Luka said.

I sat on the windowsill, catching my breath. For one moment, I wondered if it all might be a mistake.

"I saw Anna earlier," I said. "Have you spoken to her?"

"Of course not," Jenny said.

"What do you mean?"

"After going through all this trouble to get her home," Jenny said, "why would I call her now?"

I gripped the sill, leaning against the cold window.

"So you did call Arthur. And told him . . . what did you tell him?"

In a swift, graceful manner only a certain type of woman can pull off, Jenny sat up, finished her full glass of wine, and placed the vessel delicately beside her.

"Luka," she said, patting her chest delicately. "Do you mind going out for some more of that Montefalco?"

"Well . . . normally, I'd tell you to fuck off. But."

"Yes, exactly." Jenny smiled.

"All right. I'll be back." Luka looked at me, then bundled up laboriously and clattered loudly out the door.

Jenny rose and crossed over to the kitchen. She pulled down an empty glass for me and poured us both drinks.

"All right, Taz. First, just hear the story. It's not as bad as you think." She smiled and pushed the wine toward me.

"Okay," I said. I took the glass and settled into one of Luka's overstuffed chairs, as if Jenny and I were about to settle into one of our intimate gossip sessions. For a fleeting moment, I again rode that bubble of hope that all of this was a mistake. "So?"

Jenny installed herself on the sofa. "I'm sure you've seen how Anna's been acting."

"She's been really upset."

"Upset and unreasonable. Having an awful time. I kept encouraging her just to go home, but she wouldn't. She's unstable, Taz. A bit ill in the head, poor girl. So I had to solve the problem."

I looked at my wine, which seemed darker than it should have been. Burnished. "It seems to me you could have just called her mother."

"Too complicated. There was that ugly thing with her mum, you see. Hard to get over, when your daughter sleeps with your husband. Excusable as it is, with her horrible childhood. Poor girl watched her father suffocate. Lung cancer, you know."

"I didn't." I could hear a rumbling nearby. Thunder? Maybe a sweeper, cleaning the street. Two pigeons huddled on the iron balcony outside. There were a few untended flowerpots lining the railing, covered in their droppings.

"Besides, we know Arthur already, don't we? And it had to be something serious. Something to get him physically *here*."

She looked at me expectantly. I said nothing, which seemed to distress her.

"Truthfully, Taz, Anna did this to herself. She's got quite a self-destructive streak, in case you hadn't noticed."

"But she's your friend." The words came out sharply, like bullets.

Jenny got up and looked at one of Luka's paintings. "Oh, she was begging for this, Taz."

"Didn't seem that way this morning, when I found her out of her head."

"Trust me, she wanted out," Jenny said. "This was the nicest thing we could have done. Look, Luka said you overheard it. Anna said, on no uncertain terms, that she was out of the arrangement. Which was so silly, because she really didn't have to do anything. When I told her it wasn't a great idea, she threatened to go to the police. I had to protect her."

"And you think she won't go to the police now, after this?"

"She might," Jenny said, moving to another picture. I noticed the apartment was dirtier than I'd ever seen it. There were dishes piled in the sink, and a thin coat of dust on the television and shelves. "But what credibility does she have? Her godfather and mother clearly think she's a dealer. Arthur found all of that evidence. So who's going to believe her now?"

"But—"

"Listen, I love Anna. I was looking out for her. I could have called the police and just had Anna's place searched. With that much stuff, she'd be in an Italian prison for quite a while. Nasty places, I hear."

"I could tell on you. Luka could."

Jenny looked at me thoughtfully, then turned again to the painting. It was Luka's rendition of the lovely girl on the bathroom floor. "Do you know who this is?"

"No."

"Sure you do."

I put my fingers to my lips.

". . . Eleanor Peterfield?"

Jenny nodded.

"I guess I did know," I said, after a moment.

"And you know who she was?"

"The girl who died at our uni."

"No, Taz. She was our *you*."

I picked up a cushion and began to knead it with my fingers.

"Right. There has to be four of you. Two is too—"

"Few. Exactly. And three is bad luck—gets everything off-kilter."

"Yeah, that's what you all said at the beginning."

Outside, the rumbling was louder. Two men began shouting, then as suddenly as it came, the noise died.

"But there was this awful incident, and Eleanor overdosed. I'm telling you, never take zano again. It's poison, if you don't know the source."

"And Anna, today?"

"It was the very best stuff I sent out with Luka. The very best. The Eleanor thing was when we started. The quality control was . . . well. I warned them not to. Idiotic. And Anna and Luka were there in her room. And what did they do? Ran out. Ran out on a fucking dying friend because they were afraid of getting caught. Even I wouldn't do that."

"Are you sure?"

"Of course I'm sure," Jenny said, moving on to another painting. "I would have thought of something. Same way I did today."

"I just think you could have talked to Anna."

"Oh, we all talked to Anna. She was all about making it right for Eleanor *now.* Confess, make it right with the family, blah blah. God. You think that would have helped her family? The girl's *dead.* She and Luka would have gone to trial, my shop would have dried up, and I'd be either broke or in prison. You see that it was madnesss, right?"

"Jenny, there's no way around it." I threw the pillow away from me. "What you did is unpardonable."

"Was it?" Jenny sat down next to me. "Where is Anna now? Cozy on a train. Where are we? Here, in a nice flat, drinking wine. No one else died—not that that was my fault in the first place. No one is sick. And haven't you had a good time with us?"

I didn't have to answer that.

"Do you want Anna and Luka to go to prison?"

"Of course not."

"You've got to manage people like Anna, Taz. I love her. I love all of you. That's why I did it."

"You love us." The words were just wrong.

"It's what I said. Trust me. I'll always take care of you. I'm in front of it, love."

I think Jenny actually believed it. That she was helping us all; that she was actually taking care of things.

"So. The stuff that was at Anna's. You have it, yes?"

"No."

"No? We assumed that the professor would have tossed it to you. And that you'd have the sense to bring it over. Damn. Where is it, then?"

"I put it away," I said.

"Where?"

"I can't tell you where. Frankly, it didn't occur to me you'd want it again."

Jenny burst out laughing and put her hand on my arm.

"What?" I demanded.

"Taz, don't be an idiot. There's twenty thousand pounds worth of narcotics in that satchel. Of *course* we want it again. And so do the people who sold it to us. Not to mention the people like that little Belgian girl who have already paid for their wares. Junkies can get very nasty, you know."

"You got money in advance?"

"Anna's idea. She was quite shrewd in the beginning."

"And . . . do *I* get money if I bring it?"

"You've been *getting* money, sweetie," Jenny said. "Dresses, dinners, spending money, drinks? You already owe us thousands. Want me to tally it up for you?"

"But you wouldn't let me—"

"Pay? Of course not. It's against our code to have anyone but Luka pay. She holds all the cash. Except right now, you see, we haven't got any. We've had to lie low because of this whole Anna thing. Haven't done a sale for two bloody weeks, and we've completely gone through our reserves."

"I'm back," Luka called, her arms full of bottles of red wine. She shoved some garbage off the counter to make room. "Did I miss Armageddon?"

I pressed on, determined. "But it seems like . . . there *should* be quite a lot of money. With all of this business you're doing."

"This is how it's done, sweetie. There is enough money, when things are going well. But it's not a huge enterprise."

"And we're really bad savers," Luka said.

"It's true. Anyway, now the Anna thing is resolved."

"Right. Thanks to you, she's on a train to the loony bin."

Luka's shoulders slumped. She shook her head and opened one of the bottles.

"Drinking the guilt away, Luka?"

"Don't be mean, Taz," Jenny said. "It doesn't suit you."

"Rehab is practically a spa treatment these days," Luka said. "I went to one last year. Talky groups. Cake. It was nice. She'll like it. 'Specially because it's all a joke."

"And," Jenny said cheerfully, "she'll have her old life again. What mother wouldn't bring her daughter into the fold after drying out? Those places are all about apologies and making amends and rebuilding bridges, blah, blah, blah. Anna's mother is a public figure, sort of, and it would get around if she didn't accept Anna back. It would be downright cruel, really. No, this is everyone's big chance to make up for that horrible stepfather thing. Really this is all very cozy and clever."

I wanted so much to believe her. She really was that sort of person. She could have been an orator, or a magician. Prime minister. Maybe she will be.

"But what are we going to do?" Luka asked. "I'm so broke I can barely buy a chocolate."

"Oh, go back to the lake, obviously," Jenny said. "Now that Anna's gone home, we're not risking anything anymore. And Tazzie, we'll need to keep them in your room, same as Anna did."

Was I scared of them? Or curious? Or just tired of thinking at all?

"Can you do that?" she asked.

Both of the girls stared at me expectantly. I looked out at the balcony again. The pigeons had gone.

"I suppose I can. For a while."

"Good. Perfect. Come over tonight. You need to be here by seven, otherwise we'll be in a very bad way. Do you understand?"

"Seven," I said.

"It's important. I already have a lot of payments in, and people get quite huffy when their presents aren't delivered. So you *cannot* be late."

"Yes," I said. "Or no. I won't."

"She means it," Luka said. "These people get royally pissy."

"There should be some green boxes in the bag," Jenny said. "Everything is color coded, so it's very easy. Three green boxes. That's all I need. Leave the rest."

I was hungry, and tired, and nothing was making sense. I picked up my coat off the chair. The room had somehow gotten smaller and shabbier just during the time I was there.

"We know it's a lot," Luka said. "At least at first. But you'll be all right."

"Wait," I said, pausing at the door.

"Yes?"

"Won't we need a fourth? I mean, it's all uneven now. It's bad luck, isn't it?"

Luka and Jenny looked at each other. In that moment of charged silence, I shook with disbelief. Anna couldn't be so replaceable. She just couldn't.

"We were talking about that before you came over," Luka said.

"And?"

Jenny smiled. "Well. We thought that if you could forgive that Claire, perhaps your American flatmate isn't such a bad case after all."

•

I left the Club and walked slowly toward home, eyes trained to the ground. It was almost six. The last thing I could handle was a run-in with Claire, so I stood across the street to case out our house. I could see someone moving inside; probably Claire, waiting for me. I knew she'd have to leave soon, though, to make her shift at the bar.

As I stood there, shaking and hiding among the cars, my deviant mind raced on, far beyond the limits of decency. At last, Jenny was letting me in. But *really* in. All I'd have to do was hand her some boxes, and then we'd be back in the game. Parties, travel, maybe meet a wealthy, jet-setting boyfriend. *This is how it's done*, Jenny had said.

I left our corner and, for want of a better option, found myself walking to the leafy bar behind the *enoteca*. I desperately needed a drink. It was mostly empty at that hour, though it was pleasant, the wind blocked by the garden walls, the heat lamps already on. I ordered a small carafe of red wine and sat down in the corner. I'd made my way through about half of it when Colin came in, spotted me, and walked over.

"Oh," I said.

"Hello." To my surprise, he appeared nervous. He did look silly, towering over me there.

"Hello."

"May I sit?" he asked, after a moment.

I shrugged. He pulled out a chair and called for a drink. It took a moment for him to speak. He methodically folded a napkin, then took off his glasses to polish them.

"So," he said, finally.

"Yes. So."

"How are you?"

"I don't know," I said. "It's been a strange couple of days."

"Claire is very upset. She thinks she's hurt you in some way."

"Oh, not really."

"She says you didn't remember what happened."

"Okay. You're right. I didn't remember, and it's all turned around now. I suppose I am hurt. I thought we were on an outing, the four of us. Nice and proper. A date. And then Marcello feeds us drugs and you sit there while your girlfriend shags my—ah, what the hell."

"So you are upset."

"Sure. I'm a human. A girl, even."

"Was it the drugs?"

"Part of it. Bad trick."

"Of course, you're the one involved in a drug ring."

I slumped back in my chair. "No, I'm not," I said. "Not really. Not on purpose."

"But you're not *not* doing it on purpose either, are you?"

I didn't answer, thinking of the task I had ahead of rescuing Jenny's package from the cave.

"Tabitha, what *are* you doing on purpose?"

"I'm just here. What do you want? Jesus."

"Do you know who took you home that night?" Colin said, leaning his elbows on the table.

"Sure. Marcello did."

"No. It was me."

"Shut it."

"No really. I was sober as a stone. I didn't take anything. Not even wine. They did their thing and I took you home and got you safely to bed. Took off your cute little shoes and jacket, pulled up the covers under your cute chin."

My face was hot all over.

"Stop it."

"I waited a bit, to make certain you were all right. Then I went back home. Marcello was gone by then, and Claire was passed out."

"Very polite of you."

"But she knew. And she said it wasn't a big deal, fucking Marcello. I certainly didn't think so. But then she ran into you and now she's all done in. Loves you more than me, you see. Oh, she loves you the world over."

"Why did you pick her?" I said, suddenly. The girls at the table next to us glanced over and smirked. "I knew you *first*."

Colin paused, playing with his glass. "Because she's the most beautiful girl I've ever seen."

The mist was turning into drops of rain. The customers huddled under the umbrellas.

"She's also smart, you know," I said. "And a damned good person."

"Sure."

"I hate you."

"I'm sorry. I know we had a flirtation."

"I need to go."

"Do you really like him all that much?" Colin asked. "Marcello, I mean?"

"I don't know. I suppose."

"Because I think you don't. I think you're just humiliated."

I put my hands over my eyes. He was still leaning forward, talking to me steadily.

"You know, from the beginning I knew we were the same in some way. I think we think about the same things. That we watch from the sides. That we're curious. That we know this place—Grifonia—is more than just a bunch of bars and parties and tourists. That this place is extraordinary. That there are layers here, thousands of years of life and death and secrets and untold history."

"You're laying it on thick."

"Tabitha," he said, grabbing my hand.

"Don't. I just told you—I hate you."

"No you don't. You know you don't."

"How can you say that?"

"Because you came after me. Before Claire. You just said it."

Everything was changing too fast for me. *I'm just a girl from Lucan,* I thought frantically. *I like tea with milk. Cake. Silly shows on the telly.*

"There's one way to make this all even."

"You're insane."

"You'll like it. You won't be mad at Claire, you'll piss off Marcello. You'll feel better. Trust me."

"And what about Claire? She's my friend. She didn't mean to shag my boyfriend. She was out of her head."

Colin cocked his head. "So she *never* showed interest in Marcello before?"

*You can have him if you want him.*

"God, I really liked you," I said. "But you're not a nice person at all."

"Why don't you come over, Tabitha? Just for a bit." He leaned in closer. "Come on. Come even things out."

"I . . . well." I struggled for some way to get out of the hole I was falling into. "The thing is, I'm supposed to meet Jenny. I need to get her something."

"So be late," Colin said.

I looked at his shirt, so clean, so free of wrinkles. His soft dark hair, his expensive belt, the tiny lines around his eyes. But all of that was nothing, compared to the way he was staring at me.

It's a dangerous thing, to be wanted.

"All right, then," I said. "Let's go."

•

I wish it weren't true. I wish I could tell you I was a perfect person. That we were all perfect people. Especially since Claire and I have both been so flattened by time—one into a martyr, one into alternating versions of wronged prisoner and bloodthirsty monster. But, you see, Claire and I—as well as Jenny, Luka, and Anna—we were real live women with brains and souls and beating hearts. It meant even though we loved one another, we often fouled things up.

I betrayed Claire. I knew she was in love with Colin—really, out of her head in *love*. Our being together would break her. And I knew that she had only had sex with Marcello to please Colin. But I was finally wanted. And that trumped everything.

And, worse, I betrayed my mother, by playing out yet another unworthy love scene. How would I ever spin this? He was supposed to be the one, the final one. But how could it be so? The sheets, already soiled from the lovemaking of my friend. The empty bottles on the counter from previous nights, Claire's cigarette butts, the odd knife display on the wall.

It wasn't that Colin wasn't trying. Claire's lover—it was impossible for me not to think of him that way—was savoring me. He spent ten minutes on my neck alone, and then moved lower, then lower. He murmured my name through his teeth. *Ti voglio. Sei bellissima. Ti adoro.* At first there was satisfaction, knowing I had taken the thing Claire so wanted. But the more he went on, the more repulsed I became. Not by Colin, but by myself.

*What a stupid circle we're caught in*, I thought. Claire for Colin, Colin for me, me for Marcello, Marcello for Claire. I let out a bitter laugh.

Colin took it as encouragement. He arched his back, pressing his pelvis harder into mine.

"Just finish," I begged. "Please. I want you to finish."

He let out a strangled cry and started pumping until he shuddered with a dull moan. Finally, he collapsed onto me. I struggled out from under him and rolled out of bed.

"Tabitha," he said. "Come on. Stay."

I shook my head, searching for my clothes. He put his arm over his head, staring at me.

"You're a good girl, you know," he said.

And yet, the blackness in my heart. I couldn't even look at the man on the bed, so thick was my revulsion with the thing I had done to my friend. I pulled on my jeans, shirt, and trainers, not even bothering to shower.

"You're panicking," he said. "But in a little while you'll see this will all be all right. Now you and Claire can forgive each other, move on with things."

"I don't think so," I said, zipping my jacket. "I'm sorry, but this is ruined, all of it."

"Are you sure?"

"Yes," I said, with a certainty that surprised me. "*Yes.*" I did not want to see Colin again. I had thought of him for so long, but everything about him repulsed me now. Was it the narrowness of his cheekbones? The sharpness of his nose? Or simply the notion that I had done something so horrible?

*Hysteria.*

"I'm sorry. I'm just a bit mad."

"Listen, why don't we go talk to her," Colin said. "Together. It's not like she hasn't fucked up herself. She'll understand, I promise you."

"I don't want her to," I said. "You don't understand. This isn't me at all." The room was dank, airless. I was in a deepening panic to leave. "Goodbye, then."

It was eight when I scurried down Colin's steps. There, just on the other side of the street, I could see Claire walking to our lover's flat, texting madly. *I'll make this up to you*, I whispered. I put up my hood and hurried past her, head down, breaking into a run toward the safety of home.

# 26

Ervin Bogdani. Just a small player in my story. And yet, he was the one who stole everything.

I'd met him only a few times. The police and reporters bent over backward trying to link us together, but I had danced with him just once, and after that barely remembered him in passing. Each time I ran into him, including the last, fatal incident, he was little more than a stranger to me.

I should have paid more attention, I suppose, to the boy with the white-tipped hair. Objectively, Ervin Bogdani, who was born to a poor but loving home in Albania, was a pleasant-looking person, born with good intentions. He had a sister and a mother, though his father was dead. Ervin was brought up in one of the poorer neighborhoods of Gjirokastra. When he was eleven, during the 1997 rebellion over Ponzi schemes, his mother and sister were accidentally killed at a demonstration when a truck was turned over by protesters. Ervin's uncle managed to get his nephew a manufactured visa, and the boy was sent to Italy to live with a distant cousin.

A poor Albanian in Italy. What does it mean? The Italians see their country as the big brother of Albania, but the truth is, unless they are paying tourists, foreigners are far from beloved. To be an immigrant means you are one of hundreds of thousands, many who have come to escape violence, hunger, disease, famine. It means, in many parts of Italy, the locals won't speak with you. It means employment is unlikely. If you are lucky, you'll make your way to one of the more cosmopolitan cities, where work is more plentiful and minds are more open. Rome, or Florence, or a university town, like Grifonia.

Ervin's cousin was an unmarried bartender, uninterested in fatherly duties. He lived in a flat on the edge of the city. It was a grim place, and the boy took to slipping into the other apartments in the building and making himself at home. The neighbors didn't seem to mind. He was quiet. Polite. By the time Ervin was fifteen the cousin had disappeared. And so when Ervin wasn't sleeping on the sofa or guest room of a friend, he was hiding at the train station, his things stored in a locker.

Ervin learned how to disappear. To flatten himself against the walls of alleyways, to dart into the shadows. Once he was dragged by a well-meaning postal policewoman to a homeless shelter, where he was beaten and raped. After that he became impossible to catch, a master at slipping away.

As Ervin got older, Grifonia became a sea of collegiate opportunity. He began sleeping with the girls who streamed down to the universities, staying at their houses, borrowing his friends' sweatshirts and clothes. He played basketball at the public court. No one knew if he went to school, or who he was, or where he was from. He spoke pretty good English. He spoke Italian like a native. Though what everyone later recounted was that he rarely spoke at all.

To make ends meet, Ervin sold drugs. He had nothing to lose, and the opportunity came without hassle. He was at a party, and someone suggested, as he knew everyone and came and went so easily, that he get into the business. Only he didn't like dealing on his own, so he started working for the Enteria connection. That year, his boss was a cold, intimidating blonde named Jenny Cole. Ervin didn't like her much but was scared of her. She told him not to approach her in public, so he didn't.

Ervin Bogdani was not a cruel person. Deep under his façade of indifference was a terrified boy pressed flat on the cement shower floor of a homeless shelter, arms pinned, a foot against his head. The memory motivated him to constantly carry a knife in his back pocket. He slept with it clenched in his hand.

I am not suggesting that Ervin Bogdani be pardoned. After all, he is alive and I am not. I wish it were the other way around. What I am trying to say is that he was a person. Killers are always people. It's no excuse. Still, it's important to remember, particularly if one is going to try at all to understand this strange nebula that was the end.

•

I walked down the alley, crossed the street, and came into the gate. It was unlocked, as usual. There was a light on, but then, I often left the kitchen light on, as I hated coming home to a dark house. Alessandra sometimes scolded me for the practice, as it offended her Italian sense of conservation. She grew up in a house where Ziploc bags were washed and reused, where every possible piece of food was used for compost. But she was gone that weekend, as was everyone else in the cottage, including the boys downstairs. It was the first time since I'd lived there that the building was completely empty, as all the Italians had gone home for the holiday. I opened the door, entered, and locked it from the inside with my key. Then I went to my room to get ready to shower.

The silence was heavy; it made me uneasy, and soon I began to imagine someone else was there. I was, by now, used to being chased by spirits. Their presence wasn't something I could articulate, exactly, but since scratching the surface of the ancients and their tombs, I'd accepted that perhaps dimensions were deeper than I had believed before. So perhaps these apparitions I came across from time to time were not just my imagination, but something different I wasn't meant to understand.

Only that night, there was a person in my house.

At seven o'clock, when I hadn't arrived at the Club, Jenny called Ervin, who had worked for her since her arrival. She really did have expectant clients waiting—people who would be angry with her, who might call the Enteria administrators and inform them of some version of what she was doing. Hurriedly, she told Ervin that my house was always unlocked.

"And what if she's home?" he'd asked her.

"She'll give it to you," Jenny told him. "She's not unreasonable. She's just always bloody *late*."

But I hadn't been home. No one had. He walked in as easily as if he'd been invited. For a man who lived nowhere, the coziness of our female nest must have been too much for temptation. Ervin poured himself a glass of juice and sat on the sofa. He poked about in our rooms, looking at our clothes, our books, our underthings. He hadn't properly searched for the satchel yet, but he believed he had time, so he went into the bathroom and closed the door. A moment later, he heard the front door open and shut, and heard me walk into my bedroom.

Could there have been a day more filled with misunderstandings? There are so many *perhapses*. Perhaps if I had just gone straight to Jenny's . . . Perhaps if I hadn't slept with Colin . . . Perhaps if I had been a little less jumpy . . . Perhaps if Ervin hadn't chosen to use the bathroom just then. For if I had opened the door and seen him there, I could have run, or waited for him, in his usual, unassuming, genial manner, to explain himself.

But those scenarios are not the story. This is the story.

I was undressing for my shower, my mind rife with guilt about the person I had clearly become. Mostly, I was thinking of Babs. I wouldn't be able to tell her what I'd done. Craving unconditional love and forgiveness, I put my phone to my ear as I kicked off my pants, dialed my mother's line, and, as I waited for her to pick up, pulled my shirt around my shoulders. That's when I saw a man in the doorway.

The phone fell to the floor, cutting off. I screamed. I wasn't a screamer, but it seemed important to make noise, so I did, at the top of my lungs. He wasn't a large man, Ervin, but the years of basketball had made him strong. He had even played for the city team for a few months. His local sponsors—men fueled by newspaper stats and grappa—sometimes talked of his going for the national league. What I am trying to tell you is that he had inordinately large hands. At that moment, to stop my yowling, he brought his wide palm back and, with all his strength, knocked me down.

My head hit the corner of the bedside table. I felt an enormous burst of shooting pain and an alarming inability to move. The man, whom I now placed as the boy from the club, was kneeling over me, shaking me, trying to get me to be quiet. And that's when I remembered his name.

"Ervin," I said. Slowly. Clearly, so he would know I knew him. "*Ervin*."

Mother, you were the last person I called. The other call to the bank, the one the police traced later, wasn't me, of course. I knew you'd be sitting there on your sofa, the phone beside you, reading a book among your cozy litany of pillows. I was going to tell you, before I saw the boy in the doorway, that I was in trouble. That I had done something of which I wasn't proud. I was going to let you mother me, perhaps fly me home for the weekend and feed me dolmas and ice cream. I would have let you love me and, by doing so, would have loved you back.

I don't know if you picked up the call or not, but now you are reduced to such sorrow, the world can barely watch. You wander back and forth between Lucan and the haunted streets of Grifonia, a mortal Demeter, demanding justice, devastating mothers across the world with your bleak gazes. "I still see her," you told the papers. They printed the words as a headline, blaring and bold. I wish I could talk to you, to tell you that the end was not, in fact, as terrifying as you believe. It was simple, really: I screamed a name, and the owner of that name had to quiet me. He had grabbed a knife from our kitchen. I didn't even see it coming.

Two stabs to the neck. Blood shot forth in the form of a red geyser, scaring Ervin enough to send him backward. It was fascinating: the blood was inside of me, and then it was there, pulsing onto both of our bodies, pooling beside me in slick red sheets. Ervin did a panicked dance. He stepped in the blood, then jumped out of it again. He ran to the bathroom, grabbed a towel, and tried to mop it off his shoes. But it kept coming, and coming, and he gave up.

He knelt, staring at my face. When I blinked, he hit me. I suppose he thought it would help me die. I knew enough to lie still, and that seemed to satisfy him. He was not good at killing. It's an art, you see.

He stood up, as if remembering his task, and grabbed my purse. He emptied my wallet—three hundred euros were inside, as I had gone to the bank just after Jenny's admitting her lack of funds—then grabbed my phone off the floor. When he looked down at me, I could see that he was terrified yet resigned—he was the sort of person who leaves a mess, no matter how dire, out of laziness. I heard him run out of the flat, cursing. He was gone.

I lay there for a long time, feeling myself growing weaker, and—Mother, I'm sorry to tell you this—I was beginning to suffer. The wounds burned and ached, and I could feel my brain slowly ceasing to function. In truth, I was already dead, but I faced another hour or two of painful expiration. And then I heard someone at the door again.

"Look, we all love each other," I heard Claire say. "I just think we all need to fucking talk this out."

"You're pretty drunk for this endeavor, love."

"I needed to calm down," she said. "I'm not too bad. Just some shots and pot."

"Perhaps when you're sober—"

"No. You ass. I love you and I love her. But I fucking hate you both, too. You *had* to even it out? This is too fucked up. I want everything worked out *now*."

"Fine," Colin said. "But she's not—"

"Holy shit, there's blood in here. Gross. She must have pierced her ear, or has her period or something—"

"No," Colin said. "Oh, God. No. Oh, no. Claire, she's right here."

Tabitha Deacon, a girl from Ireland, studying abroad. She came home one night to an empty house, where a man was waiting. He stabbed her twice in the neck, then ran out the door, covered in her blood, taking her for dead.

But she wasn't dead. Her friends came upon her—her flatmate and her lover. She was there, still breathing, blood burbling at her throat.

How did Colin know I was beyond saving? Which was the truth—no ambulance would have gotten to me in time; no doctor would have pumped enough blood back in. Was it the thin trickle of air escaping from my windpipe? Something in my eyes? The fact that I couldn't even speak?

I could hear Claire sobbing from the doorway. Colin told her to stay away. *Take off your shoes*, he said. Ervin, in his haste and perhaps out of horror, had left the knife right beside me. Colin took my jeans and, using them to keep his fingerprints off it, picked it up. He cleaned the blade on the cloth, then cut off my bra, which was up around my neck. I suppose this was to help my breathing. It didn't. He looked at me, holding that knife with a shaking hand, then leaned over me and whispered something.

"What did you say?" Claire screamed. "Did you just fucking say you loved her?"

"*Misericordia*," the man whispered to the dying girl. "*Et ego ducam te. Iam ut relinquamus. Ut in aeternum dormias.*"

Tabitha understood. It was the same Latin she had heard him chanting in the meeting. It was important, what she had seen. It meant something.

For Colin Bancordia was one of the youngest members of the Compagnia. An order, two thousand years old, that was now only ritualistic. The men met for tradition; they learned the ritual of mercy killing as an homage to history. They held balls that raised money for hospices and burial of the poor. But in this era of peace and modernity, there was no practical reason for the Compagnia. Not anymore.

Yet here Colin was. A girl, suffering in his arms. He had an oath, one he'd been told was a formality. To serve a good death, so that the trapped soul could go into the next life.

"Tabitha, I'm going to help you," he said. "Are you ready for me to help you?"

—

Claire had run to the bathroom to get towels. As I've said, she had a tracker's walk, thereby, just by sheer habit, leaving no presence at the crime scene. She brought towels in and was stuffing them under me, trying to stop the blood.

"Don't you fucking die on me!" she screamed in my ear. "Oh, God, I can't believe I'm actually saying that. *Fuck!* You fucking bitch! I love, you, okay? *Wake the fuck up!*"

What is it, really, that feeds a friendship between women? Perhaps the place to look is in their very beginnings. When Babs and I were three—babies, still—we would clutch each other in our cribs like lovers. Our mothers would come in spilling glasses of gin, pulling us apart with embarrassed laughs. Then, minutes later in the kitchen, we'd be screaming—grape-faced, Medea cries—beating each other on the head savagely with wooden spoons. There must be something rabid about the love of a true friend, something poisonous in order to sustain it. Sweet friendships, they dull and eventually sputter out to a point of inertia. Yes, I believe this. You can't love another woman honestly without some element of hate.

And it *was* love, between Claire and me. We had done this horrible thing to each other, yet her cries were the last human sounds I heard on earth, and at the time there was no one else I'd rather have had near. And I needed to hear something. I clung to the sound, tinged as it was with despair. Dying is a private matter, and I can no more explain it to you as I could losing my virginity at sixteen all those years ago. But I can tell you that in my case, I knew what I would be missing. I would never fight with my sister again over clothes, or hear my father chastise me for being late, or feel the steaming water of a good shower. I would never be split open to have a baby, never struggle through my first job. There would be no wrinkles, no arthritis, no more letting my mother cuddle me, no more hushed Hebrew songs. I knew all of it was ending, and the knowledge was unbearable. It's not the pain that's the hardest. It's all the things you suddenly know you won't ever have.

Claire will never know what she did for me. Later, drunk and high as she was, she wouldn't even remember it. But we were there, together in the bleeding place, and it was as if it *had* to be her. Babs would have been too sweet to bear it, and the others, as dazzling as they'd appeared, were liars. I knew that now. But of course, at that point, I knew everything. When dying, you're separate. You are the most knowledgeable person on earth.

"Stay still," Colin commanded sharply. "Leave us alone, Claire. You're too high to help."

My flatmate slumped over, her face in her hands.

"Tabitha?" he said. "Are you ready?"

She was fading. A bit of black was hovering to the right of her field of vision. She was drowning in her own blood.

"It hurts," she whispered.

"Hold on," he said. "*Adducam te.*"

Colin raised the knife.

"Fuck, no!" Claire screamed. "Please, no."

It was a quick but large incision, eight centimeters long. Colin had paid close attention in his meetings, had learned well a skill no Italian ever believed he would use. The girl's eyes closed instantly. Colin stood and said another prayer.

The American, sobbing, pulled the girl's white duvet off her mattress and threw it over her friend's body. Colin drew her gently away. As if offering a last moment of privacy, Claire pressed the inside lock on the bedroom door before closing it. In the mornings, Claire knew, Taz liked it quiet. Soon there would be a storm here. Her flatmate would want to be alone.

*Tabitha Deacon, twenty-one years old, 21st century AD*

# 27

According to Arthur, Etruscan funerals, particularly for those from important families, were celebrated with a typically audacious feast and party. Game was killed and served over three-day banquets; rivers of wine flowed; men, women, and children took turns sleeping and eating on sumptuous cushions; perhaps a stray orgy sprang up in the odd hours of the night. The men took the opportunity to stage huge funerary games—running, discus, and perhaps even a gladiator match. This all culminated in taking the body down to the tomb below, prepared decades before so that the dead could live in comfort. The corpse was then surrounded by his or her favorite objects, and the tomb was sealed until it was time for the next member to enter.

My own funeral was not nearly as grand or amusing, though it was a large Catholic affair in St. Andrew's in Dublin. I became something of a martyr, though no one could make out what happened, exactly, and hundreds of people came. Jenny and Luka flew in for it, though Anna remained at her facility. My family, lined up in a grim row. Sean came from Oxford. In the afternoon, a small Hebrew ceremony as well. There were reporters there, who dispersed after a day or two, after which my hometown sank back into its pocket of quiet, albeit a bit more somber than usual.

As for the situation back in Grifonia: it would be safe to say that, in the days after my death, things unraveled for certain players at a blazing pace.

Jenny and Luka fled the day after I was found. The British consulate, upon hearing from the Enteria administrators that we were close, offered them flights to London. The girls took them without hesitation. They finished up their Enteria year in Portugal. They didn't speak that language either, but the administration made an exception, given their claims of trauma.

Gia and Alessandra also put distance between themselves and the situation, by fleeing to their parents' homes. They were Italian, and they knew the court system, how these things could work. Claire tried to contact them, but the girls didn't reply, upon advisement of their families. They sent their friends for their things and never entered the cottage again.

Colin, also, went back to England shortly after he was questioned by the police. He told his father, who was always rather puzzled by his son's interest in his heritage, that he was going back for a job.

The drugs, as far as I know—all twenty-thousand euros' worth—still remain in the tomb behind the farmer's house in the valley.

Claire was the only one who stayed. She wanted to be near Colin, not knowing that he was leaving. But more than that, she wanted to help find the man who had stabbed me. She really thought she could help the police, and that they actually would want to hear from her. Claire was a girl with strong, unshakable ideals—the sort formed under the cold, clear skies of Montana. For her, love meant loyalty. And for that, in the end, she paid.

•

This is all years ago now. And, likely, you know the rest. How I was found by Gia and Alessandra, whose lovers kicked in the bedroom door and discovered me there, dead in my blood under my comforter. How my flatmate's uncharacteristic drinking binge that night ended up being the factor to condemn her. How, due to the whiskey, she never could quite remember what she had done that night, or where she had been. How it all came back to her in jumbled scenes of horror. How she clung to Colin outside of the murder scene and at the police station, increasingly damned by watching Italian eyes. How, pressed by the increasingly irritated authorities shouting in a language she couldn't understand, she gave several different stories of what she remembered. How, after just one hour of the same interrogation, Colin—who had spent some time studying Italian law—gave a very clear, concise account of being at his apartment, an account in which Claire did not factor. How Jenny Cole, in a phone interview from Lisbon, said Claire had always been a strange, unbalanced girl. How the press, the police, and the public jumped on the American in order to formulate an answer to this mystery as neat as those in the thrillers I used to love. How there wasn't one, because in real life, murders usually don't work that way.

It wasn't that they didn't find the man who killed me. They did, easily. Ervin Bogdani was not a smart man. He left his DNA everywhere, called his friends and told them about me, even confessed to the crime. He claimed connections with the B4, but of course, Jenny had been clever enough never to have been seen in public with Ervin. And besides, she was gone. No matter how much he protested, nobody could believe that he actually knew such upstanding girls.

"Who else did you know?" the police goaded.

"Tabitha. We danced."

"Yes, yes. Who else?"

"Claire," he said.

"You knew her well?" they asked, suddenly interested.

"I—"

"If she helped you, your sentence will be much shorter. But tell the truth, of course."

"Of course," Ervin said, looking at his barrister, who was nodding. "Yes. Her, I knew."

•

Where are they now, my friends and lovers?

Older. A bit more tired. Jenny is working in an advertising office, though she doesn't mind it as much as she thought. It turns out her ruthless business sense serves her well in the real world. Though I doubt she entirely appreciates the irony of it, given the elegance of her building and the rewarding pace of her social life, she is, in fact, a happy spinster. She works at a desk and lives alone with a cat.

Luka is dead. Such a wasteful surprise. Upon returning to London that fall, she stopped calling Jenny back. She had adopted a fondness for her father's sedatives, which helped blot out the faces of Eleanor Peterfield and Tabitha Deacon. The housekeeper found her one morning three summers after my murder, facedown in her father's modest swimming pool.

Anna is doing well. She moved to America to study classics in New Haven, where she married a fellow scholar in another department, an expert on Proust. She makes her own money through grants, never tells anyone about her father's title, and hasn't spoken to her mother or Professor Korloff in years.

Sweet Babs is a scientist, though she never did marry George. This story has proved that a person can, most certainly, change another's life by entering it; the same can happen, it seems, when a dear sister violently exits. Babs was altered by my murder. She stopped wearing colors and took to living in the university lab most hours of the day. Her skin is almost blue from lack of sun, her hair a greasy brown. There's a protein she is searching for; something to do with light hitting the eyes. She is almost thirty and one of the most promising biochemists in England.

Marcello stayed in the apartment below. He went to my makeshift Grifonian memorial with some friends, then went home with an Italian girl. He stopped going out with foreigners, as the consequences seemed complicated. He gained brief fame as my lover, but after university moved home and faded into Naples. He married a distant cousin. They run a small restaurant.

Claire was pardoned at twenty-seven, after six years in an Italian prison. She finally got what she wanted, I suppose, though hardly how she wanted it, in that she felt like a real Italian. She became harder, and so fluent it was difficult to remember her English when she got out. After her release she sank deep into the sharp mountains of Montana and married a rancher. She had a daughter, whom she briefly considered naming Tabitha. But after some conversations with her husband, that idea was abandoned.

Colin went back to England, choosing to finish his dissertation there. He teaches medieval Italian history at the University of London. He went on to marry a British law student. The two never go back to Grifonia. The wife, who knows vaguely that he knew Claire and me, never asks why.

Other than my mother, everyone in my family moved on as well. My parents divorced and my father remarried; my sister had a baby; my cousins also married and had babies of their own. My mother, unable to live with my ghost anymore, left my childhood home and put it on the market. There is a new family there now. They fear they will never be able to escape my shadow; the story remains too notorious for that. Still, life continues. The children, miraculously, don't know of what happened to me yet.

My room, which has been freshly painted a sparkling white, is now occupied by a stout five-year-old named Melinda. As I once did, she favors toys that are expectedly female—dolls, plush animals, play houses. She found the ten pounds I left, caught in the edge of the carpet. She is meticulously organized and lines up her dolls on her wooden shelf, calling them nightly by name. Good*night*, Melly. Good*night*, Shira. She collects glass jars of buttons, and has two of mine that she found in corners of the room. One was to a blue shirt I wore as my school uniform; the other a shiny, fat black button that once belonged to the sleeve of a coat. She snatches them up, looking at each one carefully before placing it in its proper glass vessel. She is now up to three jars full, and they really are quite beautiful, particularly in the afternoon light.

•

And me? Where am *I* now? My body was taken back to Lucan, Ireland, but in truth, I remain in Italy, where most of the blood left my veins. After the crime scene was closed, the landlord hired a washerwoman to scrub the cottage. She collected pail after pail of bloody water and threw it in the garden, as she was afraid to pour the red liquid down the toilet or the shower. Down it trickled, into the soil under the olive trees. And so I stay here, abroad.

But I'm not alone. The Compagnia remains a secret, but we are still here: Thainia, who died in the sheep fields; Adriana, the baker's daughter; Althea, the pigeon catcher; Maria, the midwife. You don't know us. In the history books, it's Nicolai the bishop you read about, not Althea. You know the Inquisition, but you don't know Maria's name. There is a portrait in Samuel's castle of the cardinal, yet Lucretia remains faceless. You know about the sieges, the warriors, the family feuds. And in my case, you know about Claire, whose incredible moon face outshone mine in death as well as in life. As the trial went on, my name fell out of the papers. Few people, in fact, can remember it, despite my family's indignant public protests. There is a small Enteria scholarship dedicated to me, and sometimes tourists gather in the petrol station to gawk at the cottage where I expired. Other than that, to the world I am just a shadow of a life.

Listen. My name is Tabitha Deacon. I am here, and there are others. Girlhoods cut short, steeped in desire. We are the sun that blinds your eyes when you come out of a massive, stone archway; the ancient smell that rushes up from the cracks when it rains; the wind that bites your cheeks in the great piazza on autumn nights. I thought I heard voices in those enchanted days, that I glimpsed ghosts, and I did. I did. We were all alive, and we loved and hated and lived brilliant, messy existences. The air is thick with our wanting.

Yet you're the one still here, aren't you? Still looking, though my story is long over. So perhaps I'm wrong about everything. Perhaps the wanting is yours.

# AUTHOR'S NOTE

In 2007, a British student was killed while studying abroad in Perugia, Italy. As is true in many works of fiction, this book was thematically inspired by various accounts of some people's experiences. However, all the incidents in this work, as well as all the characters, are products of the author's imagination.

The Compagnia della Morte, now called the Compagnia della Misericordia, meaning "mercy," is an actual organization, though its nature is much different from that invented for this novel. Founded in 1570 with the aim of providing burials and masses for those who died in poverty, eventually the Compagnia became watchdogs against Perugia's use of the death penalty. The Compagnia kept the executioners' tools in its custody. Once a year, on the festival of Saint John the Baptist, the members of the order would process through the town in black robes; then they would burn the ropes that had held that years' executed prisoners and place the remaining ashes in a grave.

Today, the Compagnia della Misericordia is solely a historical institution. In Corso Vannucci, Perugia's main square, there is an artifact still visible: a small tile painted with a skull and crossbones on the outside of house number thirty-eight.

## ACKNOWLEDGMENTS

I'd like to thank the MacDowell Colony and Civitella Ranieri for their great kindness to our family. A big thanks to my students at San Francisco State University for keeping me in line. Thank you to the playwright Diego Mencaroni and the poet Riccardo Duranti for their insights into Italian history and culture. Grady Hendrix, Michelle Gagnon, Molly Antopol, Helena Echlin—cruel, brilliant readers all. And Sarah Crichton, my editor. You are the real deal.

Rob McQuilkin, agent. We know where this book would be without you. You are the old guard, the gregarious bitch-slapper, the sort that sweet talks and bullies a writer, and then stands behind her, fangs bared. In the era of the easy online gush, this, friend, in print. It's been ten years. Thank you.

The family: cheers to Mom for running the house in Italy, and to my brother, sister-in-law, and father for believing in me. Thank you, Peter, for pushing me as an author, and otherwise. I love you so much, and should say it more. And finally, thank you, Phoebe Kaplan Crouch Orner, for being such a good little Boo.

## A Note About the Author

Katie Crouch is the *New York Times* bestselling author of *Girls in Trucks*, among other novels. She contributes to *The Guardian, McSweeney's, Tin House, Slate, The Rumpus*, and *Salon*. A MacDowell fellow, Crouch teaches at San Francisco State University and lives in Bolinas, California.